D0746805

"WHAT IS THIS ...... by Isaac Asimov—The aliens had captured the beings called "male" and "female," and if they ever figured out how the species continued its existence it could prove the end of the human race. . . .

"DEATH AND THE SENATOR" by Arthur C. Clarke—He had been betrayed by his own body, and his only chance for survival rested with the Soviet space program. . . .

"A PLANET NAMED SHAYOL" by Cordwainer Smith—It was the ultimate punishment for crimes against the Empire, a life sentence on a world that would never let you die. . . .

These are just a few of the masterful tales that will capture your imagination in—

ISAAC ASIMOV PRESENTS THE GREAT SF STORIES: 23

Watch for these exciting DAW anthologies:

ASIMOV PRESENTS THE GREAT SF
STORIES
    Classics of short fiction from the golden age
of science fiction.
*Edited by Isaac Asimov and Martin H.
Greenberg.*

THE YEAR'S BEST HORROR STORIES
    The finest, most spine-chilling terror stories
of the current year.
Edited by Karl Edward Wagner.

SWORD AND SORCERESS
    Original tales of fantasy and adventure,
stories of warrior women and sorceresses,
wielding their powers in the war against evil.
Edited by Marion Zimmer Bradley.

CATFANTASTIC I AND II
    All new tales of those long-tailed, furry
keepers of mankind, practitioners of magi-
cal arts beyond human ken.
*Edited by Andre Norton and Martin H.
Greenberg.*

ISAAC ASIMOV
PRESENTS
THE GREAT
SF STORIES
#23

(1961)

EDITED BY ISAAC ASIMOV
AND MARTIN H. GREENBERG

D A W   B O O K S ,   I N C .
DONALD A. WOLLHEIM, FOUNDER
375 Hudson Street, New York, NY 10014
ELIZABETH R. WOLLHEIM
SHEILA E. GILBERT
PUBLISHERS

Copyright © 1991 by Nightfall, Inc. and Martin H. Greenberg.

All rights reserved

Complete list of acknowledgments will be found on the following page.

Cover art by Angus McKie.

DAW Book Collectors No. 856.

First Printing, July, 1991

1 2 3 4 5 6 7 8 9

DAW TRADEMARK REGISTERED
U.S. PAT. OFF. AND FOREIGN COUNTRIES
—MARCA REGISTRADA.
HECHO EN U.S.A.

PRINTED IN THE U.S.A.

ACKNOWLEDGMENTS

THE HIGHEST TREASON by Randall Garrett—Copyright © 1961 by Street & Smith Publications, Inc.; reprinted by permission of the Scott Meredith Literary Agency, Inc., 845 Third Avenue, New York, NY 10022.

HOTHOUSE by Brian W. Aldiss—Copyright © 1961 by Mercury Press, Inc.; renewed © 1989 by Brian W. Aldiss. Reprinted by permission of the Scott Meredith Literary Agency, Inc., 845 Third Avenue, New York, NY 10022.

HIDING PLACE by Poul Anderson—Copyright © 1961 by Street & Smith Publications, Inc.; renewed © 1989 by Poul Anderson. Reprinted by permission of the author and his agents, the Scott Meredith Literary Agency, Inc., 845 Third Avenue, New York, NY 10022.

WHAT IS THIS THING CALLED LOVE? by Isaac Asimov—Copyright © 1961; renewed © 1989 by Isaac Asimov. Reprinted by permission of the author.

A PRIZE FOR EDIE by J. F. Bone—Copyright © 1961 by Street & Smith Publications, Inc.; renewed © 1989 by J. F. Bone. Reprinted by permission of the author and his agents, the Scott Meredith Literary Agency, Inc., 845 Third Avenue, New York, NY 10022.

THE SHIP WHO SANG by Anne McCaffrey—Copyright © 1961 by Mercury Press, Inc.; renewed © 1989 by Anne McCaffrey. Reprinted by permission of the author and her agent, Virginia Kidd.

DEATH AND THE SENATOR by Arthur C. Clarke—Copyright © 1961 by Street & Smith Publications, Inc.; renewed © 1989 by Arthur C. Clarke. Reprinted by permission of the author and his agents, the Scott Meredith Literary Agency, Inc., 845 Third Avenue, New York, NY 10022.

THE QUAKER CANNON by Frederik Pohl and C. M. Kornbluth—Copyright © 1961 by Street & Smith Publications, Inc.; renewed © 1989 by Frederik Pohl. Reprinted by permission of Frederik Pohl.

THE MOON MOTH by Jack Vance—Copyright © 1961 by Galaxy Publishing Corporation; renewed © 1989 by Jack Vance. Reprinted by permission of Ralph Vicinanza, Inc.

A PLANET NAMED SHAYOL by Cordwainer Smith—Copyright © 1961 by Galaxy Publshiing Corporation; renewed © 1989 by the Estate of Cordwainer Smith. Reprinted by permission of the agents for the author's Estate, the Scott Meredith Literary Agency, Inc., 845 Third Avenue, New York, NY 10022.

RAINBIRD by R. A. Lafferty—Copyright © 1961 by Galaxy Publishing Corporation; renewed © 1989 by R. A. Lafferty. Reprinted by permission of the author and his agent, Virginia Kidd.

WALL OF CRYSTAL, EYE OF NIGHT by Algis Budrys—Copyright © 1961 by Galaxy Publishing Corporation; renewed © 1989 by Algis Budrys. Reprinted by permission of the author.

REMEMBER THE ALAMO! by R. R. Fehrenbach—Copyright © 1961 by Street & Smith Publications, Inc.; renewed © 1989 by R. R. Fehrenbach. Reprinted by permission of the author and his agents, the Scott Meredith Literary Agency, Inc., 845 Third Avenue, New York, NY 10022. The editors would like to thank Barry N. Malzberg for reminding us of this story.

CONTENTS

INTRODUCTION

In the world outside reality it was another *relatively* quiet year, which opened with the inauguration of John F. Kennedy as 35th President of the United States. It was a year that saw the United States break off diplomatic relations with Castro's Cuba, then arrange a disastrous attempt to overthrow the bearded dictator at the Bay of Pigs. The infamous Berlin Wall (really a deep barrier of electrified fencing and mines all along the border) was constructed, and the Peace Corps was formed.

Other highlights and lowlights included the assassination of Patrice Lumumba of the Congo and Rafael Trujilio of the Dominican Republic; the activities of the "Freedom Riders" in the southern United States; the trial and conviction of Adolf Eichmann in Jerusalem; and great strides in the conquest of space with the flights of Yuri Gagarin and Alan B. Shepard (the latter aboard Freedom 7) in orbit and suborbit around the Earth.

The Cold War continued unabated, and President Kennedy told Americans that it would be "prudent" for each and every American family to have a bomb shelter.

During 1961 the top box-office stars were Elizabeth Taylor and Rock Hudson; inflation in the U.S. was at 1.9%; the top movies of the year included *West Side Story* (which copped the Oscar for Best Picture), *The Misfits*, directed by John Huston and Clark Gable's last film, *The Guns of Navarone*, *One-Eyed Jacks* starring Marlon Brando as actor and director, Robert Rossen's *The Hustler*, *Splendor in the*

Grass, Stanley Kramer's *Judgment at Nuremberg,* and *Breakfast at Tiffany's.* Melvin Calvin won the Nobel Prize in Chemistry for his work in analyzing photosynthesis.

In sports, Roy Emerson and Darlene Hard were tops at the U.S. Tennis Open, Jim Brown led the NFL in rushing, "Carry Back" won the Kentucky Derby, the Boston Celtics with Bill Russell won the NBA championship, Roberto Clemente led the majors with a .351 average, the Green Bay Packers routed the New York Giants 37-0 to take the NFL title, the damn Yankees won the World Series four games to one over the Reds, while Roger Maris hit 61 home runs in a season. The first group of McDonald's fast food restaurants was bought by Ray Kroc in 1961, beginning an era of high cuisine in America.

Timothy Leary was fired from Harvard for using undergraduates in drug experiments while Larry Rivers painted *Parts of the Face* and Andrew Wyeth drew *Distant Thunder.* Outstanding and/or bestselling books included Marty's favorite book, *Calories Don't Count, Catch-22* by Joseph Heller, *The Making of the President, 1960* by Theodore H. White, *Tropic of Cancer* by Henry Miller, *The Death and Life of Great American Cities* by Jane Jacobs, *The Agony and the Ecstasy* by Irving Wallace, *A Nation of Sheep* by William Lederer, *The Carpetbaggers* by Harold Robbins, *The City in History* by Lewis Mumford, *To Kill a Mockingbird* by Harper Lee, and *The Rise and Fall of the Third Reich* by William L. Shirer. Seventeen-year-old Bobby Fischer won his fourth U.S. Chess Championship; and the IUD (the intrauterine device) was introduced.

Hit songs of 1961 included "Cryin' " by Roy Orbison, Ferlin Husky's great "Wings of a Dove," Elvis' "Don't Be Cruel", "Tossin' and Turning' " by Bobby Lewis, Del Shannon's "Runaway", the theme from "Exodus", "Where the Boys Are" by Connie Francis, and the beautiful "I Fall to Pieces" by Patsy Cline. President Eisenhower, in his farewell address, warned the country of the dangers of what was called the "military industrial complex."

Popular television shows included "The Dick Van Dyke Show," "Dr. Kildare," "Wide World of Sports," "The Defenders," with E. G. Marshall, Vince Edwards as "Ben Casey," and the number one rated show of the year, "Wagon Train." The population of the United States was

209,000,000, while IBM introduced the Selectric electric typewriter, boosting the productivity of many writers.

In 1961 the first disco, "Le Club," opened in New York. The theater was enriched by the opening of Harold Pinter's *The Caretaker*, Ossie Davis' *Purlie Victorious*, Frank Loesser's *How to Succeed in Business Without Really Trying*, Robert Bolt's *A Man for All Seasons*, and Tennessee Williams' *The Night of the Iguana*. The top ticket price for a Broadway musical was $8.60.

Death took Lee De Forest, the inventor of the vacuum tube; Richard Wright; Gary Cooper; Ty Cobb; "Grandma Moses"; Chico Marx; James Thurber; Marion Davies; Dashiell Hammett; George S. Kaufman; Sam Rayburn; Joan Davis; U.N. Secretary-General Dag Hammarskjold; Carl Jung; and, by his own hand, Ernest Hemingway.

In the real world it was a below average year as the paperback explosion continued.

Notable books published in 1961 include *Pilgrimage: The Book of the People* by Zenna Henderson, *The Lovers* by Phillip Jose Farmer, *Three Hearts and Three Lions* by Poul Anderson, *Star Hunter* by Andre Norton, *A Cupful of Space* by Mildred Clingerman, *A Fall of Moondust* by Arthur C. Clarke, *Nightmares and Geezenstacks* by Fredric Brown, *The Primal Urge* by Brian W. Aldiss, the wonderful *The Big Time* by Fritz Leiber, *Solaris* by Stanislaw Lem, and two especially important novels, *Stranger in a Strange Land* by Robert A. Heinlein, and, perhaps the best novel of the year, *Dark Universe*, by the regretfully forgotten Daniel F. Galouye.

Only five science fiction magazines remained on the newsstands, although there was no shortage of plans to launch new titles. One very important development was the retirement of the legendary H. L. Gold as editor of the *Galaxy* group of magazines; he was followed by Frederik Pohl, who although technically Managing Editor, began to make his editorial influence felt, a sign of good things to come.

In the real world, some important people made their maiden voyages into reality; in February—Fred Saberhagen with "Volume Paa-Pyx"; and in May—Sterling E. Lanier with "Join Our Gang."

Fantastic films (in terms of category, not always quality) included *Gorgo*; Greenberg's life story depicted in *The*

Absent Minded Professor; *Konga*; the elusive *Atlantis, The Lost Continent*; Jules Verne's (well, he did write the book) *Master of the World*; *The Fabulous World of Jules Verne*, an interesting film from Czechoslovakia; *Mysterious Island*, yet another film based on a Verne story—it really "pays" to be out-of-copyright, doesn't it? *The Beast of Yucca Flats*; the underrated and noirish *Most Dangerous Man Alive*; *Voyage to the Bottom of the Sea*, yet another water-logged epic; and a real sleeper not to be missed, *The Day the Earth Caught Fire*.

The Family (all 300 of them) gathered in Seattle for the Nineteenth World Science Fiction Convention—the Seacon. Hugos (awarded for achievements in 1960) included *A Canticle for Leibowitz* by Walter M. Miller, Jr. as Best Novel; "The Longest Voyage" by Poul Anderson for Best Short Fiction; *The Twilight Zone* for Best Dramatic Presentation; *Analog* for Best Professional Magazine; Ed Emshwiller for Best Professional Artist; and for Earl Kemp's *Who Killed Science Fiction?* as Best Fanzine.

Let us travel back to that honored year of 1961 and enjoy the best stories that the real world bequeathed to us.

THE HIGHEST TREASON

BY RANDALL GARRETT (1927-1987)

ANALOG
JANUARY

John W. Campbell's Astounding/Analog *was an enthusiastic participant in the Cold War of beloved memory. Its pages were filled with stories about the search for powerful weapons, military matters, totalitarian countries and civilizations obviously patterned after the Soviet Union, and espionage tales posing as science fiction. This is one of the reasons that the 1950s and 1960s were not the greatest years in the magazine's history, but to be fair, much excellent material appeared.*

A lot of it was written by such writers as David Gordon, Walter Bupp, Darrell T. Langart, Robert Randall, and Mark Phillips, all of whom were at least, in part, Randall Garrett, who also had dozens of stories in the magazine under his own name. And although Garrett was clever, and capable of producing some of the funniest sf ever written, he was also a pro who knew what Campbell wanted and knew how to give it to him.

"The Highest Treason" is a fine example of his ability to play to an editor's biases and still produce a thoughtful and exciting story. (MHG)

Poor Randall. He and I hung about together at science fiction conventions in the 1950s. In fact, Randall and I reduced the 1955 convention to a noisy shambles and helped make it the most pleasurable in history (so everyone who attended agreed.)

Randall was one of the cleverest and wittiest fellows I ever

13

*met. Talking with him was like a series of explosions as we
tried to top each other.*

*However, it always seemed to me that he didn't really capi-
talize on his cleverness. So much of it was wasted, so little
of it put to work. It didn't help, of course, that he was a
little too fond of the bottle, but I suppose it is hard living in
a world of dullards and a man like Randall had to find an
escape.*

*And then in the 1980s, he suffered an attack of meningitis
that destroyed first his mind and finally him. It was a sad
ending he didn't deserve. (IA)*

The Prisoner

The two rooms were not luxurious, but MacMaine hadn't
expected that they would be. The walls were a flat metallic
gray, unadorned and windowless. The ceilings and floors
were simply continuations of the walls, except for the glow-
plates overhead. One room held a small cabinet for his personal possessions, a wide, reasonably soft bed, a small but
adequate desk, and, in one corner, a cubicle that contained
the necessary sanitary plumbing facilities.

The other room held a couch, two big easy-chairs, a low
table, some bookshelves, a squat refrigerator containing
food and drink for his occasional snacks—his regular meals
were brought in hot from the main kitchen—and a closet
that contained his clothing—the insignialess uniforms of a
Kerothi officer.

No, thought Sebastian MacMaine, it was not luxurious,
but neither did it look like the prison cell it was.

There was comfort here, and even the illusion of privacy,
although there were TV pickups in the walls, placed so that
no movement in either room would go unnoticed. The
switch which cut off the soft white light from the glow plates
did not cut off the infrared radiation which enabled his hosts
to watch him while he slept. Every sound was heard and
recorded.

But none of that bothered MacMaine. On the contrary,
he was glad of it. He wanted the Kerothi to know that he
had no intention of escaping or hatching any plot against
them.

He had long since decided that, if things continued as

they had, Earth would lose the war with Keroth, and Sebastian MacMaine had no desire whatever to be on the losing side of the greatest war ever fought. The problem now was to convince the Kerothi that he fully intended to fight with them, to give them the full benefit of his ability as a military strategist, to do his best to win every battle for Keroth.

And that was going to be the most difficult task of all.

A telltale glow of red blinked rapidly over the door, and a soft chime pinged in time with it.

MacMaine smiled inwardly, although not a trace of it showed on his broad-jawed, blocky face. To give him the illusion that he was a guest rather than a prisoner, the Kerothi had installed an announcer at the door and invariably used it. Not once had any one of them ever simply walked in on him.

"Come in," MacMaine said.

He was seated in one of the easy-chairs in his "living room," smoking a cigarette and reading a book on the history of Keroth, but he put the book down on the low table as a tall Kerothi came in through the doorway.

MacMaine allowed himself a smile of honest pleasure. To most Earthmen, "all the Carrot-skins look alike," and, MacMaine admitted honestly to himself, he hadn't yet trained himself completely to look beyond the strangenesses that made the Kerothi different from Earthmen and see the details that made them different from each other. But this was one Kerothi that MacMaine would never mistake for any other.

"Tallis!" He stood up and extended both hands in the Kerothi fashion. The other did the same, and they clasped hands for a moment. "How are your guts?" he added in Kerothic.

"They function smoothly, my sibling-by-choice," answered Space General Polan Tallis. "And your own?"

"Smoothly, indeed. It's been far too long a time since we have touched."

The Kerothi stepped back a pace and looked the Earthman up and down. "You look healthy enough—for a prisoner. You're treated well, then?"

"Well enough. Sit down, my sibling-by-choice." MacMaine waved toward the couch nearby. The general sat down and looked around the apartment.

"Well, well. You're getting preferential treatment, all right. This is as good as you could expect as a battleship commander. Maybe you're being trained for the job."

MacMaine laughed, allowing the touch of sardonicism that he felt to be heard in the laughter. "I might have hoped so once, Tallis. But I'm afraid I have simply come out even. I have traded nothing for nothing."

General Tallis reached into the pocket of his uniform jacket and took out the thin aluminum case that held the Kerothi equivalent of cigarettes. He took one out, put it between his lips, and lit it with the hotpoint that was built into the case.

MacMaine took an Earth cigarette out of the package on the table and allowed Tallis to light it for him. The pause and the silence, MacMaine knew, were for a purpose. He waited. Tallis had something to say, but he was allowing the Earthman to "adjust to surprise." It was one of the fine points of Kerothi etiquette.

A sudden silence on the part of one participant in a conversation, under these particular circumstances, meant that something unusual was coming up, and the other person was supposed to take the opportunity to brace himself for shock.

It could mean anything. In the Kerothi Space Forces, a superior informed a junior officer of the junior's forthcoming promotion by just such tactics. But the same tactics were used when informing a person of the death of a loved one.

In fact, MacMaine was well aware that such a period of silence was *de rigueur* in a Kerothi court, just before sentence was pronounced, as well as a preliminary to a proposal of marriage by a Kerothi male to the light of his love.

MacMaine could do nothing but wait. It would be indelicate to speak until Tallis felt that he was ready for the surprise.

It was not, however, indelicate to watch Tallis' face closely; it was expected. Theoretically, one was supposed to be able to discern, at least, whether the news was good or bad.

With Tallis, it was impossible to tell, and MacMaine knew it would be useless to read the man's expression. But he watched, nonetheless.

In one way, Tallis' face was typically Kerothi. The orange-pigmented skin and the bright, grass-green eyes were common to all Kerothi. The planet Keroth, like Earth, had evolved several different "races" of humanoid, but, unlike Earth, the distinction was not one of color.

MacMaine took a drag off his cigarette and forced himself to keep his mind off whatever it was that Tallis might be about to say. He was already prepared for a death sentence—even a death sentence by torture. Now, he felt, he could not be shocked. And, rather than build up the tension within himself to an unbearable degree, he thought about Tallis rather than about himself.

Tallis, like the rest of the Kerothi, was unbelievably humanoid. There were internal differences in the placement of organs, and differences in the functions of those organs. For instance, it took two separate organs to perform the same function that the liver performed in Earthmen, and the kidneys were completely absent, that function being performed by special tissues in the lower colon, which meant that the Kerothi were more efficient with water-saving than Earthmen, since the waste products were excreted as relatively dry solids through an all-purpose cloaca.

But, externally, a Kerothi would need only a touch of plastic surgery and some makeup to pass as an Earthman in a stage play. Close up, of course, the job would be much more difficult—as difficult as a Negro trying to disguise himself as a Swede or *vice versa*.

But Tallis was—

"I would have a word," Tallis said, shattering Mac-Maine's carefully neutral train of thought. It was a standard opening for breaking the pause of adjustment, but it presaged good news rather than bad.

"I await your word," MacMaine said. Even after all this time, he still felt vaguely proud of his ability to handle the subtle idioms of Kerothic.

"I think," Tallis said carefully, "that you may be offered a commission in the Kerothi Space Forces."

Sebastian MacMaine let out his breath slowly, and only then realized that he had been holding it. "I am grateful, my sibling-by-choice," he said.

General Tallis tapped his cigarette ash into a large blue

ceramic ashtray. MacMaine could smell the acrid smoke from the alien plant matter that burned in the Kerothi cigarette—a chopped-up inner bark from a Kerothi tree. MacMaine could no more smoke a Kerothi cigarette than Tallis could smoke tobacco, but the two were remarkably similar in their effects.

The "surprise" had been delivered. Now, as was proper, Tallis would move adroitly all around the subject until he was ready to return to it again.

"You have been with us . . . how long, Sepastian?" he asked.

"Two and a third *Kronet*."

Tallis nodded. "Nearly a year of your time."

MacMaine smiled. Tallis was as proud of his knowledge of Earth terminology as MacMaine was proud of his mastery of Kerothic.

"Lacking three weeks," MacMaine said.

"What? Three . . . oh, yes. Well. A long time," said Tallis.

Damn it! MacMaine thought, in a sudden surge of impatience, *get to the point!* His face showed only calm.

"The Board of Strategy asked me to tell you," Tallis continued. "After all, my recommendation was partially responsible for the decision." He paused for a moment, but it was merely a conversational hesitation, not a formal hiatus.

"It was a hard decision, Sepastian—you must realize that. We have been at war with your race for ten years now. We have taken thousands of Earthmen as prisoners, and many of them have agreed to co-operate with us. But, with one single exception, these prisoners have been the moral dregs of your civilization. They have been men who had no pride of race, no pride of society, no pride of self. They have been weak, self-centered, small-minded, cowards who had no thought for Earth and Earthmen, but only for themselves.

"Not," he said hurriedly, "that all of them are that way—or even the majority. Most of them have the minds of warriors, although, I must say, not *strong* warriors."

That last, MacMaine knew, was a polite concession. The Kerothi had no respect for Earthmen. And MacMaine could hardly blame them. For three long centuries, the people of

Earth had had nothing to do but indulge themselves in the pleasures of material wealth. It was a wonder that any of them had any moral fiber left.

"But none of those who had any strength agreed to work with us," Tallis went on. "With one exception. You."

"Am I weak, then?" MacMaine asked.

General Tallis shook his head in a peculiarly humanlike gesture. "No. No, you are not. And that is what has made us pause for three years." His grass-green eyes looked candidly into MacMaine's own. "You aren't the type of person who betrays his own kind. It looks like a trap. After a whole year, the Board of Strategy still isn't sure that there is no trap."

Tallis stopped, leaned forward, and ground out the stub of his cigarette in the blue ashtray. Then his eyes again sought MacMaine's.

"If it were not for what I, personally, know about you, the Board of Strategy would not even consider your proposition."

"I take it, then, that they have considered it?" MacMaine asked with a grin.

"As I said, Sepastian," Tallis said, "you have won your case. After almost a year of your time, your decision has been justified."

MacMaine lost his grin. "I am grateful, Tallis," he said gravely. "I think you must realize that it was a difficult decision to make."

His thoughts went back, across long months of time and longer light-years of space, to the day when that decision had been made.

The Decision

Colonel Sebastian MacMaine didn't feel, that morning, as though this day were different from any other. The sun, faintly veiled by a few wisps of cloud, shone as it always had; the guards at the doors of the Space Force Administration Building saluted him as usual; his brother officers nodded politely, as they always did; his aide greeted him with the usual "Good morning, sir."

The duty list lay on his desk, as it had every morning for years. Sebastian MacMaine felt tense and a little irritated with himself, but he felt nothing that could be called a premonition.

When he read the first item on the duty list, his irritation became a little stronger.

"Interrogate Kerothi general."

The interrogation duty had swung round to him again. He didn't want to talk to General Tallis. There was something about the alien that bothered him, and he couldn't place exactly what it was.

Earth had been lucky to capture the alien officer. In a space war, there's usually very little left to capture after a battle—especially if your side lost the battle.

On the other hand, the Kerothi general wasn't so lucky. The food that had been captured with him would run out in less than six months, and it was doubtful that he would survive on Earth food. It was equally doubtful that any more Kerothi food would be captured.

For two years, Earth had been fighting the Kerothi, and for two years Earth had been winning a few minor skirmishes and losing the major battles. The Kerothi hadn't hit any of the major colonies yet, but they had swallowed up outpost after outpost, and Earth's space fleet was losing ships faster than her factories could turn them out. The hell of it was that nobody on Earth seemed to be very much concerned about it at all.

MacMaine wondered why he let it concern him. If no one else was worried, why did he let it bother him? He pushed the thought from his mind and picked up the questionnaire form that had been made out for that morning's session with the Kerothi general. Might as well get it over with.

He glanced down the list of further duties for the day. It looked as though the routine interrogation of the Kerothi general was likely to provide most of the interest in the day's work at that.

He took the dropchute down to the basement of the building, to the small prison section where the alien officer was being held. The guards saluted nonchalantly as he went in. The routine questioning sessions were nothing new to them.

MacMaine turned the lock on the prisoner's cell door and went in. Then he came to attention and saluted the Kerothi general. He was probably the only officer in the place who did that, he knew; the others treated the alien general as though he were a criminal. Worse, they treated him as though he were a petty thief or a common pickpocket—criminal, yes, but of a definitely inferior type.

General Tallis, as always, stood and returned the salute. "Cut mawnik, Cunnel MacMaine," he said. The Kerothi language lacked many of the voiced consonants of English and Russian, and, as a result, Tallis' use of *B, D, G, J V,* and *Z* made them come out as *P, T, K, CH, F,* and *S.* The English *R,* as it is pronounced in *run* or *rat,* eluded him entirely, and he pronounced it only when he could give it the guttural pronunciation of the German *R.* The terminal *NG* always came out as *NK.* The nasal *M* and *N* were a little more drawn out than in English, but they were easily understandable.

"Good morning, General Tallis," MacMaine said. "Sit down. How do you feel this morning?"

The general sat again on the hard bunk that, aside from the single chair, was the only furniture in the small cell. "Ass well ass coot pe expectct. I ket ferry little exercisse. I . . . how iss it set? . . . I pecome soft? Soft? Iss correct?"

"Correct. You've learned our language very well for so short a time."

The general shrugged off the compliment. "When it iss a matteh of learrn in orrter to surfife, one learrnss."

"You think, then, that your survival has depended on your learning our language?"

The general's orange face contrived a wry smile. "Opfiously. Your people fill not learn Kerothic. If I cannot answerr questionss, I am uff no use. Ass lonk ass I am uff use, I will liff. Not?"

MacMaine decided he might as well spring his bomb on the Kerothi officer now as later. "I am not so certain but that you might have stretched out your time longer if you had forced us to learn Kerothic, general," he said in Kerothic. He knew his Kerothic was bad, since it had been learned from the Kerothi spaceman who had been captured with the general, and the man had been badly wounded and had survived only two weeks. But that little bit of basic instruction, plus the work he had done on the books and tapes from the ruined Kerothi ship, had helped him.

"Ah?" The general blinked in surprise. Then he smiled. "Your accent," he said in Kerothic, "is atrocious, but certainly no worse than mine when I speak your *Inklitch*. I suppose you intend to question me in Kerothic now, eh? In the hope that I may reveal more in my own tongue?"

"Possibly you may," MacMaine said with a grin, "but I learned it for my own information."

"For your own what? Oh. I see. Interesting. I know no others of your race who would do such a thing. Anything which is difficult is beneath them."

"Not so, general. I'm not unique. There are many of us who don't think that way."

The general shrugged. "I do not deny it. I merely say that I have met none. Certainly they do not tend to go into military service. Possibly that is because you are not a race of fighters. It takes a fighter to tackle the difficult just because it is difficult."

MacMaine gave him a short, hard laugh. "Don't you think getting information out of *you* is difficult? And yet, we tackle that."

"Not the same thing at all. Routine. You have used no pressure. No threats, no promises, no torture, no stress."

MacMaine wasn't quite sure of his translation of the last two negative phrases. "You mean the application of physical pain? That's barbaric."

"I won't pursue the subject," the general said with sudden irony.

"I can understand that. But you can rest assured that we would never do such a thing. It isn't civilized. Our civil police do use certain drugs to obtain information, but we have so little knowledge of Kerothi body chemistry that we hesitate to use drugs on you."

"The application of stress, you say, is not civilized. Not, perhaps, according to your definition of"—he used the English word—"*cifiliced*. No. Not *cifiliced*—but it works." Again he smiled. "I said that I have become soft since I have been here, but I fear that your civilization is even softer."

"A man can lie, even if his arms are pulled off or his feet crushed," MacMaine said stiffly.

The Kerothi looked startled. When he spoke again, it was in English. "I will say no morr. If you haff questionss to ask, ko ahet. I will not take up time with furtherr talkink."

A little angry with himself and with the general, Mac-Maine spent the rest of the hour asking routine questions and getting nowhere, filling up the tape in his minicorder with the same old answers that others had gotten.

He left, giving the general a brisk salute and turning before the general had time to return it.

Back in his office, he filed the tape dutifully and started on Item Two of the duty list: *Strategy Analysis of Battle Reports*.

Strategy analysis always irritated and upset him. He knew that if he'd just go about it in the approved way, there would be no irritation—only boredom. But he was constitutionally incapable of working that way. In spite of himself, he always played a little game with himself and with the General Strategy Computer.

The only battle of significance in the past week had been the defense of an Earth outpost called Bennington IV. Theoretically, MacMaine was supposed to check over the entire report, find out where the losing side had erred, and feed correctional information into the Computer. But he couldn't resist stopping after he had read the first section: *Information Known to Earth Commander at Moment of Initial Contact*.

Then he would stop and consider how he, personally, would have handled the situation if he had been the Earth commander. So many ships in such-and-such places. Enemy fleet approaching at such-and-such velocities. Battle array of enemy thus-and-so.

Now what?

MacMaine thought over the information on the defense of Bennington IV and devised a battle plan. There was a weak point in the enemy's attack, but it was rather obvious. MacMaine searched until he found another weak point, much less obvious than the first. He knew it would be there. It was.

Then he proceeded to ignore both weak points and concentrate on what he would do if he were the enemy commander. The weak points were traps; the computer could see them and avoid them. Which was just exactly what was wrong with the computer's logic. In avoiding the traps, it also avoided the best way to hit the enemy. A weak point *is* weak, no matter how well it may be booby-trapped. In baiting a rat trap, you have to use real cheese because an imitation won't work.

Of course, MacMaine thought to himself, *you can always poison the cheese, but let's not carry the analogy too far.*

All right, then. How to hit the traps?

It took him half an hour to devise a completely wacky and unorthodox way of hitting the holes in the enemy advance. He checked the time carefully, because there's no point in devising a strategy if the battle is too far gone to use it by the time you've figured it out.

Then he went ahead and read the rest of the report. Earth had lost the outpost. And, worse, MacMaine's strategy would have won the battle if it had been used. He fed it through his small office computer to make sure. The odds were good.

And that was the thing that made MacMaine hate Strategy Analysis. Too often, he won; too often, Earth lost. A computer was fine for working out the logical outcome of a battle if it was given the proper strategy, but it couldn't devise anything new.

Colonel MacMaine had tried to get himself transferred to space duty, but without success. The Commanding Staff didn't want him out there.

The trouble was that they didn't believe MacMaine actually devised his strategy before he read the complete report. How could anyone outthink a computer?

He'd offered to prove it. "Give me a problem," he'd told his immediate superior, General Matsukuo. "Give me the Initial Contact information of a battle I haven't seen before, and I'll show you."

And Matsukuo had said, testily: "Colonel, I will not permit a member of my staff to make a fool of himself in front of the Commanding Staff. Setting yourself up as someone superior to the Strategy Board is the most antisocial type of egocentrism imaginable. You were given the same education at the Academy as every other officer; what makes you think you are better than they? As time goes on, your automatic promotions will put you in a position to vote on such matters—provided you don't prejudice the Promotion

Board against you by antisocial behavior. I hold you in the highest regard, colonel, and I will say nothing to the Promotion Board about this, but if you persist I will have to do my duty. Now, I don't want to hear any more about it. Is that clear?"

It was.

All MacMaine had to do was wait, and he'd automatically be promoted to the Commanding Staff, where he would have an equal vote with the others of his rank. One unit vote to begin with and an additional unit for every year thereafter.

It's a great system for running a peacetime social club, maybe, MacMaine thought, *but it's no way to run a fighting force*.

Maybe the Kerothi general was right. Maybe *homo sapiens* just wasn't a race of fighters.

They had been once. Mankind had fought its way to domination of Earth by battling every other form of life on the planet, from the smallest virus to the biggest carnivore. The fight against disease was still going on, as a matter of fact, and Man was still fighting the elemental fury of Earth's climate.

But Man no longer fought with Man. Was that a bad thing? The discovery of atomic energy, two centuries before, had literally made war impossible, if the race was to survive. Small struggles bred bigger struggles—or so the reasoning went. Therefore, the society had unconsciously sought to eliminate the reasons for struggle.

What bred the hatreds and jealousies among men? What caused one group to fight another?

Society had decided that intolerance and hatred were caused by inequality. The jealousy of the inferior toward his superior; the scorn of the superior toward his inferior. The Have-not envies the Have, and the Have looks down upon the Have-not.

Then let us eliminate the Have-not. Let us make sure that everyone is a Have.

Raise the standard of living. Make sure that every human being has the necessities of life—food, clothing, shelter, proper medical care, and proper education. More, give them the luxuries, too—let no man be without anything that is poorer in quality or less in quantity than the possessions

of any other. There was no longer any middle class simply
because there were no other classes for it to be in the middle of.

"The poor you will have always with you," Jesus of Naza-
reth had said. But, in a material sense, that was no longer
true. The poor were gone—and so were the rich.

But the poor in mind and the poor in spirit were still
there—in ever-increasing numbers.

Material wealth could be evenly distributed, but it could
not remain that way unless Society made sure that the man
who was more clever than the rest could not increase his
wealth at the expense of his less fortunate brethren.

Make it a social stigma to show more ability than the
average. Be kind to your fellow man; don't show him up as
a stupid clod, no matter how cloddish he may be.

All men are created equal, and let's make sure they stay
that way!

There could be no such thing as a classless society, of
course. That was easily seen. No human being could do
everything, learn everything, be everything. There had to
be doctors and lawyers and policemen and bartenders and
soldiers and machinists and laborers and actors and writers
and criminals and bums.

But let's make sure that the differentiation between
classes is horizontal, not vertical. As long as a person does
his job the best he can, he's as good as anybody else. A
doctor is as good as a lawyer, isn't he? Then a garbage
collector is just as good as a nuclear physicist, and an
astronomer is no better than a street sweeper.

And what of the loafer, the bum, the man who's too lazy
or weak-willed to put out any more effort than is absolutely
necessary to stay alive? Well, my goodness, the poor chap
can't *help* it, can he? It isn't *his* fault, is it? He has to be
helped. There is always *something* he is both capable of
doing and willing to do. Does he like to sit around all day
and do nothing but watch television? Then give him a sheet
of paper with all the programs on it and two little boxes
marked *Yes* and *No*, and he can put an X in one or the
other to indicate whether he likes the program or not. Useful? Certainly. All these sheets can be tallied up in order

to find out what sort of program the public likes to see. After all, his vote is just as good as anyone else's, isn't it?

And a Program Analyst is just as good, just as important, and just as well cared-for as anyone else.

And what about the criminal? Well, what *is* a criminal? A person who thinks he's superior to others. A thief steals because he thinks he has more right to something than its real owner. A man kills because he has an idea that he has a better right to live than someone else. In short, a man breaks the law because he feels superior, because he thinks he can outsmart Society and The Law. Or, simply, because he thinks he can outsmart the policeman on the beat.

Obviously, that sort of antisocial behavior can't be allowed. The poor fellow who thinks he's better than anyone else has to be segregated from normal society and treated for his aberrations. But not punished! Heavens no! His erratic behavior isn't *his* fault, is it?

It was axiomatic that there had to be some sort of vertical structure to society, naturally. A child can't do the work of an adult, and a beginner can't be as good as an old hand. Aside from the fact that it was actually impossible to force everyone into a common mold, it was recognized that there had to be some incentive for staying with a job. What to do?

The labor unions had solved that problem two hundred years before. Promotion by seniority. Stick with a job long enough, and you'll automatically rise to the top. That way, everyone had as good a chance as everyone else.

Promotion tables for individual jobs were worked out on the basis of longevity tables, so that by the time a man reached the automatic retirement age he was automatically at the highest position he could hold. No fuss, no bother, no trouble. Just keep your nose clean and live as long as possible.

It eliminated struggle. It eliminated the petty jockeying for position that undermined efficiency in an organization. Everybody deserves an equal chance in life, so make sure everybody gets it.

Colonel Sebastian MacMaine had been born and reared in that society. He could see many of its faults, but he didn't have the orientation to see all of them. As he'd grown older, he'd seen that, regardless of the position a man held according to seniority, a smart man could exercise more power than those above him if he did it carefully.

A man is a slave if he is held rigidly in a pattern and not permitted to step out of that pattern. In ancient times, a slave was born at the bottom of the social ladder, and he remained there all his life. Only rarely did a slave of exceptional merit manage to rise above his assigned position.

But a man who is forced to remain on the bottom step of a stationary stairway is no more a slave than a man who is forced to remain on a given step of an escalator, and no less so.

Slavery, however, has two advantages—one for the individual, and one which, in the long run, can be good for the race. For the individual, it offers security, and that is the goal which by far the greater majority of mankind seeks.

The second advantage is more difficult to see. It operates only in favor of the exceptional individual. There are always individuals who aspire to greater heights than the one they occupy at any given moment, but in a slave society, they are slapped back into place if they act hastily. Just as the one-eyed man in the kingdom of the blind can be king if he taps the ground with a cane, so the gifted individual can gain his ends in a slave society—provided he thinks out the consequences of any act in advance.

The Law of Gravity is a universal edict which enslaves, in a sense, every particle of matter in the cosmos. The man who attempts to defy the "injustice" of that law by ignoring the consequences of its enforcement will find himself punished rather severely. It may be unjust that a bird can fly under its own muscle power, but a man who tries to correct that injustice by leaping out of a skyscraper window and flapping his arms vigorously will find that overt defiance of the Law of Gravity brings very serious penalties indeed. The wise man seeks the loopholes in the law, and loopholes are caused by other laws which counteract—*not defy!*—the given law. A balloon full of hydrogen "falls up" in obedience to the Law of Gravity. A contradiction? A paradox? No. It is the Law of Gravity which causes the density and pressure of a planet's atmosphere to decrease with altitude, and that decrease in pressure forces the balloon upwards until the balance point between atmospheric density and the internal density of the balloon is reached.

The illustration may seem obvious and elementary to the modern man, but it seems so only because he understands, at least to some extent, the laws involved. It was not obvious to even the most learned man of, say, the Thirteenth Century.

Slavery, too, has its laws, and it is as dangerous to defy the laws of a society as it is to defy those of nature, and the only way to escape the punishment resulting from those laws is to find the loopholes. One of the most basic laws of any society is so basic that it is never, *ever* written down.

And that law, like all basic laws, is so simple in expression and so obvious in application that any man above the moron level has an intuitive grasp of it. It is the first law one learns as a child.

Thou shalt not suffer thyself to be caught.

The unthinking man believes that this basic law can be applied by breaking the laws of his society in secret. What he fails to see is that such lawbreaking requires such a fantastic network of lies, subterfuges, evasions, and chicanery that the structure itself eventually breaks down and his guilt is obvious to all. The very steps he has taken to keep from getting caught eventually become signposts that point unerringly at the lawbreaker himself.

Like the loopholes in the law of gravity, the loopholes in the laws of society can not entail a *defiance* of the law. Only compliance with those laws will be ultimately successful.

The wise man works within the framework of the law—not only the written, but the unwritten law—of his society. In a slave society, any slave who openly rebels will find that he gets squashed pretty quickly. But many a slave-owner has danced willingly to the tune of a slave who was wiser and cleverer than he, without ever knowing that the tune played was not his own.

And that is the second advantage of slavery. It teaches the exceptional individual to think.

When a wise, intelligent individual openly and violently breaks the laws of his society, there are two things which are almost certain: One: he knows that there is no other way to do the thing he feels must be done, and—

Two: he knows that he will pay the penalty for his crime in one way or another.

Sebastian MacMaine knew the operations of those laws. As a member of a self-enslaved society, he knew that to betray any sign of intelligence was dangerous. A slight slip could bring the scorn of the slaves around him; a major offense could mean death. The war with Keroth had thrown him slightly off balance, but after his one experience with General Matsukuo, he had quickly regained his equilibrium.

At the end of his work day, MacMaine closed his desk and left his office precisely on time, as usual. Working overtime, except in the gravest emergencies, was looked upon as antisocialism. The offender was suspected of having Ambition—obviously a Bad Thing.

It was during his meal at the Officers' Mess that Colonel Sebastian MacMaine heard the statement that triggered the decision in his mind.

There were three other officers seated with MacMaine around one of the four-place tables in the big room. MacMaine only paid enough attention to the table conversation to be able to make the appropriate noises at the proper times. He had long since learned to do his thinking under cover of general banalities.

Colonel VanDeusen was a man who would never have made Private First Class in an army that operated on a strict merit system. His thinking was muddy, and his conversation betrayed it. All he felt comfortable in talking about was just exactly what he had been taught. Slogans, banalities, and bromides. He knew his catechism, and he knew it was safe.

"What I mean is, we got nothing to worry about. We all stick together, and we can do anything. As long as we don't rock the boat, we'll come through O.K."

"Sure," said Major Brock, looking up from his plate in blank-faced surprise. "I mean, who says different?"

"Guy on my research team," said VanDeusen, plying his fork industriously. "A wise-guy second looie. One of them."

"Oh," said the major knowingly. "One of them." He went back to his meal.

"What'd he say?" MacMaine asked, just to keep his oar in.

"Ahhh, nothing serious, I guess," said VanDeusen, around a mouthful of steak. "Said we were all clogged up with paper work, makin' reports on tests, things like that. Said, why don't we figure out something to pop those Carrot-skins outa the sky. So I said to him, 'Look, Lootenant,' I said, 'you got your job to do, I got mine. If the paper work's pilin' up,' I said, 'it's because somebody isn't pulling his share. And it better not be you,' I said." He chuckled and speared another cube of steak with his fork. "That settled him down. He's all right, though. Young yet, you know. Soon's he gets the hang of how the Space Force operates, he'll be O.K."

Since VanDeusen was the senior officer at the table, the others listened respectfully as he talked, only inserting a word now and then to show that they were listening.

MacMaine was thinking deeply about something else entirely, but VanDeusen's influence intruded a little. MacMaine was wondering what it was that bothered him about General Tallis, the Kerothi prisoner.

The alien was pleasant enough, in spite of his position. He seemed to accept his imprisonment as one of the fortunes of war. He didn't threaten or bluster, although he tended to maintain an air of superiority that would have been unbearable in an Earthman.

Was that the reason for his uneasiness in the general's presence? No. MacMaine could accept the reason for that attitude; the general's background was different from that of an Earthman, and therefore he could not be judged by Terrestrial standards. Besides, MacMaine could acknowledge to himself that Tallis *was* superior to the norm—not only the norm of Keroth, but that of Earth. MacMaine wasn't sure he could have acknowledged superiority in another Earthman, in spite of the fact that he knew that there must be men who were his superiors in one way or another.

Because of his social background, he knew that he would probably form an intense and instant dislike for any Earthman who talked the way Tallis did, but he found that he actually *liked* the alien officer.

It came as a slight shock when the realization hit MacMaine that his liking for the general was exactly why he was uncomfortable around him. Dammit, a man isn't supposed to like his enemy—and most especially when that enemy does and says things that one would despise in a friend.

Come to think of it, though, did he, MacMaine, actually have any friends? He looked around him, suddenly clearly conscious of the other men in the room. He searched through his memory, thinking of all his acquaintances and relatives.

It was an even greater shock to realize that he would not be more than faintly touched emotionally if any or all of them were to die at that instant. Even his parents, both of whom were now dead, were only dim figures in his memory. He had mourned them when an aircraft accident had taken both of them when he was only eleven, but he found himself wondering if it had been the loss of loved ones that had caused his emotional upset or simply the abrupt vanishing of a kind of security he had taken for granted.

And yet, he felt that the death of General Polan Tallis would leave an empty place in his life.

Colonel VanDeusen was still holding forth.

". . . So I told him. I said, 'Look, Lootenant,' I said, 'don't rock the boat. You're a kid yet, you know,' I said. 'You got equal rights with everybody else,' I said, 'but if you rock the boat, you aren't gonna get along so well.'

" 'You just behave yourself,' I said, 'and pull your share of the load and do your job right and keep your nose clean, and you'll come out all right.

" 'Time I get to be on the General Staff,' I told him, 'why, you'll be takin' over my job, maybe. That's the way it works,' I said.

"He's a good kid. I mean, he's a fresh young punk, that's all. He'll learn, O.K. He'll climb right up, once he's got the right attitude. Why, when I was—"

But MacMaine was no longer listening. It was astonishing to realize that what VanDeusen had said was perfectly true. A blockhead like VanDeusen would simply be lifted to a position of higher authority, only to be replaced by another blockhead. There would be no essential change in the *status quo*.

The Kerothi were winning steadily, and the people of Earth and her colonies were making no changes whatever in their way of living. The majority of people were too blind to be able to see what was happening, and the rest were afraid to admit the danger, even to themselves. It required no great understanding of strategy to see what the inevitable outcome must be.

At some point in the last few centuries, human civilization had taken the wrong path—a path that led only to oblivion.

It was at that moment that Colonel Sebastian MacMaine made his decision.

The Escape

"Are you sure that you understand, Tallis?" MacMaine asked in Kerothic.

The alien general nodded emphatically. "Perfectly. Your Kerothic is not so bad that I could misunderstand your instructions. I still don't understand why you are doing this. Oh I know the reasons you've given me, but I don't completely believe them. However, I'll go along with you. The worst that could happen would be for me to be killed, and I would sooner face death in trying to escape than in waiting for your executioners. If this is some sort of trap, some sort of weird way your race's twisted idea of kindness has evolved to dispose of me, then I'll accept your sentence. It's better than starving to death or facing a firing squad."

"Not a firing squad," MacMaine said. "That wouldn't be kind. An odorless, but quite deadly gas would be pumped into this cell while you slept."

"That's worse. When death comes, I want to face it and fight it off as long as possible, not have it sneaking up on me in my sleep. I think I'd rather starve."

"You would," said MacMaine. "The food that was captured with you has nearly run out, and we haven't been able to capture any more. But rather than let you suffer, they would have killed you painlessly." He glanced at the watch on his instrument cuff. "Almost time."

MacMaine looked the alien over once more. Tallis was dressed in the uniform of Earth's Space Force, and the insignia of a full general gleamed on his collar. His face and hands had been sprayed with an opaque, pink-tan film, and his hairless head was covered with a black wig. He wouldn't pass a close inspection, but MacMaine fervently hoped that he wouldn't need to.

Think it out, be sure you're right, then go ahead. Sebastian MacMaine had done just that. For three months, he had worked over the details of his plan, making sure that they were as perfect as he was capable of making them. Even so, there was a great deal of risk involved, and there were too many details that required luck for MacMaine to be perfectly happy about the plan.

But time was running out. As the general's food supply dwindled, his execution date neared, and now it was only two days away. There was no point in waiting until the last minute; it was now or never.

There were no spying TV cameras in the general's cell, no hidden microphones to report and record what went on. No one had ever escaped from the Space Force's prison, therefore, no one ever would.

MacMaine glanced again at his watch. It was time. He reached inside his blouse and took out a fully loaded handgun.

For an instant, the alien officer's eyes widened, and he stiffened as if he were ready to die in an attempt to disarm the Earthman. Then he saw that MacMaine wasn't holding it by the butt; his hand was clasped around the middle of the weapon.

"This is a chance I have to take," MacMaine said evenly. "With this gun, you can shoot me down right here and try to escape alone. I've told you every detail of our course of action, and, with luck, you might make it alone." He held out his hand, with the weapon resting on his open palm.

General Tallis eyed the Earthman for a long second. Then, without haste, he took the gun and inspected it with a professional eye.

"Do you know how to operate it?" MacMaine asked, forcing calmness into his voice.

"Yes. We've captured plenty of them." Tallis thumbed the stud that allowed the magazine to slide out of the butt and into his hand. Then he checked the mechanism and the power cartridges. Finally, he replaced the magazine and put the weapon into the empty sleeve holster that MacMaine had given him.

MacMaine let his breath out slowly. "All right," he said. "Let's go."

*　　*　　*

He opened the door of the cell, and both men stepped out into the corridor. At the far end of the corridor, some thirty yards away, stood the two armed guards who kept watch over the prisoner. At that distance, it was impossible to tell that Tallis was not what he appeared to be.

The guard had been changed while MacMaine was in the prisoner's cell, and he was relying on the lax discipline of the soldiers to get him and Tallis out of the cell block. With luck, the guards would have failed to listen too closely to what they had been told by the men they replaced; with even greater luck, the previous guardsmen would have failed to be too explicit about who was in the prisoner's cell. With no luck at all, MacMaine would be forced to shoot to kill.

MacMaine walked casually up to the two men, who came to an easy attention.

"I want you two men to come with me. Something odd has happened, and General Quinby and I want two witnesses as to what went on."

"What happened, sir?" one of them asked.

"Don't know for sure," MacMaine said in a puzzled voice. "The general and I were talking to the prisoner, when all of a sudden he fell over. I think he's dead. I couldn't find a heartbeat. I want you to take a look at him so that you can testify that we didn't shoot him or anything."

Obediently, the two guards headed for the cell, and Mac-Maine fell in behind them. "You couldn't of shot him, sir," said the second guard confidently. "We would of heard the shot."

"Besides," said the other, "it don't matter much. He was going to be gassed day after tomorrow."

As the trio approached the cell, Tallis pulled the door open a little wider and, in doing so, contrived to put himself behind it so that his face couldn't be seen. The young guards weren't too awed by a full general; after all, they'd be generals themselves someday. They were much more interested in seeing the dead alien.

As the guards reached the cell door, MacMaine unholstered his pistol from his sleeve and brought it down hard on the head of the nearest youth. At the same time, Tallis stepped from behind the door and clouted the other.

Quickly, MacMaine disarmed the fallen men and dragged them into the open cell. He came out again and locked the door securely. Their guns were tossed into an empty cell nearby.

"They won't be missed until the next change of watch, in four hours," MacMaine said. "By then, it won't matter, one way or another."

Getting out of the huge building that housed the administrative offices of the Space Force was relatively easy. A lift chute brought the pair to the main floor, and, this late in the evening, there weren't many people on that floor. The officers and men who had night duty were working on the upper floors. Several times, Tallis had to take a handkerchief from his pocket and pretend to blow his nose in order to conceal his alien features from someone who came too close, but no one appeared to notice anything out of the ordinary.

As they walked out boldly through the main door, fifteen minutes later, the guards merely came to attention and relaxed as a tall colonel and a somewhat shorter general strode out. The general appeared to be having a fit of sneezing, and the colonel was heard to say: "That's quite a cold you've picked up, sir. Better get over to the dispensary and take an anti-coryza shot."

"Mmmf," said the general. "*Ha-CHOO!*"

Getting to the spaceport was no problem at all. Mac-Maine had an official car waiting, and the two sergeants in the front seat didn't pay any attention to the general getting in the back seat because Colonel MacMaine was talking to them. "We're ready to roll, sergeant," he said to the driver. "General Quinby wants to go straight to the *Manila*, so let's get him there as fast as possible. Take-off is scheduled in ten minutes." Then he got into the back seat himself. The one-way glass partition that separated the back seat from the front prevented either of the two men from looking back at their passengers.

Seven minutes later, the staff car was rolling unquestioned through the main gate of Waikiki Spaceport.

It was all so incredibly easy, MacMaine thought. Nobody questioned an official car. Nobody checked anything too closely. Nobody wanted to risk his lifelong security by doing or saying something that might be considered antisocial by a busy general. Besides, it never entered anyone's mind that there could be anything wrong. If there was a war on, apparently no one had been told about it yet.

MacMaine thought, *Was I ever that stubbornly blind? Not quite, I guess, or I'd never have seen what is happening.* But he knew he hadn't been too much more perceptive than those around him. Even to an intelligent man, the mask of stupidity can become a barrier to the outside world as well as a concealment from it.

The Interstellar Ship *Manila* was a small, fast, ten-man blaster-boat, designed to get in to the thick of a battle quickly, strike hard, and get away. Unlike the bigger, more powerful battle cruisers, she could be landed directly on any planet with less than a two-gee pull at the surface. The really big babies had to be parked in an orbit and loaded by shuttle; they'd break up of their own weight if they tried to set down on anything bigger than a good-sized planetoid. As long as their antiacceleration fields were on, they could take unimaginable thrusts along their axes, but the A-A fields were the cause of those thrusts as well as the protection against them. The ships couldn't stand still while they were operating, so they were no protection at all against a planet's gravity. But a blaster-boat was small enough and compact enough to take the strain.

It had taken careful preparation to get the *Manila* ready to go just exactly when MacMaine needed it. Papers had to be forged and put into the chain of command communication at precisely the right times; others had had to be taken out and replaced with harmless near-duplicates so that the Commanding Staff wouldn't discover the deception. He had had to build up the fictional identity of a "General Lucius Quinby" in such a way that it would take a thorough check to discover that the officer who had been put in command of the *Manila* was nonexistent.

It was two minutes until take-off time when the staff car pulled up at the foot of the ramp that led up to the main air lock of the ISS *Manila*. A young-looking captain was standing nervously at the foot of it, obviously afraid that his new commander might be late for the take-off and wondering what sort of decision he would have to make if the general wasn't there at take-off time. MacMaine could imagine his feelings.

"General Quinby" developed another sneezing fit as he stepped out of the car. This was the touchiest part of Mac-Maine's plan, the weakest link in the whole chain of action. For a space of perhaps a minute, the disguised Kerothi general would have to stand so close to the young captain that the crudity of his make-up job would be detectable. He had to keep that handkerchief over his face, and yet do it in such a way that it would seem natural

As Tallis climbed out of the car, chuffing windily into the kerchief, MacMaine snapped an order to the sergeant behind the wheel. "That's all. We're taking off almost immediately, so get that car out of here."

Then he walked rapidly over to the captain, who had snapped to attention. There was a definite look of relief on his face, now that he knew his commander was on time.

"All ready for take-off, captain? Everything checked out? Ammunition? Energy packs all filled to capacity? All the crew aboard? Full rations and stores stowed away?"

The captain kept his eyes on MacMaine's face as he answered "Yes, sir; yes, sir; yes, sir," to the rapid fire of questions. He had no time to shift his gaze to the face of his new C.O., who was snuffling his way toward the foot of the landing ramp. MacMaine kept firing questions until Tallis was halfway up the ramp.

Then he said: "Oh, by the way, captain—was the large package containing General Quinby's personal gear brought aboard?"

"The big package? Yes, sir. About fifteen minutes ago."

"Good," said MacMaine. He looked up the ramp. "Are there any special orders at this time, sir?" he asked.

"No," said Tallis, without turning. "Carry on, colonel." He went on up to the air lock. It had taken Tallis hours of practice to say that phrase properly, but the training had been worth it.

After Tallis was well inside the air lock, MacMaine whispered to the young captain, "As you can see, the general has got a rather bad cold. He'll want to remain in his cabin until he's over it. See that anti-coryza shots are sent up from the dispensary as soon as we are out of the Solar System. Now, let's go; we have less than a minute till take-off."

MacMaine went up the ramp with the captain scrambling up behind him.

Tallis was just stepping into the commander's cabin as the two men entered the air lock. MacMaine didn't see him again until the ship was twelve minutes on her way—nearly five billion miles from Earth and still accelerating.

He identified himself at the door and Tallis opened it cautiously.

"I brought your anti-coryza shot, sir," he said. In a small ship like the *Manila*, the captain and the seven crew members could hear any conversation in the companionways. He stepped inside and closed the door. Then he practically collapsed on the nearest chair and had a good case of the shakes.

"So-so f-f-far, s-so good," he said.

General Tallis grasped his shoulder with a firm hand. "Brace up, Sepastian," he said gently in Kerothic. "You've done a beautiful job. I still can't believe it, but I'll have to admit that if this is an act it's a beautiful one." He gestured toward the small desk in one corner of the room and the big package that was sitting on it. "The food is all there. I'll have to eat sparingly, but I can make it. Now, what's the rest of the plan?"

MacMaine took a deep breath, held it, and let it out slowly. His shakes subsided to a faint, almost imperceptible quiver. "The captain doesn't know our destination. He was told that he would receive secret instructions from you." His voice, he noticed thankfully, was almost normal. He reached into his uniform jacket and took out an official-looking sealed envelope. "These are the orders. We are going out to arrange a special truce with the Kerothi."

"What?"

"That's what it says here. You'll have to get on the subradio and do some plain and fancy talking. Fortunately, not a man jack aboard this ship knows a word of your language, so they'll think you're arranging truce terms.

"They'll be sitting ducks when your warship pulls up alongside and sends in a boarding party. By the time they realize what has happened, it will be too late."

"You're giving us the ship, too?" Tallis looked at him wonderingly. "And eight prisoners?"

"Nine," said MacMaine. "I'll hand over my sidearm to you just before your men come through the air lock."

General Tallis sat down in the other small chair, his eyes still on the Earthman. "I can't help but feel that this is some sort of trick, but if it is, I can't see through it. Why are you doing this, Sepastian?"

"You may not understand this, Tallis," MacMaine said evenly, "but I am fighting for freedom. The freedom to think."

The Traitor

Convincing the Kerothi that he was in earnest was more difficult than MacMaine had at first supposed. He had done his best, and now, after nearly a year of captivity, Tallis had come to tell him that his offer had been accepted.

General Tallis sat across from Colonel MacMaine, smoking his cigarette absently.

"Just why are they accepting my proposition?" MacMaine asked bluntly.

"Because they can afford to," Tallis said with a smile. "You will be watched, my sibling-by-choice. Watched every moment, for any sign of treason. Your flagship will be a small ten-man blaster-boat—one of our own. You gave us one; we'll give you one. At the worst, we will come out even. At the best, your admittedly brilliant grasp of tactics and strategy will enable us to save thousands of Kerothi lives, to say nothing of the immense savings in time and money."

"All I ask is a chance to prove my ability and my loyalty."

"You've already proven your ability. All of the strategy problems that you have been given over the past year were actual battles that had already been fought. In eighty-seven per cent of the cases, your strategy proved to be superior to our own. In most of the others, it was just as good. In only three cases was the estimate of your losses higher than the actual losses. Actually, we'd be fools to turn you down. We have everything to gain and nothing to lose."

"I felt the same way a year ago," said MacMaine. "Even being watched all the time will allow me more freedom than

I had on Earth—if the Board of Strategy is willing to meet my terms."

Tallis chuckled. "They are. You'll be the best-paid officer in the entire fleet; none of the rest of us gets a tenth of what you'll be getting, as far as personal value is concerned. And yet, it costs us practically nothing. You drive an attractive bargain, Sepastian."

"Is that the kind of pay you'd like to get, Tallis?" Mac-Maine asked with a smile.

"Why not? You'll get your terms: full pay as a Kerothi general, with retirement on full pay after the war is over. The pick of the most beautiful—by your standards—of the Earthwomen we capture. A home on Keroth, built to your specifications, and full citizenship, including the freedom to enter into any business relationships you wish. If you keep your promises, we can keep ours and still come out ahead."

"Good. When do we start?"

"Now," said Tallis rising from his chair. "Put on your dress uniform, and we'll go down to see the High Commander. We've got to give you a set of general's insignia, my sibling-by-choice."

Tallis waited while MacMaine donned the blue trousers and gold-trimmed red uniform of a Kerothi officer. When he was through, MacMaine looked at himself in the mirror. "There's one more thing, Tallis," he said thoughtfully.

"What's that?"

"This hair. I think you'd better arrange to have it permanently removed, according to your custom. I can't do anything about the color of my skin, but there's no point in my looking like one of your wild hillmen."

"You're very gracious," Tallis said. "And very wise. Our officers will certainly come closer to feeling that you are one of us."

"I am one of you from this moment," MacMaine said. "I never intend to see Earth again, except, perhaps, from space—when we fight the final battle of the war."

"That may be a hard battle," Tallis said.

"Maybe," MacMaine said thoughtfully. "On the other hand, if my overall strategy comes out the way I think it will, that battle may never be fought at all. I think that complete and total surrender will end the war before we ever get that close to Earth."

"I hope you're right," Tallis said firmly. "This war is costing far more than we had anticipated, in spite of the weakness of your—that is, of Earth."

"Well," MacMaine said with a slight grin, "at least you've been able to capture enough Earth food to keep me eating well all this time."

Tallis' grin was broad. "You're right. We're not doing too badly at that. Now, let's go; the High Commander is waiting."

MacMaine didn't realize until he walked into the big room that what he was facing was not just a discussion with a high officer, but what amounted to a Court of Inquiry.

The High Commander, a dome-headed, wrinkled, yellow-skinned, hard-eyed old Kerothi, was seated in the center of a long, high desk, flanked on either side by two lower-ranking generals who had the same deadly, hard look. Off to one side, almost like a jury in a jury box, sat twenty or so lesser officers, none of them ranking below the Kerothi equivalent of lieutenant-colonel.

As far as MacMaine could tell, none of the officers wore the insignia of fleet officers, the spaceship-and-comet that showed that the wearer was a fighting man. These were the men of the Permanent Headquarters Staff—the military group that controlled, not only the armed forces of Keroth, but the civil government as well.

"What's this?" MacMaine hissed in a whispered aside, in English.

"Pearr up, my prrotherr," Tallis answered softly, in the same tongue, "all is well."

MacMaine had known, long before he had ever heard of General Polan Tallis, that the Hegemony of Keroth was governed by a military junta, and that all Kerothi were regarded as members of the armed forces. Technically, there were no civilians; they were legally members of the "unorganized reserve," and were under military law. He had known that Kerothi society was, in its own way, as much a slave society as that of Earth, but it had the advantage over Earth in that the system did allow for advance by merit. If a man had the determination to get ahead, and the ability to cut the throat—either literally or figuratively—of the man above him in rank, he could take his place.

On a more strictly legal basis, it was possible for a common trooper to become an officer by going through the schools set up for that purpose, but, in practice, it took both pull and pressure to get into those schools.

In theory, any citizen of the Hegemony could become an officer, and any officer could become a member of the Permanent Headquarters Staff. Actually, a much greater preference was given to the children of officers. Examinations were given periodically for the purpose of recruiting new members for the elite officers' corps, and any citizen could take the examination—once.

But the tests were heavily weighted in favor of those who were already well-versed in matters military, including what might be called the "inside jokes" of the officers' corps. A common trooper had some chance of passing the examination; a civilian had a very minute chance. A noncommissioned officer had the best chance of passing the examination, but there were age limits which usually kept NCO's from getting a commission. By the time a man became a noncommissioned officer, he was too old to be admitted to the officers training schools. There were allowances made for "extraordinary merit," which allowed common troopers or upper-grade NCO's to be commissioned in spite of the general rules, and an astute man could take advantage of those allowances.

Ability could get a man up the ladder, but it had to be a particular kind of ability.

During his sojourn as a "guest" of the Kerothi, Mac-Maine had made a point of exploring the history of the race. He knew perfectly well that the histories he had read were doctored, twisted, and, in general, totally unreliable in so far as presenting anything that would be called a history by an unbiased investigator.

But, knowing this, MacMaine had been able to learn a great deal about the present society. Even if the "history" was worthless as such, it did tell something about the attitudes of a society that would make up such a history. And, too, he felt that, in general, the main events which had been catalogued actully occurred; the details had been blurred, and the attitudes of the people had been misrepresented, but the skeleton was essentially factual.

MacMaine felt that he knew what kind of philosophy had produced the mental attitudes of the Court he now faced, and he felt he knew how to handle himself before them.

Half a dozen paces in front of the great desk, the color of the floor tiling was different from that of the rest of the floor. Instead of a solid blue, it was a dead black. Tallis, who was slightly ahead of MacMaine, came to a halt as his toes touched the edge of the black area.

Uh-oh! a balk line, MacMaine thought. He stopped sharply at the same point. Both of them just stood there for a full minute while they were carefully inspected by the members of the Court.

Then the High Commander gestured with one hand, and the officer to his left leaned forward and said: "Why is this one brought before us in the uniform of an officer, bare of any insignia of rank?"

It could only be a ritual question, MacMaine decided; they must know why he was there.

"I bring him as a candidate for admission to our Ingroup," Tallis replied formally, "and ask the indulgence of Your Superiorities therefor."

"And who are you who ask our indulgence?"

Tallis identified himself at length—name, rank, serial number, military record, et cetera, et cetera, et cetera.

By the time he had finished, MacMaine was beginning to think that the recitation would go on forever. The High Commander had closed his eyes, and he looked as if he had gone to sleep.

There was more formality. Through it all, MacMaine stood at rigid attention, flexing his calf muscles occasionally to keep the blood flowing in his legs. He had no desire to disgrace himself by passing out in front of the Court.

Finally the Kerothi officer stopped asking Tallis questions and looked at the High Commander. MacMaine got the feeling that there was about to be a departure from the usual procedure.

Without opening his eyes, the High Commander said, in a brittle, rather harsh voice, "These circumstances are unprecedented." Then he opened his eyes and looked directly at MacMaine. "Never has an animal been proposed for such an honor. In times past, such a proposal would have been mockery of this Court and this Ingroup, and a crime of such monstrous proportions as to merit Excommunication."

MacMaine knew what that meant. The word was used literally; the condemned one was cut off from all communication by having his sensory nerves surgically severed. Madness followed quickly; psychosomatic death followed eventually, as the brain, cut off from any outside stimuli except those which could not be eliminated without death following instantly, finally became incapable of keeping the body alive. Without feedback, control was impossible, and the organism-as-a-whole slowly deteriorated until death was inevitable.

At first, the victim screamed and thrashed his limbs as the brain sent out message after message to the rest of the body, but since the brain had no way of knowing whether the messages had been received or acted upon, the victim soon went into a state comparable to that of catatonia and finally died.

If it was not the ultimate in punishment, it was a damned close approach, MacMaine thought. And he felt that the word "damned" could be used in that sense without fear of exaggeration.

"However," the High Commander went on, gazing at the ceiling, "circumstances change. It would once have been thought vile that a machine should be allowed to do the work of a skilled man, and the thought that a machine might do the work with more precision and greater rapidity would have been almost blasphemous.

"This case must be viewed in the same light. As we are replacing certain of our workers on our outer planets with Earth animals simply because they are capable of doing the work more cheaply, so we must recognize that the same interests of economy govern in this case.

"A computing animal, in that sense, is in the same class as a computing machine. It would be folly to waste their abilities simply because they are not human.

"There also arises the question of command. It has been represented to this court, by certain officers who have been active in investigating the candidate animal, that it would be as degrading to ask a human officer to take orders from an animal as it would be to ask him to take orders from a commoner of the Unorganized Reserve, if not more so. And, I must admit, there is, on the surface of it, some basis for this reasoning.

"But, again, we must not let ourselves be misled. Does not a spaceship pilot, in a sense, take orders from the computer that gives him his orbits and courses? In fact, do not all computers give orders, in one way or another, to those who use them?

"Why, then, should we refuse to take orders from a computing animal?"

He paused and appeared to listen to the silence in the room before going on.

"Stand at ease until the High Commander looks at you again," Tallis said in a low aside.

This was definitely the pause for adjusting to surprise.

It seemed interminable, though it couldn't have been longer than a minute later that the High Commander dropped his gaze from the ceiling to MacMaine. When Mac-Maine snapped to attention again, the others in the room became suddenly silent.

"We feel," the hard-faced old Kerothi continued, as if there had been no break, "that, in this case, we are justified in employing the animal in question.

"However, we must make certain exceptions to our normal procedure. The candidate is not a machine, and therefore cannot be treated as a machine. Neither is it human, and therefore cannot be treated as human.

"Therefore, this is the judgment of the Court of the Ingroup:

"The animal, having shown itself to be capable of behaving, in some degree, as befits an officer—including, as we have been informed, voluntarily conforming to our custom as regards superfluous hair—it shall henceforth be considered as having the same status as an untaught child or a barbarian, insofar as social conventions are concerned, and shall be entitled to the use of the human pronoun, he.

"Further, he shall be entitled to wear the uniform he now wears, and the insignia of a General of the Fleet. He shall be entitled, as far as personal contact goes, to the privileges of that rank, and shall be addressed as such.

"He will be accorded the right of punishment of an officer of that rank, insofar as disciplining his inferiors is concerned, except that he must first secure the concurrence of his Guardian Officer, as hereinafter provided.

"He shall also be subject to punishment in the same way and for the same offenses as humans of his rank, taking into account physiological differences, except as hereinafter provided.

"His reward for proper service"—The High Commander listed the demands MacMaine had made—"are deemed fitting, and shall be paid, provided his duties in service are carried out as proposed.

"Obviously, however, certain restrictions must be made. General MacMaine, as he is entitled to be called, is employed solely as a Strategy Computer. His ability as such and his knowledge of the psychology of the Earth animals are, as far as we are concerned at this moment, his only useful attributes. Therefore, his command is restricted to that function. He is empowered to act only through the other officers of the Fleet as this Court may appoint; he is not to command directly.

"Further, it is ordered that he shall have a Guardian Officer, who shall accompany him at all times and shall be directly responsible for his actions.

"That officer shall be punished for any deliberate crime committed by the aforesaid General MacMaine as if he had himself committed the crime.

"Until such time as this Court may appoint another officer for the purpose, General Polan Tallis, previously identified in these proceedings, is appointed as Guardian Officer."

The High Commander paused for a moment, then he said: "Proceed with the investment of the insignia."

The Strategy

General Sebastian MacMaine, sometime Colonel of Earth's Space Force, and presently a General of the Kerothi Fleet, looked at the array of stars that appeared to drift by the main viewplate of his flagship, the blaster-boat *Shudos*.

Behind him, General Tallis was saying, "You've done well, Sepastian. Better than anyone could have really expected. Three battles so far, and every one of them won by a margin far greater than anticipated. Any ideas that anyone may have had that you were not wholly working for the Kerothi cause have certainly been dispelled."

"Thanks, Tallis." MacMaine turned to look at the Kerothi officer. "I only hope that I can keep it up. Now that we're ready for the big push, I can't help but wonder what would happen if I were to lose a battle."

"Frankly," Tallis said, "that would depend on several things, the main one being whether or not it appeared that you had deliberately thrown the advantage to the enemy. But nobody expects you, or anyone else, to win every time. Even the most brilliant commander can make an honest mistake, and if it can be shown that it *was* an honest mistake, and one, furthermore, that he could not have been expected to avoid, he wouldn't be punished for it. In your case, I'll admit that the investigation would be a great deal more thorough than normal, and that you wouldn't get as much of the benefit of the doubt as another officer might, but unless there is a deliberate error I doubt that anything serious would happen."

"Do you really believe that, Tallis, or is it just wishful thinking on your part, knowing as you do that your punishment will be the same as mine if I fail?" MacMaine asked flatly.

Tallis didn't hesitate. "If I didn't believe it, I would ask to be relieved as your Guardian. And the moment I did that, you would be removed from command. The moment I feel that you are not acting for the best interests of Keroth, I will act—not only to protect myself, but to protect my people."

"That's fair enough," MacMaine said. "But how about the others?"

"I cannot speak for my fellow officers—only for myself." Then Tallis' voice became cold. "Just keep your hands clean, Sepastian, and all will be well. You will not be punished for mistakes—only for crimes. If you are planning no crimes, this worry of yours is needless."

"I ceased to worry about myself long ago," MacMaine said coolly. "I do not fear personal death, not even by Excommunication. My sole worry is about the ultimate outcome of the war if I should fail. That, and nothing more."

"I believe you," Tallis said. "Let us say no more about it. Your actions are difficult for us to understand, in some ways, that's all. No Kerothi would ever change his allegiance as you have. Nor has any Earth officer that we have captured shown any desire to do so. Oh, some of them have agreed to do almost anything we wanted them to, but these were not the intelligent ones, and even they were only doing it to save their own miserable hides.

"Still, you are an exceptional man, Sepastian, unlike any other of your race, as far as we know. Perhaps it is simply that you are the only one with enough wisdom to seek your intellectual equals rather than remain loyal to a mass of stupid animals who are fit only to be slaves."

"It was because I foresaw their eventual enslavement that I acted as I did," MacMaine admitted. "As I saw it, I had only two choices—to remain as I was and become a slave to the Kerothi or to put myself in your hands willingly and hope for the best. As you—"

He was interrupted by a harsh voice from a nearby speaker.

"Battle stations! Battle stations! Enemy fleet in detector range! Contact in twelve minutes!"

Tallis and MacMaine headed for the Command Room at a fast trot. The three other Kerothi who made up the Strategy Staff came in at almost the same time. There was a flurry of activity as the computers and viewers were readied for action, then the Kerothi looked expectantly at the Earthman.

MacMaine looked at the detector screens. The deployment of the approaching Earth fleet was almost as he had expected it would be. There were slight differences, but they would require only minor changes in the strategy he had mapped out from the information brought in by the Kerothi scout ships.

Undoubtedly, the Kerothi position had been relayed to the Earth commander by their own advance scouts buzzing about in tiny, one-man shells just small enough to be undetectable at normal range.

Watching the positions on the screens carefully, MacMaine called out a series of numbers in an unhurried voice and watched as the orders, relayed by the Kerothi staff, changed the position of parts of the Kerothi fleet. Then, as the computer-led Earth fleet jockeyed to compensate for the change in the Kerothi deployment, MacMaine called out more orders.

The High Commander of Keroth had called MacMaine a "computing animal," but the term was far from accurate. MacMaine couldn't possibly have computed all the variables in that battle, and he didn't try. It was a matter of human intuition against mechanical logic. The advantage lay with MacMaine, for, while the computer could not logically fathom the intuitive processes of its human opponent, Mac-Maine could and did have an intuitive grasp of the machine's logic. MacMaine didn't need to know every variable in the pattern; he only needed to know the pattern as a whole.

The *Shudos* was well in the rear of the main body of the Kerothi fleet. There was every necessity for keeping MacMaine's flagship out of as much of the fighting as possible.

When the first contact was made, MacMaine was certain of the outcome. His voice became a steady drone as he called out instructions to the staff officers; his mind was so fully occupied with the moving pattern before him that he noticed nothing else in the room around him.

Spaceship against spaceship, the two fleets locked in battle. The warheads of ultralight torpedoes flared their eye-searing explosions soundlessly into the void; ships exploded like overcharged beer bottles as blaster energy caught them and smashed through their screens; men and machines flamed and died, scattering the stripped nuclei of their component atoms through the screaming silence of space.

And through it all, Sebastian MacMaine watched dispassionately, calling out his orders as ten Earthmen died for every Kerothi death.

This was a crucial battle. The big push toward the center of Earth's cluster of worlds had begun. Until now, the Kerothi had been fighting the outposts, the planets on the fringes of Earth's sphere of influence which were only lightly colonized, and therefore relatively easy to take. Earth's strongest fleets were out there, to protect planets that could not protect themselves.

Inside that periphery were the more densely populated planets, the self-sufficient colonies which were more or less able to defend themselves without too much reliance on

space fleets as such. But now that the backbone of the
Earth's Space Force had been all but broken, it would be
a relatively easy matter to mop up planet after planet, since
each one could be surrounded separately, pounded into surrender, and secured before going on to the next.

That, at least, had been the original Kerothi intention.
But MacMaine had told them that there was another way—
a way which, if it succeeded, would save time, lives, and
money for the Kerothi. And, if it failed, MacMaine said,
they would be no worse off, they would simply have to
resume the original plan.

Now, the first of the big colony planets was to be taken.
When the protecting Earth fleet was reduced to tatters, the
Kerothi would go on to Houston's World as the first step
in the big push toward Earth itself.

But MacMaine wasn't thinking of that phase of the war.
That was still in the future, while the hellish space battle
was still at hand.

He lost track of time as he watched the Kerothi fleet take
advantage of their superior tactical position and tear the
Earth fleet to bits. Not until he saw the remains of the
Earth fleet turn tail and run did he realize that the battle
had been won.

The Kerothi fleet consolidated itself. There was no point
in pursuing the fleeting Earth ships; that would only break
up the solidity of the Kerothi deployment. The losers could
afford to scatter; the winners could not. Early in the war,
the Kerothi had used that trick against Earth; the Kerothi
had broken and fled, and the Earth fleet had split up to
chase them down. The scattered Earth ships had suddenly
found that they had been led into traps composed of hidden
clusters of Kerothi ships. Naturally, the trick had never
worked again for either side.

"All right," MacMaine said when it was all over, "let's
get on to Houston's World."

The staff men, including Tallis, were already on their
feet, congratulating MacMaine and shaking his hands. Even
General Hokotan, the Headquarters Staff man, who had
been transferred temporarily to the Fleet Force to keep an
eye on both MacMaine and Tallis, was enthusiastically
pounding MacMaine's shoulder.

No one aboard was supposed to know that Hokotan was a Headquarters officer, but MacMaine had spotted the spy rather easily. There was a difference between the fighters of the Fleet and the politicoes of Headquarters. The politicoes were no harder, perhaps, nor more ruthless, than the fighters, but they were of a different breed. Theirs was the ruthlessness of the bully who steps on those who are weaker rather than the ruthlessness of the man who kills only to win a battle. MacMaine had the feeling that the Headquarters Staff preferred to spend their time browbeating their underlings rather than risk their necks with someone who could fight back, however weakly.

General Hokotan seemed to have more of the fighting quality than most HQ men, but he wasn't a Fleet Officer at heart. He couldn't be compared to Tallis without looking small and mean.

As a matter of cold fact, very few of the officers were in anyway comparable to Tallis—not even the Fleet men. The more MacMaine learned of the Kerothi, the more he realized just how lucky he had been that it had been Tallis, and not some other Kerothi general, who had been captured by the Earth forces. He was not at all sure that his plan would have worked at all with any of the other officers he had met.

Tallis, like MacMaine, was an unusual specimen of his race.

MacMaine took the congratulations of the Kerothi officers with a look of pleasure on his face, and when they had subsided somewhat, he grinned and said:

"Let's get a little work done around here, shall we? We have a planet to reduce yet."

They laughed. Reducing a planet didn't require strategy—only firepower. The planet-based defenses couldn't maneuver, but the energy reserve of a planet is greater than that of any fleet, no matter how large. Each defense point would have to be cut down individually by the massed power of the fleet, cut down one by one until the planet was helpless. The planet as a whole might have more energy reserve than the fleet, but no individual defense point did. The problem was to avoid being hit by the rest of the defense points while one single point was bearing the brunt of the fleet's attack. It wasn't without danger, but it could be done.

And for a job like that, MacMaine's special abilities weren't needed. He could only watch and wait until it was over.

So he watched and waited. Unlike the short-time fury of a space battle, the reduction of a planet took days of steady pounding. When it was over, the blaster-boats of the Kerothi fleet and the shuttles from the great battle cruisers landed on Houston's World and took possession of the planet.

MacMaine was waiting in his cabin when General Hokotan brought the news that the planet was secured.

"They are ours," the HQ spy said with a superior smile. "The sniveling animals didn't even seem to want to defend themselves. They don't even know how to fight a hand-to-hand battle. How could such things have ever evolved intelligence enough to conquer space?" Hokotan enjoyed making such remarks to MacMaine's face, knowing that since MacMaine was technically a Kerothi he couldn't show any emotion when the enemy was insulted.

MacMaine showed none. "Got them all, eh?" he said.

"All but a few who scattered into the hills and forests. But not many of them had the guts to leave the security of their cities, even though we were occupying them."

"How many are left alive?"

"An estimated hundred and fifty million, more or less."

"Good. That should be enough to set an example. I picked Houston's World because we can withdraw from it without weakening our position; its position in space is such that it would constitute no menace to us even if we never reduced it. That way, we can be sure that our little message is received on Earth."

Hokotan's grin was wolfish. "And the whole weak-hearted race will shake with fear, eh?"

"Exactly. Tallis can speak English well enough to be understood. Have him make the announcement to them. He can word it however he likes, but the essence is to be this: Houston's World resisted the occupation by Kerothi troops; an example must be made of them to show them what happens to Earthmen who resist."

"That's all?"

"That's enough. Oh, by the way, make sure that there are plenty of their cargo spaceships in good working order; I doubt that we've ruined them all, but if we have, repair some of them.

"And, too, you'd better make sure that you allow some of the merchant spacemen to 'escape,' just in case there are no space pilots among those who took to the hills. We want to make sure that someone can use those ships to take the news back to Earth."

"And the rest?" Hokotan asked, with an expectant look. He knew what was to be done, but he wanted to hear MacMaine say it again.

MacMaine obliged.

"Hang them. Every man, every woman, every child. I want them to be decorating every lamppost and roof-beam on the planet, dangling like overripe fruit when the Earth forces return."

The Results

"I don't understand it," said General Polan Tallis worriedly. "Where are they coming from? How are they doing it? What's happened?"

MacMaine and the four Kerothi officers were sitting in the small dining room that doubled as a recreation room between meals. The nervous strain of the past few months was beginning to tell on all of them.

"Six months ago," Tallis continued jerkily, "we had them beaten. One planet after another was reduced in turn. Then, out of nowhere, comes a fleet of ships we didn't even know existed, and they've smashed us at every turn."

"If they *are* ships," said Loopat, the youngest officer of the *Shudos* staff. "Who ever heard of a battleship that was undetectable at a distance of less than half a million miles? It's impossible!"

"Then we're being torn to pieces by the impossible!" Hokotan snapped. "Before we even know they are anywhere around, they are blasting us with everything they've got! Not even the strategic genius of General MacMaine can help us if we have no time to plot strategy!"

The Ketrothi had been avoiding MacMaine's eyes, but

now, at the mention of his name, they all looked at him as if their collective gaze had been drawn to him by some unknown attractive force.

"It's like fighting ghosts," MacMaine said in a hushed voice. For the first time, he felt a feeling of awe that was almost akin to fear. What had he done?

In another sense, that same question was in the mind of the Kerothi.

"Have you any notion at all what they are doing or how they are doing it?" asked Tallis gently.

"None," MacMaine answered truthfully. "None at all, I swear to you."

"They don't even behave like Earthmen," said the fourth Kerothi, a thick-necked officer named Ossif. "They not only outfight us, they outthink us at every turn. Is it possible, General MacMaine, that the Earthmen have allies of another race, a race of intelligent beings that we don't know of?" He left unsaid the added implication: *"And that you have neglected to tell us about?"*

"Again," said MacMaine, "I swear to you that I know nothing of any third intelligent race in the galaxy."

"If there were such allies," Tallis said, "isn't it odd that they should wait so long to aid their friends?"

"No odder than that the Earthmen should suddenly develop superweapons that we cannot understand, much less fight against," Hokotan said, with a touch of anger.

"Not 'superweapons'," MacMaine corrected almost absently. "All they have is a method of making their biggest ships indetectable until they're so close that it doesn't matter. When they do register on our detectors, it's too late. But the weapons they strike with are the same weapons as they've always used, I believe."

"All right, then," Hokotan said, his voice showing more anger. "One weapon or whatever you want to call it. Practical invisibility. But that's enough. An invisible man with a knife is more deadly than a dozen ordinary men with modern armament. Are you sure you know nothing of this, General MacMaine?"

Before MacMaine could answer, Tallis said, "Don't be ridiculous, Hokotan! If he had known that such a weapon existed, would he have been fool enough to leave his people? With that secret, they stand a good chance of beating us in less than half the time it took us to wipe out their fleet—or, rather, to wipe out as much of it as we did."

"They got a new fleet somewhere," said young Loopat, almost to himself.

Tallis ignored him. "If MacMaine deserted his former allegiance, knowing that they had a method of rendering the action of a space drive indetectable, then he was and is a blithering idiot. And we know he isn't."

"All right, all right! I concede that," snapped Hokotan. "He knows nothing. I don't say that I fully trust him, even now, but I'll admit that I cannot see how he is to blame for the reversals of the past few months.

"If the Earthmen had somehow been informed of our activities, or if we had invented a superweapon and they found out about it, I would be inclined to put the blame squarely on MacMaine. But—"

"How would he get such information out?" Tallis cut in sharply. "He has been watched every minute of every day. We know he couldn't send any information to Earth. How could he?"

"Telepathy, for all I know!" Hokotan retorted. "But that's beside the point! I don't trust him any farther than I can see him, and not completely, even then. But I concede that there is no possible connection between this new menace and anything MacMaine might have done.

"This is no time to worry about that sort of thing; we've got to find some way of getting our hands on one of those ghost ships!"

"I do suggest," put in the thick-necked Ossif, "that we keep a closer watch on General MacMaine. Now that the Earth animals are making a comeback, he might decide to turn his coat now, even if he has been innocent of any acts against Keroth so far."

Hokotan's laugh was a short, hard bark. "Oh, we'll watch him, all right, Ossif. But, as Tallis has pointed out, Mac-Maine is not a fool, and he would certainly be a fool to return to Earth if his leaving it was a genuine act of desertion. The last planet we captured, before this invisibility thing came up to stop us, was plastered all over with notices that the Earth fleet was concentrating on the capture of the arch-traitor MacMaine.

"The price on his head, as a corpse, is enough to allow an Earthman to retire in luxury for life. The man who brings him back alive gets ten times that amount.

"Of course, it's possible that the whole thing is a put-up job—a smoke screen for our benefit. That's why we must and will keep a closer watch. But only a few of the Earth's higher-up would know that it was a smoke screen; the rest believe it, whether it is true or not. MacMaine would have to be very careful not to let the wrong people get their hands on him if he returned."

"It's no smoke screen," MacMaine said in a matter-of-fact tone. "I assure you that I have no intention of returning to Earth. If Keroth loses this war, then I will die—either fighting for the Kerothi or by execution at the hands of Earthmen if I am captured. Or," he added musingly, "perhaps even at the hands of the Kerothi, if someone decides that a scapegoat is needed to atone for the loss of the war."

"If you are guilty of treason," Hokotan barked, "you will die as a traitor! If you are not, there is no need for your death. The Kerothi do not need scapegoats!"

"Talk, talk, talk!" Tallis said with a sudden bellow. "We have agreed that MacMaine has done nothing that could even remotely be regarded as suspicious! He has fought hard and loyally; he has been more ruthless than any of us in destroying the enemy. Very well, we will guard him more closely. We can put him in irons if that's necessary.

"But let's quit yapping and start thinking! We've been acting like frightened children, not knowing what it is we fear, and venting our fear-caused anger on the most handy target!

"Let's act like men—not like children!"

After a moment, Hokotan said: "I agree." His voice was firm, but calm. "Our job will be to get our hands on one of those new Earth ships. Anyone have any suggestions?"

They had all kinds of suggestions, one after another. The detectors, however, worked because they detected the distortion of space which was necessary for the drive of a ship as the distortion of air was necessary for the movement of a propellor-driven aircraft. None of them could see how a ship could avoid making that distortion, and none of them could figure out how to go about capturing a ship that no one could even detect until it was too late to set a trap.

The discussion went on for days. And it was continued the next day and the next. And the days dragged out into weeks.

Communications with Keroth broke down. The Fleet-to-Headquarters courier ships, small in size, without armament, and practically solidly packed with drive mechanism, could presumably outrun anything but another unarmed courier. An armed ship of the same size would have to use some of the space for her weapons, which meant that the drive would have to be smaller; if the drive remained the same size, then the armament would make the ship larger. In either case, the speed would be cut down. A smaller ship might outrun a standard courier, but if they got much smaller, there wouldn't be room inside for the pilot.

Nonetheless, courier after courier never arrived at its destination.

And the Kerothi Fleet was being decimated by the hit-and-run tactics of the Earth's ghost ships. And Earth never lost a ship; by the time the Kerothi ships knew their enemy was in the vicinity, the enemy had hit and vanished again. The Kerothi never had a chance to ready their weapons.

In the long run, they never had a chance at all.

MacMaine waited with almost fatalistic complacence for the inevitable to happen. When it did happen, he was ready for it.

The *Shudos*, tiny flagship of what had once been a mighty armada and was now only a tattered remnant, was floating in orbit, along with the other remaining ships of the fleet, around a bloated red-giant sun. With their drives off, there was no way of detecting them at any distance, and the chance of their being found by accident was microscopically small. But they could not wait forever. Water could be recirculated, and energy could be tapped from the nearby sun, but food was gone once it was eaten.

Hokotan's decision was inevitable, and, under the circumstances, the only possible one. He simply told them what they had already known—that he was a Headquarters Staff officer.

"We haven't heard from Headquarters in weeks," he said at last. "The Earth fleet may already be well inside our periphery. We'll have to go home." He produced a document which he had obviously been holding in reserve for another purpose and handed it to Tallis. "Headquarters Staff Orders, Tallis. It empowers me to take command of the Fleet in the event of an emergency, and the decision as to what constitutes an emergency was left up to my discretion. I must admit that this is not the emergency any of us at Headquarters anticipated."

Tallis read through the document. "I see that it isn't," he said dryly. "According to this, MacMaine and I are to be placed under immediate arrest as soon as you find it necessary to act."

"Yes," said Hokotan bitterly. "So you can both consider yourselves under arrest. Don't bother to lock yourselves up—there's no point in it. General MacMaine, I see no reason to inform the rest of the Fleet of this, so we will go on as usual. The orders I have to give are simple: The Fleet will head for home by the most direct possible geodesic. Since we cannot fight, we will simply ignore attacks and keep going as long as we last. We can do nothing else." He paused thoughtfully.

"And, General MacMaine, in case we do not live through this, I would like to extend my apologies. I do not like you; I don't think I could ever learn to like an anim . . . to like a non-Kerothi. But I know when to admit an error in judgment. You have fought bravely and well—better, I know, than I could have done myself. You have shown yourself to be loyal to your adopted planet; you are a Kerothi in every sense of the word except the physical. My apologies for having wronged you."

He extended his hands and MacMaine took them. A choking sensation constricted the Earthman's throat for a moment, then he got the words out—the words he had to say. "Believe me, General Hokotan, there is no need for an apology. No need whatever."

"Thank you," said Hokotan. Then he turned and left the room.

"All right, Tallis," MacMaine said hurriedly, "let's get moving."

The orders were given to the remnants of the Fleet, and they cut in their drives to head homeward. And the instant they did, there was chaos. Earth's fleet of "ghost ships" had been patrolling the area for weeks, knowing that the Kerothi fleet had last been detected somewhere in the vicinity. As soon as the spatial distortions of the Kerothi drives flashed on the Earth ships' detectors, the Earth fleet, widely scattered over the whole circumambient volume of space, coalesced toward the center of the spatial disturbance like a cloud of bees all heading for the same flower.

Where there had been only the dull red light of the giant star, there suddenly appeared the blinding, blue-white brilliance of disintegrating matter, blossoming like cruel, deadly, beautiful flowers in the midst of the Kerothi ships, then fading slowly as each expanding cloud of plasma cooled.

Sebastian MacMaine might have died with the others except that the *Shudos*, as the flagship, was to trail behind the fleet, so her drive had not yet been activated. The *Shudos* was still in orbit, moving at only a few miles per second when the Earth fleet struck.

Her drive never did go on. A bomb, only a short distance away as the distance from atomic disintegration is measured, sent the *Shudos* spinning away, end over end, like a discarded cigar butt flipped toward a gutter, one side caved in near the rear, as if it had been kicked in by a giant foot.

There was still air in the ship, MacMaine realized groggily as he awoke from the unconsciousness that had been thrust upon him. He tried to stand up, but he found himself staggering toward one crazily-slanted wall. The stagger was partly due to his grogginess, and partly due to the Coriolis forces acting within the spinning ship. The artificial gravity was gone, which meant that the interstellar drive engines had been smashed. He wondered if the emergency rocket drive was still working—not that it would take him anywhere worth going to in less than a few centuries. But, then, Sebastian MacMaine had nowhere to go, anyhow.

Tallis lay against one wall, looking very limp. MacMaine half staggered over to him and knelt down. Tallis was still alive.

The centrifugal force caused by the spinning ship gave an effective pull of less than one Earth gravity, but the weird twists caused by the Coriolis forces made motion and orientation difficult. Besides, the ship was spinning slightly on her long axis as well as turning end-for-end.

MacMaine stood there for a moment, trying to think. He had expected to die. Death was something he had known was inevitable from the moment he made his decision to leave Earth. He had not known how or when it would come, but he had known that it would come soon. He had known that he would never live to collect the reward he had demanded of the Kerothi for "faithful service." Traitor he might be, but he was still honest enough with himself to know that he would never take payment for services he had not rendered.

Now death was very near, and Sebastian MacMaine almost welcomed it. He had no desire to fight it. Tallis might want to stand and fight death to the end, but Tallis was not carrying the monstrous weight of guilt that would stay with Sebastian MacMaine until his death, no matter how much he tried to justify his actions.

On the other hand, if he had to go, he might as well do a good job of it. Since he still had a short time left, he might as well wrap the whole thing up in a neat package. How?

Again, his intuitive ability to see pattern gave him the answer long before he could have reasoned it out.

They will know, he thought, *but they will never be sure they know. I will be immortal. And my name will live forever, although no Earthman will ever again use the surname MacMaine or the given name Sebastian.*

He shook his head to clear it. No use thinking like that now. There were things to be done.

Tallis first. MacMaine made his way over to one of the emergency medical kits that he knew were kept in every compartment of every ship. One of the doors of a wall locker hung open, and the blue-green medical symbol used by the Kerothi showed darkly in the dim light that came from the three unshattered glow plates in the ceiling. He opened the kit, hoping that it contained something equivalent to adhesive tape. He had never inspected a Kerothi medical kit before. Fortunately, he could read Kerothi. If a military government was good for nothing else, at least it was capable of enforcing a simplified phonetic orthography so that words were pronounced as they were spelled. And—

He forced his wandering mind back to his work. The blow

on the head, plus the crazy effect the spinning was having on his inner ears, plus the cockeyed gravitational orientation that made his eyes feel as though they were seeing things at two different angles, all combined to make for more than a little mental confusion.

There was adhesive tape, all right. Wound on its little spool, it looked almost homey. He spent several minutes winding the sticky plastic ribbon around Tallis' wrists and ankles.

Then he took the gun from the Kerothi general's sleeve holster—he had never been allowed one of his own—and, holding it firmly in his right hand, he went on a tour of the ship.

It was hard to move around. The centrifugal force varied from point to point throughout the ship, and the corridors were cluttered with debris that seemed to move with a life of its own as each piece shifted slowly under the effects of the various forces working on it. And, as the various masses moved about, the rate of spin of the ship changed as the law of conservation of angular momentum operated. The ship was full of sliding, clattering, jangling noises as the stuff tried to find a final resting place and bring the ship to equilibrium.

He found the door to Ossif's cabin open and the room empty. He found Ossif in Loopat's cabin, trying to get the younger officer to his feet.

Ossif saw MacMaine at the door and said: "You're alive! Good! Help me—" Then he saw the gun in MacMaine's hand and stopped. It was the last thing he saw before Mac-Maine shot him neatly between the eyes.

Loopat, only half conscious, never even knew he was in danger, and the blast that drilled through his brain prevented him from ever knowing anything again in this life.

Like a man in a dream, MacMaine went on to Hokotan's cabin, his weapon at the ready. He was rather pleased to find that the HQ general was already quite dead, his neck broken as cleanly as if it had been done by a hangman. Hardly an hour before, MacMaine would cheerfully have shot Hokotan where it would hurt the most and watch him die slowly. But the memory of Hokotan's honest apology made the Earthman very glad that he did not have to shoot the general at all.

There remained only the five-man crew, the NCO technician and his gang, who actually ran the ship. They would be at the tail of the ship, in the engine compartment. To get there, he had to cross the center of spin of the ship, and the change of gravity from one direction to another, decreasing toward zero, passing the null point, and rising again on the other side, made him nauseous. He felt better after his stomach had emptied itself.

Cautiously, he opened the door to the drive compartment and then slammed it hard in sudden fear when he saw what had happened. The shielding had been torn away from one of the energy converters and exposed the room to high-energy radiation. The crewmen were quite dead.

The fear went away as quickly as it had come. So maybe he'd dosed himself with a few hundred Roentgens—so what? A little radiation never hurt a dead man.

But he knew now that there was no possibility of escape. The drive was wrecked, and the only other means of escape, the one-man courier boat that every blaster-boat carried, had been sent out weeks ago and had never returned.

If only the courier boat were still in its cradle—

MacMaine shook his head. No. It was better this way. Much better.

He turned and went back to the dining cabin where Tallis was trussed up. This time, passing the null-gee point didn't bother him much at all.

Tallis was moaning a little and his eyelids were fluttering by the time MacMaine got back. The Earthman opened the medical kit again and looked for some kind of stimulant. He had no knowledge of medical or chemical terms in Kerothic, but there was a box of glass ampoules bearing instructions to "crush and allow patient to inhale fumes." That sounded right.

The stuff smelled like a mixture of spirits of ammonia and butyl mercaptan, but it did the job. Tallis coughed convulsively, turned his head away, coughed again, and opened his eyes. MacMaine tossed the stinking ampoule out into the corridor as Tallis tried to focus his eyes.

"How do you feel?" MacMaine asked. His voice sounded oddly thick in his own ears.

"All right. I'm all right. What happened?" He looked wonderingly around. "Near miss? Must be. Anyone hurt?"

"They're all dead but you and me," MacMaine said.

"Dead? Then we'd better—" He tried to move and then realized that he was bound hand and foot. The sudden realization of his position seemed to clear his brain completely. "Sepastian, what's going on here? Why am I tied up?"

"I had to tie you," MacMaine explained carefully, as though to a child. "There are some things I have to do yet, and I wouldn't want you to stop me. Maybe I should have just shot you while you were unconscious. That would have been kinder to both of us, I think. But . . . but, Tallis, I had to tell somebody. Someone else has got to know. Someone else has to judge. Or maybe I just want to unload it on someone else, someone who will carry the burden with me for just a little while. I don't know."

"Sepastian, what are you talking about?" The Kerothi's face shone dully orange in the dim light, his bright green eyes looked steadily at the Earthman, and his voice was oddly gentle.

"I'm talking about treason," said MacMaine. "Do you want to listen?"

"I don't have much choice, do I?" Tallis said. "Tell me one thing first: Are we going to die?"

"You are, Tallis. But I won't. I'm going to be immortal."

Tallis looked at him for a long moment. Then, "All right, Sepastian. I'm no psych man, but I know you're not well. I'll listen to whatever you have to say. But first, untie my hands and feet."

"I can't do that, Tallis. Sorry. But if our positions were reversed, I know what I would do to you when I heard the story. And I can't let you kill me, because there's something more that has to be done."

Tallis knew at that moment that he was looking at the face of Death. And he also knew that there was nothing whatever he could do about it. Except talk. And listen.

"Very well, Sepastian," he said levelly. "Go ahead. Treason, you say? How? Against whom?"

"I'm not quite sure," said Sebastian MacMaine. "I thought maybe you could tell me."

The Reason

"Let me ask you one thing, Tallis," MacMaine said. "Would you do anything in your power to save Keroth from destruction? Anything, no matter how drastic, if you knew that it would save Keroth in the long run?"

"A foolish question. Of course I would. I would give my life."

"Your life? A mere nothing. A pittance. Any man could give his life. Would you consent to live forever for Keroth?"

Tallis shook his head as though he were puzzled. "Live forever? That's twice or three times you've said something about that. I *don't* understand you."

"Would you consent to live forever as a filthy curse on the lips of every Kerothi old enough to speak? Would you consent to be a vile, inhuman monster whose undead spirit would hang over your homeland like an evil miasma for centuries to come, whose very name would touch a flame of hatred in the minds of all who heard it?"

"That's a very melodramatic way of putting it," the Kerothi said, "but I believe I understand what you mean. Yes, I would consent to that if it would be the only salvation of Keroth."

"Would you slaughter helpless millions of your own people so that other billions might survive? Would you ruthlessly smash your system of government and your whole way of life if it were the only way to save the people themselves?"

"I'm beginning to see what you're driving at," Tallis said slowly. "And if it is what I think it is, I think I would like to kill you—very slowly."

"I know, I know. But you haven't answered my question. Would you do those things to save your people?"

"I would," said Tallis coldly. "Don't misunderstand me. I do not loathe you for what you have done to your own people; I hate you for what you have done to mine."

"That's as it should be," said MacMaine. His head was clearing up more now. He realized that he had been talking a little wildly at first. Or was he really insane? Had he been insane from the beginning? No. He knew with absolute clarity that every step he had made had been cold, calculating, and ruthless, but utterly and absolutely sane.

He suddenly wished that he had shot Tallis without wakening him. If his mind hadn't been in such a state of shock, he would have. There was no need to torture the man like this.

"Go on," said Tallis, in a voice that had suddenly become devoid of all emotion. "Tell it all."

"Earth was stagnating," MacMaine said, surprised at the sound of his own voice. He hadn't intended to go on. But he couldn't stop now. "You saw how it was. Every standard had become meaningless because no standard was held to be better than any other standard. There was no beauty because beauty was superior to ugliness and we couldn't allow superiority or inferiority. There was no love because in order to love someone or something you must feel that it is in some way superior to that which is not loved. I'm not even sure I know what those terms mean, because I'm not sure I ever thought anything was beautiful, I'm not sure I ever loved anything. I only read about such things in books. But I know I felt the emptiness inside me where those things should have been.

"There was no morality, either. People did not refrain from stealing because it was wrong, but simply because it was pointless to steal what would be given to you if you asked for it. There was no right or wrong.

"We had a form of social contract that we called 'marriage,' but it wasn't the same thing as marriage was in the old days. There was no love. There used to be a crime called 'adultery,' but even the word had gone out of use on the Earth I knew. Instead, it was considered antisocial for a woman to refuse to give herself to other men; to do so might indicate that she thought herself superior or thought her husband to be superior to other men. The same thing applied to men in their relationships with women other than their wives. Marriage was a social contract that could be made or broken at the whim of the individual. It served no purpose because it meant nothing, neither party gained anything by the contract that they couldn't have had without it. But a wedding was an excuse for a gala party at which the couple were the center of attention. So the contract was entered into lightly for the sake of a gay time for a while, then broken again so that the game could be played with someone else—the game of Musical Bedrooms."

He stopped and looked down at the helpless Kerothi. "That doesn't mean much to you, does it? In your society, women are chattel, to be owned, bought, and sold. If you see a woman you want, you offer a price to her father or brother or husband—whoever the owner might be. Then she's yours until you sell her to another. Adultery is a very serious crime on Kerothi, but only because it's an infringement of property rights. There's not much love lost there, either, is there?

"I wonder if either of us knows what love is, Tallis?"

"I love my people," Tallis said grimly.

MacMaine was startled for a moment. He'd never thought about it that way. "You're right, Tallis," he said at last. "You're right. We *do* know. And because I loved the human race, in spite of its stagnation and its spirit of total mediocrity, I did what I had to do."

"You will pardon me," Tallis said, with only the faintest bit of acid in his voice, "if I do not understand exactly what it is that you did." Then his voice grew softer. "Wait. Perhaps I do understand. Yes, of course."

"You think you understand?" MacMaine looked at him narrowly.

"Yes. I said that I am not a psychomedic, and my getting angry with you proves it. You fought hard and well for Keroth, Sepastian, and, in doing so, you had to kill many of your own race. It is not easy for a man to do, no matter how much your reason tells you it *must* be done. And now, in the face of death, remorse has come. I do not completely understand the workings of the Earthman's mind, but I—"

"That's just it; you don't," MacMaine interrupted. "Thanks for trying to find an excuse for me, Tallis, but I'm afraid it isn't so. Listen.

"I had to find out what Earth was up against. I had a pretty good idea already that the Kerothi would win—would wipe us out or enslave us to the last man. And, after I had seen Keroth, I was certain of it. So I sent a message back to Earth, telling them what they were up against, because, up 'til then they hadn't known. As soon as they knew, they reacted as they have always done when they are certain that they face danger. They fought. They unleashed the chained-down intelligence of the few extraordinary Earthmen, and they released the fighting spirit of even the ordinary Earthmen. And they won!"

Tallis shook his head. "You sent no message, Sepastian. You were watched. You know that. You could not have sent a message."

"You saw me send it," MacMaine said. "So did everyone else in the fleet. Hokotan helped me send it—made all the arrangements at my orders. But because you do not understand the workings of the Earthman's mind, you didn't even recognize it as a message.

"Tallis, what would your people have done if an invading force, which had already proven that it could whip Keroth easily, did to one of your planets what we did on Houston's World?"

"If the enemy showed us that they could easily beat us and then hanged the whole population of a planet for resisting? Why, we would be fools to resist. Unless, of course, we had a secret weapon in a hidden pocket, the way Earth had."

"No, Tallis; no. That's where you're making your mistake. Earth didn't have that weapon until *after* the massacre on Houston's World. Let me ask you another thing: Would any Kerothi have ordered that massacre?"

"I doubt it," Tallis said slowly. "Killing that many potential slaves would be wasteful and expensive. We are fighters, not butchers. We kill only when it is necessary to win; the remainder of the enemy is taken care of as the rightful property of the conqueror."

"Exactly. Prisoners were part of the loot, and it's foolish to destroy loot. I noticed that in your history books. I noticed, too, that in such cases, the captives recognized the right of the conqueror to enslave them, and made no trouble. So, after Earth's forces get to Keroth, I don't think we'll have any trouble with you."

"Not if they set us an example like Houston's World," Tallis said, "and can prove that resistance is futile. But I don't understand the message. What was the message and how did you send it?"

"The massacre on Houston's World was the message, Tallis. I even told the Staff, when I suggested it. I said that such an act would strike terror into the minds of Earthmen.

"And it did, Tallis; it did. But that terror was just the

goad they needed to make them fight. They had to sit up and take notice. If the Kerothi had gone on the way they were going, taking one planet after another, as they planned, the Kerothi would have won. The people of each planet would think, 'It can't happen here.' And, since they felt that nothing could be superior to anything else, they were complacently certain that they couldn't be beat. Of course, maybe Earth couldn't beat you, either, but that was all right; it just proved that there was no such thing as superiority.

"But Houston's World jarred them—badly. It had to. 'Hell does more than Heaven can to wake the fear of God in man.' They didn't recognize beauty, but I shoved ugliness down their throats; they didn't know love and friendship, so I gave them hatred and fear.

"The committing of atrocities has been the mistake of aggressors throughout Earth's history. The battle cries of countless wars have called upon the people to remember an atrocity. Nothing else hits an Earthman as hard as a vicious, brutal, unnecessary murder.

"So I gave them the incentive to fight, Tallis. That was my message."

Tallis was staring at him wide eyed. "You *are* insane."

"No. It worked. In six months, they found something that would enable them to blast the devil Kerothi from the skies. I don't know what the society of Earth is like now—and I never will. But at least I know that men are allowed to think again. And I know they'll survive."

He suddenly realized how much time had passed. Had it been too long? No. There would still be Earth ships prowling the vicinity, waiting for any sign of a Kerothi ship that had hidden in the vastness of space by not using its engines.

"I have some things I must do, Tallis," he said, standing up slowly. "Is there anything else you want to know?"

Tallis frowned a little, as though he were trying to think of something, but then he closed his eyes and relaxed. "No, Sepastian. Nothing. Do whatever it is you have to do."

"Tallis," MacMaine said. Tallis didn't open his eyes, and MacMaine was very glad of that. "Tallis, I want you to know that, in all my life, you were the only friend I ever had."

The bright green eyes remained closed. "That may be so.
Yes, Sepastian, I honestly think you believe that."

"I do," said MacMaine, and shot him carefully through
the head.

The End

—and Epilogue.

"Hold it!" The voice bellowed thunderingly from the
loud-speakers of the six Earth ships that had boxed in the
derelict. "Hold it! *Don't bomb that ship!* I'll personally have
the head of any man who damages that ship!"

In five of the ships, the commanders simply held off the
bombardment that would have vaporized the derelict. In the
sixth, Major Thornton, the Group Commander, snapped off
the microphone. His voice was shaky as he said: "That was
close! Another second, and we'd have lost that ship
forever."

Captain Verenski's Oriental features had a half-startled,
half-puzzled look. "I don't get it. You grabbed that mike
control as if you'd been bitten. I know that she's only a
derelict. After that burst of fifty-gee acceleration for fifteen
minutes, there couldn't be anyone left alive on her. But
there must have been a reason for using atomic rockets
instead of their antiacceleration fields. What makes you
think she's not dangerous?"

"I didn't say she wasn't dangerous," the major snapped.
"She may be. Probably is. But we're going to capture her
if we can. Look!" He pointed at the image of the ship in
the screen.

She wasn't spinning now, or looping end-over-end. After
fifteen minutes of high acceleration, her atomic rockets had
cut out, and now she moved serenely at constant velocity,
looking as dead as a battered tin can.

"I don't see anything," Captain Verenski said.

"The Kerothic symbols on the side. Palatal unvoiced sibi-
lant, rounded—"

"I don't read Kerothic, major," said the captain. "I—"
Then he blinked and said, *"Shudos!"*

"That's it. The *Shudos* of Keroth. The flagship of the
Kerothi Fleet."

The look in the major's eyes was the same look of hatred that had come into the captain's.

"Even if its armament is still functioning, we have to take the chance," Major Thornton said. "Even if they're all dead, we have to try to get The Butcher's body." He picked up the microphone again.

"Attention, Group. Listen carefully and don't get itchy trigger fingers. That ship is the *Shudos*. The Butcher's ship. It's a ten-man ship, and the most she could have aboard would be thirty, even if they jammed her full to the hull. I don't know of any way that anyone could be alive on her after fifteen minutes at fifty gees of atomic drive, but remember that they don't have any idea of how our counter-action generators damp out spatial distortion either. Remember what Dr. Pendric said: 'No man is superior to any other in *all* ways. Every man is superior to every other in *some* way.' We may have the counteraction generator, but they may have something else that we don't know about. So stay alert.

"I am going to take a landing-party aboard. There's a reward out for The Butcher, and that reward will be split proportionately among us. It's big enough for us all to enjoy it, and we'll probably get citations if we bring him in.

"I want ten men from each ship. I'm not asking for volunteers; I want each ship commander to pick the ten men he thinks will be least likely to lose their heads in an emergency. I don't want anyone to panic and shoot when he should be thinking. I don't want anyone who had any relatives on Houston's World. Sorry, but I can't allow vengeance yet.

"We're a thousand miles from the *Shudos* now; close in slowly until we're within a hundred yards. The boarding parties will don armor and prepare to board while we're closing in. At a hundred yards, we stop and the boarding parties will land on the hull. I'll give further orders then.

"One more thing. I don't think her A-A generators could possibly be functioning, judging from that dent in her hull, but we can't be sure. If she tries to go into A-A drive, she is to be bombed—no matter who is aboard. It is better that sixty men die than that The Butcher escape.

"All right, let's go. Move in."

*   *   *

Half an hour later, Major Thornton stood on the hull of the *Shudos*, surrounded by the sixty men of the boarding party. "Anybody see anything through those windows?" he asked.

Several of the men had peered through the direct-vision ports, playing spotlight beams through them.

"Nothing alive," said a sergeant, a remark which was followed by a chorus of agreement.

"Pretty much of a mess in there," said another sergeant. "That fifty gees mashed everything to the floor. Why'd anyone want to use acceleration like that?"

"Let's go in and find out," said Major Thornton.

The outer door to the air lock was closed, but not locked. It swung open easily to disclose the room between the outer and inner doors. Ten men went in with the major, the others stayed outside with orders to cut through the hull if anything went wrong.

"If he's still alive," the major said, "we don't want to kill him by blowing the air. Sergeant, start the air-lock cycle."

There was barely room for ten men in the air lock. It had been built big enough for the full crew to use it at one time, but it was only just big enough.

When the inner door opened, they went in cautiously. They spread out and searched cautiously. The caution was unnecessary, as it turned out. There wasn't a living thing aboard.

"Three officers shot through the head, sir," said the sergeant. "One of 'em looks like he died of a broken neck, but it's hard to tell after that fifty gees mashed 'em. Crewmen in the engine room—five of 'em. Mashed up, but I'd say they died of radiation, since the shielding on one of the generators was ruptured by the blast that made that dent in the hull."

"Nine bodies," the major said musingly. "All Kerothi. And all of them probably dead *before* the fifty-gee acceleration. Keep looking, sergeant. We've got to find the tenth man."

Another twenty-minute search gave them all the information they were ever to get.

"No Earth food aboard," said the major. "One spacesuit missing. Handweapons missing. Two emergency survival kits and two medical kits missing. *And*—most important of all—the courier boat is missing." He bit at his lower lip for a moment, then went on. "Outer air lock door left unlocked. Three Kerothi shot—*after* the explosion that ruined the A-A drive, and *before* the fifty-gee acceleration." He looked at the sergeant. "What do you think happened?"

"He got away," the tough-looking noncom said grimly. "Took the courier boat and scooted away from here."

"Why did he set the timer on the drive, then? What was the purpose of that fifty-gee blast?"

"To distract us, I'd say, sir. While we were chasing this thing, he hightailed it out."

"He might have, at that," the major said musingly. "A one-man courier *could* have gotten away. Our new detection equipment isn't perfect yet. But—"

At that moment, one of the troopers pushed himself down the corridor toward them. "Look, sir! I found this in the pocket of the Carrot-skin who was taped up in there!" He was holding a piece of paper.

The major took it, read it, then read it aloud. "Greetings, fellow Earthmen: When you read this, I will be safe from any power you may think you have to arrest or punish me. But don't think *you* are safe from *me*. There are other intelligent races in the galaxy, and I'll be around for a long time to come. You haven't heard the last of me. With love—Sebastian MacMaine."

The silence that followed was almost deadly.

"He *did* get away!" snarled the sergeant at last.

"Maybe," said the major. "But it doesn't make sense." He sounded agitated. "Look. In the first place, how do we know the courier boat was even aboard? They've been trying frantically to get word back to Keroth; does it make sense that they'd save this boat? And why all the fanfare? Suppose he did have a boat? Why would he attract our attention with that fifty-gee flare? Just so he could leave us a note?"

"What do you think happened, sir?" the sergeant asked.

"I don't think he had a boat. If he did, he'd want us to think he was dead, not the other way around. I think he set the drive timer on this ship, went outside with his supplies, crawled up a drive tube and waited until that atomic rocket blast blew him into plasma. He was probably badly wounded and didn't want us to know that we'd won. That way, we'd never find him."

There was no belief on the faces of the men around him.

"Why'd he want to do that, sir?" asked the sergeant.

"Because as long as we don't *know*, he'll haunt us. He'll be like Hitler or Jack the Ripper. He'll be an immortal menace instead of a dead villain who could be forgotten."

"Maybe so, sir," said the sergeant, but there was an utter lack of conviction in his voice. "But we'd still better comb this area and keep our detectors hot. We'll know what he was up to when we catch him."

"But if we *don't* find him," the major said softly, "we'll *never* know. That's the beauty of it, sergeant. If we don't find him, then he's won. In his own fiendish, twisted way, he's won."

"If we don't find him," said the sergeant stolidly, "I think we better keep a sharp eye out for the next intelligent race we meet. He might find 'em first."

"Maybe," said the major very softly, "that's just what he wanted. I wish I knew why."

HOTHOUSE

BY BRIAN W. ALDISS (1925-   )

THE MAGAZINE OF FANTASY AND SCIENCE FICTION
FEBRUARY

Brian W. Aldiss is an Englishman who is highly regarded as a mainstream novelist as well as one of the premier science fiction writers in Great Britain. His long career began in the mid-1950s and continues to this day; his masterpiece is usually considered to be the three Helliconia *books (1982-1985), which well illustrate his talent for creating alien civilizations.*

His long career has been marked by critical acclaim and literary criticism, since he has devoted considerable energy to evaluating the work of others, first as Literary Editor of the Oxford Mail *and as the author of* Billion Year Spree: A History of Science Fiction *(1973; revised and expanded as* Trillion Year Spree) *for which he won the Pilgrim Award of The Science Fiction Research Association.*

"Hothouse" constitutes part of his fix-up novel The Long Afternoon of Earth *(1962), and is an excellent example of his ability to effectively render the most alien (even though it is on Earth) societies. (MHG)*

When we speak of alien life in science fiction, we almost always deal with intelligent animal life. Since we are ourselves intelligent animals, this is simply a measure of self-absorption.

Even when we deal with unintelligent life, it is almost always animal in nature. Plants somehow are only background. Except for supplying us with food, they are as unimportant for story purposes as rocks and soil.

This is true even on Earth. Plants are by all odds the dominant life form on Earth. They can live without animals *(at least some of them can) but animals cannot live without plants. Plants supply us with the ultimate food source and with oxygen and, by and large, we ignore them just the same.*

It is a pleasure, then, to read of a world in which plants are really dominant. One of the great feats of science fiction is to allow you to approach the Universe from a new perspective, and this story is exactly what we mean when we say that. (IA)

My vegetable love should grow
Vaster than empires and more slow.

ANDREW MARVELL

I

The heat, the light, the humidity—these were constant and had remained constant for . . . but nobody knew how long. Nobody cared any more for the big questions that begin "How long . . . ?" or "Why . . . ?" It was no longer a place for mind. It was a place for growth, for vegetables. It was like a hothouse.

In the green light, some of the children came out to play. Alert for enemies, they ran along the branch, calling to each other in soft voices. A fast-growing berrywhisk moved upwards to one side, its sticky crimson mass of berries gleaming. Clearly it was intent on seeding and would offer the children no harm. They scuttled past it. Beyond the margin of the group strip, some nettlemoss had sprung up during their period of sleep. It stirred as the children approached.

"Kill it," Toy said simply. She was the head child of the group. She was ten. The others obeyed her. Unsheathing the sticks every child carried in imitation of every adult, they scraped at the nettlemoss. They scraped at it and hit it. Excitement grew in them as they beat down the plant, squashing its poisoned tips.

Clat fell forward in her excitement. She was only five, the youngest of the group's children. Her hands fell among the poisonous stuff. She cried aloud and rolled aside. The other children also cried, but did not venture into the nettlemoss to save her.

Struggling out of the way, little Clat cried again. Her fingers clutched at the rough bark—then she was tumbling from the branch.

The children saw her fall onto a great spreading leaf several lengths below, clutch it, and lie there quivering on the quivering green. She looked up pitifully.

"Fetch Lily-yo," Toy told Gren. Gren sped back along the branch to get Lily-yo. A tigerfly swooped out of the air at him, humming its anger deeply. He struck it aside with a hand, not pausing. He was nine, a rare man child, very brave already, and fleet and proud. Swiftly he ran to the Headwoman's hut.

Under the branch, attached to its underside, hung eighteen great homemaker nuts. Hollowed out they were, and cemented into place with the cement distilled from the acetoyle plant. Here lived the eighteen members of the group, one to each homemaker's nut—the Headwoman, her five women, their man, and the eleven surviving children.

Hearing Gren's cry, out came Lily-yo from her nuthut, climbing up a line to stand on the branch beside him.

"Clat falls!" cried Gren.

With her stick, Lily-yo rapped sharply on the bough before running on ahead of the child.

Her signal called out the other six adults, the women Flor, Daphe, Hy, Ivin, and Jury, and the man Haris. They hastened from their nuthuts, weapons ready, poised for attack or flight.

As Lily-yo ran, she whistled on a sharp split note.

Instantly to her from the thick foliage nearby came a dumbler, flying to her shoulder. The dumbler rotated, a fleecy umbrella whose separate spokes controlled its direction. It matched its flight to her movement.

Both children and adults gathered round Lily-yo when she looked down at Clat, still sprawled some way below on her leaf.

"Lie still, Clat! Do not move!" called Lily-yo. "I will come to you." Clat obeyed that voice, though she was in pain and fear.

Lily-yo climbed astride the hooked base of the dumbler, whistling softly to it. Only she of the group had fully mastered the art of commanding dumblers. These dumblers were the half-sentient spores of the whistlethistle. The tips of their feathered spokes carried seeds; the seeds were strangely shaped, so that a light breeze whispering in them made them into ears that listened to every advantage of the wind that would spread their propagation. Humans, after long years of practice, could use these crude ears for their own purposes and instructions, as Lily-yo did now.

The dumbler bore her down to the rescue of the helpless child. Clat lay on her back, watching them come, hoping to herself. She was still looking up when green teeth sprouted through the leaf all about her.

"Jump, Clat!" Lily-yo cried.

The child had time to scramble to her knees. Vegetable predators are not so fast as humans. Then the green teeth snapped shut about her waist.

Under the leaf, a trappersnapper had moved into position, sensing the presence of prey through the single layer of foliage. It was a horny, caselike affair, just a pair of square jaws hinged and with many long teeth. From one corner of it grew a stalk, very muscular and thicker than a human. It looked like a neck. Now it bent, carrying Clat away, down to its true mouth, which lived with the rest of the plant far below on the unseen forest Ground, slobbering in darkness and wetness and decay.

Whistling, Lily-yo directed her dumbler back up to the home bough. Nothing now could be done for Clat. It was the way.

Already the rest of the group was dispersing. To stand in a bunch was to invite trouble from the unnumbered enemies of the forest. Besides, Clat's was not the first death they had witnessed.

Lily-yo's group had once been of seven underwomen and two men. Two women and one man had fallen to the green. Among them, the eight women had born twenty-two children to the group, four of them being man children. Deaths of children were many, always. Now that Clat was gone, over half the children had fallen to the green. Only two man children were left, Gren and Veggy.

Lily-yo walked back along the branch in the green light. The dumbler drifted from her unheeded, obeying the silent instructions of the forest air, listening for word of a seeding place. Never had there been such an overcrowding of the world. No bare places existed. The dumblers sometimes drifted through the jungles for centuries waiting to alight.

Coming to a point above one of the nuthuts, Lily-yo lowered herself into it by the creeper. This had been Clat's nuthut. The headwoman could hardly enter it, so small was the door. Humans kept their doors as narrow as possible, enlarging them as they grew. It helped to keep out unwanted visitors.

All was tidy in the nuthut. From the interior soft fibre a bed had been cut; there the five year old had slept, when a feeling for sleep came among the unchanging forest green. On the cot lay Clat's soul. Lily-yo took it and thrust it into her belt.

She climbed out onto the creeper, took her knife, and began to slash at the place where the bark of the tree had been cut away and the nuthut was attached to the living wood. After several slashes, the cement gave. Clat's nuthut hinged down, hung for a moment, then fell.

As it disappeared among huge coarse leaves, there was a flurry of foliage. Something was fighting for the privilege of devouring the huge morsel.

Lily-yo climbed back onto the branch. For a moment she paused to breathe deeply. Breathing was more trouble than it had been. She had gone on too many hunts, borne too many children, fought too many fights. With a rare and fleeting knowledge of herself, she glanced down at her bare green breasts. They were less plump than they had been when she first took the man Haris to her; they hung lower. Their shape was less beautiful.

By instinct she knew her youth was over. By instinct she knew it was time to Go Up.

The group stood near the Hollow, awaiting her. She ran to them. The Hollow was like an upturned armpit, formed where the branch joined the trunk. In the Hollow collected their water supply.

Silently, the group was watching a line of termights climb the trunk. One of the termights now and again signalled greetings to the humans. The humans waved back. As far as they had allies at all, the termights were their allies. Only five great families survived here in the all-conquering vegetable world; the tigerflies, the treebees, the plantants and the termights were social insects, mighty and invincible.

And the fifth family was man, lowly and easily killed, not organised as the insects were, but not extinct—the last animal species remaining.

Lily-yo came up to the group. She too raised her eyes to follow the moving line of termights until it disappeared into the layers of green. The termights could live on any level of the great forest, in the Tips or down on the Ground. They were the first and last of insects; as long as anything lived, the termights and tigerflies would.

Lowering her eyes, Lily-yo called to the group.

When they looked, she brought out Clat's soul, lifting it above her head to show to them.

"Clat has fallen to the green," she said. "Her soul must go to the Tips, according to the custom. Flor and I will take it at once, so that we can go with the termights. Daphe, Hy, Ivin, Jury, you guard well the man Haris and the children till we return."

The women nodded solemnly. Then they came one by one to touch Clat's soul.

The soul was roughly carved of wood into the shape of a woman. As a child was born, so with rites its male parent carved it a soul, a doll, a totem soul—for in the forest when one fell to the green there was scarcely ever a bone surviving to be buried. The soul survived for burial in the Tips.

As they touched the soul, Gren adventurously slipped from the group. He was nearly as old as Toy, as active and as strong. Not only had he power to run. He could climb. He could swim. Ignoring the cry of his friend Veggy, he scampered into the Hollow and dived into the pool.

Below the surface, opening his eyes, he saw a world of bleak clarity. A few green things like clover leaves grew at his approach, eager to wrap round his legs. Gren avoided them with a flick of his hand as he shot deeper. Then he saw the crocksock—before it saw him.

The crocksock was an aquatic plant, semi-parasitic by nature. Living in hollows, it sent down its saw-toothed suckers into the trees' sap. But the upper section of it, rough and tongue-shaped like a sock, could also feed. It unfolded, wrapping round Gren's left arm, its fibres instantly locking to increase the grip.

Gren was ready for it.

With one slash of his knife, he clove the crocksock in two, leaving the lower half to thrash uselessly at him. Before he could rise to the surface, Daphe the skilled huntress was beside him, her face angered, bubbles flashing out silver like fish from between her teeth. Her knife was ready to protect him.

He grinned at her as he broke surface and climbed out onto the dry bank. Nonchalantly he shook himself as she climbed beside him.

" 'Nobody runs or swims or climbs alone,' " Daphe called to him, quoting one of the laws. "Gren, have you no fear? Your head is an empty burr!"

The other women too showed anger. Yet none of them touched Gren. He was a man child. He was tabu. He had the magic powers of carving souls and bringing babies—or would have when fully grown, which would be soon now.

"I am Gren, the man child!" he boasted to them. His eyes sought Haris's for approval. Haris merely looked away. Now that Gren was so big, Haris did not cheer as once he had, though the boy's deeds were braver than before.

Slightly deflated, Gren jumped about, waving the strip of crocksock still wrapped round his left arm. He called and boasted at the women to show how little he cared for them.

"You are a baby yet," hissed Toy. She was ten, his senior by one year. Gren fell quiet.

Scowling, Lily-yo said, "The children grow too old to manage. When Flor and I have been to the Tips to bury Clat's soul, we shall return and break up the group. Time has come for us to part. Guard yourselves!"

It was a subdued group that watched their leader go. All knew that the group had to split; none cared to think about it. Their time of happiness and safety—so it seemed to all of them—would be finished, perhaps forever. The children would enter a period of lonely hardship, fending for themselves. The adults embarked on old age, trial, and death when they Went Up into the unknown.

II

Lily-yo and Flor climbed the rough bark easily. For them it was like going up a series of more or less symmetrically placed rocks. Now and again they met some kind of vegetable enemy, a thinpin or a pluggyrug, but these were small fry, easily dispatched into the green gloom below. Their enemies were the termights' enemies, and the moving column had already dealt with the foes in its path. Lily-yo and Flor climbed close to the termights, glad of their company.

They climbed for a long while. Once they rested on an empty branch, capturing two wandering burrs, splitting them, and eating their oily white flesh. On the way up, they had glimpsed one or two groups of humans on different branches; sometimes these groups waved shyly, sometimes not. Now they were too high for humans.

Nearer the Tips, new danger threatened. In the safer middle layers of the forest the humans lived, avoiding the perils of the Tips or the Ground.

"Now we move on," Lily-yo told Flor, getting to her feet when they had rested. "Soon we will be at the Tips."

A commotion silenced the two women. They looked up, crouching against the trunk for protection. Above their heads, leaves rustled as death struck.

A leapycreeper flailed the rough bark in a frenzy of greed, attacking the termight column. The leapycreeper's roots and stems were also tongues and lashes. Whipping round the trunk, it thrust its sticky tongues into the termights.

Against this particular plant, flexible and hideous, the insects had little defence. They scattered but kept doggedly climbing up, each perhaps trusting in the blind law of averages to survive.

For the humans, the plant was less of a threat—at least when met on a branch. Encountered on a trunk, it could easily dislodge them and send them helplessly falling to the green.

"We will climb on another trunk," Lily-yo said.

She and Flor ran deftly along the branch, once jumping a bright parasitic bloom round which treebees buzzed, a forerunner of the world of colour above them.

A far worse obstacle lay waiting in an innocent-looking hole in the branch. As Flor and Lily-yo approached, a tigerfly zoomed up at them. It was all but as big as they were, a terrible thing that possessed both weapons and intelligence—and malevolence. Now it attacked only through viciousness, its eyes large, its mandibles working, its transparent wings beating. Its head was a mixture of shaggy hair

and armour-plating, while behind its slender waist lay the
great swivel-plated body, yellow and black, sheathing a
lethal sting on its tail.

It dived between the women, aiming to hit them with its
wings. They fell flat as it sped past. Angrily, it tumbled
against the branch as it turned on them again; its golden-
brown sting flicked in and out.

"I'll get it!" Flor said. A tigerfly had killed one of her
babes.

Now the creature came in fast and low. Ducking, Flor
reached up and seized its shaggy hair, swinging the tigerfly
off balance. Quickly she raised her sword. Bringing it down
in a mighty sweep, she severed that chitinous and narrow
waist.

The tigerfly fell away in two parts. The two women ran
on.

The branch, a main one, did not grow thinner. Instead,
it ran on for another twenty yards and grew into another
trunk. The tree, vastly old, the longest lived organism ever
to flourish on this little world, had a myriad trunks. Very
long ago—two thousand million years past—trees had
grown in many kinds, depending on soil, climate, and other
conditions. As temperatures climbed, they proliferated and
came into competition with each other. The banyan, thriv-
ing in the heat, using its complex system of self-rooting
branches, gradually established ascendancy over the other
species. Under pressure, it evolved and adapted. Each banyan spread out further and further, sometimes doubling
back on itself for safety. Always it grew higher and crept
wider, protecting its parent stem as its rivals multiplied,
dropping down trunk after trunk, throwing out branch after
branch, until at last it learnt the trick of growing into its
neighbour banyan, forming a thicket against which no other
tree could strive. Their complexity became unrivalled, their
immortality established.

On this great continent where the humans lived, only one
banyan tree grew now. It had become first King of the forest, then it had become the forest itself. It had conquered
the deserts and the mountains and the swamps. It filled the
continent with its interlaced scaffolding. Only before the
wider rivers or at the margins of the sea, where the deadly
seaweeds could assail it, did the tree not go.

And at the terminator, where all things stopped and night began, there too the tree did not go.

The women climbed slowly now, alert as the odd tigerfly zoomed in their direction. Splashes of colour grew everywhere, attached to the tree, hanging from lines, or drifting free. Lianas and fungi blossomed. Dumblers moved mournfully through the tangle. As they gained height, the air grew fresher and colour rioted, azures and crimsons, yellows and mauves, all the beautifully tinted snares of nature.

A dripperlip sent its scarlet dribbles of gum down the trunk. Several thinpins, with vegetable skill, stalked the drops, pounced, and died. Lily-yo and Flor went by on the other side.

Slashweed met them. They slashed back and climbed on.

Many fantastic plant forms there were, some like birds, some like butterflies. Ever and again, whips and hands shot out.

"Look!" Flor whispered. She pointed above their heads.

The tree's bark was cracked almost invisibly. Almost invisibly, a part of it moved. Thrusting her stick out at arm's length, Flor eased herself up until stick and crack were touching. Then she prodded.

A section of the bark gaped wide, revealing a pale deadly mouth. An oystermaw, superbly camouflaged, had dug itself into the tree. Jabbing swiftly, Flor thrust her stick into the trap. As the jaws closed, she pulled with all her might, Lily-yo steadying her. The oystermaw, taken by surprise, was wrenched from its socket.

Opening its maw in shock, it sailed outward through the air. A rayplane took it without trying.

Lily-yo and Flor climbed on.

The Tips was a strange world of its own, the vegetable kingdom at its most imperial and most exotic.

If the banyan ruled the forest, *was* the forest, then the traversers ruled the Tips. The traversers had formed the typical landscape of the Tips. Theirs were the great webs trailing everywhere, theirs the nests built on the tips of the tree.

When the traversers deserted their nests, other creatures built there, other plants grew, spreading their bright colours to the sky. Debris and droppings knitted these nests into solid platforms. Here grew the burnurn plant, which Lily-yo sought for the soul of Clat.

Pushing and climbing, the two women finally emerged onto one of these platforms. They took shelter from the perils of the sky under a great leaf and rested from their exertions. Even in the shade, even for them, the heat of the Tips was formidable. Above them, paralysing half the heaven, burned a great sun. It burnt without cease, always fixed and still at one point in the sky, and so would burn until that day—now no longer impossibly distant—when it burnt itself out.

Here in the Tips, relying on that sun for its strange method of defence, the burnurn ruled among stationary plants. Already its sensitive roots told it that intruders were near. On the leaf above them, Lily-yo and Flor saw a circle of light move. It wandered over the surface, paused, contracted. The leaf smouldered and burst into flames. Focussing one of its urns on them, the plant was fighting them with its terrible weapon—fire.

"Run!" Lily-yo commanded, and they dashed behind the top of a whistlethistle, hiding beneath its thorns, peering out at the burnurn plant.

It was a splendid sight.

High reared the plant, displaying perhaps half a dozen cerise flowers, each flower larger than a human. Other flowers, fertilized, had closed together, forming many-sided urns. Later stages still could be seen, where the colour drained from the urns as seed swelled at the base of them. Finally, when the seed was ripe, the urn—now hollow and immensely strong—turned transparent as glass and became a heat weapon the plant could use even after its seeds were scattered.

Every vegetable and creature shrank from fire—except humans. They alone could deal with the burnurn plant and use it to advantage.

Moving cautiously, Lily-yo stole forth and cut off a big leaf which grew through the platform on which they stood. A pluggyrug launched a spine at her from underneath, but she dodged it. Seizing the leaf, so much bigger than herself, she ran straight for the burnurn, hurling herself among its foliage and shinning to the top of it in an instant, before it could bring its urn-shaped lenses up to focus on her.

"Now!" she cried to Flor.

Flor was already on the move, sprinting forward.

Lily-yo raised the leaf above the burnurn, holding it between the plant and the sun. As if realising that this ruined its method of defence, the plant drooped in the shade as though sulking. Its flowers and its urns hung down limply.

Her knife out ready, Flor darted forward and cut off one of the great transparent urns. Together the two women dashed back for the cover of the whistlethistle while the burnurn came back to furious life, flailing its urns as they sucked in the sun again.

They reached cover just in time. A vegbird swooped out of the sky at them—and impaled itself on a thorn.

Instantly, a dozen scavengers were fighting for the body. Under cover of the confusion, Lily-yo and Flor attacked the urn they had won. Using both their knives and all their strength, they prized up one side far enough to put Clat's soul inside the urn. The side instantly snapped back into place again, an airtight join. The soul stared woodenly out at them through the transparent facets.

"May you Go Up and reach heaven," Lily-yo said.

It was her business to see the soul stood at least a sporting chance of doing so. With Flor, she carried the urn across to one of the cables spun by a traverser. The top end of the urn, where the seed had been, was enormously sticky. The urn adhered easily to the cable and hung there in the sun.

Next time a traverser climbed up the cable, the urn stood an excellent chance of sticking like a burr to one of its legs. Thus it would be carried away to heaven.

As they finished the work, a shadow fell over them. A mile-long body drifted down towards them. A traverser, a gross vegetable-equivalent of a spider, was descending to the Tips.

Hurriedly, the women burrowed their way through the platform. The last rites for Clat had been carried out: it was time to return to the group.

Before they climbed down again to the green world of middle levels, Lily-yo looked back.

The traverser was descending slowly, a great bladder with legs and jaws, fibery hair covering most of its bulk. To her it was like a god, with the powers of a god. It came down a cable, floated nimbly down the strand trailing up into the sky.

As far as could be seen, cables slanted up from the jungle, pointing like slender drooping fingers to heaven. Where the sun caught them, they glittered. They all trailed up in the same direction, toward a floating silver half-globe, remote and cool, but clearly visible even in the glare of eternal sunshine.

Unmoving, steady, the half-moon remained always in the same sector of the sky.

Through the eons, the pull of this moon had gradually slowed the axial revolution of its parent planet to a standstill, until day and night slowed, and became fixed forever, day always on one side of the planet, night on the other. At the same time, a reciprocal braking effect had checked the moon's apparent flight. Drifting further from Earth, the moon had shed its role as Earth's satellite and rode along in Earth's orbit, an independent planet in its own right. Now the two bodies, for what was left of the afternoon of eternity, faced each other in the same relative position. They were locked face to face, and so would be, until the sands of time ceased to run, or the sun ceased to shine.

And the multitudinous strands of cable floated across the gap, uniting the worlds. Back and forth the traversers could shuttle at will, vegetable astronauts huge and insensible, with Earth and Luna both enmeshed in their indifferent net.

With surprising suitability, the old age of the Earth was snared about with cobwebs.

III

The journey back to the group was fairly uneventful. Lily-yo and Flor travelled at an easy pace, sliding down again into the middle levels of the tree. Lily-yo did not press forward as hard as usual, for she was reluctant to face the breakup of the group.

She could not express her few thoughts easily.

"Soon we must Go Up like Clat's soul," she said to Flor, as they climbed down.

"It is the way," Flor answered, and Lily-yo knew she would get no deeper word on the matter than that. Nor could she frame deeper words herself; human understandings trickled shallow these days.

The group greeted them soberly when they returned. Being weary, Lily-yo offered them a brief salutation and retired to her nuthut. Jury and Ivin soon brought her food, setting not so much as a finger inside her home, that being tabu. When she had eaten and slept, she climbed again onto the home strip of branch and summoned the others.

"Hurry!" she called, staring fixedly at Haris, who was not hurrying. Why should a difficult thing be so precious—or a precious thing be so difficult?

At that moment, while her attension was diverted, a long green tongue licked out from behind the tree trunk. Uncurling, it hovered daintily for a second. It took Lily-yo round the waist, pinning her arms to her side, lifting her off the branch. Furiously she kicked and cried.

Haris pulled a knife from his belt, leapt forward with eyes slitted, and hurled the blade. Singing, it pierced the tongue and pinned it to the rough trunk of the tree.

Haris did not pause after throwing. As he ran towards the pinioned tongue, Daphe and Jury ran behind him, while Flor scuttled the children to safety. In its agony, the tongue eased its grip on Lily-yo.

Now a terrific thrashing had set in on the other side of the tree trunk: the forest seemed full of its vibrations. Lily-yo whistled up two dumblers, fought her way out of the green coils round her, and was now safely back on the branch. The tongue, writhing in pain, flicked about meaninglessly. Weapons out, the four humans moved forward to deal with it.

The tree itself shook with the wrath of the trapped creature. Edging cautiously round the trunk, they saw it. Its great vegetable mouth distorted, a wiltmilt stared back at them with the hideous palmate pupil of its single eye. Furiously it hammered itself against the tree, foaming and mouthing. Though they had faced wiltmilts before, yet the humans trembled.

The wiltmilt was many times the girth of the tree trunk at its present extension. If necessary, it could have extended itself up almost to the Tips, stretching and becoming thinner as it did so. Like an obscene jack-in-the-box, it sprang up from the Ground in search of food, armless, brainless, goug-

ing its slow way over the forest floor on wide and rooty
legs.

"Pin it!" Lily-yo cried.

Concealed all along the branch were sharp stakes kept
for such emergencies. With these they stabbed the writhing
tongue that cracked like a whip about their heads. At last
they had a good length of it secured, staked down to the
tree. Though the wiltmilt writhed, it would never get free
now.

"Now we must leave and Go Up," Lily-yo said.

No human could ever kill a wiltmilt. But already its struggles were attracting predators, the thinpins—those mindless
sharks of the middle levels—rayplanes, trappersnappers,
gargoyles, and smaller vegetable vermin. They would tear
the wiltmilt to living pieces and continue until nothing of it
remained—and if they happened on a human at the same
time . . . well, it was the way.

Lily-yo was angry. She had brought on this trouble. She
had not been alert. Alert, she would never have allowed
the wiltmilt to catch her. Her mind had been tied with
thought of her own bad leadership. For she had caused two
dangerous trips to be made to the Tips where one would
have done. If she had taken all the group with her when
Clat's soul was disposed of, she would have saved this second ascent. What ailed her brain that she had not seen this
beforehand?

She clapped her hands. Standing for shelter under a giant
leaf, she made the group come about her. Sixteen pairs of
eyes stared trustingly at her. She grew angry to see how
they trusted her.

"We adults grow old," she told them. "We grow stupid.
I grow stupid. I let a slow wiltmilt catch me. I am not fit
to lead. Not any more. The time is come for the adults to
Go Up and return to the gods who made us. Then the
children will be on their own. They will be the group. Toy
will lead the group. By the time you are sure of your group,
Gren and soon Veggy will be old enough to give you children. Take care of the man children. Let them not fall to
the green, or the group dies. Better to die yourself than let
the group die."

Lily-yo had never made, the others had never heard, so
long a speech. Some of them did not understand it all. What

of this talk about falling to the green? One did or one did not: it needed no talk. Whatever happened was the way, and talk could not touch it.

May, a girl child, said cheekily, "On our own we can enjoy many things."

Reaching out, Flor clapped her on an ear.

"First you make the hard climb to the Tips," she said.

"Yes, move," Lily-yo said. She gave the order for climbing, who should lead, who follow.

About them the forest throbbed, green creatures sped and snapped as the wiltmilt was devoured.

"The climb is hard. Begin quickly," Lily-yo said, looking restlessly about her.

"Why climb?" Gren asked rebelliously. "With dumblers we can fly easily to the Tips and suffer no pain."

It was too complicated to explain to him that a human drifting in the air was far more vulnerable than a human shielded by a trunk, with the good rough bark nodules to squeeze between in case of attack.

"While I lead, you climb," Lily-yo said. She could not hit Gren. He was a tabu man child.

They collected their souls from their nuthuts. There was no pomp about saying goodbye to their old home. Their souls went in their belts, their swords—the sharpest, hardest, thorns available—went in their hands. They ran along the branch after Lily-yo, away from the disintegrating wiltmilt, away from their past.

Slowed by the younger children, the journey up to the Tips was long. Although the humans fought off the usual hazards, the tiredness growing in small limbs could not be fought. Half way to the Tips, they found a side branch to rest on, for there grew a fuzzypuzzle, and they sheltered in it.

The fuzzypuzzle was a beautiful, disorganised fungus. Although it looked like nettlemoss on a larger scale, it did not harm humans, drawing in its poisoned pistils as if with disgust when they came to it. Ambling in the eternal branches of the tree, fuzzypuzzles desired only vegetable food. So the group climbed into the middle of it and slept. Guarded among the waving viridian and yellow stalks, they were safe from nearly all forms of attack.

Flor and Lily-yo slept most deeply of the adults. They were tired by their previous journey. Haris the man was the first to awake, knowing something was wrong. As he roused, he woke up Jury by poking her with his stick. He was lazy; besides, it was his duty to keep out of danger. Jury sat up. She gave a shrill cry of alarm and jumped at once to defend the children.

Four winged things had invaded the fuzzypuzzle. They had seized Veggy, the man child, and Bain, one of the younger girl children, gagging and typing them before the pair could wake properly.

At Jury's cry, the winged ones looked round.

They were flymen!

In some aspects they resembled humans. They had one head, two long and powerful arms, stubby legs, and strong fingers on hands and feet. But instead of smooth green skin, they were covered in a glittering horny substance, here black, here pink. And large scaly wings resembling those of a vegbird grew from their wrists to their ankles. Their faces were sharp and clever. Their eyes glittered.

When they saw the humans waking, the flymen grabbed up the two captive children. Bursting through the fuzzypuzzle, which did not harm them, they ran towards the edge of the branch to jump off.

Flymen were crafty enemies, seldom seen but much dreaded by the group. They worked by stealth. Though they did not kill unless forced to, they stole children. Catching them was hard. Flymen did not fly properly, but the crash glides they fell into carried them swiftly away through the forest, safe from human reprisal.

Jury flung herself forward with all her might, Ivin behind her. She caught an ankle, seized part of the leathery tendon of wing where it joined the foot, and clung on. One of the flymen holding Veggy staggered with her weight, turning as he did so to free himself. His companion, taking the full weight of the boy child, paused, dragging out a knife to defend himself.

Ivin flung herself at him with savagery. She had mothered Veggy: he should not be taken away. The flyman's blade came to meet her. She threw herself on it. It ripped her stomach till the brown entrails showed, and she toppled from the branch with no cry. There was a commotion in the foliage below as trappersnappers fought for her.

Deciding he had done enough, the flyman dropped the bound Veggy and left his friend still struggling with Jury. He spread his wings, taking off heavily after the two who had born Bain away between them into the green thicket.

All the group were awake now. Lily-yo silently untied Veggy, who did not cry, for he was a man child. Meanwhile, Haris knelt by Jury and her winged opponent, who fought without words to get away. Quickly, Haris brought out a knife.

"Don't kill me. I will go!" cried the flyman. His voice was harsh, his words hardly understandable. The mere strangeness of him filled Haris with savagery, so that his lips curled back and his tongue came thickly between his bared teeth.

He thrust his knife deep between the flyman's ribs, four times over, till the blood poured over his clenched fist.

Jury stood up gasping and leant against Ivin. "I grow old," she said. "Once it was no trouble to kill a flyman."

She looked at the man Haris with gratitude. He had more than one use.

With one foot she pushed the limp body over the edge of the branch. It rolled messily, then dropped. Its old wizened wings tucked uselessly about its head, the flyman fell to the green.

IV

They lay among the sharp leaves of two whistlethistle plants, dazed by the bright sun but alert for new dangers. Their climb had been completed. Now the nine children saw the Tips for the first time—and were struck mute by it.

Once more Lily-yo and Flor lay siege to a burnurn, with Daphe helping them. As the plant slumped defencelessly in the shadow of their upheld leaves, Daphe severed six of the great transparent pods that were to be their coffins. Hy helped her carry them to safety, after which Lily-yo and Flor dropped their leaves and ran for the shelter of the whistlethistles.

A cloud of paperwings drifted by, their colours startling

to eyes generally submerged in green: sky blues and yellows and bronzes and a viridian that flashed like water.

One of the paperwings alighted fluttering on a tuft of emerald foliage near the watchers. The foliage was a dripperlip. Almost at once the paperwing turned grey as its small nourishment content was sucked out. It disintegrated like ash.

Rising cautiously, Lily-yo led the group over to the nearest cable of traverser web. Each adult carried her own urn.

The traversers, largest of all creatures, vegetable or otherwise, could never go into the forest. They spurted out their line among the upper branches, securing it with side strands.

Finding a suitable cable with no traverser in sight, Lily-yo turned, signalling for the urns to be put down. She spoke to Toy, Gren, and the seven other children.

"Now help us climb with our souls into our burnurns. See us tight in. Then carry us to the cable and stick up to it. Then good-bye. We Go Up. You are the group now."

Toy momentarily hesitated. She was a slender girl, her breasts like pearfruit.

"Do not go, Lily-yo," she said. "We still need you."

"It is the way," Lily-yo said firmly.

Prizing open one of the facets of her urn, she slid into her coffin. Helped by the children, the other adults did the same. From habit, Lily-yo glanced to see that Haris was safe.

They were all in now, and helpless. Inside the urns it was surprisingly cool.

The children carried the coffins between them, glancing nervously up at the sky meanwhile. They were afraid. They felt helpless. Only the bold man child Gren looked as if he was enjoying their new sense of independence. He more than Toy directed the others in the placing of the urns upon the traverser's cable.

Lily-yo smelt a curious smell in the urn. As it soaked through her lungs, her senses became detached. Outside, the scene which had been clear clouded and shrank. She saw she hung suspended on a traverser cable above the tree tops, with Flor, Haris, Daphe, Hy and Jury in other urns nearby, hanging helplessly. She saw the children, the new group, run to shelter. Without looking back, they dived into the muddle of foliage on the platform and disappeared.

* * *

The traverser hung ten and a half miles above the Tops, safe from its enemies. All about it, space was indigo, and the invisible rays of space bathed it and nourished it. Yet the traverser was still dependent on Earth for some food. After many hours of vegetative dreaming, it swung itself over and climbed down a cable.

Other traversers hung motionless nearby. Occasionally one would blow a globe of oxygen or hitch a leg to try and dislodge a troublesome parasite. Theirs was a leisureliness never attained before. Time was not for them; the sun was theirs, and would ever be until it became unstable, turned nova, and burnt both them and itself out.

The traverser fell fast, its feet twinkling, hardly touching the cable, fell straight to the forest, plunging towards the leafy cathedrals of the forest. Here in the air lived its enemies, enemies many times smaller, many times more vicious, many times more clever. Traversers were prey to one of the last families of insect, the tigerflies.

Only tigerflies could kill traversers—kill in their own insidious, invincible way.

Over the long slow eons as the sun's radiation increased, vegetation had evolved to undisputed supremacy. The wasps had developed too, keeping pace with the new developments. They grew in numbers and size as the animal kingdom fell into eclipse and dwindled into the rising tide of green. In time they became the chief enemies of the spider-like traversers. Attacking in packs, they could paralyse the primitive nerve centres, leaving the traversers to stagger to their own destruction. The tigerflies also laid their eggs in tunnels bored into the stuff of their enemies' bodies; when the eggs hatched, the larvae fed happily on living flesh.

This threat it was, more than anything, that had driven the traversers further and further into space many millenia past. In this seemingly inhospitable region, they reached their full and monstrous flowering.

Hard radiation became a necessity for them. Nature's first astronauts, they changed the face of the firmament. Long after man had rolled up his affairs and retired to the trees from whence he came, the traversers reconquered that vacant pathway he had lost. Long after intelligence had died from its peak of dominance, the traversers linked indissolubly the green globe and the white—with that antique symbol of neglect, a spider's web.

The traverser scrambled down among the upper leaves, erecting the hairs on its back, where patchy green and black afforded it natural camouflage. On its way down it had collected several creatures caught fluttering in its cables. It sucked them peacefully. When the soupy noises stopped, it vegetated.

Buzzing roused it from its doze. Yellow and black stripes zoomed before its crude eyes. A pair of tigerflies had found it.

With great alacrity, the traverser moved. Its massive bulk, contracted in the atmosphere, had an overall length of over a mile, yet it moved lightly as pollen, scuttling up a cable back to the safety of vacuum.

As it retreated, its legs brushing the web, it picked up various spores, burrs, and tiny creatures that adhered there. It also picked up six burnurns, each containing an insensible human, which swung unregarded from its shin.

Several miles up, the traverser paused. Recovering from its fright, it ejected a globe of oxygen, attaching it gently to a cable. It paused. Its palps trembled. Then it headed out towards deep space, expanding all the time as pressure dropped.

Its speed increased. Folding its legs, the traverser began to eject fresh web from the spinnerets under its abdomen. So it propelled itself, a vast vegetable almost without feeling, rotating slowly to stabilise its temperature.

Hard radiations bathed it. The traverser basked in them. It was in its element.

Daphe roused. She opened her eyes, gazing without intelligence. What she saw had no meaning. She only knew she had Gone Up. This was a new existence and she did not expect it to have meaning.

Part of the view from her urn was eclipsed by stiff yellowy whisps that might have been hair or straw. Everything else was uncertain, being washed either in blinding light or deep shadow. Light and shadow revolved.

Gradually Daphe identified other objects. Most notable was a splendid green half-ball mottled with white and blue. Was it a fruit? To it trailed cables, glinting here and there, many cables, silver or gold in the crazy light. Two traversers she recognised at some distance, travelling fast, looking mummified. Bright points of lights sparkled painfully. All was confusion.

This was where gods lived.

Daphe had no feeling. A curious numbness kept her without motion or the wish to move. The smell in the urn was strange. Also the air seemed thick. Everything was like an evil dream. Daphe opened her mouth, her jaw sticky and slow to respond. She screamed. No sound came. Pain filled her. Her sides in particular ached.

Even when her eyes closed again, her mouth hung open.

Like a great shaggy balloon, the traverser floated down to the moon.

It could hardly be said to think, being a mechanism or little more. Yet somewhere in it the notion stirred that its pleasant journey was too brief, that there might be other directions in which to sail. After all, the hated tigerflies were almost as many now, and as troublesome, on the moon as on the earth. Perhaps somewhere there might be a peaceful place, another of these half-round places with green stuff, in the middle of warm delicious rays. . . .

Perhaps some time it might be worth sailing off on a full belly and a new course. . . .

Many traversers hung above the moon. Their nets straggled untidily everywhere. This was their happy base, better liked than the earth, where the air was thick and their limbs were clumsy. This was the place they had discovered first— except for some puny creatures who had been long gone before they arrived. They were the last lords of creation. Largest and lordliest, they enjoyed their long lazy afternoon's supremacy.

The traverser slowed, spinning out no more cable. In leisurely fashion, it picked its way through a web and drifted down to the pallid vegetation of the moon. . . .

Here were conditions very unlike those on the heavy planet. The many-trunked banyans had never gained supremacy here; in the thin air and low gravity they outgrew their strength and collapsed. In their place, monstrous celeries and parsleys grew, and it was into a bed of these that the traverser settled. Hissing from its exertions, it blew off a great cloud of oxygen and relaxed.

As it settled down into the foliage, its great sack of body rubbed against the stems. Its legs too scraped into the mass of leaves. From legs and body a shower of light debris was dislodged—burrs, seeds, grit, nuts, and leaves caught up in its sticky fibres back on distant earth. Among this detritus were six seed casings from a burnurn plant. They rolled over the ground and came to a standstill.

Haris the man was the first to awaken. Groaning with an unexpected pain in his sides, he tried to sit up. Pressure on his forehead reminded him of where he was. Doubling up knees and arms, he pushed against the lid of his coffin.

Momentarily, it resisted him. Then the whole urn crumbled into pieces, sending Haris sprawling. The rigours of total vacuum had destroyed its cohesive powers.

Unable to pick himself up, Haris lay where he was. His head throbbed, his lungs were full of an unpleasant odour. Eagerly he gasped in fresh air. At first it seemed thin and chill, yet he sucked it in with gratitude.

After a while, he was well enough to look about him.

Long yellow tendrils were stretching out of a nearby thicket, working their way gingerly towards him. Alarmed, he looked about for a woman to protect him. None was there. Stiffly, his arms so stiff, he pulled his knife from his belt, rolled over on one side, and lopped the tendrils off as they reached him. This was an easy enemy!

Haris cried. He screamed. He jumped unsteadily to his feet, yelling in disgust at himself. Suddenly he had noticed he was covered in scabs. Worse, as his clothes fell in shreds from him, he saw that a mass of leathery flesh grew from his arms, his ribs, his legs. When he lifted his arms, the mass stretched out almost like wings. He was spoilt, his handsome body ruined.

A sound made him turn, and for the first time he remembered his fellows. Lily-yo was struggling from the remains of her burnurn. She raised a hand in greeting.

To his horror, Haris saw that she bore disfigurements like his own. In truth, at first he scarcely recognised her. She resembled nothing so much as one of the hated flymen. He flung himself to the ground and wept as his heart expanded in fear and loathing.

Lily-yo was not born to weep. Disregarding her own painful deformities, breathing laboriously, she cast about, seeking the other four coffins.

Flor's was the first she found, half buried though it was. A blow with a stone shattered it. Lily-yo lifted up her friend, as hideously transformed as she, and in a short while Flor roused. Inhaling the strange air raucously, she too sat up. Lily-yo left her to seek the others. Even in her dazed state, she thanked her aching limbs for feeling so light.

Daphe was dead. She lay stiff and purple in her urn. Though Lily-yo shattered it and called aloud, Daphe did not stir. Her swollen tongue stayed dreadfully protruding from her mouth. Daphe was dead, Daphe who had lived, Daphe who had been the sweet singer.

Hy also was dead, a poor shrivelled thing lying in a coffin that had cracked on its arduous journey between the two worlds. When that coffin shattered under Lily-yo's blow, Hy fell away to powder. Hy was dead. Hy who had born a man child. Hy always so fleet of foot.

Jury's urn was the last. She stirred as the headwoman reached her. A minute later, she was sitting up, eying her deformities with a stoical distaste, breathing the sharp air. Jury lived.

Haris staggered over to the women. In his hand he carried his soul.

"Four of us!" he exclaimed. "Have we been received by the gods or no?"

"We feel pain—so we live," Lily-yo said. "Daphe and Hy have fallen to the green."

Bitterly, Haris flung down his soul and trampled it underfoot.

"Look at us! Better be dead!" he said.

"Before we decide that, we will eat," said Lily-yo.

Painfully, they retreated into the thicket, alerting themselves once more to the idea of danger. Flor, Lily-yo, Jury, Haris, each supported the other. The idea of tabu had somehow been forgotten.

V

"No proper trees grow here," Flor protested, as they pushed among giant celeries whose crests waved high above their heads.

"Take care!" Lily-yo said. She pulled Flor back. Something rattled and snapped like a chained dog, missing Flor's leg by inches.

A trappersnapper, having missed its prey, was slowly reopening its jaws, baring its green teeth. This one was only a shadow of the terrible trappersnappers spawned on the jungle floors of earth. Its jaws were weaker, its movements far more circumscribed. Without the shelter of the giant banyans, the trappersnappers were disinherited.

Something of the same feeling overcame the humans. They and their ancestors for countless generations had lived in the high trees. Safety was arboreal. Here there were only celery and parsley trees, offering neither the rock-steadiness nor the unlimited boughs of the giant banyan.

So they journeyed, nervous, lost, in pain, knowing neither where they were nor why they were.

They were attacked by leapycreepers and sawthorns, and beat them down. They skirted a thicket of nettlemoss taller and wider than any to be met with on earth. Conditions that worked against one group of vegetation favoured others. They climbed a slope and came on a pool fed by a stream. Over the pool hung berries and fruits, sweet to taste, good to eat.

"This is not so bad," Haris said. "Perhaps we can still live."

Lily-yo smiled at him. He was the most trouble, the most lazy; yet she was glad he was still here. When they bathed in the pool, she looked at him again. For all the strange scales that covered him, and the two broad sweeps of flesh that hung by his side, he was still good to look on just because he was Haris. She hoped she was also comely. With a burr she raked her hair back; only a little of it fell out.

When they had bathed, they ate. Haris worked then, collecting fresh knives from the bramble bushes. They were not as tough as the ones on earth, but they would have to do. Then they rested in the sun.

The pattern of their lives was completely broken. More

by instinct than intelligence they had lived. Without the group, without the tree, without the earth, no pattern guided them. What was the way or what was not became unclear. So they lay where they were and rested.

As she lay there, Lily-yo looked about her. All was strange, so that her heart beat faintly.

Though the sun shone bright as ever, the sky was as deep blue as a vandalberry. And the half-globe in the sky was monstrous, all streaked with green and blue and white, so that Lily-yo could not know it for somewhere she had lived. Phantom silver lines pointed to it, while nearer at hand the tracery of traverser webs glittered, veining the whole sky. Traversers moved over it like clouds, their great bodies slack.

All this was their empire, their creation. On their first journeys here, many millenia ago, they had literally laid the seeds of this world. To begin with, they had withered and died by the thousand on the inhospitable ash. But even the dead had brought their little legacies of oxygen, soil, spores, and seed, some of which later sprouted on the fruitful corpses. Under the weight of dozing centuries, they gained a sort of foothold.

They grew. Stunted and ailing in the beginning, they grew. With vegetal tenacity, they grew. They exhaled. They spread. They thrived. Slowly the broken wastes of the moon's lit face turned green. In the craters creepers grew. Up the ravaged slopes the parsleys crawled. As the atmosphere deepened, so the magic of life intensified, its rhythm strengthened, its tempo increased. More thoroughly than another dominant species had once managed to do, the traversers colonised the moon.

Lily-yo could know or care little about any of this. She turned her face from the sky.

Flor had crawled over to Haris the man. She lay against him in the circle of his arms, half under the shelter of his new skin, and she stroked his hair.

Furious, Lily-yo jumped up, kicked Flor on the shin, and then flung herself upon her, using teeth and nails to pull her away. Jury ran to join in.

"This is not time for mating!" Lily-yo cried.

"Let me *go!*" cried Flor.

Haris in his startlement jumped up. He stretched his arms, waved them, and rose effortlessly into the air.

"Look!" he shouted in alarmed delight.

Over their heads he circled once, perilously. Then he lost his balance and came sprawling head first, mouth open in fright. Head first he pitched into the pool.

Three anxious, awe-struck, lovestuck female humans dived after him in unison.

While they were drying themselves, they heard noises in the forest. At once they became alert, their old selves. They drew their new swords and looked to the thicket.

The wiltmilt when it appeared was not like its Earthly brothers. No longer upright like a jack-in-the-box, it groped its way along like a caterpillar.

The humans saw its distorted eye break from the celeries. Then they turned and fled.

Even when the danger was left behind, they moved rapidly, not knowing what they sought. Once they slept, ate, and then again pressed on through the unending growth, the undying daylight, until they came to where the jungle gaped.

Ahead of them, everything seemed to cease and then go on again.

Cautiously they approached. The ground underfoot had been badly uneven. Now it broke altogether into a wide crevasse. Beyond the crevasse the vegetation grew again— but how did humans pass the gulf? The four of them stood anxiously where the ferns ended, looking across at the far side.

Haris the man screwed his face in pain to show he had a troublesome idea in his head.

"What I did before—going up in the air," he began awkwardly. "If we do it again now, all of us, we go in the air across to the other side."

"No!" Lily-yo said. "When you go up you come down hard. You will fall to the green!"

"I will do better than before."

"No!" repeated Lily-yo. "You are not to go."

"Let him go," Flor said.

The two women turned to glare at each other. Taking his

chance, Haris raised his arms, waved them, rose slightly from the ground, and began to use his legs too. He moved forward over the crevasse before his nerve broke.

As he fluttered down, Flor and Lily-yo, moved by instinct, dived into the gulf after him. Spreading their arms, they glided about him, shouting. Jury remained behind, crying in baffled anger down to them.

Regaining a little control, Haris landed heavily on an outcropping ledge. The two women alighted chattering and scolding beside him. They looked up. Two lips fringed with green fern sucked a narrow purple segment of sky. Jury could not be seen, though her cries still echoed down to them.

Behind the ledge on which they stood a tunnel ran into the cliff. All the rock face was peppered with similar holes, so that it resembled a sponge. From the hole behind the ledge ran three flymen, two male and one female. They rushed out with ropes and spears.

Flor and Lily-yo were bending over Haris. Before they had time to recover, they were knocked sprawling and tied with the ropes. Helpless, Lily-yo saw other flymen launch themselves from other holes and come gliding in to help secure them. Their flight seemed more sure, more graceful, than it had on earth. Perhaps the way humans were lighter here had something to do with it.

"Bring them in!" the flymen cried to each other. Their sharp, clever faces jostled round eagerly as they hoisted up their captives and bore them into the tunnel.

In their alarm, Lily-yo, Flor and Haris forgot about Jury, still crouching on the lip of the crevasse. They never saw her again. A pack of thinpins got her.

The tunnel sloped gently down. Finally it curved and led into another which ran level and true. This in its turn led into an immense cavern with regular sides and a regular roof. Grey daylight flooded in at one end, for the cavern stood at the bottom of the crevasse.

To the middle of this cavern the three captives were brought. Their knives were taken from them and they were released. As they huddled together uneasily, one of the flymen stood forward and spoke.

"We will not harm you unless we must," he said. "You

come by traverser from the Heavy World. You are new here. When you learn our ways, you will join us."

"I am Lily-yo," Lily-yo proudly said. "Let me go. We three are humans. You are flymen."

"Yes, you are humans, we are flymen. Also we are humans, you are flymen. Now you know nothing. Soon you will know, when you have seen the Captives. They will tell you many things."

"I am Lily-yo. I know many things."

"The Captives will tell you many more things."

"If there were many more things, then I should know them."

"I am Band Appa Bondi and I say come to see the Captives. Your talk is stupid Heavy World talk, Lily-yo."

Several flymen began to look aggressive, so that Haris nudged Lily-yo and muttered, "Let us do what he asks."

Grumpily, Lily-yo let herself and her two companions be led to another chamber. This one was partially ruined, and stank. At the far end of it, a fall of cindery rock marked where the roof had fallen in, while a shaft of the unremitting sunlight burnt on the floor, sending up a curtain of golden light about itself. Near this light were the Captives.

"Do not fear to see them. They will not harm you," Band Appa Bondi said, going forward.

The encouragement was needed, for the Captives were not prepossessing.

Eight of them there were, eight Captives, kept in eight great burnurns big enough to serve them as narrow cells. The cells stood grouped in a semicircle. Band Appa Bondi led Lily-yo, Flor and Haris into the middle of this semicircle, where they could survey and be surveyed.

The Captives were painful to look on. All had some kind of deformity. One had no legs. One had no flesh on his lower jaw. One had four gnarled dwarf arms. One had short wings of flesh connecting ear lobes and thumbs, so that he lived perpetually with hands half raised to his face. One had boneless arms trailing at his side and one boneless leg. One had monstrous wings which trailed about him like carpet. One was hiding his ill-shaped form away behind a screen of his own excrement, smearing it onto the transparent walls of his cell. And one had a second head, a small wizened thing growing from the first that fixed Lily-yo with a malevolent eye. This last captive, who seemed to lead the others, spoke now, using the mouth of his main head.

"I am the Chief Captive. I greet you. You are of the Heavy World. We are of the True World. Now you join us because you are of us. Though your wings and your scars are new, you may join us."

"I am Lily-yo. We three are humans. You are only fly-men. We will not join you."

The Captives grunted in boredom. The Chief Captive spoke again.

"Always this talk from you of the Heavy World! You *have* joined us! You are flymen, we are human. You know little, we know much."

"But we—"

"Stop your stupid talk, woman!"

"We are—"

"Be silent, woman, and listen," Band Appa Bondi said.

"We know much," repeated the Chief Captive. "Some things we will tell you. All who make the journey from the Heavy World become changed. Some die. Most live and grow wings. Between the worlds are many strong rays, not seen or felt, which change our bodies. When you come here, when you come to the True World, you become a true human. The grub of the tigerfly is not a tigerfly until it changes. So humans change."

"I cannot know what he says," Haris said stubbornly, throwing himself down. But Lily-yo and Flor were listening.

"To this True World, as you call it, we come to die," Lily-yo said, doubtingly.

The Captive with the fleshless jaw said, "The grub of the tigerfly thinks it dies when it changes into a tigerfly."

"You are still young," said the Chief Captive. "You begin newly here. Where are your souls?"

Lily-yo and Flor looked at each other. In their flight from the wiltmilt they had heedlessly thrown down their souls. Haris had trampled on his. It was unthinkable!

"You see. You needed them no more. You are still young. You may be able to have babies. Some of those babies may be born with wings."

The Captive with the boneless arms added, "Some may be born wrong, as we are. Some may be born right."

"You are too foul to live!" Haris growled. "Why are you not killed?"

"Because we know all things," the Chief Captive said. Suddenly his second head roused itself and declared, "To be a good shape is not all in life. To know is also good. Because we cannot move well we can—*think*. This tribe of the True World is good and knows these things. So it lets us rule it."

Flor and Lily-yo muttered together.

"Do you say that you poor Captives *rule* the True World?" Lily-yo asked at last.

"We do."

"Then why are you captives?"

The flyman with ear lobes and thumbs connected, making his perpetual little gesture of protest, spoke for the first time.

"To rule is to serve, woman. Those who bear power are slaves to it. Only an outcast is free. Because we are Captives, we have the time to talk and think and plan and know. Those who know command the knives of others."

"No hurt will come to you, Lily-yo," Band Appa Bondi added. "You will live among us and enjoy your life free from harm."

"No!" the Chief Captive said with both mouths. "Before she can enjoy, Lily-yo and her companion Flor—this other man creature is plainly useless—must help our great plan."

"The invasion?" Bondi asked.

"What else? Flor and Lily-yo, you arrive here at a good time. Memories of the Heavy World and its savage life are still fresh in you. We need such memories. So we ask you to go back there on a great plan we have."

"Go back?" gasped Flor.

"Yes. We plan to attack the Heavy World. You must help to lead our force."

VI

The long afternoon of eternity wore on, that long golden road of an afternoon that would somewhere lead to everlasting night. Motion there was, but motion without event—except for those negligible events that seemed so large to the creatures participating in them.

For Lily-yo, Flor and Haris there were many events.
Chief of these was that they learned to fly properly.

The pains associated with their wings soon died away as
the wonderful new flesh and tendon strengthened. To sail
up in the light gravity became an increasing delight—the
ugly flopping movements of flymen on the Heavy World
had no place here.

They learned to fly in packs, and then to hunt in packs.
In time they were trained to carry out the Captives' plan.

The series of accidents that had first delivered humans to
this world in burnurns had been a fortunate one, growing
more fortunate as millennia tolled away. For gradually the
humans adapted better to the True World. Their survival
factor became greater, their power surer. And all this as on
the Heavy World conditions grew more and more adverse
to anything but the giant vegetables.

Lily-yo at least was quick to see how much easier life was
in these new conditions. She sat with Flor and a dozen
others eating pulped pluggyrug, before they did the Captives' bidding and left for the Heavy World.

It was hard to express all she felt.

"Here we are safe," she said, indicating the whole green
land that sweltered under the silver network of webs.

"Except from the tigerflies," Flor agreed.

They rested on a bare peak, where the air was thin and
even the giant creepers had not climbed. The turbulent
green stretched away below them, almost as if they were
on Earth—although here it was continually checked by the
circular formations of rock.

"This world is smaller," Lily-yo said, trying again to make
Flor know what was in her head. "Here we are bigger. We
do not need to fight so much."

"Soon we must fight."

"Then we can come back here again. This is a good place,
with nothing so savage and with not so many enemies. Here
the groups could live without so much fear. Veggy and Toy
and May and Gren and the other little ones would like it
here."

"They would miss the trees."

"We shall soon miss the trees no longer. We have wings
instead."

This idle talk took place beneath the unmoving shadow

of a rock. Overhead, silver blobs against a purple sky, the traversers went, walking their networks, descending only occasionally to the celeries far below. As Lily-yo fell to watching these creatures, she thought in her mind of the grand plan the Captives had hatched, she flicked it over in a series of vivid pictures.

Yes, the Captives knew. They could see ahead as she could not. She and those about her had lived like plants, doing what came. The Captives were not plants. From their cells they saw more than those outside.

This, the Captives saw: that the few humans who reached the True World bore few children, because they were old, or because the rays that made their wings grow made their seed die; that it was good here, and would be better still with more humans; that one way to get more humans here was to bring babies and children from the Heavy World.

For countless time, this had been done. Brave flymen had travelled back to that other world and stolen children. The flymen who had once attacked Lily-yo's group on their climb to the Tips had been on that mission. They had taken Bain to bring her to the True World in burnurns—and had not been heard of since.

Many perils and mischances lay in that long double journey. Of those who set out, few returned.

Now the Captives had thought of a better and more daring scheme.

"Here comes a traverser," Band Appa Bondi said. "Let us be ready to move."

He walked before the pack of twelve flyers who had been chosen for this new attempt. He was the leader. Lily-yo, Flor, and Haris were in support of him, together with eight others, three male, five female. Only one of them, Band Appa Bondi himself, had been carried to the True World as a boy.

Slowly the pack stood up, stretching their wings. The moment for their great adventure was here. Yet they felt little fear; they could not look ahead as the Captives did, except perhaps for Band Appa Bondi and Lily-yo. She strengthened her will by saying, "It is the way." Then they all spread their arms wide and soared off to meet the traverser.

                        *   *   *

The traverser had eaten.

It had caught one of its most tasty enemies, a tigerfly, in a web, and had sucked it till only a shell was left. Now it sank down into a bed of celeries, crushing them under its great bulk. Gently, it began to bud. Afterwards, it would head out for the great black gulfs, where heat and radiance called it. It had been born on this world. Being young, it had never yet made that dreaded, desired journey.

Its buds burst up from its back, hung over, popped, fell to the ground, and scurried away to bury themselves in the pulp and dirt where they might begin their ten thousand years' growth in peace.

Young though it was, the traverser was sick. It did not know this. The enemy tigerfly had been at it, but it did not know this. Its vast bulk held little sensation.

The twelve humans glided down and landed on its back, low down on the abdomen in a position hidden from the creature's cluster of eyes. They sank among the tough shoulder-high fibres that served the traverser as hair, and looked about them. A rayplane swooped overhead and disappeared. A trio of tumbleweeds skittered into the fibres and were seen no more. All was as quiet as if they lay on a small deserted hill.

At length they spread out and moved along in line, heads down, eyes searching, Band Appa Bondi at one end, Lily-yo at the other. The great body was streaked and pitted and scarred, so that progress down the slope was not easy. The fibre grew in patterns of different shades, green, yellow, black, breaking up the traverser's bulk when seen from the air, serving it as natural camouflage. In many places, tough parasitic plants had rooted themselves, drawing their nourishment entirely from their host; most of them would die when the traverser launched itself out between worlds.

The humans worked hard. Once they were thrown flat when the traverser changed position. As the slope down which they moved grew steeper, so progress became more slow.

"Here!" cried Y Coyin, one of the women.

At last they had found what they sought, what the Captives sent them to seek.

Clustering round Y Coyin with their knives out, the pack looked down.

Here the fibres had been neatly champed away in swathes, leaving a bare patch as far across as a human was long. In this patch was a round scab. Lily-yo felt it. It was immensely hard.

Lo Jint put his ear to it. Silence.

They looked at each other.

No signal was needed, none given.

Together they knelt, prizing with their knives round the scab. Once the traverser moved, and they threw themselves flat. A bud rose nearby, popped, rolled down the slope and fell to the distant ground. A thinpin devoured it as it ran. The humans continued prising.

The scab moved. They lifted it off. A dark and sticky tunnel was revealed to them.

"I go first," Band Appa Bondi said.

He lowered himself into the hole. The others followed. Dark sky showed roundly above them until the twelfth human was in the tunnel. Then the scab was drawn back into place. A soft slobber of sound came from it, as it began to heal back into position again.

They crouched where they were for a long time. They crouched, their knives ready, their wings folded round them, their human hearts beating strongly.

In more than one sense they were in enemy territory. At the best of times, traversers were only allies by accident; they ate humans as readily as they devoured anything else. But this burrow was the work of that yellow and black destroyer, the tigerfly. One of the last true insects to survive, the tough and resourceful tigerflies had instinctively made the most invincible of all living things its prey.

The female tigerfly alights and bores her tunnel into the traverser. Working her way down, she at last stops and prepares a natal chamber, hollowing it from the living traverser, paralysing the matter with her needletail to prevent it healing again. There she lays her store of eggs before climbing back to daylight. When the eggs hatch, the larvae have fresh and living stuff to nourish them.

After a while, Band Appa Bondi gave a sign and the pack moved forward, climbing awkwardly down the tunnel. A faint luminescence guided their eyes. The air lay heavy and green in their chests. They moved very slowly, very quietly, for they heard movement ahead.

Suddenly the movement was on them.

"Look out!" Band Appa Bondi cried.

From the terrible dark, something launched itself at them.

Before they realised it, the tunnel had curved and widened into the natal chamber. The tigerfly's eggs had hatched. Two hundred larvae with jaws as wide as a man's reach turned on the intruders, snapping in fury and fear.

Even as Band Appa Bondi sliced his first attacker, another had his head off. He fell, and his companions launched themselves over him. Pressing forward, they dodged those clicking jaws.

Behind their hard heads, the larvae were soft and plump. One slash of a sword and they burst, their entrails flowing out. They fought, but knew not how to fight. Savagely the humans stabbed, ducked and stabbed. No other human died. With backs to the wall they cut and thrust, breaking jaws, ripping flimsy stomachs. They killed unceasingly with neither hate nor mercy until they stood knee deep in slush. The larvae snapped and writhed and died. Uttering a grunt of satisfaction, Haris slew the last of them.

Wearily then, eleven humans crawled back to the tunnel, there to wait until the mess drained away—and then to wait a longer while.

The traverser stirred in its bed of celeries. Vague impulses drifted through its being. Things it had done. Things it had to do. The things it had done had been done, the things it had to do were still to do. Blowing off oxygen, it heaved itself up.

Slowly at first, it swung up a cable, climbing to the network where the air thinned. Always, always before in the eternal afternoon it had stopped here. This time there seemed no reason for stopping. Air was nothing, heat was all, the heat that blistered and prodded and chafed and coaxed increasingly with height. . . .

It blew a jet of cable from a spinneret. Gaining speed, gaining intention, it rocketed its mighty vegetable self out and away from the place where the tigerflies flew. Ahead of it floated a semicircle of light, white and blue and green, that was a useful thing to look at to avoid getting lost.

For this was a lonely place for a young traverser, a terrible-wonderful bright-dark place, so full of nothing. Turn as you speed and you fry well on all sides . . . nothing to trouble you. . . .

. . . Except that deep in your core a little pack of humans use you as an ark for their own purposes. You carry them back to a world that once—so staggeringly long ago—belonged to their kind; you carry them back so that they may eventually—who knows?—fill another world with their own kind.

For remember, there is always plenty of time.

HIDING PLACE

BY POUL ANDERSON (1926-   )

ANALOG
MARCH

I'm going to let Poul Anderson introduce this story. The following is his headnote from The Best of Poul Anderson *(1976):*

"One danger science fiction faces in this era of growing respectability stems from the fact that some people are taking it too bloody seriously. I don't mean that it should never, or seldom, treat serious themes. Nor do I mean that the writer should not give every story he writes the very best he has to give at the time. But where in today's critical essays, academic conferences, and the fictional dooms and frustrations with which they are concerned is there any room for old-fashioned fun?

"Oh well, whether or not English professors do, the reading public continues to like adventures, exotic settings, and—in science fiction—exploration of a few of the infinite possible forms which worlds and the life upon them may take. With every respect, and, indeed, admiration for my colleagues whose interests lie elsewhere, I'll continue to spend a good part of my time as a spinner of yarns."

"Hiding Place" is an excellent example of his ability to spin with the best of them. (MHG)

By 1991, the Science Fiction Writers of America had chosen eleven science fiction writers to receive their Grand Masters award. This is a really coveted award, despite the fact that the phrase is a cliché. I know because I coveted it like crazy until I got mine in 1987.

All the Grand Masters have received the award not for this story or that but for a lifetime of science fictional achievement, and all of them were worthy of the award.

It is my opinion that of all the science fiction writers who have not yet received the award, the most worthy is Poul Anderson. He has been writing science fiction steadily for over forty years and has run the gamut from the hardest of hard science fiction to the softest of fantasy. To prove that this is not merely an exercise in quantity, he has won more Hugos and other awards than almost anyone else in the field.

What's more, he has established a dynasty of sorts. His daughter is married to Greg Bear, who is now one of the most prominent of the younger science fiction writers. (IA)

Captain Bahadur Torrance received the news as befitted a Lodgemaster in the Federated Brotherhood of Spacemen. He heard it out, interrupting only with a few knowledgeable questions. At the end, he said calmly, "Well done, Freeman Yamamura. Please keep this to yourself till further notice. I'll think about what's to be done. Carry on." But when the engineer officer had left the cabin—the news had not been the sort you tell on the intercom—he poured himself a triple whiskey, sat down, and stared emptily at the viewscreen.

He had traveled far, seen much, and been well rewarded. However, promotion being swift in his difficult line of work, he was still too young not to feel cold at hearing his death sentence.

The screen showed such a multitude of stars, hard and winter-brilliant, that only an astronaut could recognize individuals. Torrance sought past the Milky Way until he identified Polaris. Then Valhalla would lie so-and-so-many degrees away, in that direction. Not that he could see a type-G sun at this distance, without optical instruments more powerful than any aboard the *Hebe G.B.* But he found a certain comfort in knowing his eyes were sighted toward the nearest League base (houses, ships, humans, nestled in a green valley on Freya) in this almost uncharted section of our galactic arm. Especially when he didn't expect to land there, ever again.

The ship hummed around him, pulsing in and out of four-space with a quasi-speed that left light far behind and yet was still too slow to save him.

Well . . . it became the captain to think first of the others. Torrance sighed and stood up. He spent a moment checking his appearance; morale was important, never more so than now. Rather than the usual gray coverall of shipboard, he preferred full uniform: blue tunic, white cape and culottes, gold braid. As a citizen of Ramanujan planet, he kept a turban on his dark aquiline head, pinned with the Ship-and-Sunburst of the Polesotechnic League.

He went down a passageway to the owner's suite. The steward was just leaving, a tray in his hand. Torrance signaled the door to remain open, clicked his heels and bowed. "I pray pardon for the interruption, sir," he said. "May I speak privately with you? Urgent."

Nicholas van Rijn hoisted the two-liter tankard which had been brought him. His several chins quivered under the stiff goatee; the noise of his gulping filled the room, from the desk littered with papers to the Huy Brasealian jewel-tapestry hung on the opposite bulkhead. Something by Mozart lilted out of a taper. Blond, big-eyed, and thoroughly three-dimensional, Jeri Kofoed curled on a couch, within easy reach of him where he sprawled in his lounger. Torrance, who was married but had been away from home for some time, forced his gaze back to the merchant.

"Ahhh!" Van Rijn banged the empty mug down on a table and wiped foam from his mustaches. "Pox and pestilence, but the first beer of the day is good! Something with it is so quite cool and—um—by damn, what word do I want?" He thumped his sloping forehead with one hairy fist. "I get more absent in the mind every week. Ah, Torrance, when you are too a poor old lonely fat man with all powers failing him, you will look back and remember me and wish you was more good to me. But then is too late." He sighed like a minor tornado and scratched the pelt on his chest. In the near tropic temperature at which he insisted on maintaining his quarters, he need wrap only a sarong about his huge body. "Well, what begobbled stuping is it I must be dragged from my all-too-much work to fix up for you, ha?"

His tone was genial. He had, in fact, been in a good mood

ever since they escaped the Adderkops. (Who wouldn't be? For a mere space yacht, even an armed one with ultrapowered engines, to get away from three cruisers was more than an accomplishment; it was nearly a miracle. Van Rijn still kept four grateful candles burning before his Martian sandroot statuette of St. Dismas.) True, he sometimes threw crockery at the steward when a drink arrived later than he wished, and he fired everybody aboard ship at least once a day. But that was normal.

Jeri Kofoed arched her brows. "Your first beer, Nicky?" she murmured. "Now really! Two hours ago—"

"*Ja*, but that was before midnight time. If not Greenwich midnight, then surely on some planet somewhere, *nie?* So is a new day." Van Rijn took his churchwarden off the table and began stuffing it. "Well, sit down, Captain Torrance, make yourself to be comfortable and lend me your lighter. You look like a dynamited custard, boy. All you youngsters got no stamina. When I was a working spaceman, by Judas, we made solve our own problems. These days, death and damnation, you come ask me how to wipe your noses! Nobody has any guts but me." He slapped his barrel belly. "So what is be-jingle-bang gone wrong now?"

Torrance wet his lips. "I'd rather speak to you alone, sir."

He saw the color leave Jeri's face. She was no coward. Frontier planets, even the pleasant ones like Freya, didn't breed that sort. She had come along on what she knew would be a hazardous trip because a chance like this—to get an in with the merchant prince of the Solar Spice & Liquors Company, which was one of the major forces within the whole Polesotechnic League—was too good for an opportunistic girl to refuse. She had kept her nerve during the fight and the subsequent escape, though death came very close. But they were still far from her planet, among unknown stars, with the enemy hunting them.

"So go in the bedroom," van Rijn ordered her.

"Please," she whispered. "I'd be happier hearing the truth."

The small black eyes, set close to van Rijn's hook nose, flared. "Foulness and fulminate!" he bellowed. "What is this poppies with cocking? When I say frog, by billy damn, you jump!"

She sprang to her feet, mutinous. Without rising, he slapped her on the appropriate spot. It sounded like a pistol going off. She gasped, choked back an indignant screech, and stamped into the inner suite. Van Rijn rang for the steward.

"More beer this calls for," he said to Torrance. "Well, don't stand there making bug's eyes! I got no time for fumblydiddles, even if you overpaid loafers do. I got to make revises of all price schedules on pepper and nutmeg for Freya before we get there. Satan and stenches! At least ten percent more that idiot of a factor could charge them, and not reduce volume of sales. I swear it! All good saints, hear me and help a poor old man saddled with oatmeal-brained squatpots for workers!"

Torrance curbed his temper with an effort. "Very well, sir. I just had a report from Yamamura. You know we took a near miss during the fight, which hulled us at the engine room. The converter didn't seem damaged, but after patching the hole, the gang's been checking to make sure. And it turns out that about half the circuitry for the infrashield generator was fused. We can't replace more than a fraction of it. If we continue to run at full quasi-speed, we'll burn out the whole converter in another fifty hours."

"Ah, s-s-so." Van Rijn grew serious. The snap of the lighter, as he touched it to his pipe, came startlingly loud. "No chance of stopping altogether to make fixings? Once out of hyperdrive, we would be much too small a thing for the bestinkered Adderkops to find. Hey?"

"No, sir. I said we haven't enough replacement parts. This is a yacht, not a warship."

"Hokay, we must continue in hyperdrive. How slow must we go, to make sure we come within calling distance of Freya before our engine burns out?"

"One-tenth of top speed. It'd take us six months."

"No, my captain friend, not that long. We never reach Valhalla star at all. The Adderkops find us first."

"I suppose so. We haven't got six months' stores aboard anyway." Torrance stared at the deck. "What occurs to me is, well, we could reach one of the nearby stars. There barely might be a planet with an industrial civilization, whose people could eventually be taught to make the circuits we need. A habitable planet, at least—maybe . . ."

"Nie!" Van Rijn shook his head till the greasy black ringlets swirled about his shoulders. "All us men and one woman, for life on some garbagey rock where they have not even wine grapes? I'll take an Adderkop shell and go out like a gentleman, by damn!" The steward appeared. "Where you been snoozing? Beer, with God's curses on you! I need to make thinks! How you expect I can think with a mouth like a desert in midsummer?"

Torrance chose his words carefully. Van Rijn would have to be reminded that the captain, in space, was the final boss. And yet the old devil must not be antagonized, for he had a record of squirming between the horns of dilemmas. "I'm open to suggestions, sir, but I can't take the responsibility of courting enemy attack."

Van Rijn rose and lumbered about the cabin, fuming obscenities and volcanic blue clouds. As he passed the shelf where St. Dismas stood, he pinched the candles out in a marked manner. That seemed to trigger something in him. He turned about and said, "Ha! Industrial civilizations, *ja,* maybe. Not only the pest-begotten Adderkops ply this region of space. Gives some chance perhaps we can come in detection range of an un-beat-up ship, *nie?* You go get Yamamura to jack up our detector sensitivities till we can feel a gnat twiddle its wings back in my Djakarta office on Earth, so lazy the cleaners are. Then we go off this direct course and run a standard naval search pattern at reduced speed."

"And if we find a ship? Could belong to the enemy, you know."

"That chance we take."

"In all events, sir, we'll lose time. The pursuit will gain on us while we follow a search-helix. Especially if we spend days persuading some nonhuman crew who've never heard of the human race that we have to be taken to Valhalla immediately if not sooner."

"We burn that bridge when we come to it. You have might be a more hopeful scheme?"

"Well. . . ." Torrance pondered awhile, blackly.

The steward came in with a fresh tankard. Van Rijn snatched it.

"I think you're right, sir," said Torrance. "I'll go and—"

"Virginal!" bellowed van Rijn.

Torrance jumped. "What?"

"Virginal! That's the word I was looking for. The first beer of the day, you idiot!"

The cabin door chimed. Torrance groaned. He'd been hoping for some sleep, at least, after more hours on deck than he cared to number. But when the ship prowled through darkness, seeking another ship which might or might not be out there, and the hunters drew closer. . . . "Come in."

Jeri Kofoed entered. Torrance gaped, sprang to his feet, and bowed. "Freelady! What—what—what a surprise! Is there anything I can do?"

"Please." She laid a hand on his. Her gown was of shimmerite and shameless in cut, because van Rijn hadn't provided any different sort, but the look she gave Torrance had nothing to do with that. "I had to come, Lodgemaster. If you've any pity at all, you'll listen to me."

He waved her to a chair, offered cigarettes, and struck one for himself. The smoke, drawn deep into his lungs, calmed him a little. He sat down on the opposite side of the table. "If I can be of help to you, Freelady Kofoed, you know I'm happy to oblige. Uh . . . Freeman van Rijn . . ."

"He's asleep. Not that he has any claims on me. I haven't signed a contract or any such thing." Her irritation gave way to a wry smile. "Oh, admitted, we're all his inferiors, in fact as well as in status. I'm not contravening his wishes, not really. It's just that he won't answer my questions, and if I don't find out what's going on I'll have to start screaming."

Torrance weighed a number of factors. A private explanation, in more detail than the crew had required, might indeed be best for her. "As you wish, Freelady," he said, and related what had happened to the converter. "We can't fix it ourselves," he concluded. "If we continued traveling at high quasi-speed, we'd burn it out before we arrived; and then, without power, we'd soon die. If we proceed slowly enough to preserve it, we'd need half a year to reach Valhalla, which is more time than we have supplies for. Though the Adderkops would doubtless track us down within a week or two."

She shivered. "Why? I don't understand." She stared at her glowing cigarette end for a moment, until a degree of composure returned, and with it a touch of humor. "I may pass for a fast, sophisticated girl on Freya, Captain. But you know even better than I, Freya is a jerkwater planet on the very fringe of human civilization. We've hardly any spatial traffic, except the League merchant ships, and they never stay long in port. I really know nothing about military or political technology. No one told me this was anything more important than a scouting mission, because I never thought to inquire. Why should the Adderkops be so anxious to catch us?"

Torrance considered the total picture before framing a reply. As a spaceman of the League, he must make an effort before he could appreciate how little the enemy actually meant to colonists who seldom left their home world. The name "Adderkop" was Freyan, a term of scorn for outlaws who'd been booted off the planet a century ago. Since then, however, the Freyans had had no direct contact with them. Somewhere in the unexplored deeps beyond Valhalla, the fugitives had settled on some unknown planet. Over the generations, their numbers grew, and the numbers of their warships. But Freya was still too strong for them to raid, and had no extraplanetary enterprises of her own to be harried. Why should Freya care?

Torrance decided to explain systematically, even if he must repeat the obvious. "Well," he said, "the Adderkops aren't stupid. They keep somewhat in touch with events, and know the Polesotechnic League wants to expand its operations into this region. They don't like that. It'd mean the end of their attacks on planets which can't fight back, their squeezing of tribute and their overpriced trade. Not that the League is composed of saints; we don't tolerate that sort of thing, but merely because freebooting cuts into the profits of our member companies. So the Adderkops undertook not to fight a full-dress war against us, but to harass our outposts till we gave it up as a bad job. They have the advantage of knowing their own sector of space, which we hardly do at all. And we were, indeed, at the point of writing this whole region off and trying someplace else. Freeman van Rijn wanted to make one last attempt.

The opposition to this was so great that he had to come here and lead the expedition himself.

"I suppose you know what he did: used an unholy skill at bribery and bluff, at extracting what little information the prisoners we'd taken possessed, at fitting odd facts together. He got a clue to a hitherto untried segment. We flitted there, picked up a neutrino trail, and followed it to a human-colonized planet. As you know, it's almost certainly their own home world.

"If we bring back that information, there'll be no more trouble with the Adderkops. Not after the League sends in a few Star-class battleships and threatens to bombard their planet. They realize as much. We were spotted; several warcraft jumped us; we were lucky to get away. Their ships are obsolete, and so far we've shown them a clean pair of heels. But I hardly think they've quit hunting for us. They'll send their entire fleet cruising in search. Hyperdrive vibrations transmit instantaneously, and can be detected out to about one light-year distance. So if any Adderkop observes our 'wake' and homes in on it—with us crippled—that's the end."

She drew hard on her cigarette, but remained otherwise calm. "What are your plans?"

"A countermove. Instead of trying to make Freya—uh—I mean, we're proceeding in a search-helix at medium speed, straining our own detectors. If we discover another ship, we'll use the last gasp of our engines to close in. If it's an Adderkop vessel, well, perhaps we can seize it or something; we do have a couple of light guns in our turrets. It may be a nonhuman craft, though. Our intelligence reports, interrogation of prisoners, evaluation of explorers' observations, et cetera, indicate that three or four different species in this region possess the hyperdrive. The Adderkops themselves aren't certain about all of them. Space is so damned huge."

"If it does turn out to be nonhuman?"

"Then we'll do what seems indicated."

"I see." Her bright head nodded. She sat for a while, unspeaking, before she dazzled him with a smile. "Thanks, Captain. You don't know how much you've helped me."

Torrance suppressed a foolish grin. "A pleasure, Freelady."

"I'm coming to Earth with you. Did you know that? Freeman van Rijn has promised me a very good job."

He always does, thought Torrance.

Jeri leaned closer. "I hope we'll have a chance on the Earthward trip to get better acquainted, Captain. Or even right now."

The alarm bell chose that moment to ring.

The *Hebe G.B.* was a yacht, not a buccaneer frigate. When Nicholas van Rijn was aboard, though, the distinction sometimes got a little blurred. Thus she had more legs than most ships, detectors of uncommon sensitivity, and a crew experienced in the tactics of overhauling.

She was able to get a bearing on the hyperemission of the other craft long before her own vibrations were observed. Pacing the unseen one, she established the set course it was following, then poured on all available juice to intercept. If the stranger had maintained quasi-velocity, there would have been contact in three or four hours. Instead, its wake indicated a sheering off, an attempt to flee. The *Hebe G.B.* changed course too, and continued gaining on her slower quarry.

"They're afraid of us," decided Torrance. "And they're not running back toward the Adderkop sun. Which two facts indicate they're not Adderkops themselves, but do have reason to be scared of strangers." He nodded, rather grimly, for during the preliminary investigations he had inspected a few backward planets which the bandit nation had visited.

Seeing that the pursuer kept shortening her distance, the pursued turned off their hyperdrive. Reverting to intrinsic sublight velocity, converter throttled down to minimal output, their ship became an infinitesimal speck in an effectively infinite space. The maneuver often works; after casting about futilely for a while, the enemy gives up and goes home. The *Hebe G.B.*, though, was prepared. The known superlight vector, together with the instant of cutoff, gave her computers a rough idea of where the prey was. She continued to that volume of space and then hopped about in a well-designed search pattern, reverting to normal state at intervals to sample the neutrino haze which any nuclear engine emits. Those nuclear engines known as stars provided most; but by statistical analysis, the computers presently isolated one feeble nearby source. The yacht went thither . . . and wan against the glittering sky, the other ship appeared in her screens.

It was several times her size, a cylinder with bluntly rounded nose and massive drive cones, numerous housings for auxiliary boats, a single gun turret. The principles of physics dictate that the general conformation of all ships intended for a given purpose shall be roughly the same. But any spaceman could see that this one had never been built by members of Technic civilization.

Fire blazed. Even with the automatic stopping-down of his viewscreen, Torrance was momentarily blinded. Instruments told him that the stranger had fired a fusion shell which his own robogunners had intercepted with a missile. The attack had been miserably slow and feeble. This was not a warcraft in any sense; it was no more a match for the *Hebe G.B.* than the yacht was for one of the Adderkops chasing her.

"Hokay, now we got that foolishness out of the way and we can talk business," said van Rijn. "Get them on the telecom and develop a common language. Fast! Then explain we mean no harm but want just a lift to Valhalla." He hesitated before adding, with a distinct wince, "We can pay well."

"Might prove difficult, sir," said Torrance. "Our ship is identifiably human-built, but chances are that the only humans they've ever met are Adderkops."

"Well, so if it makes needful, we can board them and force them to transport us, *nie?* Hurry up, for Satan's sake! If we wait too long here, like bebobbled snoozers, we'll get caught."

Torrance was about to point out they were safe enough. The Adderkops were far behind the swifter Terrestrial ship. They could have no idea that her hyperdrive was now cut off; when they began to suspect it, they could have no measurable probability of finding her. Then he remembered that the case was not so simple. If the parleying with these strangers took unduly long—more than a week, at best— Adderkop squadrons would have penetrated this general region and gone beyond. They would probably remain on picket for months, which the humans could not do for lack of food. When a hyperdrive did start up, they'd detect it and run down this awkward merchantman with ease. The only hope was to hitch a ride to Valhalla *soon*, using the head start already gained to offset the disadvantage of reduced speed.

"We're trying all bands, sir," he said. "No response so far." He frowned worriedly. "I don't understand. They must know we've got them cold, and they must have picked up our calls and realize we want to talk. Why don't they respond? Wouldn't it cost them anything."

"Maybe they abandoned ship," suggested the communications officer. "They might have hyperdriven lifeboats."

"No." Torrance shook his head. "We'd have spotted that. . . . Keep trying, Freeman Betancourt. If we haven't gotten an answer in an hour, we'll lay alongside and board."

The receiver screens remained blank. But at the end of the grace period, when Torrance was issuing space armor, Yamamura reported something new. Neutrino output had increased from a source near the stern of the alien. Some process involving moderate amounts of energy was being carried out.

Torrance clamped down his helmet. "We'll have a look at that."

He posted a skeleton crew—van Rijn himself, loudly protesting, took over the bridge—and led his boarding party to the main air lock. Smooth as a gliding shark (the old swine was a blue-ribbon spaceman after all, the captain realized in some astonishment), the *Hebe G.B.* clamped on a tractor beam and hauled herself toward the bigger vessel.

It disappeared. Recoil sent the yacht staggering.

"Beelzebub and botulism!" snarled van Rijn. "He went back into hyper, ha? We see about that!" The ulcerated converter shrieked as he called upon it, but the engines were given power. On a lung and a half, the Terrestrial ship again overtook the foreigner. Van Rijn phased in so casually that Torrance almost forgot this was a job considered difficult by master pilots. He evaded a frantic pressor beam and tied his yacht to the larger hull with unshearable bands of force. He cut off his hyperdrive again, for the converter couldn't take much more. Being within the force-field of the alien, the *Hebe G.B.* was carried along, though the "drag" of extra mass reduced quasi-speed considerably. If he had hoped the grappled vessel would quit and revert to normal state, he was disappointed. The linked hulls continued plunging faster than light toward an unnamed constellation.

Torrance bit back an oath, summoned his men, and went outside.

He had never forced entry on a hostile craft before, but assumed it wasn't much different from burning his way into a derelict. Having chosen his spot, he set up a balloon tent to conserve air; no use killing the alien crew. The torches of his men spewed flame; blue actinic sparks fountained backward and danced through zero gravity. Meanwhile the rest of the squad stood by with blasters and grenades.

Beyond, the curves of the two hulls dropped off to infinity. Without compensating electronic viewscreens, the sky was weirdly distorted by aberration and Doppler effect, as if the men were already dead and beating through the other existence toward Judgment. Torrance held his mind firmly to practical worries. Once inboard, the nonhumans made prisoner, how was he to communicate? Especially if he first had to gun down several of them . . .

The outer shell was peeled back. He studied the inner structure of the plate with fascination. He'd never seen anything like it before. Surely this race had developed space travel quite independently of mankind. Though their engineering must obey the same natural laws, it was radically different in detail. What was that tough but corky substance lining the inner shell? And was the circuitry embedded in it, for he didn't see any elsewhere?

The last defense gave way. Torrance swallowed hard and shot a flashbeam into the interior. Darkness and vacuum met him. When he entered the hull, he floated, weightless; artificial gravity had been turned off. The crew was hiding someplace and . . .

Torrance returned to the yacht in an hour. When he came on the bridge, he found van Rijn seated by Jeri. The girl started to speak, took a closer look at the captain's face, and clamped her teeth together.

"Well?" snapped the merchant peevishly.

Torrance cleared his throat. His voice sounded unfamiliar

and faraway to him. "I think you'd better come have a look, sir."

"You found the crew, wherever the sputtering hell they holed up? What are they like? What kind of ship is this we've gotten us, ha?"

Torrance chose to answer the last question first. "It seems to be an interstellar animal collector's transport vessel. The main hold is full of cages—environmentally controlled compartments, I should say—with the damnedest assortment of creatures I've ever seen outside Luna City Zoo."

"So what the pox is that to me? Where is the collector himself, and his fig-plucking friends?"

"Well, sir." Torrance gulped. "We're pretty sure by now they're hiding from us. Among the other animals."

A tube was run between the yacht's main lock and the entry cut into the other ship. Through this, air was pumped and electric lines were strung, to illuminate the prize. By some fancy juggling with the gravitic generator of the *Hebe G.B.*, Yamamura supplied about one-fourth Earth-weight to the foreigner, though he couldn't get the direction uniform and its decks felt canted in wildly varying degrees.

Even under such conditions, van Rijn walked ponderously. He stood with a salami in one hand and a raw onion in the other, glaring around the captured bridge. It could only be that, though it was in the bows rather than the waist. The viewscreens were still in operation, smaller than human eyes found comfortable, but revealing the same pattern of stars, surely by the same kind of optical compensators. A control console made a semicircle at the forward bulkhead, too big for a solitary human to operate. Yet presumably the designer had only had one pilot in mind, for a single seat had been placed in the middle of the arc.

Had been. A short metal post rose from the deck. Similar structures stood at other points, and boltholes showed where chairs were once fastened to them. But the seats had been removed.

"Pilot sat there at the center, I'd guess, when they weren't simply running on automatic," Torrance hazarded. "Navigator and communications officer . . . here and here? I'm not sure. Anyhow, they probably didn't use a copilot, but that chair bollard at the after end of the room suggests that an extra officer sat in reserve, ready to take over."

Van Rijn munched his onion and tugged his goatee. "Pestish big, this panel," he said. "Must be a race of bloody-be-damned octopussies, ha? Look how complicated."

He waved the salami around the half circle. The console, which seemed to be of some fluorocarbon polymer, held very few switches or buttons, but scores of flat luminous plates, each about twenty centimeters square. Some of them were depressed. Evidently these were the controls. Cautious experiment had shown that a stiff push was needed to budge them. The experiment had ended then and there, for the ship's cargo lock had opened and a good deal of air was lost before Torrance slapped the plate he had been testing hard enough to make the hull reseal itself. One should not tinker with the atomic-powered unknown, most especially not in galactic space.

"They must be strong like horses, to steer by this system without getting exhausted," went on van Rijn. "The size of everything tells likewise, *nie?*"

"Well, not exactly, sir," said Torrance. "The viewscreens seem made for dwarfs. The meters even more so." He pointed to a bank of instruments, no larger than buttons, on each of which a single number glowed. (Or letter, or ideogram, or what? They looked vaguely Old Chinese.) Occasionally a symbol changed value. "A human couldn't use these long without severe eyestrain. Of course, having eyes better adapted to close work than ours doesn't prove they are not giants. Certainly that switch couldn't be reached from here without long arms, and it seems meant for big hands." By standing on tiptoe, he touched it himself, an outsize double-pole affair set overhead, just above the pilot's hypothetical seat.

The switch fell open.

A roar came from aft. Torrance lurched backward under a sudden force. He caught at a shelf on the after bulkhead to steady himself. Its thin metal buckled as he clutched. "Devilfish and dunderheads!" cried van Rijn. Bracing his columnar legs, he reached up and shoved the switch back into position. The noise ended. Normality returned. Torrance hastened to the bridge doorway, a tall arch, and shouted down the corridor beyond: "It's okay! Don't worry! We've got it under control!"

"What the blue blinking blazes happened?" demanded van Rijn, in somewhat more high-powered words.

Torrance mastered a slight case of the shakes. "Emergency switch, I'd say." His tone wavered. "Turns on the gravitic field full speed ahead, not wasting any force on acceleration compensators. Of course, we being in hyperdrive, it wasn't very effective. Only gave us a—uh—less than one-G push, intrinsic. In normal state we'd have accelerated several Gs, at least. It's for quick getaways and . . . and . . ."

"And you, with brains like fermented gravy and bananas for fingers, went ahead and yanked it open!"

Torrance felt himself redden. "How was I to know, sir? I must've applied less than half a kilo of force. Emergency switches aren't hair-triggered, after all. Considering how much it takes to move one of those control plates, who'd have thought the switch would respond to so little?"

Van Rijn took a closer look. "I see now there is a hook to secure it by," he said. "Must be they use that when the ship's on a high-gravity planet." He peered down a hole near the center of the panel, about one centimeter in diameter and fifteen deep. At the bottom a small key projected. "This must be another special control, ha? Safer than that switch. You would need thin-nosed pliers to make a turning of it." He scratched his pomaded curls. "But then, why is not the pliers hanging handy? I don't see even a hook or bracket or drawer for them."

"I don't care," said Torrance. "When the whole interior's been stripped— There's nothing but a slagheap in the engine room, I tell you—fused metal, carbonized plastic . . . bedding, furniture, anything they thought might give us a clue to their identity, all melted down in a jury-rigged cauldron. They used their own converter to supply heat. That was the cause of the neutrino flux Yamamura observed. They must have worked like demons."

"But they did not destroy all needful tools and machines, surely? Simpler then they should blow up their whole ship, and us with it. I was sweating like a hog, me, for fear they would do that. Not so good a way for a poor sinful old man to end his days, blown into radioactive stinks three hundred light-years from the vineyards of Earth."

"N-n-no. As far as we can tell from a cursory examination, they didn't sabotage anything absolutely vital. We can't be sure, of course. Yamamura's gang would need weeks just to get a general idea of how this ship is put together, let alone the practical details of operating it. But I agree, the crew isn't bent on suicide. They've got us more neatly trapped than they know, even. Bound helplessly through space—toward their home star, maybe. In any event, almost at right angles to the course we want."

Torrance led the way out. "Suppose we go have a more thorough look at the zoo, sir," he went on. "Yamamura talked about setting up some equipment . . . to help us tell the crew from the animals!"

The main hold comprised almost half the volume of the great ship. A corridor below, a catwalk above, ran through a double row of two-decker cubicles. These numbered ninety-six, and were identical. Each was about five meters on a side, with adjustable fluorescent plates in the ceiling and a springy, presumably inert plastic on the floor. Shelves and parallel bars ran along the side walls, for the benefit of creatures that liked jumping or climbing. The rear wall was connected to well-shielded machines; Yamamura didn't dare tamper with these, but said they obviously regulated atmosphere, temperature, gravity, sanitation, and other environmental factors within each "cage." The front wall, facing on corridor and catwalk, was transparent. It held a stout air lock, almost as high as the cubicle itself, motorized but controlled by simple wheels inside and out. Only a few compartments were empty.

The humans had not strung fluoros in this hold, for it wasn't necessary. Torrance and Van Rijn walked through shadows, among monsters;the simulated light of a dozen different suns streamed around them: red, orange, yellow, greenish, and harsh electric blue.

A thing like a giant shark, save that tendrils fluttered about its head, swam in a water-filled cubicle among fronded seaweeds. Next to it was a cageful of tiny flying reptiles, their scales aglitter in prismatic hues, weaving and dodging through the air. On the opposite side, four mammals crouched among yellow mists—beautiful creatures, the size of a bear, vividly tiger-striped, walking mostly on all fours but occasionally standing up; then you noticed the retractable claws between stubby fingers, and the carnivore jaws on the massive heads. Farther on, the humans passed half a dozen sleek red beasts like six-legged otters, frolicking in a tank of water provided for them. The environmental machines must have decided this was their feeding time, for a hopper spewed chunks of proteinaceous material into a trough and the animals lolloped over to rip it with their fangs.

"Automatic feeding," Torrance observed. "I think probably the food is synthesized on the spot, according to the specifications of each individual species as determined by biochemical methods. For the crew, also. At least, we haven't found anything like a galley."

Van Rijn shuddered. "Nothing but synthetics? Not even a little glass Genever before dinner?" He brightened. "Ha, maybe here we find a good new market. And until they learn the situation, we can charge them triple prices."

"First," clipped Torrance, "we've got to find them."

Yamamura stood near the middle of the hold, focusing a set of instruments on a certain cage. Jeri stood by, handing him what he asked for, plugging and unplugging at a small powerpack. Van Rijn hove into view. "What goes on, anyhows?" he asked.

The chief engineer turned a patient brown face to him. "I've got the rest of the crew examining the shop in detail, sir," he said. "I'll join them as soon as I've gotten Freelady Kofoed trained at this particular job. She can handle the routine of it while the rest of us use our special skills to . . ." His words trailed off. He grinned ruefully. "To poke and prod gizmos we can't possibly understand in less than a month of work, with our limited research tools."

"A month we have not got," said van Rijn. "You are here checking conditions inside each individual cage?"

"Yes, sir. They're metered, of course, but we can't read the meters, so we have to do the job ourselves. I've haywired this stuff together, to give an approximate value of gravity, atmospheric pressure and composition, temperature, illumination spectrum, and so forth. It's slow work, mostly because of all the arithmetic needed to turn the dial

readings into such data. Luckily, we don't have to test every
cubicle, or even most of them."

"No," said van Rijn. "Even to a union organizer, obvious
this ship was never made by fishes or birds. In fact, some
kind of hands is always necessary."

"Or tentacles." Yamamura nodded at the compartment
before him. The light within was dim red. Several black
creatures could be seen walking restlessly about. They had
stumpy-legged quadrupedal bodies, from which torsos rose,
centaur fashion, toward heads armored in some bony material. Below the faceless heads were six thick, ropy arms, set
in triplets. Two of these ended in three boneless but probably strong fingers.

"I suspect these are our coy friends," said Yamamura.
"If so, we'll have a deuce of a time. They breathe hydrogen
under high pressure and triple gravity, at a temperature of
seventy below."

"Are they the only ones who like that kind of weather?"
asked Torrance.

Yamamura gave him a sharp look. "I see what you're
getting at, Skipper. No, they aren't. In the course of putting
this apparatus together and testing it, I've already found
three other cubicles where conditions are similar. And in
those, the animals are obviously just animals, snakes and
so on, which couldn't possibly have built this ship."

"But then these octopus-horses can't be the crew, can
they?" asked Jeri timidly. "I mean, if the crew were collecting animals from other planets, they wouldn't take home
animals along, would they?"

"They might," said van Rijn. "We have a cat and a couple parrots aboard the *Hebe G.B.*, *nie?* Or, there are many
planets with very similar conditions of the hydrogen sort,
just like Earth and Freya are much-alike oxygen planets.
So that proves nothings." He turned toward Yamamura,
rather like a rotating globe himself. "But see here, even if
the crew did pump out the air before we boarded, why not
check their reserve tanks? If we find air stored away just
like these diddlers here are breathing . . ."

"I thought of that," said Yamamura. "In fact, it was
almost the first thing I told the men to look for. They've
located nothing. I don't think they'll have any success,
either. Because what they did find was an adjustable cata-

lytic manifold. At least, it looks as if it should be, though we'd need days to find out for certain. Anyhow, my guess is that it renews exhausted air and acts as a chemosynthesizer to replace losses from a charge of simple inorganic compounds. The crew probably bled the ship's atmosphere into space before we boarded. When we go away, if we do, they'll open the door of their particular cage a crack, so its air can trickle out. The environmental adjuster will automatically force the chemosynthesizer to replace this. Eventually the ship'll be full of enough of their kind of gas for them to venture forth and adjust things more precisely." He shrugged. "That's assuming they even need to. Perhaps Earth-type conditions suit them perfectly well."

"Uh, yes," said Torrance. "Suppose we look around some more, and line up the possibly intelligent species."

Van Rijn trundled along with him. "What sort intelligence they got, these bespattered aliens?" he grumbled. "Why try this stupid masquerade in the first places?"

"It's not too stupid to have worked so far," said Torrance dryly. "We're being carried along on a ship we don't know how to stop. They must hope we'll either give up and depart, or else that we'll remain baffled until the ship enters their home region. At which time, quite probably a naval vessel—or whatever they've got—will detect us, close in, and board us to check up on what's happened."

He paused before a compartment. "I wonder . . ."

The quadruped within was the size of an elephant, though with a more slender build, indicating a lower gravity than Earth's. Its skin was green and faintly scaled, a ruff of hair along the back. The eyes with which it looked out were alert and enigmatic. It had an elephantlike trunk, terminating in a ring of pseudodactyls which must be as strong and sensitive as human fingers.

"How much could a one-armed race accomplish?" mused Torrance. "About as much as we, I imagine, if not quite as easily. And sheer strength would compensate. That trunk could bend an iron bar."

Van Rijn grunted and went past a cubicle of feathered ungulates. He stopped before the next. "Now here are some beasts might do," he said. "We had one like them on Earth once. What they called it? Quintilla? No, gorilla. Or chimpanzee, better, of gorilla size."

Torrance felt his heart thud. Two adjoining sections each held four animals of a kind which looked extremely hopeful. They were bipedal, short-legged and long-armed. Standing two meters tall, with a three-meter arm span, one of them could certainly operate that control console alone. The wrists, thick as a man's thighs, ended in proportionate hands, four-digited including a true thumb. The three-toed feet were specialized for walking, like man's feet. Their bodies were covered with brown fleece. Their heads were comparatively small, rising almost to a point, with massive snouts and beady eyes under cavernous brow ridges. As they wandered aimlessly about, Torrance saw that they were divided among males and females. On the sides of each neck he noticed two lumens closed by sphincters. The light upon them was the familiar yellowish white of a Sol-type star.

He forced himself to say, "I'm not sure. Those huge jaws must demand corresponding maxillary muscles, attaching to a ridge on top of the skull. Which'd restrict the cranial capacity."

"Suppose they got brains in their bellies," said van Rijn.

"Well, some people do," murmured Torrance. As the merchant choked, he added in haste, "No, actually, sir, that's hardly believable. Neural paths would get too long and so forth. Every animal I know of, if it has a central nervous system at all, keeps the brain close to the principal sense organs, which are usually located in the head. To be sure, a relatively small brain, within limits, doesn't mean these creatures are not intelligent. Their neurons might well be more efficient than ours."

"Humph and hassenpfeffer!" said van Rijn. "Might, might, might!" As they continued among strange shapes; "We can't go too much by atmosphere or light, either. If hiding, the crew could vary conditions quite a bit from their norm without hurting themselves. Gravity, too, by twenty or thirty percent."

"I hope they breathe oxygen, though—hoy!" Torrance stopped. After a moment, he realized what was so eerie about the several forms under the orange glow. They were chitinous-armored, not much bigger than a squarish military helmet and about the same shape. Four stumpy legs projected from beneath to carry them awkwardly about on tal-

oned feet, also a pair of short tentacles ending in a bush of
cilia. There was nothing special about them, as extraterrestrial animals go, except the two eyes which gazed from
beneath each helmet: as large and somehow human as—
well—the eyes of an octopus.

"Turtles," snorted van Rijn. "Armadillos at most."

"There can't be any harm in letting Jer—Freelady Kofoed
check their environment too," said Torrance.

"It can waste time."

"I wonder what they eat. I don't see any mouths."

"Those tentacles look like capillary suckers. I bet they
are parasites, or overgrown leeches, or something else like
one of my competitors. Come along."

"What do we do after we've established which species
could possibly be the crew?" said Torrance. "Try to communicate with each in turn?"

"Not much use, that. They hide because they don't want
to communicate. Unless we can prove to them we are not
Adderkops . . . but hard to see how."

"Wait! Why'd they conceal themselves at all, if they've
had contact with the Adderkops? It wouldn't work."

"I think I tell you that, by damn," said van Rijn. "To
give them a name, let us call this unknown race the Eksers.
So. The Eksers been traveling space for some time, but
space is so big they never bumped into humans. Then the
Adderkop nation arises, in this sector where humans never
was before. The Eksers hear about this awful new species
which has gotten into space also. They land on primitive
planets where Adderkops have made raids, talk to natives,
maybe plant automatic cameras where they think raids will
soon come, maybe spy on Adderkop camps from afar or
capture a lone Adderkop ship. So they know what humans
look like, but not much else. They do not want humans to
know about them, so they shun contact; they are not looking for trouble. Not before they are well prepared to fight
a war, at least. Hell's sputtering griddles! Torrance, we have
got to establish our bona fides with this crew, so they take
us to Freya and afterward go tell their leaders all humans
are not so bad as the slime-begotten Adderkops. Otherwise,
maybe we wake up one day with some planets attacked by
Eksers, and before the fighting ends, we have spent billions

of credits." He shook his fists in the air and bellowed like a wounded bull. "It is our duty to prevent this!"

"Our first duty is to get home alive, I'd say," Torrance answered curtly. "I have a wife and kids."

"Then stop throwing sheepish eyes at Jeri Kofoed. I saw her first."

The search turned up one more possibility. Four organisms the length of a man and the build of thick-legged caterpillars dwelt under greenish light. Their bodies were dark blue, spotted with silver. A torso akin to that of the tentacled centauroids, but stockier, carried two true arms. The hands lacked thumbs, but six fingers arranged around a three-quarter circle could accomplish much the same things. Not that adequate hands prove effective intelligence; on Earth, not only simians but a number of reptiles and amphibia boast as much, even if a man has the best, and man's apish ancestors were as well equipped in this respect as we are today. However, the round flat-faced heads of these beings, the large bright eyes beneath feathery antennae of obscure function, the small jaws and delicate lips, all looked promising.

Promising of what? thought Torrance.

Three Earth-days later, he hurried down a central corridor toward the Ekser engine room.

The passage was a great hemicylinder lined with the same rubbery gray plastic as the cages, making footfalls silent and spoken words weirdly unresonant. But a deeper vibration went through it, the almost subliminal drone of the hyperengine, driving the ship into darkness toward an unknown star, and announcing their presence to any hunter straying within a light-year of them. The flouros strung by the humans were far apart, so that one passed through bands of humming shadow. Doorless rooms opened off the hallway. Some were still full of supplies, and however peculiar the shape of tools and containers might be, however unguessable their purpose, this was a reassurance that one still lived, was not yet a ghost aboard the Flying Dutchman. Other cabins, however had been inhabited. And their bareness made Torrance's skin crawl.

Nowhere did a personal trace remain. Books, both codex and micro, survived, but in the finely printed symbology of a foreign planet. Empty places on the shelves suggested that all illustrated volumes had been sacrificed. Certainly he could see where pictures stuck on the walls had been ripped down. In the big private cabins, in the still larger one which might have been a saloon, as well as in the engine room and workshop and bridge, only the bollards to which furniture had been bolted were left. Long low niches and small cubbyholes were built into the cabin bulkheads, but when bedding had been thrown into a white-hot cauldron, how could a man guess which were the bunks . . . if either kind were? Clothing, ornaments, cooking and eating utensils, everything was destroyed. One room must have been a lavatory, but the facilities had been ripped out. Another might have been used for scientific studies, presumably of captured animals, but was so gutted that no human was certain.

By God, you've got to admire them, Torrance thought. Captured by beings whom they had every reason to think of as conscienceless monsters, the aliens had not taken the easy way out, the atomic explosion that would annihilate both crews. They might have, except for the chance of this being a zoo ship. But given a hope of survival, they snatched it, with an imaginative daring few humans could have matched. Now they sat in plain view, waiting for the monsters to depart—without wrecking their ship in mere spitefulness—or for a naval vessel of their own to rescue them. They had no means of knowing their captors were not Adderkops, or that this sector would soon be filled with Adderkop squadrons; the bandits rarely ventured even this close to Valhalla. Within the limits of available information, the aliens were acting with complete logic. But the nerve it took!

I wish we could identify them and make friends, thought Torrance. *The Eksers would be damned good friends for Earth to have. Or Ramanujan, or Freya, or the entire Polesotechnic League.* With a lopsided grin: *I'll bet they'd be nowhere near as easy to swindle as Old Nick thinks. They might well swindle him. That I'd love to see!*

My reason is more personal, though, he thought with a return of bleakness. *If we don't clear up this misunderstanding soon, neither they nor we will be around. I mean soon. If we have another three or four days of grace, we're lucky.*

The passage opened on a well, with ramps curving down either side to a pair of automatic doors. One door led to the engine room, Torrance knew. Behind it, a nuclear converter powered the ship's electrical system, gravitic cones, and hyperdrive; the principles on which this was done were familiar to him, but the actual machines were engines cased in metal and in foreign symbols. He took the other door, which opened on a workshop. A good deal of the equipment here was identifiable, however distorted to his eyes: lathe, drill press, oscilloscope, crystal tester. Much else was mystery. Yamamura sat at an improvised workbench, fitting together a piece of electronic apparatus. Several other devices, haywired on breadboards, stood close by. His face was shockingly haggard, and his hands trembled. He'd been laboring this whole time, stimpills holding him awake.

As Torrance approached, the engineer was talking with Betancourt, the communications man. The entire crew of the *Hebe G.B.* were under Yamamura's direction, in a frantic attempt to outflank the Eksers by learning on their own how to operate this ship.

"I've identified the basic electrical arrangement, sir," Betancourt was saying. "They don't tap the converter directly like us; evidently they haven't developed our step-down methods. Instead, they use a heat exchanger to run an extremely large generator—yeah, the same thing you guessed was an armature-type dynamo—and draw AC for the ship off that. Where DC is needed, the AC passes through a set of rectifier plates which, by looking at 'em, I'm sure must be copper oxide. They're bare, behind a safety screen, though so much current goes through that they're too hot to look at close up. It all seems kind of primitive to me."

"Or else merely different," sighed Yamamura. "We use a light-element fusion converter, one of whose advantages is that it can develop electric current directly. They may have perfected a power plant which utilizes moderately heavy elements with small positive packing fractions. I remember that was tried on Earth a long while ago, and given up as impractical. But maybe the Eksers are better engineers than us. Such a system would have the advantage of needing less refinement of fuel—which'd be a real advantage to a ship knocking about among unexplored planets.

Maybe enough to justify that clumsy heat exchanger and rectifier system. We simply don't know."

He stared head-shakingly at the wires he was soldering. "We don't know a damn thing," he said. Seeing Torrance: "Well, carry on, Freeman Betancourt. And remember, *festina lente*."

"For fear of wrecking the ship?" asked the captain.

Yamamura nodded. "The Eksers would've known a small craft like ours couldn't generate a big enough hyperforce field to tug their own ship home," he replied. "So they'll have made sure no prize crew could make off with it. Some of the stuff may be booby-trapped to wreck itself if it isn't handled just right; and how'd we ever make repairs? Hence we're proceeding with the utmost caution. So cautiously that we haven't a prayer of figuring out the controls before the Adderkops find us."

"It keeps the crew busy, though."

"Which is useful. Uh-huh. Well, sir, I've about got my basic apparatus set up. Everything seems to test okay. Now, let me know which animal you want to investigate first." As Torrance hesitated, the engineer explained: "I have to adapt the equipment for the creature in question, you see. Especially if it's a hydrogen breather."

Torrance shook his head. "Oxygen. In fact, they live under conditions so much like ours that we can walk right into their cages. The gorilloids. That's what Jeri and I have named them. Those woolly, two-meter-tall bipeds with the ape faces."

Yamamura made an ape face of his own. "Brutes that powerful? Have they shown any sign of intelligence?"

"No. But then, would you expect the Eksers to? Jeri Kofoed and I have been parading in front of the cages of the possible species, making signs, drawing pictures, everything we could think of, trying to get the message across that we are not Adderkops and the genuine article is chasing us. No luck, of course. All the animals did give us an interested regard, though, except the gorilloids . . . which may or may not prove anything."

"What animals, now? I've been so blinking busy—"

"Well, we call 'em the tiger apes, the tentacle centaurs, the elephantoid, the helmet beasts, and the caterpiggles. That's stretching things, I know; the tiger apes and the helmet beasts are highly improbable, to say the least, and the elephantoid isn't much more convincing. The gorilloids have the right size and the most effective-looking hands, and they're oxygen breathers, as I said, so we may well take them first. Next in order of likelihood, I'd guess, are the caterpiggles and the tentacle centaurs. But the caterpiggles, though oxygen breathers, are from a high-gravity planet; their air pressure would give us narcosis in no time. The tentacle centaurs breathe hydrogen. In either case, we'd have to work in space armor.''

"The gorilloids will be quite bad enough, thank you kindly.''

Torrance looked at the workbench. "What exactly do you plan to do?'' he asked. "I've been too busy with my own end of this affair to learn any details of yours.''

"I've adapted some things from the medical kit,'' said Yamamura. "A sort of ophthalmoscope, for example, because the ship's instruments use color codes and finely printed symbols, so that the Eksers are bound to have eyes at least as good as ours. Then this here's a nervous-impulse tracer. It detects synaptic flows and casts a three-dimensional image into yonder crystal box, shows us the whole nervous system functioning as a set of luminous traces. By correlating this with gross anatomy, we can roughly identify the sympathetic and parasympathetic systems—or their equivalents—I hope. And the brain. And, what's really to the point, the degrees of brain activity more or less independent of the other nerve paths. That is, whether the animal is thinking.''

He shrugged. "It tests out fine on me. Whether it'll work on a nonhuman, especially in a different sort of atmosphere, I do not know. I'm sure it'll develop bugs.''

" 'We can but try,' '' quoted Torrance wearily.

"I suppose Old Nick is sitting and thinking,'' said Yamamura in an edged voice. "I haven't seen him for quite some time.''

"He's not been helping Jeri and me either,'' said Torrance. "Told us our attempt to communicate was futile until we could prove to the Eksers that we know who they are. And even after that, he said, the only communication at first will be by gestures made with a pistol.''

"He's probably right.''

"He's not right! Logically, perhaps, but not psychologically. Or morally. He sits in his suite with a case of brandy and a box of cigars. The cook, who could be down here helping you, is kept aboard the yacht to fix him his damned gourmet meals. You'd think he didn't care if we're blown out of the sky!"

He remembered his oath of fealty, his official position, and so on and so on. They felt nonsensical, here on the edge of extinction. But habit was strong. He swallowed and said harshly, "Sorry. Please ignore what I said. When you're ready, Freeman Yamamura, we'll test the gorilloids."

Six men and Jeri stood by in the passage with drawn blasters. Torrance hoped fervently they wouldn't have to shoot. He hoped even more that if they did have to, he'd still be alive.

He gestured to the four crewmen at his back. "Okay, boys." He wet his lips. His heart thuttered. Being a captain and a Lodgemaster was very fine until moments like this came, when you must make a return for your special privileges.

He spun the outside control wheel. The airlock motor hummed and opened the doors. He stepped through, into a cage of gorilloids.

Pressure differentials weren't enough to worry about, but after all this time at one-fourth G, to enter a field only ten percent less than Earth's was like a blow. He lurched, almost fell, gasped in an air warm and thick and full of unnamed stenches. Sagging back against the wall, he stared across the floor at the four bipeds. Their brown fleecy bodies loomed unfairly tall, up and up to the coarse faces. Eyes overshadowed by brows glared at him. He clapped a hand on his stun pistol. He didn't want to shoot it, either. No telling what supersonics might do to a nonhuman nervous system; and if these were in truth the crewfolk, the worst thing he could do was inflict serious injury on one of them. But he wasn't used to being small and frail. The knurled handgrip was a comfort.

A male growled deep in his chest, and advanced a step. His pointed head thrust forward, the sphincters in his neck opened and shut like sucking mouths; his jaws gaped to show the white teeth.

Torrance backed toward a corner. "I'll try to attract that one in the lead away from the others," he called softly. "Then get him."

"Aye." A spacehand, a stocky slant-eyed nomad from Altai, uncoiled a lariat. Behind him, the other three spread a net woven for this purpose.

The gorilloid paused. A female hooted. The male seemed to draw resolution from her. He waved the others back with a strangely humanlike gesture and stalked toward Torrance.

The captain drew his stunner, pointed it shakily, resheathed it, and held out both hands. "Friends," he croaked.

His hope that the masquerade might be dropped became suddenly ridiculous. He sprang back toward the air lock. The gorilloid snarled and snatched at him. Torrance wasn't fast enough. The hand ripped his shirt open and left a bloody trail on his breast. He went to hands and knees, stabbed with pain. The Altaian's lasso whirled and snaked forth. Caught around the ankles, the gorilloid crashed. His weight shook the cubicle.

"Get him! Watch out for his arms! Here—"

Torrance staggered back to his feet. Beyond the melee, where four men strove to wind a roaring, struggling monster in a net, he saw the remaining three creatures. They were crowded into the opposite corner, howling in basso. The compartment was like the inside of a drum.

"Get him out," choked Torrance. "Before the others charge."

He aimed his stunner again. If intelligent, they'd know this was a weapon. They might attack anyway. . . . Deftly, the man from Altai roped an arm, snubbed his lariat around the gargantuan torso, and made it fast by a slip knot. The net came into position. Helpless in cords of wire-strong fiber, the gorilloid was dragged to the entrance. Another male advanced, step by jerky step. Torrance stood his ground. The animal ululation and human shouting surfed about him, within him. His wound throbbed. He saw with unnatural clarity the muzzle full of teeth that could snap his head off, the little dull eyes turned red with fury, the hands so much like his own but black-skinned, four-fingered, and enormous. . . .

"All clear, Skipper!"

The gorilloid lunged. Torrance scrambled through the air-lock chamber. The giant followed. Torrance braced himself in the corridor and aimed his stun pistol. The gorilloid halted, shivered, looked around in something resembling bewilderment, and retreated. Torrance closed the airlock.

Then he sat down and trembled.

Jeri bent over him. "Are you okay?" she breathed. "Oh! You've been hurt!"

"Nothing much," he mumbled. "Gimme a cigarette."

She took one from her belt pouch and said with a crispness he admired, "I suppose it is just a bruise and a deep scratch. But we'd better check it, anyway, and sterilize. Might be infected."

He nodded but remained where he was until he had finished the cigarette. Farther down the corridor, Yamamura's men got their captive secured to a steel framework. Unharmed but helpless, the brute yelped and tried to bite as the engineer approached with his equipment. Returning him to the cubicle afterward was likely to be almost as tough as getting him out.

Torrance rose. Through the transparent wall, he saw a female gorilloid viciously pulling something to shreds, and realized he had lost his turban when he was knocked over. He sighed. "Nothing much we can do till Yamamura gives us a verdict," he said. "Come on, let's go rest awhile."

"Sick bay first," said Jeri firmly. She took his arm. They went to the entry hole, through the tube, and into the steady half-weight of the *Hebe G.B.* which van Rijn preferred. Little was said while Jeri got Torrance's shirt off, swabbed the wound with universal disinfectant, which stung like hell, and bandaged it. Afterward he suggested a drink.

They entered the saloon. To their surprise, and to Torrance's displeasure, van Rijn was there. He sat at the inlaid mahogany table, dressed in snuff-stained lace and his usual sarong, a bottle in his right and a Trichinopoly cigar in his left. A litter of papers lay before him.

"Ah, so," he said, glancing up. "What gives?"

"They're testing a gorilloid now." Torrance flung himself into a chair. Since the steward had been drafted for the capture party, Jeri went after drinks. Her voice floated back, defiant:

"Captain Torrance was almost killed in the process. Couldn't you at least come watch, Nick?"

"What use I should watch, like some tourist with haddock eyes?" scoffed the merchant. "I make no skeletons about it, I am too old and fat to help chase large economy-size apes. Nor am I so technical I can twiddle knobs for Yamamura." He took a puff of his cigar and added complacently, "Besides, that is not my job. I am no kind of specialist, I have no fine university degrees, I learned in the school of hard knockers. But what I learned is how to make them do things for me, and then how to make something profitable from their doings."

Torrance breathed out, long and slow. With the tension eased, he was beginning to feel immensely tired. "What're you checking over?" he asked.

"Reports of engineer studies on the Ekser ship," said van Rijn. "I told everybody should take full notes on what they observed. Somewhere in those notes is maybe a clue we can use. If the gorilloids are not the Eksers, I mean. The gorilloids are possible, and I see no way to eliminate them except by Yamamura's checkers."

Torrance rubbed his eyes. "They're not entirely plausible," he said. "Most of the stuff we've found seems meant for big hands. But some of the tools, especially, are so small that—oh, well, I suppose a nonhuman might be as puzzled by an assortment of our own tools. Does it really make sense that the same race would use sledge hammers and etching needles?"

Jeri came back with two stiff Scotch-and-sodas. His gaze followed her. In a tight blouse and half knee-length skirt, she was worth following. She sat down next to him rather than van Rijn, whose jet eyes narrowed.

However, the older man spoke mildly. "I would like if you should list for me, here and now, the other possibilities, with your reasons for thinking of them. I have seen them too, natural, but my own ideas are not all clear yet and maybe something that occurs to you would joggle my head."

Torrance nodded. One might as well talk shop, even though he'd been over this ground a dozen times before with Jeri and Yamamura.

"Well," he said, "the tentacle centaurs appear very likely.

You know the ones I mean. They live under red light and about half again Earth's gravity. A dim sun and a low temperature must make it possible for their planet to retain hydrogen, because that's what they breathe, hydrogen and argon. You know how they look: bodies sort of like rhinoceri, torsos with bone-plated heads and fingered tentacles. Like the gorilloids, they're big enough to pilot this ship easily.

"All the rest are oxygen breathers. The ones we call caterpiggles—the long, many-legged, blue-and-silver ones, with the peculiar hands and the particularly intelligent-looking faces—they're from an oddball world. It must be big. They're under three Gs in their cage, which can't be a red herring for this length of time. Body fluid adjustment would go out of kilter, if they're used to much lower weight. Nevertheless, their planet has oxygen and nitrogen rather than hydrogen, under a dozen Earth-atmospheres' pressure. The temperature is rather high, fifty degrees. I imagine their world, though of nearly Jovian mass, is so close to its sun that the hydrogen was boiled off, leaving a clear field for evolution similar to Earth's.

"The elephantoid comes from a planet with only about half our gravity. He's the single big fellow with a trunk ending in fingers. He gets by in air too thin for us, which indicates the gravity in his cubicle isn't faked either."

Torrance took a long drink. "The others live under pretty terrestroid conditions," he resumed. "For that reason, I wish they were more probable. But actually, except for the gorilloids, they seem like long shots. The helmet beasts—"

"What's that?" asked van Rijn.

"Oh, you remember," said Jeri. "Those eight or nine things like humpbacked turtles, not much bigger than your head. They crawl around on clawed feet, waving little tentacles that end in filaments. They blot up food through those, soupy stuff the machines dump into their trough. They haven't anything like effective hands—the tentacles could only do a few very simple things—but we gave them some time because they do seem to have better developed eyes than parasites usually do."

"Parasites don't evolve intelligence," said van Rijn. "They got better ways to make a living, by damn. Better make sure the helmet beasts really are parasites—in their home environments—and got no hands tucked under those shells, before you quite write them off. Who else you got?"

"The tiger apes," said Torrance. "Those striped carnivores built something like bears. They spend most of their time on all fours, but they do stand and walk on their hind legs sometimes, and they do have hands. Clumsy, thumbless ones, with retractable claws, but on all their limbs. Are four hands without thumbs as good as two with? I don't know. I'm too tired to think."

"And that's the lot, ha?" Van Rijn tilted the bottle to his lips. After a prolonged gurgling he set it down, belched, and blew smoke through his majestic nose. "Who's to try next, if the gorilloids flunk?"

"It better be the caterpiggles, in spite of the air pressure," said Jeri. "Then . . . oh . . . the tentacle centaurs, I suppose. Then maybe the—"

"Horse maneuvers!" Van Rijn's fist struck the table. The bottle and glasses jumped. "How long it takes to catch and check each specimen? Hours, *nie?* And in between times, takes many more hours to adjust the apparatus and chase out the hiccups it develops under a new set of conditions. Also, Yamamura will collapse if he can't sleep soon, and who else we got can do this? All the whiles, the forstunken Adderkops get closer. We have not got time for that method! If the gorilloids don't pan out, then only logic will help us. We must deduce from the facts we have who the Eksers are."

"Go ahead." Torrance drained his glass. "I'm going to take a nap."

Van Rijn purpled. "That's right!" he huffed. "Be like everybody elses. Loaf and play, dance and sing, enjoy yourselfs the liver-long day. Because you always got poor old Nicholas van Rijn there, to heap the work and worry on his back. Oh, dear St. Dismas, why can't you at least make some *one* other person in this whole universe do something useful?"

Torrance was awakened by Yamamura. The gorilloids were not the Eksers. They were color blind and incapable of focusing on the ship's instruments; their brains were small, with nearly the whole mass devoted to purely animal functions. He estimated their intelligence as equal to a dog's.

The captain stood on the bridge of the yacht, because it was a familiar place, and tried to accustom himself to being doomed.

Space had never seemed so beautiful as now. He was not well acquainted with the local constellations, but his trained gaze identified Perseus, Auriga, Taurus, not much distorted since they lay in the direction of Earth (and of Ramanujan, where gilt towers rose out of mists to catch the first sunlight, blinding against blue Mount Gandhi). A few individuals could also be picked out: ruby Betelgeuse, amber Spica, the pilot stars by which he had steered through his whole working life. Otherwise the sky was aswarm with small frosty fires, across blackness unclouded and endless. The Milky Way girdled it with cool silver, a nebula glowed faint and green, another galaxy spiraled on the mysterious edge of visibility. He thought less about the planets he had trod, even his own, than about this faring between them which was soon to terminate. For end it would, in a burst of violence too swift to be felt. Better go out thus cleanly when the Adderkops came, than into their dungeons.

He stubbed out his cigarette. Returning, his hand caressed the dear shapes of controls. He knew each switch and knob as well as he knew his own fingers. This ship was his—in a way, himself. Not like that other, whose senseless control board needed a giant and a dwarf, whose emergency switch fell under a mere slap if it wasn't hooked in place, whose—

A light footfall brought him twisting around. Irrationally, so strained was he, his heart flew up within him. When he saw it was Jeri, he eased his muscles, but the pulse continued quick in his blood.

She advanced slowly. The overhead light gleamed on her yellow hair and in the blue of her eyes. But she avoided his glance, and her mouth was not quite steady.

"What brings you here?" he asked. His tone fell even more soft than he had intended.

"Oh . . . the same as you." She stared out the viewscreen. During the time since they captured the alien ship, or it captured them, a red star off the port bow had visibly grown. Now it burned baleful as they passed, a light-year distant. She grimaced and turned her back to it. "Yamamura is readjusting the test apparatus," she said thinly. "No one else knows enough about it to help him, but he has the shakes so bad from exhaustion he can scarcely do the job himself. Old Nick just sits in his suite, smoking and drinking. He's gone through that bottle already, and started another. I couldn't breathe in there any longer; it was too smoky. And he won't say a word. Except to himself, in Malay or something. I couldn't stand it."

"We may as well wait," said Torrance. "We've done everything we can, till time to check a caterpiggle. We'll have to do that spacesuited, in their own cage, and hope they don't attack us."

She slumped. "Why bother?" she said. "I know the situation as well as you. Even if the caterpiggles are the Eksers, under those conditions we'll need a couple of days to prove it. I doubt if we have that much time left. If we start toward Valhalla two days from now, I'll bet we're detected and run down before we get there. Certainly, if the caterpiggles are only animals too, we'll never get time to test a third species. Why bother?"

"We've nothing else to do," said Torrance.

"Yes, we do. Not this ugly, futile squirming about, like cornered rats. Why can't we accept that we're going to die, and use the time to . . . to be human again?"

Startled, he looked back from the sky to her. "What do you mean?"

Her lashes fluttered downward. "I suppose that would depend on what we each prefer. Maybe you'll want to, well, get your thoughts in order or something."

"How about you?" he asked through his heartbeat.

"I'm not a thinker." She smiled forlornly. "I'm afraid I'm just a shallow sort of person. I'd like to enjoy life while I have it." She half turned from him. "But I can't find anyone I'd like to enjoy it with."

He, or his hands, grabbed her bare shoulders and spun her around to face him. She felt silken under his palms. "Are you sure you can't?" he said roughly. She closed her eyes and stood with face tilted upward, lips half parted. He kissed her. After a second she responded.

After a minute, Nicholas van Rijn appeared in the doorway.

He stood an instant, pipe in hand, gun belted to his waist, before he flung the churchwarden shattering to the deck. "So!" he bellowed.

"Oh!" wailed Jeri.

She disengaged herself. A tide of rage mounted in Torrance. He knotted his fists and started toward van Rijn.

"So!" repeated the merchant. The bulkheads seemed to quiver with his voice. "By louse-bitten damn, this is a fine thing for me to come on. Satan's tail in a mousetrap! I sit hour by hour sweating my brain to the bone for the sake of your worthless life, and all whiles you, you illegitimate spawn of a snake with dandruff and a cheese mite, here you are making up to my own secretary hired with my own hard-earned money! Gargoyles and *Götterdämmerung!* Down on your knees and beg my pardon, or I mash you up and sell you for dogfood!"

Torrance stopped, a few centimeters from van Rijn. He was slightly taller than the merchant, if less bulky, and at least thirty years younger. "Get out," he said in a strangled voice.

Van Rijn turned puce and gobbled at him.

"Get out," repeated Torrance. "I'm still the captain of this ship. I'll do what I damned well please, without interference from any loud-mouthed parasite. Get off the bridge, or I'll toss you out on your fat bottom!"

The color faded in van Rijn's cheeks. He stood motionless for whole seconds. "Well, by damn," he whispered at last. "By damn and death, cubical. He has got the nerve to talk back."

His left fist came about in a roundhouse swing. Torrance blocked it, though the force nearly threw him off his feet. His own left smacked the merchant's stomach, sank a short way into fat, encountered the muscles, and rebounded bruised. Then van Rijn's right fist clopped. The cosmos exploded around Torrance. He flew up in the air, went over backward, and lay where he fell.

When awareness returned, van Rijn was cradling his head and offering brandy which a tearful Jeri had fetched. "Here, boy. Go slow there. A little nip of this, ha? That goes good. There, now, you only lost one tooth and we get that fixed at Freya. You can even put it on expense account. There, that makes you feel more happy, *nie?* Now, girl, Jarry, Jelly, whatever your name is, give me that stimpill. Down the hatchworks, boy. And then, upsy-rosy, onto your feet. You should not miss the fun."

One-handed, van Rijn heaved Torrance erect. The captain leaned awhile on the merchant, until the stimpill removed aches and dizziness. Then, huskily through swollen lips, he asked, "What's going on? What d' you mean?"

"Why, I know who the Eksers are. I came to get you, and we fetch them from their cage." Van Rijn nudged Torrance with a great splay thumb and whispered almost as softly as a hurricane, "Don't tell anyone or I have too many fights, but I like a brass-bound nerve like you got. When we get home, I think you transfer off this yacht to command of a trading squadron. How you like that, ha? But come, we still got a damn plenty of work to do."

Torrance followed him in a daze through the small ship and the tube, into the alien, down a corridor and a ramp to the zoological hold. Van Rijn gestured at the spacemen posted on guard lest the Eksers make a sally. They drew their guns and joined him, their weary slouch jerking to alertness when he stopped before an air lock.

"Those?" sputtered Torrance. "But—I thought—"

"You thought what they hoped you would think," said van Rijn grandly. "The scheme was good. Might have worked, not counting the Adderkops, except that Nicholas van Rijn was here. Now, then. We go in and carry them all out, making a good show of our weapons. I hope we need not get too tough with them. I expect not, when we explain by drawings how we understand their secret. Then they should take us to Valhalla, as we can show by those pretty astronautical diagrams Captain Torrance has already prepared. They will cooperate under threats, as prisoners, at first. But on the voyage, we can use the standard means to establish alimentary communications . . . no, terror and taxes, I mean rudimentary . . . anyhows, we get the idea across that all humans are not Adderkops and we want to be friends and sell them things. Hokay? We go!"

He marched through the air lock, scooped up a helmet beast, and bore it kicking out of its cage.

*   *   *

Torrance didn't have time for anything en route except his work. First the entry hole in the prize must be sealed, while supplies and equipment were carried over from the *Hebe G.B.* Then the yacht must be cast loose under her own hyperdrive; in the few hours before her converter quite burned out, she might draw an Adderkop in chase. Then the journey commenced, and though the Eksers laid a course as directed, they must be constantly watched lest they try some suicidal stunt. Every spare moment must be devoted to the urgent business of achieving a simple common language with them. Torrance must also supervise his crew, calm their fears, and maintain a detector-watch for enemy vessels. If any had been detected, the humans would have gone off hyperdrive and hoped they could lie low. None were, but the strain was considerable.

Occasionally he slept.

Thus he got no chance to talk to van Rijn at length. He assumed the merchant had had a lucky hunch, and let it go at that.

Until Valhalla was a tiny yellow disc, outshining every other star; a League patrol ship closed on them; and, explanation being made, it gave them escort as they moved at sublight speed toward Freya.

The patrol captain intimated he'd like to come aboard. Torrance stalled him. "When we're in orbit, Freeman Agilik, I'll be delighted. But right now, things are pretty disorganized. You can understand that, I'm sure."

He switched off the alien telecom he had now learned to operate. "I'd better go below and clean up," he said. "Haven't had a bath since we abandoned the yacht. Carry on, Freeman Lafarge." He hesitated. "And—uh—Freeman Jukh-Barklakh."

Jukh grunted something. The gorilloid was too busy to talk, squatting where a pilot seat should have been, his big hands slapping control plates as he edged the ship into a hyperbolic path. Barklakh, the helmet beast on his shoulders, who had no vocal cords of his own, waved a tentacle before he dipped it into the protective shaft to turn a delicate adjustment key. The other tentacle remained buried on its side of the gorilloid's massive neck, drawing nourishment from the bloodstream, receiving sensory impulses, and emitting the motor-nerve commands of a skilled space pilot.

At first the arrangement had looked vampirish to Torrance. But though the ancestors of the helmet beasts might once have been parasites on the ancestors of the gorilloids, they were no longer. They were symbionts. They supplied the effective eyes and intellect, while the big animals supplied strength and hands. Neither species was good for much by itself; in combination, they were something rather special. Once he got used to the idea, Torrance found the sight of a helmet beast using its claws to climb up a gorilloid no more unpleasant than a man in a historical stereopic mounting a horse. And once the helmet beasts were used to the idea that these humans were not enemies, they showed a positive affection for them.

Doubtless they're thinking what lovely new specimens we can sell them for their zoo, reflected Torrance. He slapped Barklakh on the shell, patted Jukh's fur, and left the bridge.

A sponge bath of sorts and fresh garments took the edge off his weariness. He thought he'd better warn van Rijn, and knocked at the cabin which the merchant had curtained off as his own.

"Come in," boomed the bass voice. Torrance entered a cubicle blue with smoke. Van Rijn sat on an empty brandy case, one hand holding a cigar, the other holding Jeri, who was snuggled on his lap.

"Well, sit down, sit down," he roared cordially. "You find a bottle somewhere under those dirty clothes in the corner."

"I stopped by to tell you, sir, we'll have to receive the captain of our escort when we're in orbit around Freya, which'll be soon. Professional courtesy, you know. He's naturally anxious to meet the Eks—uh—the Togru-Kon-Tanakh."

"Hokay, pipe him aboard, lad." Van Rijn scowled. "Only make him bring his own bottle, and not take too long. I want to land, me; I'm sick of space. I think I'll run barefoot over the soft cool acres and acres of Freya, by damn!"

"Maybe you'd like to change clothes?" hinted Torrance.

"Ooh!" squeaked Jeri, and ran off to the cabin she sometimes occupied. Van Rijn leaned back against the wall, hitched up his sarong and crossed his shaggy legs as he said: "If that captain comes to meet the Eksers, let him meet the Eksers. I stay comfortable like I am. And I will not entertain him with how I figured out who they were. That I keep exclusive, for sale to what news syndicate bids highest. Understand?"

His eyes grew unsettlingly sharp. Torrance gulped. "Yes, sir."

"Good. Now do sit down, boy. Help me put my story in order. I have not your fine education, I was a poor lonely hard-working old man from I was twelve, so I would need some help making my words as elegant as my logic."

"Logic?" echoed Torrance, puzzled. He tilted the flask, chiefly because the tobacco haze in here made his eyes smart. "I thought you guessed—"

"What? You know me so little as that? No, no, by damn. Nicholas van Rijn never guesses. I *knew*." He reached for the bottle, took a hefty swig, and added magnanimously, "That is, after Yamamura found the gorilloids alone could not be the peoples we wanted. Then I sat down and uncluttered my brains and thought it over.

"See, it was simple eliminations. The elephantoid was out right away. Only one of him. Maybe, in emergency, one could pilot this ship through space—but not land it, and pick up wild animals, and care for them, and all else. Also, if somethings go wrong, he is helpless."

Torrance nodded. "I did consider it from the spaceman's angle," he said. "I was inclined to rule out the elephantoid on that ground. But I admit I didn't see the animal-collecting aspect made it altogether impossible that this could be a one-being expedition."

"He was pretty too big anyhow," said van Rijn. "As for the tiger apes, like you, I never took them serious. Maybe their ancestors was smaller and more biped, but this species is reverting to quadruped again. Animals do not specialize in being everything. Not brains and size and carnivore teeth and cat claws, all to once.

"The caterpiggles looked hokay till I remembered that time you accidental turned on the bestonkered emergency acceleration switch. Unless hooked in place, what such a switch would not be except in special cases, it fell rather easy. So easy that its own weight would make it drop open under three Earth gravities. Or at least there would always be serious danger of this. Also, that shelf you bumped into—they wouldn't build shelves so light on high-gravity planets."

He puffed his cigar back to furnace heat. "Well, might be the tentacle centaurs," he continued. "Which was bad for us, because hydrogen and oxygen explode. I checked hard through the reports on the ship, hoping I could find something that would eliminate them. And by damn, I did. For this I will give St. Dismas an altar cloth, not too expensive. You see, the Eksers is kind enough to use copper oxide rectifiers, exposed to the air. Copper oxide and hydrogen, at a not very high temperature such as would soon develop from strong electricking, they make water and pure copper. Poof, no more rectifier. Therefore ergo, this shop was not designed for hydrogen breathers." He grinned. "You has had so much high scientific education you forgot your freshlyman chemistry."

Torrance snapped his fingers and swore at himself.

"By eliminating, we had the helmet beasts," said van Rijn. "Only they could not possible be the builders. True, they could handle certain tools and controls, like that buried key, but never all of it. And they are too slow and small. How could they ever stayed alive long enough to invent spaceships? Also, animals that little don't get room for real brains. And neither armored animals nor parasites ever get much. Nor do they get good eyes. And yet the helmet beasts seemed to have very good eyes, as near as we could tell. They looked like human eyes, anyhows.

"I remembered there was both big and little cubbyholes in these cabins. Maybe bunks for two kinds of sleeper? And I thought, is the human brain a turtle just because it is armored in bone? A parasite just because it lives off blood from other places? Well, maybe some people I could name but won't, like Juan Harleman of the Venusian Tea & Coffee Growers, Inc., has parasite turtles for brains. But not me. So there I was. Q.," said van Rijn smugly, "E.D."

Hoarse from talking, he picked up the bottle. Torrance sat a few minutes more, but as the other seemed disinclined to conversation, he got up to go.

Jeri met him in the doorway. In a slit and topless blue gown which fitted like a coat of lacquer, she was a fourth-order stunblast. Torrance stopped in his tracks. Her gaze slid slowly across him, as if reluctant to depart.

"Mutant sea-otter coats," murmured van Rijn dreamily. "Martian firegems. An apartment in the Stellar Towers."

She scampered to him and ran her fingers through his hair. "Are you comfortable, Nicky, darling?" she purred. "Can't I do something for you?"

Van Rijn winked at Torrance. "Your technique, that time on the bridge—I watched and it was lousy," he said to the captain. "Also, you are not old and fat and lonesome; you have a happy family for yourself."

"Uh—yes," said Torrance. "I do." He let the curtain drop and returned to the bridge.

WHAT IS THIS THING CALLED LOVE?

BY ISAAC ASIMOV (1920-   )

AMAZING STORIES
MARCH (AS "THE PLAYBOY AND THE SLIME GOD")

This story was written at editorial request.

It seems that the magazine Playboy *published a satire on science fiction—and an uncommonly stupid one. Whoever wrote it had picked up copies of an old science fiction magazine,* Marvel Science Fiction, *which, for a few issues (before dying a most deserved death) published some sleazy soft-porn stories.*

The Playboy *piece quoted from these stories and made it appear that they were typical of science fiction.*

I did not see the satire because I don't read Playboy, *but Cele Goldsmith, then editor of* Amazing Stories *either saw it or had her attention called to it. She was highly indignant, sent me a copy, and I was highly indignant, too.*

She asked me to write a counter-satire, making fun of Playboy's *foul deed, and I did, and here it is. (IA)*

"But these are two species," said Captain Garm, peering closely at the creatures that had been brought up from the planet below. His optic organs adjusted focus to maximum sharpness, bulging outwards as they did so. The color patch above them gleamed in quick flashes.

Botax felt warmly comfortable to be following color-changes once again, after months in a spy cell on the planet, trying to make sense out of the modulated sound waves emitted by the natives. Communication by flash was almost like being home in the far-off Perseus arm of the Galaxy. "Not two species," he said, "but two forms of one species."

154

"Nonsense, they look quite different. Vaguely Perse-like, thank the Entity, and not as disgusting in appearance as so many out-forms are. Reasonable shape, recognizable limbs. But no color-patch. Can they speak?"

"Yes, Captain Garm," Botax indulged in a discreetly disapproving prismatic interlude. "The details are in my report. These creatures form sound waves by way of throat and mouth, something like complicated coughing. I have learned to do it myself." He was quietly proud. "It is very difficult."

"It must be stomach-turning. Well, that accounts for their flat, unextensible eyes. Not to speak by color makes eyes largely useless. Meanwhile, how can you insist these are a single species? The one on the left is smaller and has longer tendrils, or whatever it is, and seems differently proportioned. It bulges where this other does not. Are they alive?"

"Alive but not at the moment conscious, Captain. They have been psycho-treated to repress fright in order that they might be studied easily."

"But are they worth study? We are behind our schedule and have at least five worlds of greater moment than this one to check and explore. Maintaining a Time-stasis unit is expensive and I would like to return them and go on—"

But Botax's moist spindly body was fairly vibrating with anxiety. His tubular tongue flicked out and curved up and over his flat nose, while his eyes sucked inward. His splayed three-fingered hand made a gesture of negation as his speech went almost entirely into the deep red.

"Entity save us, Captain, for no world is of greater moment to us than this one. We may be facing a supreme crisis. These creatures could be the most dangerous life-forms in the Galaxy, Captain, just *because* there are two forms."

"I don't follow you."

"Captain, it has been my job to study this planet, and it has been most difficult, for it is unique. It is so unique that I can scarcely comprehend its facets. For instance, almost all life on the planet consists of species in two forms. There are no words to describe it, no concepts even. I can only speak of them as first form and second form. If I may use their sounds, the little one is called 'female,' and the big one, here, 'male,' so the creatures themselves are aware of the difference."

Garm winced, "What a disgusting means of communication."

"And, Captain, in order to bring forth young, the two forms must cooperate."

The Captain, who had bent forward to examine the specimens closely with an expression compounded of interest and revulsion, straightened at once. "Cooperate? What nonsense is this? There is no more fundamental attribute of life than that each living creature bring forth its young in innermost communication with itself. What else makes life worth living?"

"The one form does bring forth life but the other form must cooperate."

"How?"

"That has been difficult to determine. It is something very private and in my search through the available forms of literature I could find no exact and explicit description. But I have been able to make reasonable deductions."

Garm shook his head. "Ridiculous. Budding is the holiest, most private function in the world. On tens of thousands of worlds it is the same. As the great photo-bard, Levuline, said, 'In budding-time, in budding time, in sweet, delightful budding time; when—' "

"Captain, you don't understand. This cooperation between forms brings about somehow (and I am not certain exactly how) a mixture and recombination of genes. It is a device by which in every generation, new combinations of characteristics are brought into existence. Variations are multiplied; mutated genes hastened into expression almost at once where under the usual budding system, millennia might pass first."

"Are you trying to tell me that the genes from one individual can be combined with those of another? Do you know how completely ridiculous that is in the light of all the principles of cellular physiology?"

"It must be so," said Botax nervously under the other's pop-eyed glare. "Evolution *is* hastened. This planet is a riot of species. There are supposed to be a million and a quarter different species of creatures."

"A dozen and a quarter more likely. Don't accept too completely what you read in the native literature."

"I've seen dozens of radically different species myself in just a small area. I tell you, Captain, give these creatures a short space of time and they will mutate into intellects powerful enough to overtake us and rule the Galaxy."

"Prove that this cooperation you speak of exists, Investigator, and I shall consider your contentions. If you cannot, I shall dismiss all your fancies as ridiculous and we will move on."

"I can prove it." Botax's color-flashes turned intensely yellow-green. "The creatures of this world are unique in another way. They foresee advances they have not yet made, probably as a consequence of their belief in rapid change which, after all, they constantly witness. They therefore indulge in a type of literature involving the space-travel they have never developed. I have translated their term for the literature as 'science-fiction.' Now I have dealt in my readings almost exclusively with science-fiction, for there I thought, in their dreams and fancies, they would expose themselves and their danger to us. And it was from that science-fiction that I deduced the method of their inter-form cooperation."

"How did you do that?"

"There is a periodical on this world which sometimes publishes science-fiction which is, however, devoted almost entirely to the various aspects of the cooperation. It does not speak entirely freely, which is annoying, but persists in merely hinting. Its name as nearly as I can put it into flashes is 'Recreationlad.' The creature in charge, I deduce, is interested in nothing but inter-form cooperation and searches for it everywhere with a systematic and scientific intensity that has roused my awe. He has found instances of cooperation described in science-fiction and I let material in his periodical guide me. From the stories he instanced I have learned how to bring it about.

"And, Captain, I beg of you, when the cooperation is accomplished and the young are brought forth before your eyes, give orders not to leave an atom of this world in existence."

"Well," said Captain Garm, wearily, "bring them into full consciousness and do what you must do quickly."

*   *   *

Marge Skidmore was suddenly completely aware of her surroundings. She remembered very clearly the elevated station at the beginning of twilight. It had been almost empty, one man standing near her, another at the other end of the platform. The approaching train had just made itself known as a faint rumble in the distance.

There had then come the flash, a sense of turning inside out, the half-seen vision of a spindly creature, dripping mucus, a rushing upward, and now—

"Oh, God," she said, shuddering. "It's still here. And there's another one, too."

She felt a sick revulsion, but no fear. She was almost proud of herself for feeling no fear. The man next to her, standing quietly as she herself was, but still wearing a battered fedora, was the one that had been near her on the platform.

"They got you, too?"she asked. "Who else?"

Charlie Grimwold, feeling flabby and paunchy, tried to lift his hand to remove his hat and smooth the thin hair that broke up but did not entirely cover the skin of his scalp and found that it moved only with difficulty against a rubbery but hardening resistance. He let his hand drop and looked morosely at the thin-faced woman facing him. She was in her middle thirties, he decided, and her hair was nice and her dress fit well, but at the moment, he just wanted to be somewhere else and it did him no good at all that he had company, even female company.

He said, "I don't know, lady. I was just standing on the station platform."

"Me, too."

"And then I see a flash. Didn't hear nothing. Now here I am. Must be little men from Mars or Venus or one of them places."

Marge nodded vigorously, "That's what I figure. A flying saucer? You scared?"

"No. That's funny, you know. I think maybe I'm going nuts or I *would* be scared."

"Funny thing. I ain't scared, either. Oh, God, here comes one of them now. If he touches me, I'm going to scream. Look at those wiggly hands. And that wrinkled skin, all slimy; makes me nauseous."

Botax approached gingerly and said, in a voice at once rasping and screechy, this being the closest he could come to imitating the native timbre, "Creatures! We will not hurt you. But we must ask you if you would do us the favor of cooperating."

"Hey, it talks!" said Charlie. "What do you mean, cooperate."

"Both of you. With each other," said Botax.

"Oh?" He looked at Marge. "You know what he means, lady?"

"Ain't got no idea whatsoever," she answered loftily.

Botax said, "What I mean—" and he used the short term he had once heard employed as a synonym for the process.

Marge turned red and said, "What!" in the loudest scream she could manage. Both Botax and Captain Garm put their hands over their mid-regions to cover the auditory patches that trembled painfully with the decibels.

Marge went on rapidly, and nearly incoherently. "Of all things. I'm a married woman, you. If my Ed was here, you'd hear from *him*. And you, wise guy," she twisted toward Charlie against rubbery resistance, "whoever you are, if you think—"

"Lady, lady," said Charlie in uncomfortable desperation. "It ain't my idea. I mean, far be it from me, you know, to turn down some lady, you know; but me, I'm married, too. I got three kids. Listen—"

Captain Garm said, "What's happening, Investigator Botax? These cacophonous sounds are awful."

"Well," Botax flashed a short purple patch of embarrassment. "This forms a complicated ritual. They are supposed to be reluctant at first. It heightens the subsequent result. After that initial stage, the skins must be removed."

"They have to be *skinned*?"

"Not really skinned. Those are artificial skins that can be removed painlessly, and must be. Particularly in the smaller form."

"All right, then. Tell it to remove the skins. Really, Botax, I don't find this pleasant."

"I don't think I had better tell the smaller form to remove the skins. I think we had better follow the ritual closely. I have here sections of those space-travel tales which the man

from the 'Recreationlad' periodical spoke highly of. In those
tales the skins are removed forcibly. Here is a description
of an accident, for instance, 'which played havoc with the
girl's dress, ripping it nearly off her slim body. For a second,
he felt the warm firmness of her half-bared bosom against
his cheek—' It goes on that way. You see, the ripping, the
forcible removal, acts as a stimulus."

"Bosom?" said the Captain. "I don't recognize the flash."

"I invented that to cover the meaning. It refers to the
bulges on the upper dorsal region of the smaller form."

"I see. Well, tell the larger one to rip the skins off the
smaller one. What a dismal thing this is."

Botax turned to Charlie. "Sir," he said, "rip the girl's
dress nearly off her slim body, will you? I will release you
for the purpose."

Marge's eyes widened and she twisted toward Charlie in
instant outrage. "Don't you dare do that, you. Don't you
dast touch me, you sex maniac."

"Me?" said Charlie plaintively. "It ain't my idea. You
think I go around ripping dresses? Listen," he turned to
Botax, "I got a wife and three kids. She finds out I go
around ripping dresses, I get clobbered. You know what my
wife does when I just look at some dame? *Listen*—"

"Is he still reluctant?" said the Captain, impatiently.

"Apparently," said Botax. "The strange surroundings,
you know, may be extending that stage of the cooperation.
Since I know this is unpleasant for you, I will perform this
stage of the ritual myself. It is frequently written in the
space-travel tales that an outer-world species performs the
task. For instance, here," and he riffled through his notes
finding the one he wanted, "they describe a very awful such
species. The creatures on the planet have foolish notions,
you understand. It never occurs to them to imagine handsome individuals such as ourselves, with a fine mucous
cover."

"Go on! Go on! Don't take all day," said the Captain.

"Yes, Captain. It says here that the extraterrestrial 'came
forward to where the girl stood. Shrieking hysterically, she
was cradled in the monster's embrace. Talons ripped blindly
at her body, tearing the kirtle away in rags.' You see, the
native creature is shrieking with stimulation as her skins are
removed."

"Then go ahead, Botax, remove it. But please, allow no shrieking. I'm trembling all over with the sound waves."

Botax said politely to Marge, "If you don't mind—"

One spatulate finger made as though to hook on to the neck of the dress.

Marge wiggled desperately. "Don't touch. Don't touch! You'll get slime on it. Listen, this dress cost $25.95 at Ohrbach's. Stay away, you monster. Look at those eyes on him." She was panting in her desperate efforts to dodge the groping, extraterrestrial hand. "A slimy, bug-eyed monster, that's what he is. Listen, I'll take it off myself. Just don't touch it with slime, for God's sake."

She fumbled at the zipper, and said in a hot aside to Charlie, "Don't you dast look."

Charlie closed his eyes and shrugged in resignation.

She stepped out of the dress. "All right? You satisfied?"

Captain Garm's fingers twitched with unhappiness. "Is that the bosom? Why does the other creature keep its head turned away?"

"Reluctance. Reluctance," said Botax. "Besides, the bosom is still covered. Other skins must be removed. When bared, the bosom is a very strong stimulus. It is constantly described as ivory globes, or white spheres, or otherwise after that fashion. I have here drawings, visual picturizations, that come from the outer covers of the space-travel magazines. If you will inspect them, you will see that upon every one of them, a creature is present with a bosom more or less exposed."

The Captain looked thoughtfully from the illustrations to Marge and back. "What is ivory?"

"That is another made-up flash of my own. It represents the tusky material of one of the large sub-intelligent creatures on the planet."

"Ah," and Captain Garm went into a pastel green of satisfaction. "That explains it. This small creature is one of a warrior sect and those are tusks with which to smash the enemy."

"No, no. They are quite soft, I understand." Botax's small brown hand flicked outward in the general direction of the objects under discussion and Marge screamed and shrank away.

"Then what other purpose do they have?"

"I think," said Botax with considerable hesitation, "that they are used to feed the young."

"The young eat them?" asked the Captain with every evidence of deep distress.

"Not exactly. The objects produce a fluid which the young consume."

"Consume a fluid from a living body? Yech-h-h." The Captain covered his head with all three of his arms, calling the central supernumerary into use for the purpose, slipping it out of its sheath so rapidly as almost to knock Botax over.

"A three-armed, slimy, bug-eyed monster," said Marge.

"Yeah," said Charlie.

"All right you, just watch those eyes. Keep them to yourself."

"Listen, lady. I'm trying not to look."

Botax approached again. "Madam, would you remove the rest?"

Marge drew herself up as well as she could against the pinioning field. "Never!"

"I'll remove it, if you wish."

"Don't touch! For God's sake, don't touch. Look at the slime on him, will you? All right, I'll take it off." She was muttering under her breath and looking hotly in Charlie's direction as she did so.

"Nothing is happening," said the Captain, in deep dissatisfaction, "and this seems an imperfect specimen."

Botax felt the slur on his own efficiency. "I brought you two perfect specimens. What's wrong with the creature?"

"The bosom does not consist of globes or spheres. I know what globes or spheres are and in these pictures you have shown me, they are so depicted. Those are large globes. On this creature, though, what we have are nothing but small flaps of dry tissue. And they're discolored, too, partly."

"Nonsense," said Botax. "You must allow room for natural variation. I will put it to the creature herself."

He turned to Marge, "Madame, is your bosom imperfect?"

Marge's eyes opened wide and she struggled vainly for moments without doing anything more than gasp loudly. "*Really!*" she finally managed. "Maybe I'm no Gina Lollobrigida or Anita Ekberg, but I'm perfectly all right, thank you. Oh boy, if my Ed were only here." She turned to Charlie. "Listen, you, you tell this bug-eyed slimy thing here, there ain't nothing wrong with my development."

"Lady," said Charlie, softly, "I ain't looking, remember?"

"Oh, sure, you ain't looking. You been peeking enough, so you might as well just open your crummy eyes and stick up for a lady, if you're the least bit of a gentleman, which you probably ain't."

"Well," said Charlie, looking sideways at Marge, who seized the opportunity to inhale and throw her shoulders back, "I don't like to get mixed up in a kind of delicate matter like this, but you're all right—I guess."

"You *guess*? You blind or something? I was once runner-up for Miss Brooklyn, in case you don't happen to know, and where I missed out was on waistline, *not* on—"

Charlie said, "All right, all right. They're fine. Honest." He nodded vigorously in Botax's direction. "They're okay. I ain't that much of an expert, you understand, but they're okay by me."

Marge relaxed.

Botax felt relieved. He turned to Garm. "The bigger form expresses interest, Captain. The stimulus is working. Now for the final step."

"And what is that?"

"There is no flash for it, Captain. Essentially, it consists of placing the speaking-and-eating apparatus of one against the equivalent apparatus of the other. I have made up a flash for the process, thus: kiss."

"Will nausea never cease?" groaned the Captain.

"It is the climax. In all the tales, after the skins are removed by force, they clasp each other with limbs and indulge madly in burning kisses, to translate as nearly as possible the phrase most frequently used. Here is one example, just one, taken at random: 'He held the girl, his mouth avid on her lips.' "

"Maybe one creature was devouring the other," said the Captain.

"Not at all," said Botax impatiently. "Those were burning kisses."

"How do you mean burning? Combustion takes place?"

"I don't think literally so. I imagine it is a way of expressing the fact that the temperature goes up. The higher the temperature, I suppose, the more successful the production of young. Now that the big form is properly stimulated, he need only place his mouth against her to produce young. The young will not be produced without that step. It is the cooperation I have been speaking of."

"That's all? Just this—" The Captain's hands made motions of coming together, but he could not bear to put the thought into flash form.

"That's all," said Botax. "In none of the tales, not even in 'Recreationlad,' have I found a description of any further physical activity in connection with young-bearing. Sometimes after the kissing, they write a line of symbols like little stars, but I suppose that merely means more kissing; one kiss for each star, when they wish to produce a multitude of young."

"Just one, please, right now."

"Certainly, Captain."

Botax said with grave distinctness, "Sir, would you kiss the lady?"

Charlie said, "Listen, I can't move."

"I will free you, of course."

"The lady might not like it."

Marge glowered. "You bet your damn boots I won't like it. You just stay away."

"I would like to, lady, but what do they do if I don't? Look, I don't want to get them mad. We can just—you know—make like a little peck."

She hesitated, seeing the justice of the caution. "All right. No funny stuff, though. I ain't in the habit of standing around like this in front of every Tom, Dick and Harry, you know."

"I know that, lady. It was none of my doing. You got to admit that."

Marge muttered angrily, "Regular slimy monsters. Must think they're some kind of gods or something, the way they order people around. Slime gods is what they are!"

Charlie approached her. "If it's okay now, lady." He made a vague motion as though to tip his hat. Then he put his hands awkwardly on her bare shoulders and leaned over in a gingerly pucker.

Marge's head stiffened so that lines appeared in her neck. Their lips met.

Captain Garm flashed fretfully. "I sense no rise in temperature." His heat-detecting tendril had risen to full extension at the top of his head and remained quivering there.

"I don't either," said Botax, rather at a loss, "but we're doing it just as the space travel stories tell us to. I think his limbs should be more extended— Ah, like that. See, it's working."

Almost absently, Charlie's arm had slid around Marge's soft, nude torso. For a moment, Marge seemed to yield against him and then she suddenly writhed hard against the pinioning field that still held her with fair firmness.

"Let go." The words were muffled against the pressure of Charlie's lips. She bit suddenly, and Charlie leaped away with a wild cry, holding his lower lip, then looking at his fingers for blood.

"What's the idea, lady?" he demanded plaintively.

She said, "We agreed just a peck, is all. What were you starting there? You some kind of playboy or something? What am I surrounded with here? Playboy and the slime gods?"

Captain Garm flashed rapid alternations of blue and yellow. "Is it done? How long do we wait now?"

"It seems to me it must happen at once. Throughout all the universe, when you have to bud, you bud, you know. There's no waiting."

"Yes? After thinking of the foul habits you have been describing, I don't think I'll ever bud again. Please get this over with."

"Just a moment, Captain."

But the moments passed and the Captain's flashes turned slowly to a brooding orange, while Botax's nearly dimmed out altogether.

Botax finally asked hesitantly, "Pardon me, madam, but when will you bud?"

"When will I *what*?"

"Bear young?"

"I've got a kid."

"I mean bear young now."

"I should say not. I ain't ready for another kid yet."

"What? What?" demanded the Captain. "What's she saying?"

"It seems," said Botax, "she does not intend to have young at the moment."

The Captain's color patch blazed brightly. "Do you know what I think, Investigator? I think you have a sick, perverted mind. Nothing's happening to these creatures. There is no cooperation between them, and no young to be borne. I think they're two different species and that you're playing some kind of foolish game with me."

"But, Captain—" said Botax.

"Don't but Captain me," said Garm. "I've had enough. You've upset me, turned my stomach, nauseated me, disgusted me with the whole notion of budding and wasted my time. You're just looking for headlines and personal glory and I'll see to it that you don't get them. Get rid of these creatures now. Give that one its skins back and put them back where you found them. I ought to take the expense of maintaining Time-stasis all this time out of your salary."

"But, Captain—"

"Back, I say. Put them back in the same place and at the same instant of time. I want this planet untouched, and I'll see to it that it stays untouched." He cast one more furious glance at Botax. "One species, two forms, bosoms, kisses, cooperation. BAH—You are a fool, Investigator, a dolt as well and, most of all, a sick, sick, sick creature."

There was no arguing. Botax, limbs trembling, set about returning the creatures.

They stood there in the elevated station, looking around wildly. It was twilight over them, and the approaching train was just making itself known as a faint rumble in the distance.

Marge said, hesitantly, "Mister, did it really happen?"

Charlie nodded. "I remember it."

Marge said, "We can't tell anybody."

"Sure not. They'd say we was nuts. Know what I mean?"

"Uh-huh. Well." She edged away.

Charlie said, "Listen. I'm sorry you was embarrassed. It was none of my doing."

"That's all right. I know." Marge's eyes considered the

wooden platform at her feet. The sound of the train was louder.

"I mean, you know, lady, you wasn't really bad. In fact, you looked good, but I was kind of embarrassed to say that."

Suddenly, she smiled. "It's all right."

"You want maybe to have a cup of coffee with me just to relax you? My wife, she's not really expecting me for a while."

"Oh? Well, Ed's out of town for the weekend so I got only an empty apartment to go home to. My little boy is visiting at my mother's," she explained.

"Come on, then. We been kind of introduced."

"I'll say." She laughed.

The train pulled in, but they turned away, walking down the narrow stairway to the street.

They had a couple of cocktails actually, and then Charlie couldn't let her go home in the dark alone, so he saw her to her door. Marge was bound to invite him in for a few moments, naturally.

Meanwhile, back in the spaceship, the crushed Botax was making a final effort to prove his case. While Garm prepared the ship for departure Botax hastily set up the tight-beam visiscreen for a last look at his specimens. He focused in on Charlie and Marge in her apartment. His tendril stiffened and he began flashing in a coruscating rainbow of colors.

"Captain Garm! Captain! Look what they're doing now!"

But at that very instant the ship winked out of Time-stasis.

A PRIZE FOR EDIE

BY J.F. BONE (1916-   )

ANALOG SCIENCE FICTION
APRIL

Jesse Bone is a Doctor of Veterinary Medicine and was a Professor in his specialty at Oregon State University from 1965 to 1979. He also served as a Fulbright Lecturer in Kenya and Egypt, and advised the government of Zimbabwe in modern veterinary practices.

As a science fiction writer, Dr. Bone is the author of some five novels, the most noteworthy of which is The Lani People *(1962). His short stories are much more important, and it is a shame that he has not had a collection, since such stories as "Triggerman" and "Founding Father" deserve to be widely read. "A Prize for Edie" shows that he possesses a hearty sense of humor. (MHG)*

It's impossible to discuss this story in any way without at once giving away the point, which I don't want to do. Nor can I find refuge by talking about J.F. Bone instead, for I have never met him.

So, since the story deals with the Nobel Prize (as you'll find out in the third line) I'll talk about that.

When I was very young and very foolish, I dreamed about getting a Nobel Prize someday. I thought of myself taking my degree in chemistry, making an enormous discovery, and having to go to Stockholm in a tuxedo. Wow!

There was only one catch. It turned out that I was an absolutely miserable chemist, and I gladly turned my career in the direction of writing. To be sure, there is such a thing as a Nobel Prize for Literature but not all my incredible self-

assurance could persuade me that my chances were higher than a flat zero. So I gave up.

You can imagine how delighted I was when I received a fan letter from someone who, after praising me highly, congratulated me on my Nobel Prize for Literature. There was only one catch. My first name confused her. She thought I was Isaac Bashevis Singer. (IA)

The letter from America arrived too late. The Committee had regarded acceptance as a foregone conclusion, for no one since Boris Pasternak had turned down a Nobel Prize. So when Professor Doctor Nels Christianson opened the letter, there was not the slightest fear on his part, or on that of his fellow committeemen, Dr. Eric Carlstrom and Dr. Sven Eklund, that the letter would be anything other than the usual routine acceptance.

"At last we learn the identity of this great research worker," Christianson murmured as he scanned the closely typed sheets. Carlstrom and Eklund waited impatiently, wondering at the peculiar expression that fixed itself on Christianson's face. Fine beads of sweat appeared on the professor's high, narrow forehead as he laid the letter down. "Well," he said heavily, "now we know."

"Know what?" Eklund demanded. "What does it say? Does she accept?"

"She accepts," Christianson said in a peculiar half-strangled tone as he passed the letter to Eklund. "See for yourself."

Eklund's reaction was different. His face was a mottled reddish white as he finished the letter and handed it across the table to Carlstrom. "Why," he demanded of no one in particular, "did this have to happen to us?"

"It was bound to happen sometime," Carlstrom said. "It's just our misfortune that it happened to us." He chuckled as he passed the letter back to Christianson. "At least this year the presentation should be an event worth remembering."

"It seems that we have a little problem," Christianson said, making what would probably be the understatement of the century. Possibly there would be greater understatements in the remaining ninety-nine years of the twenty-first century, but Carlstrom doubted it. "We certainly have our necks out," he agreed.

"We can't do it!" Eklund exploded. "We simply can't award the Nobel Prize in medicine and physiology to that . . . that *C. Edie!*" He sputtered into silence.

"We can hardly do anything else," Christianson said. "There's no question as to the identity of the winner. Dr. Hanson's letter makes that unmistakably clear. And there's no question that the award is deserved."

"We still could award it to someone else," Eklund said.

"Not a chance. We've already said too much to the press. It's known all over the world that the medical award is going to the discoverer of the basic cause of cancer, to the founder of modern neoplastic therapy." Christianson grimaced. "If we changed our decision now, there'd be all sorts of embarrassing questions from the press."

"I can see it now," Carlstrom said, "the banquet, the table, the flowers, and Professor Doctor Nels Christianson in formal dress with the Order of St. Olaf gleaming across his white shirtfront, standing before that distinguished audience and announcing: 'The Nobel Prize in Medicine and Physiology is awarded to—' and then that deadly hush when the audience sees the winner."

"You needn't rub it in," Christianson said unhappily. "I can see it, too."

"These Americans!" Eklund said bitterly. He wiped his damp forehead. The picture Carlstrom had drawn was accurate but hardly appealing. "One simply can't trust them. Publishing a report as important as that as a laboratory release. They should have given proper credit."

"They did," Carlstrom said. "They did—precisely. But the world, including us, was too stupid to see it. We have only ourselves to blame."

"If it weren't for the fact that the work was inspired and effective," Christianson muttered, "we might have a chance of salvaging this situation. But through its application ninety-five percent of cancers are now curable. It is obviously the outstanding contribution to medicine in the past five decades."

"But we must consider the source," Eklund protested. "This award will make the prize for medicine a laughingstock. No doctor will ever accept another. If we go through with this, we might as well forget about the medical award from now on. This will be its swan song. It hits too close to home. Too many people have been saying similar things about our profession and its trend toward specialization. And to have the Nobel Prize confirm them would alienate every doctor in the world. We simply can't do it."

"Yet who else has made a comparable discovery? Or one that is even half as important?" Christianson asked.

"That's a good question," Carlstrom said, "and a good answer to it isn't going to be easy to find. For my part, I can only wish that Alphax Laboratories had displayed an interest in literature rather than medicine. Then our colleagues at the Academy could have had the painful decision."

"Their task would be easier than ours," Christianson said wearily. "After all, the criteria of art are more flexible. Medicine, unfortunately, is based upon facts."

"That's the hell of it," Carlstrom said.

"There must be some way to solve this problem," Eklund said. "After all it was a perfectly natural mistake. We never suspected that Alphax was a physical rather than a biological sciences laboratory. Perhaps that might offer grounds—"

"I don't think so," Carlstrom interrupted. "The means in this case aren't as important as the results, and we can't deny that the cancer problem is virtually solved."

"Even though cancer men have been saying for the past two generations that the answer was probably in the literature and all that was needed was someone with the intelligence and the time to put the facts together, the fact remains that it was C. Edie who did the job. And it required quite a bit more than merely collecting facts. Intelligence and original thinking of a high order were involved." Christianson sighed.

"Some*one*," Eklund said bitterly. "Some *thing* you mean. C. Edie—C.E.D.—Computer, Extrapolating, Discriminatory. Manufactured by Alphax Laboratories, Trenton, New Jersey, U.S.A. C. Edie! Americans!—always naming things. A machine wins the Nobel Prize. It's fantastic!"

Christianson shook his head. "It's not fantastic, unfortunately. And I see no way out. We can't even award the prize to the team of engineers who designed and built Edie. Dr. Hanson is right when he says the discovery was Edie's

and not the engineers'. It would be like giving the prize to
Albert Einstein's parents because they created him."

"Is there any way we can keep the presentation secret?"
Eklund asked.

"I'm afraid not. The presentations are public. We've done
too good a job publicizing the Nobel Prize. As a telecast
item, it's almost the equal of the motion picture Academy
award."

"I can imagine the reaction when our candidate is revealed in all her metallic glory. A two-meter cube of steel
filled with microminiaturized circuits, complete with flashing
lights and cogwheels," Carlstrom chuckled. "And where are
you going to hang the medal?"

Christianson shivered. "I wish you wouldn't give that
metal nightmare a personality," he said. "It unnerves me.
Personally, I wish that Dr. Hanson, Alphax Laboratories,
and Edie were all at the bottom of the ocean—in some nice
deep spot like the Marianas Trench." He shrugged. "Of
course, we won't have that sort of luck, so we'll have to
make the best of it."

"It just goes to show that you can't trust Americans,"
Eklund said. "I've always thought we should keep our
awards on this side of the Atlantic where people are sane
and civilized. Making a personality out of a computer—ugh!
I suppose it's their idea of a joke."

"I doubt it," Christianson said. "They just like to name
things—preferably with female names. It's a form of insecu-
rity, the mother fixation. But that's not important. I'm
afraid, gentlemen, that we shall have to make the award as
we have planned. I can see no way out. After all, there's
no reason why the machine cannot receive the prize. The
conditions merely state that it is to be presented to the one,
regardless of nationality, who makes the greatest contribution to medicine or physiology."

"I wonder how His Majesty will take it," Carlstrom said.

"The king! I'd forgotten that!" Eklund gasped.

"I expect he'll have to take it," Christianson said. "He
might even appreciate the humor in the situation."

"Gustaf Adolf is a good king, but there are limits,"
Eklund observed.

"There are other considerations," Christianson replied.

"After all, Edie is the reason the Crown Prince is still alive, and Gustaf is fond of his son."

"After all these years?"

Christianson smiled. Swedish royalty *was* long-lived. It was something of a standing joke that King Gustaf would probably outlast the pyramids, providing the pyramids lived in Sweden. "I'm sure His Majesty will cooperate. He has a strong sense of duty and since the real problem is his, not ours, I doubt if he will shirk it."

"How do you figure that?" Eklund asked.

"We merely select the candidates according to the rules, and according to the nature of their contribution. Edie is obviously the outstanding candidate in medicine for this year. It deserves the prize. We would be compromising with principle if we did not award it fairly."

"I suppose you're right," Eklund said gloomily. "I can't think of any reasonable excuse to deny the award."

"Nor I," Carlstrom said. "But what did you mean by that remark about this being the king's problem?"

"You forget," Christianson said mildly. "Of all of us, the king has the most difficult part. As you know, the Nobel Prize is formally presented at a state banquet."

"Well?"

"His Majesty is the host," Christianson said. "And just how does one eat dinner with an electronic computer?"

THE SHIP WHO SANG

BY ANNE MCCAFFREY (1926-   )

THE MAGAZINE OF FANTASY AND SCIENCE FICTION
APRIL

Anne McCaffrey is the creator of several memorable universes and characters, including her bestselling Pern series of telepathic dragonlike creatures and their riders. An American who has long resided in Ireland where she raises thoroughbred horses, she is well-known among fans for her beautiful operatic singing voice.

I believe that her greatest creation is "Helva," whose disfigured body is the basis of a cybornetic transformation that results in her being merged into the hull of a great spaceship. She is one of the great female characters in the history of the genre.

The Helva stories were "fixed-up" into a novel, also called The Ship Who Sang, *in 1969. (MHG)*

For a period of time in the 1960s, Anne McCaffrey was by far my favorite science fiction writer. For one thing, she was a very attractive female as compared with the others, almost all of whom were ugly males. For another, she did indeed have a beautiful singing voice and could outsing me, to my chagrin. Nor did she ever tell me she had had operatic training until she decided my chagrin was total. What's more, she had extraordinarily beautiful pectoral development and I always insisted they were actually a pair of spare lungs.

But I got even. I got even. She came to me at a Nebula banquet and asked me to hand out the award that was going to her, because it would embarrass her to give herself an

174

award. (Why? I wondered. I would cheerfully give myself a dozen awards and simply feel I deserved them.)

I agreed, of course. *Holding her award, I said, "Everyone's name has the syllables and stress that would fit it into a particular song. Please note that the rhythm of 'Anne McCaffrey' is the same as that of 'San Francisco.' Therefore, let me sing—*

> *"Anne McCaffrey, open your golden gate,*
> *"I can no longer wait*
> *"Frustratedly here—"*

And she came running up and snatched her award from my fingers, yowling, "Never trust a tenor." Served her right.

But then she moved to Ireland, darn it, and we lost touch. (IA)

She was born a thing and as such would be condemned if she failed to pass the encephalograph test required of all newborn babies. There was always the possibility that though the limbs were twisted, the mind was not, that though the ears would hear only dimly, the eyes see vaguely, the mind behind them was receptive and alert.

The electroencephalogram was entirely favorable, unexpectedly so, and the news was brought to the waiting, grieving parents. There was the final, harsh decision: to give their child euthanasia or permit it to become an encapsulated "brain," a guiding mechanism in any one of a number of curious professions. As such, their offspring would suffer no pain, live a comfortable existence in a metal shell for several centuries, performing unusual service to Central Worlds.

She lived and was given a name, Helva. For her first three vegetable months she waved her crabbed claws, kicked weakly with her clubbed feet and enjoyed the usual routine of the infant. She was not alone, for there were three other such children in the big city's special nursery. Soon they all were removed to Central Laboratory School, where their delicate transformation began.

One of the babies died in the initial transferral, but of Helva's "class," seventeen thrived in the metal shells. Instead of kicking feet, Helva's neural responses started her wheels; instead of grabbing with hands, she manipulated mechanical extensions. As she matured, more and more neural synapses would be adjusted to operate other mechanisms that went into the maintenance and running of a spaceship. For Helva was destined to be the "brain" half of a scout ship, partnered with a man or a woman, whichever she chose, as the mobile half. She would be among the elite of her kind. Her initial intelligence tests registered above normal and her adaptation index was unusually high. As long as her development within her shell lived up to expectations, and there were no side effects from the pituitary tinkering, Helva would live a rewarding, rich and unusual life, a far cry from what she would have faced as an ordinary, "normal" being.

However, no diagram of her brain patterns, no early IQ tests recorded certain essential facts about Helva that Central must eventually learn. They would have to bide their official time and see, trusting that the massive doses of shell-psychology would suffice her, too, as the necessary bulwark against her unusual confinement and the pressures of her profession. A ship run by a human brain could not run rogue or insane with the power and resources Central had to build into their scout ships. Brain ships were, of course, long past the experimental stages. Most babies survived the perfected techniques of pituitary manipulation that kept their bodies small, eliminating the necessity of transfers from smaller to larger shells. And very, very few were lost when the final connection was made to the control panels of ship or industrial combine. Shell-people resembled mature dwarfs in size whatever their natal deformities were, but the well-oriented brain would not have changed places with the most perfect body in the Universe.

So, for happy years, Helva scooted around in her shell with her classmates, playing such games as Stall, Power-Seek, studying her lessons in trajectory, propulsion techniques, computation, logistics, mental hygiene, basic alien psychology, philology, space history, law, traffic, codes: all the et ceteras that eventually became compounded into a reasoning, logical, informed citizen. Not so obvious to her, but of more importance to her teachers, Helva ingested the precepts of her conditioning as easily as she absorbed her nutrient fluid. She would one day be grateful to the patient drone of the subconscious-level instruction.

Helva's civilization was not without busy, do-good associations, exploring possible inhumanities to terrestrial as well as extraterrestrial citizens. One such group—Society for the Preservation of the Rights of Intelligent Minorities—got all incensed over shelled "children" when Helva was just turning fourteen. When they were forced to, Central Worlds shrugged its shoulders, arranged a tour of the Laboratory Schools and set the tour off to a big start by showing the members case histories, complete with photographs. Very few committees ever looked past the first few photos. Most of their original objections about "shells" were overridden by the relief that these hideous (to them) bodies *were* mercifully concealed.

Helva's class was doing fine arts, a selective subject in her crowded program. She had activated one of her microscopic tools which she would later use for minute repairs to various parts of her control panel. Her subject was large— a copy of "The Last Supper"—and her canvas, small—the head of a tiny screw. She had tuned her sight to the proper degree. As she worked she absentmindedly crooned, producing a curious sound. Shell-people used their own vocal chords and diaphragms, but sound issued through microphones rather than mouths. Helva's hum, then, had a curious vibrancy, a warm, dulcet quality even in its aimless chromatic wanderings.

"Why, what a lovely voice you have," said one of the female visitors.

Helva "looked" up and caught a fascinating panorama of regular, dirty craters on a flaky pink surface. Her hum became a gurgle of surprise. She instinctively regulated her "sight" until the skin lost its cratered look and the pores assumed normal proportions.

"Yes, we have quite a few years of voice training, madam," remarked Helva calmly. "Vocal peculiarities often become excessively irritating during prolonged interstellar distances and must be eliminated. I enjoyed my lessons."

Although this was the first time that Helva had seen unshelled people, she took this experience calmly. Any other reaction would have been reported instantly.

"I meant that you have a nice singing voice . . . dear," the lady said.

"Thank you. Would you like to see my work?" Helva asked politely. She instinctively sheered away from personal discussions, but she filed the comment away for further meditation.

"Work?" asked the lady.

"I am currently reproducing 'The Last Supper' on the head of a screw."

"Oh, I say," the lady twittered.

Helva turned her vision back to magnification and surveyed her copy critically. "Of course, some of my color values do not match the old Master's and the perspective is faulty, but I believe it to be a fair copy."

The lady's eyes, unmagnified, bugged out.

"Oh, I forget," and Helva's voice was really contrite. If she could have blushed, she would have. "You people don't have adjustable vision."

The monitor of this discourse grinned with pride and amusement as Helva's tone indicated pity for the unfortunate.

"Here, this will help," said Helva, substituting a magnifying device in one extension and holding it over the picture.

In a kind of shock, the ladies and gentlemen of the committee bent to observe the incredibly copied and brilliantly executed Last Supper on the head of a screw.

"Well," remarked one gentleman who had been forced to accompany his wife, "the good Lord can eat where angels fear to tread."

"Are you referring, sir," asked Helva politely, "to the Dark Age discussions of the number of angels who could stand on the head of a pin?"

"I had that in mind."

"If you substitute 'atom' for 'angel,' the problem is not insoluble, given the metallic content of the pin in question."

"Which you are programmed to compute?"

"Of course."

"Did they remember to program a sense of humor, as well, young lady?"

"We are directed to develop a sense of proportion, sir, which contributes the same effect."

The good man chortled appreciatively and decided the trip was worth his time.

If the investigation committee spent months digesting the thoughtful food served them at the Laboratory School, they left Helva with a morsel as well.

"Singing" as applicable to herself required research. She had, of course, been exposed to and enjoyed a music-appreciation course that had included the better-known classical works, such as *Tristan und Isolde, Candide, Oklahoma,* and *Nozze di Figaro,* along with the atomic-age singers, Birgit Nilsson, Bob Dylan, and Geraldine Todd, as well as the curious rhythmic progressions of the Venusians, Capellan visual chromatics, the sonic concerti of the Altairians and Reticulan croons. But "singing" for any shell-person posed considerable technical difficulties. Shell-people were schooled to examine every aspect of a problem or situation before making a prognosis. Balanced properly between optimism and practicality, the nondefeatist attitude of the shell-people led them to extricate themselves, their ships, and personnel, from bizarre situations. Therefore to Helva, the problem that she couldn't open her mouth to sing, among other restrictions, did not bother her. She would work out a method, by-passing her limitations, whereby she could sing.

She approached the problem by investigating the methods of sound reproduction through the centuries, human and instrumental. Her own sound-production equipment was essentially more instrumental than vocal. Breath control and the proper enunciation of vowel sounds within the oral cavity appeared to require the most development and practice. Shell-people did not, strictly speaking, breathe. For their purposes, oxygen and other gases were not drawn from the surrounding atmosphere through the medium of lungs but sustained artificially by solution in their shells. After experimentation, Helva discovered that she could manipulate her diaphragmic unit to sustain tone. By relaxing the throat muscles and expanding the oral cavity well into the frontal sinuses, she could direct the vowel sounds into the most felicitous position for proper reproduction through her throat microphone. She compared the results with tape recordings of modern singers and was not unpleased, although her own tapes had a peculiar quality about them, not at all unharmonious, merely unique. Acquiring a repertoire from the Laboratory library was no problem to one trained to perfect recall. She found herself able to sing any role and any song which struck her fancy. It would not have occurred to her that it was curious for a female to sing bass, baritone, tenor, mezzo, soprano, and coloratura as she pleased. It was, to Helva, only a matter of the correct reproduction and diaphragmatic control required by the music attempted.

If the authorities remarked on her curious avocation, they did so among themselves. Shell-people were encouraged to develop a hobby so long as they maintained proficiency in their technical work.

On the anniversary of her sixteenth year, Helva was unconditionally graduated and installed in her ship, the XH-834. Her permanent titanium shell was recessed behind an even more indestructible barrier in the central shaft of the scout ship. The neural, audio, visual, and sensory connections were made and sealed. Her extendibles were diverted, connected or augmented and the final, delicate-beyond-description brain taps were completed while Helva remained anesthetically unaware of the proceedings. When she woke, she *was* the ship. Her brain and intelligence controlled every function from navigation to such loading as a scout ship of her class needed. She could take care of herself and her ambulatory half in any situation already recorded in the annals of Central Worlds and any situation its most fertile minds could imagine.

Her first actual flight, for she and her kind had made mock flights on dummy panels since she was eight, showed her to be a complete master of the techniques of her profession. She was ready for her great adventures and the arrival of her mobile partner.

There were nine qualified scouts sitting around collecting base pay the day Helva reported for active duty. There were several missions that demanded instant attention, but Helva had been of interest to several department heads in Central for some time and each bureau chief was determined to have her assigned to *his* section. No one had remembered to introduce Helva to the prospective partners. The ship always chose its own partner. Had there been another "brain" ship at the base at the moment, Helva would have been guided to make the first move. As it was, while Central wrangled among itself, Robert Tanner sneaked out of the pilots' barracks, out to the field and over to Helva's slim metal hull.

"Hello, anyone at home?" Tanner said.

"Of course," replied Helva, activating her outside scanners. "Are you my partner?" she asked hopefully, as she recognized the Scout Service uniform.

"All you have to do is ask," he retorted in a wistful tone.

"No one has come. I thought perhaps there were no partners available and I've had no directives from Central."

Even to herself Helva sounded a little self-pitying, but the truth was she was lonely, sitting on the darkened field. She had always had the company of other shells and more recently, technicians by the score. The sudden solitude had lost its momentary charm and become oppressive.

"No directives from Central is scarcely a cause for regret, but there happen to be eight other guys biting their fingernails to the quick just waiting for an invitation to board you, you beautiful thing."

Tanner was inside the central cabin as he said this, running appreciative fingers over her panel, the scout's gravity-chair, poking his head into the cabins, the galley, the head, the pressured-storage compartments.

"Now, if you want to goose Central and do *us* a favor all in one, call up the barracks and let's have a ship-warming partner-picking party. Hmmmm?"

Helva chuckled to herself. He was so completely different from the occasional visitors or the various Laboratory technicians she had encountered. He was so gay, so assured, and she was delighted by his suggestion of a partner-picking party. Certainly it was not against anything in her understanding of regulations.

"Cencom, this is XH-834. Connect me with Pilot Barracks."

"Visual?"

"Please."

A picture of lounging men in various attitudes of boredom came on her screen.

"This is XH-834. Would the unassigned scouts do me the favor of coming aboard?"

Eight figures were galvanized into action, grabbing pieces of wearing apparel, disengaging tape mechanisms, disentangling themselves from bedsheets and towels.

Helva dissolved the connection while Tanner chuckled gleefully and settled down to await their arrival.

Helva was engulfed in an unshell-like flurry of anticipation. No actress on her opening night could have been more apprehensive, fearful or breathless. Unlike the actress, she could throw no hysterics, china *objets d'art* or grease paint to relieve her tension. She could, of course, check her stores for edibles and drinks, which she did, serving Tanner from the virgin selection of her commissary.

Scouts were colloquially known as "brawns" as opposed to their ship "brains." They had to pass as rigorous a training program as the brains and only the top 1 percent of each contributory world's highest scholars were admitted to Central Worlds Scout Training Program. Consequently the eight young men who came pounding up the gantry into Helva's hospitable lock were unusually fine looking, intelligent, well-coordinated and well-adjusted young men, looking forward to a slightly drunken evening, Helva permitting, and all quite willing to do each other dirt to get possession of her.

Such a human invasion left Helva mentally breathless, a luxury she thoroughly enjoyed for the brief time she felt she should permit it.

She sorted out the young men. Tanner's opportunism amused but did not specifically attract her; the blond Nordsen seemed too simple; dark-haired Alatpay had a kind of obstinacy for which she felt no compassion; Mir-Ahnin's bitterness hinted an inner darkness she did not wish to lighten, although he made the biggest outward play for her attention. Hers was a curious courtship—this would be only the first of several marriages for her, for brawns retired after seventy-five years of service, or earlier if they were unlucky. Brains, their bodies safe from any deterioration, were indestructible. In theory, once a shell-person had paid off the massive debt of early care, surgical adaptation and maintenance charges, he or she was free to seek employment elsewhere. In practice, shell-people remained in the Service until they chose to self-destruct or died in line of duty. Helva had actually spoken to one shell-person 322 years old. She had been so awed by the contact she hadn't presumed to ask the personal questions she had wanted to.

Her choice of a brawn did not stand out from the others until Tanner started to sing a scout ditty, recounting the misadventures of the bold, dense, painfully inept Billy

Brawn. An attempt at harmony resulted in cacophony and Tanner wagged his arms wildly for silence.

"What we need is a roaring good lead tenor. Jennan, besides palming aces, what do you sing?"

"Sharp," Jennan replied with easy good humor.

"If a tenor is absolutely necessary, I'll attempt it," Helva volunteered.

"My good *woman*," Tanner protested.

"Sound your 'A,' " said Jennan, laughing.

Into the stunned silence that followed the rich, clear, high "A," Jennan remarked quietly, "Such an 'A' Caruso would have given the rest of his notes to sing."

It did not take them long to discover her full range.

"All Tanner asked for was one roaring good lead tenor," Jennan said jokingly, "and our sweet mistress supplied us an entire repertory company. The boy who gets this ship will go far, far, far."

"To the Horsehead Nebula?" asked Nordsen, quoting an old Central saw.

"To the Horsehead Nebula and back, we shall make beautiful music," said Helva, chuckling.

"Together," Jennan said. "Only you'd better make the music and, with my voice, I'd better listen."

"I rather imagined it would be I who listened," suggested Helva.

Jennan executed a stately bow with an intricate flourish of his crush-brimmed hat. He directed his bow toward the central control pillar where Helva *was*. Her own personal preference crystallized at that precise moment and for that particular reason: Jennan, alone of the men, had addressed his remarks directly at her physical presence, regardless of the fact that he knew she could pick up his image wherever he was in the ship and regardless of the fact that her body was behind massive metal walls. Throughout their partnership, Jennan never failed to turn his head in her direction no matter where he was in relation to her. In response to this personalization, Helva at that moment and from then on always spoke to Jennan only through her central mike, even though that was not always the most efficient method.

Helva didn't know that she fell in love with Jennan that evening. As she had never been exposed to love or affection, only the drier cousins, respect and admiration, she could scarcely have recognized her reaction to the warmth of his personality and thoughtfulness. As a shell-person, she considered herself remote from emotions largely connected with physical desires.

"Well, Helva, it's been swell meeting you," said Tanner suddenly as she and Jennan were arguing about the baroque quality of "Come All Ye Sons of Art." "See you in space sometime, you lucky dog, Jennan. Thanks for the party, Helva."

"You don't have to go so soon?" asked Helva, realizing belatedly that she and Jennan had been excluding the others from this discussion.

"Best man won," Tanner said wryly. "Guess I'd better go get a tape on love ditties. Might need 'em for the next ship, if there're any more at home like you."

Helva and Jennan watched them leave, both a little confused.

"Perhaps Tanner's jumping to conclusions?" Jennan asked.

Helva regarded him as he slouched against the console, facing her shell directly. His arms were crossed on his chest and the glass he held had been empty for some time. He was handsome, they all were; but his watchful eyes were unwary, his mouth assumed a smile easily, his voice (to which Helva was particularly drawn) was resonant, deep, and without unpleasant overtones or accent.

"Sleep on it, at any rate, Helva. Call me in the morning if it's your opt."

She called him at breakfast, after she had checked her choice through Central. Jennan moved his things aboard, received their joint commission, had his personality and experience file locked into her reviewer, gave her the coordinates of their first mission. The XH-834 officially became the JH-834.

Their first mission was a dull but necessary crash priority (Medical got Helva), rushing a vaccine to a distant system plagued with a virulent spore disease. They had only to get to Spica as fast as possible.

After the initial, thrilling forward surge at her maximum speed, Helva realized her muscles were to be given less of a workout than her brawn on this tedious mission. But they did have plenty of time for exploring each other's personalities. Jennan, of course, knew what Helva was capable of as a ship and partner, just as she knew what she could expect from him. But these were only facts and Helva looked forward eagerly to learning that human side of her partner which could not be reduced to a series of symbols. Nor could the give and take of two personalities be learned from a book. It had to be experienced.

"My father was a scout, too, or is that programmed?" began Jennan their third day out.

"Naturally."

"Unfair, you know. You've got all my family history and I don't know one blamed thing about yours."

"I've never known either," Helva said. "Until I read yours, it hadn't occurred to me I must have one, too, someplace in Central's files."

Jennan snorted. "Shell psychology!"

Helva laughed. "Yes, and I'm even programmed against curiosity about it. You'd better be, too."

Jennan ordered a drink, slouched into the gravity couch opposite her, put his feet on the bumpers, turning himself idly from side to side on the gimbals.

"Helva—a made-up name . . ."

"With a Scandinavian sound."

"You aren't blond," Jennan said positively.

"Well, then, there're dark Swedes."

"And blond Turks and this one's harem is limited to one."

"Your woman in purdah, yes, but you can comb the pleasure houses—" Helva found herself aghast at the edge to her carefully trained voice.

"You know," Jennan interrupted her, deep in some thought of his own, "my father gave me the impression he was a lot more married to his ship, the Silvia, than to my mother. I know I used to think Silvia was my grandmother. She was a low number, so she must have been a great-great-grandmother at least. I used to talk to her for hours."

"Her registry?" asked Helva, unwittingly jealous of everyone and anyone who had shared his hours.

"422, I think she's TS now. I ran into Tom Burgess once."

Jennan's father had died of a planetary disease, the vac-

cine for which his ship had used up in curing the local
citizens.

"Tom said she'd got mighty tough and salty. You lose
your sweetness and I'll come back and haunt you, girl,"
Jennan threatened.

Helva laughed. He startled her by stamping up to the
column panel, touching it with light, tender fingers.

"I *wonder* what you look like," he said softly, wistfully.

Helva had been briefed about this natural curiosity of
scouts. She didn't know anything about herself and neither
of them ever would or could.

"Pick any form, shape, and shade and I'll be yours obliging," she countered, as training suggested.

"Iron Maiden, I fancy blondes with long tresses," and
Jennan pantomimed Lady Godiva-like tresses. "Since
you're immolated in titanium, I'll call you Brunehilde, my
dear," and he made his bow.

With a chortle, Helva launched into the appropriate aria
just as Spica made contact.

"What'n'ell's that yelling about? Who are you? And
unless you're Central Worlds Medical, go away. We've got
a plague. No visiting privileges."

"My ship is singing, we're the JH-834 of Worlds and
we've got your vaccine. What are our landing coordinates?"

"Your *ship* is singing?"

"The greatest S.A.T.B. in organized space. Any request?"

The JH-834 delivered the vaccine but no more arias and
received immediate orders to proceed to Leviticus IV. By
the time they got there, Jennan found a reputation awaiting
him and was forced to defend the 834's virgin honor.

"I'll stop singing," murmured Helva contritely as she
ordered up poultices for his third black eye in a week.

"You will not," Jennan said through gritted teeth. "If I
have to black eyes from here to the Horsehead to keep the
snicker out of the title, we'll be the ship who sings."

After the "ship who sings" tangled with a minor but
vicious narcotic ring in the Lesser Magellanics, the title
became definitely respectful. Central was aware of each epi-
sode and punched out a "special interest" key on JH-834's
file. A first-rate team was shaking down well.

Jennan and Helva considered themselves a first-rate
team, too, after their tidy arrest.

"Of all the vices in the universe, I *hate* drug addiction," Jennan remarked as they headed back to Central Base. "People can go to hell quick enough without that kind of help."

"Is that why you volunteered for Scout Service? To redirect traffic?"

"I'll bet my official answer's on your review."

"In far too flowery wording. 'Carrying on the traditions of my family, which has been proud of four generations in Service,' if I may quote you your own words."

Jennan groaned. "I was *very* young when I wrote that. I certainly hadn't been through Final Training. And once I was in Final Training, my pride wouldn't let me fail . . .

"As I mentioned, I used to visit Dad on board the Silvia and I've a very good idea she might have had her eye on me as a replacement for my father because I had had massive doses of scout-oriented propaganda. It took. From the time I was seven, I was going to be a scout or else." He shrugged as if deprecating a youthful determination that had taken a great deal of mature application to bring to fruition.

"Ah, so? Scout Sahir Silan on the JS-422 penetrating into the Horsehead Nebula?"

Jennan chose to ignore her sarcasm.

"With *you*, I may even get that far. But even with Silvia's nudging *I* never daydreamed myself *that* kind of glory in my wildest flights of fancy. I'll leave the whoppers to your agile brain henceforth. I have in mind a smaller contribution to space history."

"So modest?"

"No. Practical. We also serve, et cetera." He placed a dramatic hand on his heart.

"Glory hound!" scoffed Helva.

"Look who's talking, my Nebula-bound friend. At least I'm not greedy. There'll only be one hero like my dad at Parsaea, but I *would* like to be remembered for some kudos. Everyone does. Why else do or die?"

"Your father died on his way back from Parsaea, if I may point out a few cogent facts. So he could never have known he was a hero for damming the flood with his ship. Which kept the Parsaean colony from being abandoned. Which gave them a chance to discover the antiparalytic qualities of Parsaea. Which *he* never knew."

"I know," said Jennan softly.

Helva was immediately sorry for the tone of her rebuttal. She knew very well how deep Jennan's attachment to his father had been. On his review a note was made that he had rationalized his father's loss with the unexpected and welcome outcome of the Affair at Parsaea.

"Facts are not human, Helva. My father was and so am I. And *basically*, so are you. Check over your dial, 834. Amid all the wires attached to you is a heart, an underdeveloped human heart. Obviously!"

"I apologize, Jennan," she said.

Jennan hesitated a moment, threw out his hands in acceptance and then tapped her shell affectionately.

"If they ever take us off the milkruns, we'll make a stab at the Nebula, huh?"

As so frequently happened in the Scout Service, within the next hour they had orders to change course, not to the Nebula, but to a recently colonized system with two habitable planets, one tropical, one glacial. The sun, named Ravel, had become unstable; the spectrum was that of a rapidly expanding shell, with absorption lines rapidly displacing toward violet. The augmented heat of the primary had already forced evacuation of the nearer world, Daphnis. The pattern of spectral emissions gave indication that the sun would sear Chloe as well. All ships in the immediate spatial vicinity were to report to Disaster Headquarters on Chloe to effect removal of the remaining colonists.

The JH-834 obediently presented itself and was sent to outlying areas on Chloe to pick up scattered settlers who did not appear to appreciate the urgency of the situation. Chloe, indeed, was enjoying the first temperatures above freezing since it had been flung out of its parent. Since many of the colonists were religious fanatics who had settled on rigorous Chloe to fit themselves for a life of pious reflection, Chloe's abrupt thaw was attributed to sources other than a rampaging sun.

Jennan had to spend so much time countering specious arguments that he and Helva were behind schedule on their way to the fourth and last settlement.

Helva jumped over the high range of jagged peaks that surrounded and sheltered the valley from the former raging snows as well as the present heat. The violent sun with its flaring corona was just beginning to brighten the deep valley as Helva dropped down to a landing.

"They'd better grab their toothbrushes and hop aboard," Helva said. "HQ says speed it up."

"All women," remarked Jennan in surprise as he walked down to meet them. "Unless the men on Chloe wear furred skirts."

"Charm 'em but pare the routine to the bare essentials. And turn on your two-way private."

Jennan advanced smiling, but his explanation of his mission was met with absolute incredulity and considerable doubt as to his authenticity. He groaned inwardly as the matriarch paraphrased previous explanations of the warming sun.

"Revered mother, there's been an overload on that prayer circuit and the sun is blowing itself up in one obliging burst. I'm here to take you to the spaceport at Rosary—"

"That Sodom?" The worthy woman glowered and shuddered disdainfully at his suggestion. "We thank you for your warning but we have no wish to leave our cloister for the rude world. We must go about our morning meditation which has been interrupted—"

"It'll be permanently interrupted when that sun starts broiling you. You must come now," Jennan said firmly

"Madame," said Helva, realizing that perhaps a female voice might carry more weight in this instance than Jennan's very masculine charm.

"Who spoke?" cried the nun, startled by the bodiless voice.

"I, Helva, the ship. Under my protection you and your sisters-in-faith may enter safely and be unprofaned by association with a male. I will guard you and take you safely to a place prepared for you."

The matriarch peered cautiously into the ship's open port. "Since only Central Worlds is permitted the use of such ships, I acknowledge that you are not trifling with us, young man. However, we are in no danger here."

"The temperature at Rosary is now 99 degrees," said Helva. "As soon as the sun's rays penetrate directly into this valley, it will also be 99 degrees, and it is due to climb to approximately 180 degrees today. I notice your buildings are made of wood with moss chinking. Dry moss. It should fire around noontime."

The sunlight was beginning to slant into the valley through the peaks, and the fierce rays warmed the restless group behind the matriarch. Several opened the throats of their furry parkas.

"Jennan," said Helva privately to him, "our time is very short."

"I can't leave them, Helva. Some of those girls are barely out of their teens."

"Pretty, too. No wonder the matriarch doesn't want to get in."

"Helva."

"It will be the Lord's will," said the matriarch stoutly and turned her back squarely on rescue.

"To burn to death?" shouted Jennan as she threaded her way through her murmuring disciples.

"They want to be martyrs? Their opt, Jennan," said Helva dispassionately, "We must leave and that is no longer a matter of option."

"How can I leave, Helva?"

"Parsaea?" Helva asked tauntingly as he stepped forward to grab one of the women. "You can't drag them *all* aboard and we don't have time to fight it out. Get on board, Jennan, or I'll have you on report."

"They'll die," muttered Jennan dejectedly as he reluctantly turned to climb on board.

"You can risk only so much," Helva said sympathetically. "As it is we'll just have time to make a rendezvous. Lab reports a critical speed up in spectral evolution."

Jennan was already in the airlock when one of the younger women, screaming, rushed to squeeze in the closing port. Her action set off the others. They stampeded through the narrow opening. Even crammed back to breast, there was not enough room inside for all the women. Jennan broke out spacesuits for the three who would have to remain with him in the airlock. He wasted valuable time explaining to the matriarch that she must put on the suit because the airlock had no independent oxygen or cooling units.

"We'll be caught," said Helva in a grim tone to Jennan on their private connection. "We've lost eighteen minutes in this last-minute rush. I am now overloaded for maximum speed and I must attain maximum speed to outrun the heat wave."

"Can you lift? We're suited."

"Lift? Yes," she said, doing so. "Run? I stagger."

Jennan, bracing himself and the women, could feel her sluggishness as she blasted upward. Heartlessly, Helva applied thrust as long as she could, despite the fact that the gravitational force mashed her cabin passengers brutally and crushed two fatally. It was a question of saving as many as possible. The only one for whom she had any concern was Jennan and she was in desperate terror about his safety. Airless and uncooled, protected by only one layer of metal, not three, the airlock was not going to be safe for the four trapped there, despite their spacesuits. These were only the standard models, not built to withstand the excessive heat to which the ship would be subjected.

Helva ran as fast as she could but the incredible wave of heat from the explosive sun caught them halfway to cold safety.

She paid no heed to the cries, moans, pleas, and prayers in her cabin. She listened only to Jennan's tortured breathing, to the missing throb in his suit's purifying system and the sucking of the overloaded cooling unit. Helpless, she heard the hysterical screams of his three companions as they writhed in the awful heat. Vainly, Jennan tried to calm them, tried to explain they would soon be safe and cool if they could be still and endure the heat. Undisciplined by their terror and torment, they tried to strike out at him despite the close quarters. One flailing arm became entangled in the leads to his power pack and the damage was quickly done. A connection, weakened by heat and the dead weight of the arm, broke.

For all the power at her disposal, Helva was helpless. She watched as Jennan fought for his breath, as he turned his head beseechingly toward *her*, and died.

Only the iron conditioning of her training prevented Helva from swinging around and plunging back into the cleansing heart of the exploding sun. Numbly she made rendezvous with the refugee convoy. She obediently transferred her burned, heat-prostrated passengers to the assigned transport.

"I will retain the body of my scout and proceed to the nearest base for burial," she informed Central dully.

"You will be provided escort," was the reply.

"I have no need of escort."

"Escort is provided, XH-834," she was told curtly. The shock of hearing Jennan's initial severed from her call number cut off her half-formed protest. Stunned, she waited by the transport until her screens showed the arrival of two other slim brain ships. The cortege proceeded homeward at unfunereal speeds.

"834? The ship who sings?"

"I have no more songs."

"Your scout was Jennan."

"I do not wish to communicate."

"I'm 422."

"Silvia?"

"Silvia died a long time ago. I'm 422. Currently MS," the ship rejoined curtly. "AH-640 is our other friend, but Henry's not listening in. Just as well—he wouldn't understand it if you wanted to turn rogue. But I'd stop *him* if he tried to deter you."

"Rogue?" The term snapped Helva out of her apathy.

"Sure. You're young. You've got power for years. Skip. Others have done it. 732 went rogue twenty years ago after she lost her scout on a mission to that white dwarf. Hasn't been seen since."

"I never heard about rogues."

"As it's exactly the thing we're conditioned against, you sure wouldn't hear about it in school, my dear," 422 said.

"Break conditioning?" cried Helva, anguished, thinking longingly of the white, white furious hot heart of the sun she had just left.

"For you I don't think it would be hard at the moment," 422 said quietly, her voice devoid of her earlier cynicism. "The stars are out there, winking."

"Alone?" cried Helva from her heart.

"Alone!" 422 confirmed bleakly.

Alone with all of space and time. Even the Horsehead Nebula would not be far enough away to daunt her. Alone with a hundred years to live with her memories and nothing . . . nothing more.

"Was Parsaea worth it?" she asked 422 softly.

"Parsaea?" 422 repeated, surprised. "With his father? Yes. We were there, at Parsaea when we were needed. Just as you . . . and his son . . . were at Chloe. When you were needed. The crime is not knowing where need is and not being there."

"But *I* need *him*. Who will supply my need?" said Helva bitterly . . .

"834," said 422 after a day's silent speeding, "Central wishes your report. A replacement awaits your opt at Regulus Base. Change course accordingly."

"A replacement?" That was certainly not what she needed . . . a reminder inadequately filling the void Jennan left. Why, her hull was barely cool of Chloe's heat. Atavistically, Helva wanted time to morn Jennan.

"Oh, none of them are impossible if *you're* a good ship," 422 remarked philosophically. "And it is just what you need. The sooner the better."

"You told them I wouldn't go rogue, didn't you?" Helva said.

"The moment passed you even as it passed me after Parsaea, and before that, after Glen Arthur, and Betelgeuse."

"We're conditioned to go on, aren't we? We *can't* go rogue. You were testing."

"Had to. Orders. Not even Psych knows why a rogue occurs. Central's very worried, and so, daughter, are your sister ships. I asked to be your escort. I . . . don't want to lose you both."

In her emotional nadir, Helva could feel a flood of gratitude for Silvia's rough sympathy.

"We've all known this grief, Helva. It's no consolation, but if we couldn't feel with our scouts, we'd only be machines wired for sound."

Helva looked at Jennan's still form stretched before her in its shroud and heard the echo of his rich voice in the quiet cabin.

"Silvia! I *couldn't* help him," she cried from her soul.

"Yes, dear, I know," 422 murmured gently and then was quiet.

The three ships sped on, wordless, to the great Central Worlds base at Regulus. Helva broke silence to acknowledge landing instructions and the officially tendered regrets.

The three ships set down simultaneously at the wooded edge where Regulus' gigantic blue trees stood sentinel over the sleeping dead in the small Service cemetery. The entire Base complement approached with measured step and formed an aisle from Helva to the burial ground. The honor detail, out of step, walked slowly into her cabin. Reverently they placed the body of her dead love on the wheeled bier, covered it honorably with the deep-blue, star-splashed flag of the Service. She watched as it was driven slowly down the living aisle which closed in behind the bier in last escort.

Then, as the simple words of interment were spoken, as the atmosphere planes dipped in tribute over the open grave, Helva found voice for her lonely farewell.

Softly, barely audible at first, the strains of the ancient song of evening and requiem swelled to the final poignant measure until black space itself echoed back the sound of the song the ship sang.

DEATH AND THE SENATOR

BY ARTHUR C. CLARKE (1917-   )

ANALOG SCIENCE FICTION
MAY

This excellent story by Arthur C. Clarke presents a senator who must decide between his responsibility to the public interest and his private interest. He is also a man with driving ambition, ruthlessness, pride, and the need to be a winner. The assumption underlying representative government is that leaders will opt for or fight for the common good, not for their own good; that they will do what is good for all the people, not what is good for just themselves or some of the people.

We all know that they have achieved that ideal.

Don't we, Isaac? (MHG)

Yes, Martin, they have achieved it. Also, pigs have wings.

Now that Robert Heinlein has gone to his reward (I hate that expression, for it is ambiguous, since no one states what the reward is going to be) Arthur Clarke and I are the Big Two, a pair of superannuated dotards who keep circling each other and wondering which will finally be the Big One.

While we engage ourselves in this absorbing pursuit, we play the game of mutual insult out of friendship and love.

The most delicious occasion I had to insult him was an occasion when he wasn't present, alas. Our styles are sufficiently similar so that it isn't uncommon for people to assign one of his books to me and one of mine to him.

In any case, a woman came up to me at a convention and said, "Dr. Asimov, I read your book 'Childhood's End' and, while I liked it, I didn't think it was as good as your other novels."

And with a perfectly straight face, I said to her, "You are quite right, madam. The book was a great disappointment to me because of its inferior nature so I insisted on having it published under the pseudonym of Arthur C. Clarke, Jr."

Ha, ha, Arthur, how do you like that? (IA)

Washington had never looked lovelier in the spring; and this was the last spring, thought Senator Steelman bleakly, that he would ever see. Even now, despite all that Dr. Jordan had told him, he could not fully accept the truth. In the past there had always been a way of escape; no defeat had been final. When men had betrayed him, he had discarded them—even ruined them, as a warning to others. But now the betrayal was within himself; already, it seemed, he could feel the labored beating of the heart that would soon be stilled. No point in planning now for the Presidential election of 1976; he might not even live to see the nominations. . . .

It was an end of dreams and ambition, and he could not console himself with the knowledge that for all men these must end someday. For him it was too soon; he thought of Cecil Rhodes, who had always been one of his heroes, crying "So much to do—so little time to do it in!" as he died before his fiftieth birthday. He was already older than Rhodes, and had done far less.

The car was taking him away from the Capitol; there was symbolism in that, and he tried not to dwell upon it. Now he was abreast of the New Smithsonian—that vast complex of museums he had never had time to visit, though he had watched it spread along the Mall throughout the years he had been in Washington. How much he had missed, he told himself bitterly, in his relentless pursuit of power. The whole universe of art and culture had remained almost closed to him, and that was only part of the price that he had paid. He had become a stranger to his family and to those who were once his friends. Love had been sacrificed on the altar of ambition, and the sacrifice had been in vain. Was there anyone in all the world who would weep at his departure?

Yes, there was. The feeling of utter desolation relaxed its

grip upon his soul. As he reached for the phone, he felt ashamed that he had to call the office to get this number, when his mind was cluttered with memories of so many less important things.

(There was the White House, almost dazzling in the spring sunshine. For the first time in his life he did not give it a second glance. Already it belonged to another world— a world that would never concern him again.)

The car circuit had no vision, but he did not need it to sense Irene's mild surprise—and her still milder pleasure.

"Hello, Renee—how are you all?"

"Fine, Dad. When are we going to see you?"

It was the polite formula his daughter always used on the rare occasions when he called. And invariably, except at Christmas or birthdays, his answer was a vague promise to drop around at some indefinite future date.

"I was wondering," he said slowly, almost apologetically, "if I could borrow the children for an afternoon. It's a long time since I've taken them out, and I felt like getting away from the office."

"But of course," Irene answered, her voice warming with pleasure. "They'll love it. When would you like them?"

"Tomorrow would be fine. I could call around twelve, and take them to the Zoo or the Smithsonian, or anywhere else they felt like visiting."

Now she was really startled, for she knew well enough that he was one of the busiest men in Washington, with a schedule planned weeks in advance. She would be wondering what had happened; he hoped she would not guess the truth. No reason why she should, for not even his secretary knew of the stabbing pains that had driven him to seek this long-overdue medical checkup.

"That would be wonderful. They were talking about you only yesterday, asking when they'd see you again."

His eyes misted, and he was glad that Renee could not see him.

"I'll be there at noon," he said hastily, trying to keep the emotion out of his voice. "My love to you all." He switched off before she could answer, and relaxed against the uphol-stery with a sigh of relief. Almost upon impulse, without conscious planning, he had taken the first step in the reshap-ing of his life. Though his own children were lost to him, a bridge across the generations remained intact. If he did nothing else, he must guard and strengthen it in the months that were left.

Taking two lively and inquisitive children through the natural-history building was not what the doctor would have ordered, but it was what he wanted to do. Joey and Susan had grown so much since their last meeting, and it required both physical and mental alertness to keep up with them. No sooner had they entered the rotunda than they broke away from him, and scampered toward the enormous elephant dominating the marble hall.

"What's that?" cried Joey.

"It's an elephant, stupid," answered Susan with all the crushing superiority of her seven years.

"I know it's an effelant," retorted Joey. "But what's its name?"

Senator Steelman scanned the label, but found no assistance there. This was one occasion when the risky adage "Sometimes wrong, never uncertain" was a safe guide to conduct.

"He was called—er—Jumbo," he said hastily. "Just look at those tusks!"

"Did he ever get toothache?"

"Oh no."

"Then how did he clean his teeth? Ma says that if I don't clean mine . . ."

Steelman saw where the logic of this was leading, and thought it best to change the subject.

"There's a lot more to see inside. Where do you want to start—birds, snakes, fish, mammals?"

"Snakes!" clamored Susan. "I wanted to keep one in a box, but Daddy said no. Do you think he'd change his mind if you asked him?"

"What's a mammal?" asked Joey, before Steelman could work out an answer to that.

"Come along," he said firmly. "I'll show you."

As they moved through the halls and galleries, the children darting from one exhibit to another, he felt at peace with the world. There was nothing like a museum for calming the mind, for putting the problems of everyday life in their true perspective. Here, surrounded by the infinite variety and wonder of Nature, he was reminded of truths he had forgotten. He was only one of a million million creatures that shared this planet Earth. The entire human race, with its hopes and fears, its triumphs and its follies, might be no more than an incident in the history of the world. As he stood before the monstrous bones of Diplodocus (the children for once awed and silent), he felt the winds of Eternity blowing through his soul. He could no longer take so seriously the gnawing of ambition, the belief that he was the man the nation needed. *What* nation, if it came to that? A mere two centuries ago this summer, the Declaration of Independence had been signed; but this old American had lain in the Utah rocks for a hundred million years. . . .

He was tired when they reached the Hall of Oceanic Life, with its dramatic reminder that Earth still possessed animals greater than any that the past could show. The ninety-foot blue whale plunging into the ocean, and all the other swift hunters of the sea, brought back memories of hours he had once spent on a tiny, glistening deck with a white sail billowing above him. That was another time when he had known contentment, listening to the swish of water past the prow, and the sighing of the wind through the rigging. He had not sailed for thirty years; this was another of the world's pleasures he had put aside.

"I don't like fish," complained Susan. "When do we get to the snakes?"

"Presently," he said. "But what's the hurry? There's plenty of time."

The words slipped out before he realized it. He checked his step, while the children ran on ahead. Then he smiled, without bitterness. For in a sense, it was true enough. There *was* plenty of time. Each day, each hour could be a universe of experience, if one used it properly. In the last weeks of his life, he would begin to live.

As yet, no one at the office suspected anything. Even his outing with the children had not caused much surprise; he had done such things before, suddenly canceling his appointments and leaving his staff to pick up the pieces. The pattern of his behavior had not yet changed, but in a few days it would be obvious to all his associates that something had happened. He owed it to them—and to the party—to break the news as soon as possible; there were, however, many personal decisions he had to make first, which he wished to settle in his own mind before he began the vast unwinding of his affairs.

There was another reason for his hesitancy. During his career, he had seldom lost a fight, and in the cut and thrust of political life he had given quarter to none. Now, facing his ultimate defeat, he dreaded the sympathy and the condolences that his many enemies would hasten to shower upon him. The attitude, he knew, was a foolish one—a remnant of his stubborn pride which was too much a part of his personality to vanish even under the shadow of death.

He carried his secret from committee room to White House to Capitol, and through all the labyrinths of Washington society, for more than two weeks. It was the finest performance of his career, but there was no one to appreciate it. At the end of that time he had completed his plan of action; it remained only to dispatch a few letters he had written in his own hand, and to call his wife.

The office located her, not without difficulty, in Rome. She was still beautiful, he thought, as her features swam on to the screen; she would have made a fine First Lady, and that would have been some compensation for the lost years. As far as he knew, she had looked forward to the prospect; but had he ever really understood what she wanted?

"Hello, Martin," she said, "I was expecting to hear from you. I suppose you want me to come back."

"Are you willing to?" he asked quietly. The gentleness of his voice obviously surprised her.

"I'd be a fool to say no, wouldn't I? But if they don't elect you, I want to go my own way again. You must agree to that."

"They won't elect me. They won't even nominate me. You're the first to know this, Diana. In six months, I shall be dead."

The directness was brutal, but it had a purpose. That fraction-of-a-second delay while the radio waves flashed up to the communication satellites and back again to Earth had never seemed so long. For once, he had broken through the beautiful mask. Her eyes widened with disbelief, her hand flew to her lips.

"You're joking!"

"About *this?* It's true enough. My heart's worn out. Dr. Jordan told me, a couple of weeks ago. It's my own fault, of course, but let's not go into that."

"So that's why you've been taking out the children: I wondered what had happened."

He might have guessed that Irene would have talked with her mother. It was a sad reflection on Martin Steelman, if so commonplace a fact as showing an interest in his own grandchildren could cause curiosity.

"Yes," he admitted frankly. "I'm afraid I left it a little late. Now I'm trying to make up for lost time. Nothing else seems very important."

In silence, they looked into each other's eyes across the curve of the Earth, and across the empty desert of the dividing years. Then Diana answered, a little unsteadily, "I'll start packing right away."

Now that the news was out, he felt a great sense of relief. Even the sympathy of his enemies was not as hard to accept as he had feared. For overnight, indeed, he had no enemies. Men who had not spoken to him in years, except with invective, sent messages whose sincerity could not be doubted. Ancient quarrels evaporated, or turned out to be founded on misunderstandings. It was a pity that one had to die to learn these things. . . .

He also learned that, for a man of affairs, dying was a full-time job. There were successors to appoint, legal and financial mazes to untangle, committee and state business to wind up. The work of an energetic lifetime could not be terminated suddenly, as one switches off an electric light. It was astonishing how many responsibilities he had acquired, and how difficult it was to divest himself of them. He had never found it easy to delegate power (a fatal flaw, many critics had said, in a man who hoped to be Chief Executive), but now he must do so, before it slipped forever from his hands.

It was as if a great clock was running down, and there was no one to rewind it. As he gave away his books, read and destroyed old letters, closed useless accounts and files, dictated final instructions, and wrote farewell notes, he sometimes felt a sense of complete unreality. There was no pain; he could never have guessed that he did not have years of active life ahead of him. Only a few lines on a cardiogram lay like a roadblock across his future—or like a curse, written in some strange language the doctors alone could read.

Almost every day now Diana, Irene, or her husband brought the children to see him. In the past he had never felt at ease with Bill, but that, he knew, had been his own fault. You could not expect a son-in-law to replace a son, and it was unfair to blame Bill because he had not been cast in the image of Martin Steelman, Jr. Bill was a person in his own right; he had looked after Irene, made her happy, and fathered her children. That he lacked ambition was a flaw—if flaw indeed it was—that the Senator could at last forgive.

He could even think, without pain or bitterness, of his own son, who had traveled this road before him and now lay, one cross among many, in the United Nations cemetery at Capetown. He had never visited Martin's grave; in the days when he had the time, white men were not popular in what was left of South Africa. Now he could go if he wished, but he was uncertain if it would be fair to harrow Diana with such a mission. His own memories would not trouble him much longer, but she would be left with hers.

Yet he would like to go, and felt it was his duty. Moreover, it would be a last treat for the children. To them it would be only a holiday in a strange land, without any tinge of sorrow for an uncle they had never known. He had started to make the arrangements when, for the second time within a month, his whole world was turned upside down.

Even now, a dozen or more visitors would be waiting for him each morning when he arrived at his office. Not as many as in the old days, but still a sizable crowd. He had never imagined, however, that Dr. Harkness would be among them.

The sight of that thin, gangling figure made him momentarily break his stride. He felt his cheeks flush, his pulse quicken at the memory of ancient battles across committee-room tables, of angry exchanges that had reverberated along the myriad channels of the ether. Then he relaxed; as far as he was concerned, all that was over.

Harkness rose to his feet, a little awkwardly, as he approached. Senator Steelman knew that initial embarrassment—he had seen it so often in the last few weeks.

Everyone he now met was automatically at a disadvantage, always on the alert to avoid the one subject that was taboo.

"Well, Doctor," he said. "This is a surprise—I never expected to see *you* here."

He could not resist that little jab, and derived some satisfaction at watching it go home. But it was free from bitterness, as the other's smile acknowledged.

"Senator," replied Harkness, in a voice that was pitched so low that he had to lean forward to hear it, "I've some extremely important information for you. Can we speak alone for a few minutes? It won't take long."

Steelman nodded; he had his own ideas of what was important now, and felt only a mild curiosity as to why the scientist had come to see him. The man seemed to have changed a good deal since their last encounter, seven years ago. He was much more assured and self-confident, and had lost the nervous mannerisms that had helped to make him such an unconvincing witness.

"Senator," he began, when they were alone in the private office, "I've some news that may be quite a shock to you. I believe that you can be cured."

Steelman slumped heavily in his chair. This was the one thing he had never expected; from the first, he had not encumbered himself with the burden of vain hopes. Only a fool fought against the inevitable, and he had accepted his fate.

For a moment he could not speak; then he looked up at his old adversary and gasped: "Who told you that? All my doctors—"

"Never mind them; it's not their fault they're ten years behind the times. Look at this."

"What does it mean? I can't read Russian."

"It's the latest issue of the USSR *Journal of Space Medicine*. It arrived a few days ago, and we did the usual routine translation. This note here—the one I've marked—refers to some recent work at the Mechnikov Station."

"What's that?"

"You don't *know*? Why, that's their Satellite Hospital, the one they've built just below the Great Radiation Belt."

"Go on," said Steelman, in a voice that was suddenly dry and constricted. "I'd forgotten they'd called it that." He had hoped to end his life in peace, but now the past had come back to haunt him.

"Well, the note itself doesn't say much, but you can read a lot between the lines. It's one of those advance hints that scientists put out before they have time to write a full-fledged paper, so they can claim priority later. The title is: 'Therapeutic Effects of Zero Gravity on Circulatory Diseases.' What they've done is to induce heart disease artificially in rabbits and hamsters, and then take them up to the space station. In orbit, of course, nothing has any weight; the heart and muscles have practically no work to do. And the result is exactly what I tried to tell you, years ago. Even extreme cases can be arrested, and many can be cured."

The tiny, paneled office that had been the center of his world, the scene of so many conferences, the birthplace of so many plans, became suddenly unreal. Memory was much more vivid: he was back again at those hearings, in the fall of 1969, when the National Aeronautics and Space Administration's first decade of activity had been under review— and, frequently, under fire.

He had never been chairman of the Senate Committee on Astronautics, but he had been its most vocal and effective member. It was here that he had made his reputation as a guardian of the public purse, as a hardheaded man who could not be bamboozled by utopian scientific dreamers. He had done a good job; from that moment, he had never been far from the headlines. It was not that he had any particular feeling for space and science, but he knew a live issue when he saw one. Like a tape-recorder unrolling in his mind, it all came back. . . .

"Dr. Harkness, you are Technical Director of the National Aeronautics and Space Administration?"

"That is correct."

"I have here the figures for NASA's expenditure over the period 1959–69; they are quite impressive. At the moment the total is $82,547,450,000, and the estimate for fiscal 69–70 is well over ten billions. Perhaps you could give us some indication of the return we can expect from all this."

"I'll be glad to do so, Senator."

That was how it had started, on a firm but not unfriendly note. The hostility had crept in later. That it was unjustified, he had known at the time; any big organization had weaknesses and failures, and one which literally aimed at the stars could never hope for more than partial success. From the beginning, it had been realized that the conquest of space would be at least as costly in lives and treasure as the conquest of the air. In ten years, almost a hundred men had died—on Earth, in space, and upon the barren surface of the Moon. Now that the urgency of the early sixties was over, the public was asking "Why?" Steelman was shrewd enough to see himself as mouthpiece for those questioning voices. His performance had been cold and calculated; it was convenient to have a scapegoat, and Dr. Harkness was unlucky enough to be cast for the role.

"Yes, Doctor, I understand all the benefits we've received from space research in the way of improved communications and weather forecasting, and I'm sure everyone appreciates them. But almost all this work has been done with automatic, unmanned vehicles. What I'm worried about—what many people are worried about—is the mounting expense of the Man-in-Space program, and its very marginal utility. Since the original Dyna-Soar and Apollo projects, almost a decade ago, we've shot billions of dollars into space. And with what result? So that a mere handful of men can spend a few uncomfortable hours outside the atmosphere, achieving nothing that television cameras and automatic equipment couldn't do—much better and cheaper. And the lives that have been lost! None of us will forget those screams we heard coming over the radio when the X-21 burned up on re-entry. What right have we to send men to such deaths?"

He could still remember the hushed silence in the committee chamber when he had finished. His questions were very reasonable ones, and deserved to be answered. What was unfair was the rhetorical manner in which he had framed them and, above all, the fact that they were aimed at a man who could not answer them effectively. Steelman would not have tried such tactics on a von Braun or a Rickover; they would have given him at least as good as they received. But Harkness was no orator; if he had deep personal feelings, he kept them to himself. He was a good scientist, an able administrator—and a poor witness. It had been like shooting fish in a barrel. The reporters had loved it; he never knew which of them coined the nickname "Hapless Harkness."

"Now this plan of yours, Doctor, for a fifty-man space laboratory—*how* much did you say it would cost?"

"I've already told you—just under one and a half billions."

"And the annual maintenance?"

"Not more than $250,000,000."

"When we consider what's happened to previous estimates, you will forgive us if we look upon these figures with some skepticism. But even assuming that they are right, what will we get for the money?"

"We will be able to establish our first large-scale research station in space. So far, we have had to do our experimenting in cramped quarters aboard unsuitable vehicles, usually when they were engaged on some other mission. A permanent, manned satellite laboratory is essential. Without it, further progress is out of the question. Astrobiology can hardly get started—"

"Asto what?"

"Astrobiology—the study of living organisms in space. The Russians really started it when they sent up the dog Laika in Sputnik II and they're still ahead of us in this field. But no one's done any serious work on insects or invertebrates—in fact, on any animals except dogs, mice, and monkeys."

"I see. Would I be correct in saying that you would like funds for building a zoo in space?"

The laughter in the committee-room had helped to kill the project. And it had helped, Senator Steelman now realized, to kill him.

He had only himself to blame, for Dr. Harkness had tried, in his ineffectual way, to outline the benefits that a space laboratory might bring. He had particularly stressed the medical aspects, promising nothing but pointing out the possibilities. Surgeons, he had suggested, would be able to develop new techniques in an environment where the organs had no weight; men might live longer, freed from the wear and tear of gravity, for the strain on heart and muscles would be enormously reduced. Yes, he had mentioned the heart; but that had been of no interest to Senator

Steelman—healthy, and ambitious, and anxious to make good copy. . . .

"Why have you come to tell me this?" he said dully. "Couldn't you let me die in peace?"

"That's the point," said Harkness impatiently. "There's no need to give up hope."

"Because the Russians have cured some hamsters and rabbits?"

"They've done much more than that. The paper I showed you only quoted the preliminary results; it's already a year out of date. They don't want to raise false hopes, so they are keeping as quiet as possible."

"How do you know this?"

Harkness looked surprised.

"Why, I called Professor Stanyukovitch, my opposite number. It turned out that he was up on the Mechnikov Station, which proves how important they consider this work. He's an old friend of mine, and I took the liberty of mentioning your case."

The dawn of hope, after its long absence, can be as painful as its departure. Steelman found it hard to breathe and for a dreadful moment he wondered if the final attack had come. But it was only excitement; the constriction in his chest relaxed, the ringing in his ears faded away, and he heard Dr. Harkness' voice saying: "He wanted to know if you could come to Astrograd right away, so I said I'd ask you. If you can make it, there's a flight from New York at ten-thirty tomorrow morning."

Tomorrow he had promised to take the children to the Zoo; it would be the first time he had let them down. The thought gave him a sharp stab of guilt, and it required almost an effort of will to answer: "I can make it."

He saw nothing of Moscow during the few minutes that the big intercontinental ramjet fell down from the stratosphere. The view-screens were switched off during the descent, for the sight of the ground coming straight up as a ship fell vertically on its sustaining jets was highly disconcerting to passengers.

At Moscow he changed to a comfortable but old-fashioned turboprop, and as he flew eastward into the night he had his first real opportunity for reflection. It was a very strange question to ask himself, but was he altogether glad that the future was no longer wholly certain? His life, which a few hours ago had seemed so simple, had suddenly become complex again, as it opened out once more into possibilities he had learned to put aside. Dr. Johnson had been right when he said that nothing settles a man's mind more wonderfully than the knowledge that he will be hanged in the morning. For the converse was certainly true—nothing unsettled it so much as the thought of a reprieve.

He was asleep when they touched down at Astrograd, the space capital of the USSR. When the gentle impact of the landing shook him awake, for a moment he could not imagine where he was. Had he dreamed that he was flying halfway around the world in search of life? No; it was not a dream, but it might well be a wild-goose chase.

Twelve hours later, he was still waiting for the answer. The last instrument reading had been taken; the spots of light on the cardiograph display had ceased their fateful dance. The familiar routine of the medical examination and the gentle, competent voices of the doctors and nurses had done much to relax his mind. And it was very restful in the softly lit reception room, where the specialists had asked him to wait while they conferred together. Only the Russian magazines, and a few portraits of somewhat hirsute pioneers of Soviet medicine, reminded him that he was no longer in his own country.

He was not the only patient. About a dozen men and women, of all ages, were sitting around the wall, reading magazines and trying to appear at ease. There was no conversation, no attempt to catch anyone's eye. Every soul in this room was in his private limbo, suspended between life and death. Though they were linked together by a common misfortune, the link did not extend to communication. Each seemed as cut off from the rest of the human race as if he was already speeding through the cosmic gulfs where lay his only hope.

But in the far corner of the room, there was an exception. A young couple—neither could have been more than twenty-five—were huddling together in such desperate misery that at first Steelman found the spectacle annoying. No matter how bad their own problems, he told himself severely, people should be more considerate. They should hide their emotions—especially in a place like this, where they might upset others.

His annoyance quickly turned to pity, for no heart can remain untouched for long at the sight of simple, unselfish love in deep distress. As the minutes dripped away in a silence broken only by the rustling of papers and the scraping of chairs, his pity grew almost to an obsession.

What was their story, he wondered? The boy had sensitive, intelligent features; he might have been an artist, a scientist, a musician—there was no way of telling. The girl was pregnant; she had one of those homely peasant faces so common among Russian women. She was far from beautiful, but sorrow and love had given her features a luminous sweetness. Steelman found it hard to take his eyes from her—for somehow, though there was not the slightest physical resemblance, she reminded him of Diana. Thirty years ago, as they had walked from the church together, he had seen that same glow in the eyes of his wife. He had almost forgotten it; was the fault his, or hers, that it had faded so soon?

Without any warning, his chair vibrated beneath him. A swift, sudden tremor had swept through the building, as if a giant hammer had smashed against the ground, many miles away. An earthquake? Steelman wondered; then he remembered where he was, and started counting seconds.

He gave up when he reached sixty; presumably the sound-proofing was so good that the slower, air-borne noise had not reached him, and only the shock wave through the ground recorded the fact that a thousand tons had just leapt into the sky. Another minute passed before he heard, distant but clear, a sound as of a thunderstorm raging below the edge of the world. It was even more miles away than he had dreamed; what the noise must be like at the launching site was beyond imagination.

Yet that thunder would not trouble him, he knew, when he also rose into the sky; the speeding rocket would leave it far behind. Nor would the thrust of acceleration be able to touch his body, as it rested in its bath of warm water— more comfortable even than this deeply padded chair.

That distant rumble was still rolling back from the edge

of space when the door of the waiting room opened and the nurse beckoned to him. Though he felt many eyes following him, he did not look back as he walked out to receive his sentence.

The news services tried to get in contact with him all the way back from Moscow, but he refused to accept the calls. "Say I'm sleeping and mustn't be disturbed," he told the stewardess. He wondered who had tipped them off, and felt annoyed at this invasion of his privacy. Yet privacy was something he had avoided for years, and had learned to appreciate only in the last few weeks. He could not blame the reporters and commentators if they assumed that he had reverted to type.

They were waiting for him when the ramjet touched down at Washington. He knew most of them by name, and some were old friends, genuinely glad to hear the news that had raced ahead of him.

"What does it feel like, Senator," said Macauley, of the *Times*, "to know you're back in harness? I take it that it's true—the Russians can cure you?"

"They *think* they can," he answered cautiously. "This is a new field of medicine, and no one can promise anything."

"When do you leave for space?"

"Within the week, as soon as I've settled some affairs here."

"And when will you be back—if it works?"

"That's hard to say. Even if everything goes smoothly, I'll be up there at least six months."

Involuntarily, he glanced at the sky. At dawn or sunset—even during the daytime, if one knew where to look—the Mechnikov Station was a spectacular sight, more brilliant than any of the stars. But there were now so many satellites of which this was true that only an expert could tell one from another.

"Six months," said a newsman thoughtfully. "That means you'll be out of the picture for seventy-six."

"But nicely in it for 1980," said another.

"*And* 1984," added a third. There was a general laugh; people were already making jokes about 1984, which had once seemed so far in the future, but would soon be a date no different from any other . . . it was hoped.

The ears and the microphones were waiting for his reply. As he stood at the foot of the ramp, once more the focus of attention and curiosity, he felt the old excitement stirring in his veins. What a comeback it would be, to return from space a new man! It would give him a glamour that no other candidate could match; there was something Olympian, almost godlike, about the prospect. Already he found himself trying to work it into his election slogans. . . .

"Give me time to make my plans," he said. "It's going to take me a while to get used to this. But I promise you a statement before I leave Earth."

Before I leave Earth. Now, there was a fine, dramatic phrase. He was still savoring its rhythm with his mind when he saw Diana coming toward him from the airport buildings.

Already she had changed, as he himself was changing; in her eyes was a wariness and reserve that had not been there two days ago. It said, as clearly as any words: "Is it going to happen, all over again?" Though the day was warm, he felt suddenly cold, as if he had caught a chill on those far Siberian plains.

But Joey and Susan were unchanged, as they ran to greet him. He caught them up in his arms, and buried his face in their hair, so that the cameras would not see the tears that had started from his eyes. As they clung to him in the innocent, unself-conscious love of childhood, he knew what his choice would have to be.

They alone had known him when he was free from the itch for power; that was the way they must remember him, if they remembered him at all.

"Your conference call, Mr. Steelman," said his secretary. "I'm routing it on to your private screen."

He swiveled round in his chair and faced the gray panel on the wall. As he did so, it split into two vertical sections. On the right half was a view of an office much like his own, and only a few miles away. But on the left—

Professor Stanyukovitch, lightly dressed in shorts and singlet, was floating in mid-air a good foot above his seat. He grabbed it when he saw that he had company, pulled himself down, and fastened a webbed belt around his waist. Behind him were ranged banks of communications equipment; and behind those, Steelman knew, was space.

Dr. Harkness spoke first, from the right-hand screen.

"We were expecting to hear from you, Senator. Professor Stanyukovitch tells me that everything is ready."

"The next supply ship," said the Russian, "comes up in two days. It will be taking me back to Earth, but I hope to see you before I leave the station."

His voice was curiously high-pitched, owing to the thin oxyhelium atmosphere he was breathing. Apart from that, there was no sense of distance, no background of interference. Though Stanyukovitch was thousands of miles away, and racing through space at four miles a second, he might have been in the same office. Steelman could even hear the faint whirring of electric motors from the equipment racks behind him.

"Professor," answered Steelman, "there are a few things I'd like to ask before I go."

"Certainly."

Now he could tell that Stanyukovitch was a long way off. There was an appreciable time lag before his reply arrived; the station must be above the far side of the Earth.

"When I was at Astrograd, I noticed many other patients at the clinic. I was wondering—on what basis do you select those for treatment?"

This time the pause was much greater than the delay due to the sluggish speed of radio waves. Then Stanyukovitch answered: "Why, those with the best chance of responding."

"But your accommodation must be very limited. You must have many other candidates besides myself."

"I don't quite see the point—" interrupted Dr. Harkness, a little too anxiously.

Steelman swung his eyes to the right hand screen. It was quite difficult to recognize, in the man staring back at him, the witness who had squirmed beneath his needling only a few years ago. That experience had tempered Harkness, had given him his baptism in the art of politics. Steelman had taught him much, and he had applied his hard-won knowledge.

His motives had been obvious from the first. Harkness would have been less than human if he did not relish this sweetest of revenges, this triumphant vindication of his faith. And as Space Administration Director, he was well aware that half his budget battles would be over when all the world knew that a potential President of the United States was in a Russian space hospital . . . because his own country did not possess one.

"Dr. Harkness," said Steelman gently, "this is *my* affair. I'm still waiting for your answer, Professor."

Despite the issues involved, he was quite enjoying this. The two scientists, of course, were playing for identical stakes. Stanyukovitch had his problems too; Steelman could guess the discussions that had taken place at Astrograd and Moscow, and the eagerness with which the Soviet astronauts had grasped this opportunity—which, it must be admitted, they had richly earned.

It was an ironic situation, unimaginable only a dozen years before. Here were NASA and the USSR Commission of Astronautics working hand in hand, using him as a pawn for their mutual advantage. He did not resent this, for in their place he would have done the same. But he had no wish to be a pawn; he was an individual who still had some control of his own destiny.

"It's quite true," said Stanyukovitch, very reluctantly, "that we can only take a limited number of patients here in Mechnikov. In any case, the station's a research laboratory, not a hospital."

"How many?" asked Steelman relentlessly.

"Well—fewer than ten," admitted Stanyukovitch, still more unwillingly.

It was an old problem, of course, though he had never imagined that it would apply to him. From the depths of memory there flashed a newspaper item he had come across long ago. When penicillin had been first discovered, it was so rare that if both Churchill and Roosevelt had been dying for lack of it, only one could have been treated. . . .

Fewer than ten. He had seen a dozen waiting at Astrograd, and how many were there in the whole world? Once again, as it had done so often in the last few days, the memory of those desolate lovers in the reception room came back to haunt him. Perhaps they were beyond his aid; he would never know.

But one thing he did know. He bore a responsibility that he could not escape. It was true that no man could foresee the future, and the endless consequences of his actions. Yet if it had not been for him, by this time his own country might have had a space hospital circling beyond the atmosphere. How many American lives were upon his conscience? Could he accept the help he had denied to others? Once he might have done so—but not now.

"Gentlemen," he said, "I can speak frankly with you both, for I know your interests are identical." (His mild irony, he saw, did not escape them.) "I appreciate your help and the trouble you have taken; I am sorry it has been wasted. No—don't protest; this isn't a sudden, quixotic decision on my part. If I was ten years younger, it might be different. Now I feel that this opportunity should be given to someone else—especially in view of my record." He glanced at Dr. Harkness, who gave an embarrassed smile. "I also have other, personal reasons, and there's no chance that I will change my mind. Please don't think me rude or ungrateful, but I don't wish to discuss the matter any further. Thank you again, and good-by."

He broke the circuit; and as the image of the two astonished scientists faded, peace came flooding back into his soul.

Imperceptibly, spring merged into summer. The eagerly awaited Bicentenary celebrations came and went; for the first time in years, he was able to enjoy Independence Day as a private citizen. Now he could sit back and watch the others perform—or he could ignore them if he wished.

Because the ties of a lifetime were too strong to break, and it would be his last opportunity to see many old friends, he spent hours looking in on both conventions and listening to the commentators. Now that he saw the whole world beneath the light of Eternity, his emotions were no longer involved; he understood the issues, and appreciated the arguments, but already he was as detached as an observer from another planet. The tiny, shouting figures on the screen were amusing marionettes, acting out roles in a play that was entertaining, but no longer important—at least, to him.

But it was important to his grandchildren, who would one day move out onto this same stage. He had not forgotten that; they were his share of the future, whatever strange form it might take. And to understand the future, it was necessary to know the past.

He was taking them into that past, as the car swept along Memorial Drive. Diana was at the wheel, with Irene beside her, while he sat with the children, pointing out the familiar sights along the highway. Familiar to him, but not to them; even if they were not old enough to understand all that they were seeing, he hoped they would remember.

Past the marble stillness of Arlington (he thought again of Martin, sleeping on the other side of the world) and up into the hills the car wound its effortless way. Behind them, like a city seen through a mirage, Washington danced and trembled in the summer haze, until the curve of the road hid it from view.

It was quiet at Mount Vernon; there were few visitors so early in the week. As they left the car and walked toward the house, Steelman wondered what the first President of the United States would have thought could he have seen his home as it was today. He could never have dreamed that it would enter its second century still perfectly preserved, a changeless island in the hurrying river of time.

They walked slowly through the beautifully proportioned rooms, doing their best to answer the children's endless questions, trying to assimilate the flavor of an infinitely simpler, infinitely more leisurely mode of life. (But had it seemed simple or leisurely to those who lived it?) It was so hard to imagine a world without electricity, without radio, without any power save that of muscle, wind, and water. A world where nothing moved faster than a running horse, and most men died within a few miles of the place where they were born.

The heat, the walking, and the incessant questions proved more tiring than Steelman had expected. When they had reached the Music Room, he decided to rest. There were some attractive benches out on the porch, where he could sit in the fresh air and feast his eyes upon the green grass of the lawn.

"Meet me outside," he explained to Diana, "when you've done the kitchen and the stables. I'd like to sit down for a while."

"You're sure you're quite all right?" she said anxiously.

"I never felt better, but I don't want to overdo it.

Besides, the kids have drained me dry—I can't think of any more answers. You'll have to invent some; the kitchen's your department, anyway."

Diana smiled.

"I was never much good in it, was I? But I'll do my best—I don't suppose we'll be more than thirty minutes."

When they had left him, he walked slowly out onto the lawn. Here Washington must have stood, two centuries ago, watching the Potomac wind its way to the sea, thinking of past wars and future problems. And here Martin Steelman, thirty-eighth President of the United States, might have stood a few months hence, had the fates ruled otherwise.

He could not pretend that he had no regrets, but they were very few. Some men could achieve both power and happiness, but that gift was not for him. Sooner or later, his ambition would have consumed him. In the last few weeks he had known contentment, and for that no price was too great.

He was still marveling at the narrowness of his escape when his time ran out and Death fell softly from the summer sky.

THE QUAKER CANNON

BY FREDERIK POHL (1919-   )
AND C. M. KORNBLUTH (1923-1958)

ANALOG SCIENCE FICTION
AUGUST

One of the most famous writing teams in science-fiction history, Frederik Pohl and Cyril Kornbluth will always be remembered for their dystopian novels The Space Merchants *(1953) and* Gladiator-at-Law *(1955). However, they also produced much other excellent collaborative work, including the novels* Search the Sky *(1954) and* Wolfbane *(1959), as well as the stories contained in* The Wonder Effect *(1962; revised as* Critical Mass *in 1977).*

A number of the short stories were finished by Fred Pohl from fragments and ideas years after Cyril's untimely death in 1958. This is true of "The Quaker Cannon," one of their best ideas and one of the best stories of 1961. (MHG)

Back in 1938, a group of young and penurious science fiction fans got together and formed an association commonly known as the Futurians. The leading spirit was Donald A. Wollheim, who was 24 years old at the time and looked up to by the rest of us as a venerable gentleman.

Frederik Pohl, C.M. Kornbluth, Robert W. Lowndes, Damon Knight, and a number of others were also members. And so was I.

We had no way of knowing in those prehistoric days how important most of us would become in the science fiction field as writers, editors, critics, and so on.

Of all the Futurians, Cyril Kornbluth was the youngest. He was only 15 when the Futurians came into being. He was also the most brilliant and it was clear to me by the early

217

1950s that he probably would not remain in science fiction. He was edging toward the mainstream and it was my idea he would succeed there.

But as it happened, he was also the first of us to die, his giant potential remaining unused. Fred Pohl, who thought as highly of Cyril as I did has labored to keep his memory alive. (IA)

I

Lieutenant John Kramer did crossword puzzles during at least eighty percent of his waking hours. His cubicle in Bachelor Officers Quarters was untidy; one wall was stacked solid with newspapers and magazines to which he subscribed for their puzzle pages. He meant, from week to week, to clean them out but somehow never found time. The ern, or erne, a sea eagle, soared vertically through his days and by night the ai, a three-toed sloth, crept horizontally. In edes, or Dutch communes, dyers retted ecru, quaffing ades by the tun and thought was postponed.

John Kramer was in disgrace and, at thirty-eight, well on his way to becoming the oldest first lieutenant in the North American—and Allied—Army. He had been captured in '82 as an aftermath of the confused fighting around Tsingtao. A few exquisitely unpleasant months passed and he then delivered three TV lectures for the yutes. In them he announced his total conversion to Neo-Utilitarianism, denounced the North American—and Allied—military command as a loathsome pack of war-raging, anti-utilitarian mad dogs, and personally admitted the waging of viral warfare against the United Utilitarian Republics.

The yutes, or Utilitarians, had been faithful to their principles. They had wanted Kramer only for what he could do for them, not for his own sweet self, and when they had got the juice out of him they exchanged him. In '83 he came out of his fog at Fort Bradley, Utah, to find himself being court-martialed.

He was found guilty as charged, and sentenced to a reprimand. The lightness of the sentence was something to be a little proud of, if not very much. It stood as a grudging tribute to the months he had held out against involutional melancholia in the yute Blank Tanks. For exchanged PW's, the severity of their courts-martial was in inverse proportion to the duration of their ordeal in Utilitarian hands. Soldiers who caved in after a couple of days of sense-starvation could look forward only to a firing squad. Presumably a returned soldier dogged—or rigid—enough to be driven into hopeless insanity without co-operating would have been honorably acquitted by his court, but such a case had not yet come up.

Kramer's "reprimand" was not the face-to-face bawling-out suggested to a civilian by the word. It was a short letter with numbered paragraphs which said (1) you are reprimanded, (2) a copy of this reprimand will be punched on your profile card. This tagged him forever as a foul ball, destined to spend the rest of his military life shuffling from one dreary assignment to another, without hope of promotion or reward.

He no longer cared. Or thought he did not; which came to the same thing.

He was not liked in the Officers Club. He was bad company. Young officers passing through Bradley on their way to glory might ask him, "What's it *really* like in a Blank Tank, Kramer?" But beyond answering, "You go nuts," what was there to talk about? Also he did not drink, because when he drank he went on to become drunk, and if he became drunk he would cry.

So he did a crossword puzzle in bed before breakfast, dressed, went to his office, signed papers, did puzzles until lunch, and so on until the last one in bed at night. Nominally he was Commanding Officer of the 561st Provisional Reception Battalion. Actually he was—with a few military overtones—the straw boss of a gang of clerks in uniform who saw to the arrival, bedding, feeding, equipping, inoculation and transfer to a training unit of one thousand scared kids per week.

On a drizzle-swept afternoon in the spring of '85 Kramer was sounding one of those military overtones. It was his appointed day for a "surprise" inspection of Company D of his battalion. Impeccable in dress blues, he was supposed to descend like a thunderbolt on this company or that, catching them all unaware, striding arrogantly down the barracks aisle between bunks, white-gloved and eagle-eyed for dust, maddened at the sight of disarray, vengeful against such contraband as playing cards or light reading matter. Kramer knew, quite well, that one of his orderly room clerks always telephoned the doomed company to warn that he was on his way. He did not particularly mind it. What he minded was unfair definitions of key words, and ridiculously variant spellings.

The permanent-party sergeant of D Company bawled "Tench-*hut!*" when Kramer snapped the door open and stepped crisply into the barracks. Kramer froze his face into its approved expression of controlled annoyance and opened his mouth to give the noncom his orders. But the sergeant had miscalculated. One of the scared kids was still frantically mopping the aisle.

Kramer halted. The kid spun around in horror, made some kind of attempt to present arms with the mop and failed. The mop shot from his soapy hands like a slung baseball bat, and its soggy gray head schlooped against the lieutenant's dress-blue chest.

The kid turned white and seemed about to faint on the damp board floor. The other kids waited to see him destroyed.

Kramer was mildly irritated. "At ease," he said. "Pick up that mop. Sergeant, confound it, next time they buzz you from the orderly room don't cut it so close."

The kids sighed perceptibly and glanced covertly at each other in the big bare room, beginning to suspect it might not be too bad after all. Lieutenant Kramer then resumed the expression of a nettled bird of prey and strode down the aisle. Long ago he had worked out a "random" selection of bunks for special attention and now followed it through habit. If he had thought about it any more, he would have supposed that it was still spy-proof; but every noncom in his cadre had long since discovered that Kramer stopped at either every second bunk on the right and every third on the left, or every third bunk on the right and every second on the left—depending on whether the day of the month was odd or even. This would not have worried Kramer if he had known· it; but he never even noticed that the men beside the bunks he stopped at were always the best-shaved, best-policed and healthiest looking in each barracks.

Regardless, he delivered a certain quota of meaningless

demerits which were gravely recorded by the sergeant. Of blue-eyed men on the left and brown-eyed men on the right—this, at least, had not been penetrated by the noncoms—he went on to ask their names and home towns. Before discovering crossword puzzles he had memorized atlases, and so he had something to say about every home town he had yet encountered. In this respect at least he considered himself an above-average officer, and indeed he was.

It wasn't the Old Army, not by a long shot, but when the draft age went down to fifteen some of the Old Army's little ways had to go. One experimental reception station in Virginia was trying out a Barracks Mother system. Kramer, thankful for small favors, was glad they hadn't put him on that project. Even here he was expected, at the end of the inspection, to call the "men" around him and ask if anything was bothering them. Something always was. Some gangling kid would scare up the nerve to ask, gee, lieutenant, I know what the Morale Officer said, but exactly *why* didn't we ever use the megaton-head missiles, and another would want to know how come Lunar Base was such a washout, tactically speaking, sir. And then he would have to rehearse the dry "recommended discussion themes" from the briefing books; and then, finally, one of them, nudged on by others, would pipe up, "Lieutenant, what's it *like* in the Blank Tanks?" And he would know that already, forty-eight hours after induction, the kids all knew about what Lieutenant John Kramer had done.

But today he was spared. When he was halfway through the rigmarole the barracks phone rang and the sergeant apologetically answered it.

He returned from his office-cubicle on the double, looking vaguely frightened. "Compliments of General Grote's secretary, sir, and will you report to him at G-1 immediately."

"Thank you, Sergeant. Step outside with me a moment."

Out on the duckboard walk, with the drizzle trickling down his neck, he asked: "Sergeant, who is General Grote?"

"Never heard of him, sir."

Neither had Lieutenant Kramer.

* * *

He hurried to Bachelor Officers Quarters to change his sullied blue jacket, not even pausing to glance at the puzzle page of the *Times*, which had arrived while he was at "work." Generals were special. He hurried out again into the drizzle.

Around him and unnoticed were the artifacts of an army base at war. Sky-eye search radars popped from their silos to scan the horizons for a moment and then retreat, the burden of search taken up by the next in line. Helicopter sentries on guard duty prowled the barbed-wire perimeter of the camp. Fort Bradley was not all reception center. Aboveground were the barracks, warehouses and rail and highway termini for processing recruits—ninety thousand men and all their goods—but they were only the skin over the fort itself. They were, as the scared kids told each other in the dayrooms, naked to the air. If the yutes ever *did* spring a megaton attack, they would become a thin coating of charcoal on the parade ground, but they would not affect the operation of the *real* Fort Bradley a bit.

The *real* Fort Bradley was a hardened installation beneath meters of reinforced concrete, some miles of rambling warrens that held the North American—and Allied—Army's G-1. Its business was people: the past, present and future of every soul in the Army.

G-1 decided that a fifteen-year-old in Duluth was unlikely to succeed in civilian schools and drafted him. G-1 punched his Army test and civilian records on cards, consulted its card-punched tables of military requirements and assigned him, perhaps, to Machinist Training rather than Telemetering School. G-1 yanked a platoon leader halfway around the world from Formosa and handed him a commando for a raid on the yutes' Polar Station Seven. G-1 put foulball Kramer at the "head" of the 561st PRB. G-1 promoted and allocated and staffed and rewarded and punished.

Foulball Kramer approached the guardbox at the elevators to the warrens and instinctively squared his shoulders and smoothed his tie.

General Grote, he thought. He hadn't *seen* a general officer since he'd been commissioned. Not close up. Colonels and majors had court-martialed him. He didn't know who Grote was, whether he had one star or six, whether he was

Assignment, Qualifications, Training, Evaluation, Psycho-
logical—or Disciplinary.

Military Police looked him over at the elevator head.
They read him like a book. Kramer wore his record on his
chest and sleeves. Dull gold bars spelled out the overseas
months—for his age and arm, the Infantry, not enough.
"Formosa," said a green ribbon, and "the storming of the
beach" said a small bronze spearpoint on it. A brown ribbon told them "Chinese Mainland," and the stars on it
_____ engaged in three of the five mainland
_____ bly Canton, Mukden and Tsingtao,
_____ t. After that, nothing. Especially not
_____ might indicate a wound serious
_____ of further fighting.
_____ d the fact that he was still a first
_____ ough for the MPs to despise him.
_____ ould be a captain at least. Many
_____ e colonels. "You can go down,
_____ patient foulball, and he went
_____ oncrete tunnels of G-1.
_____ dered the name *General Grote*
_____ oard, and told him with a map
_____ e found. It was a longish walk
_____ e walked past banks of clicking
_____ ts he pondered other informa-
_____ ously supplied:

_____ Gen, 0-459732,

_____ ramer's puzzles. A three-star
_____ *sibly* have anything to do with
_____ Lieutenant generals ran Army
_____ mblages of up to a hundred
_____ rces, missile groups, amphibi-
_____ and missile-sub task forces.
_____ d that, whoever he was, he
_____ acious person. He had gone
_____ threshing of the wheat from
_____ and evaluation boards from
s_____ ......tenant to, say, lieutenant colonel, and then the
murderous grind of accelerated courses at Command and

General Staff School, the fanatically rigid selection for the War College, an obstacle course designed not to train the sub-standard up to competence but to keep them out. It was just this side of impossible for a human being to become a lieutenant general. And yet a few human beings in every generation did bulldoze their way through the little gap between the impossible and the almost impossible.

And such a man was unassigned?

Kramer found the office at last. A motherly, but sharp-eyed, WAC major told him to go right in.

John Kramer studied his three-star general while going through the ancient rituals of reporting-as-ordered. General Grote was an old man, straight, spare, white-haired, tanned. He wore no overseas bars. On his chest were all the meritorious ribbons his country could bestow, but none of the decorations of the combat soldier. This was explained by a modest sunburst centered over the ribbons. General Grote was, had always been, General Staff Corps. A desk man.

"Sit down, Lieutenant," Grote said, eying him casually. "You've never heard of me, I assume."

"I'm afraid not, sir."

"As I expected," said Grote complacently. "I'm not a dashing tank commander or one of those flying generals who leads his own raids. I'm one of the people who moves the dashing tank commanders and flying generals around the board like chess pieces. And now, confound it, I'm going to be a dashing combat leader at last. You may smoke if you like."

Kramer obediently lit up.

"Dan Medway," said the general, "wants me to start from scratch, build up a striking force and hit the Asian mainland across the Bering Strait."

Kramer was horrified twice—first by the reference to The Supreme Commander as "Dan" and second by the fact that he, a lieutenant, was being told about high strategy.

"Relax," the general said. "You're going to be my aide."

Kramer was horrified again. The general grinned.

"Your card popped out of the machinery," he said, and that was all there was to say about it, "and so you're going to be a highly privileged character and everybody will detest

you. That's the way it is with aides. You'll know everything
I know. And vice versa; that's the important part. You'll
run errands for me, do investigations, serve as hatchet man,
see that my pajamas are pressed without starch and make
coffee the way I like it—coarse grind, brought to the boil
for just a moment in an old-fashioned coffeepot. Actually
what you'll do is what I want you to do from day to day.
For these privileges you get to wear a blue *fourragére*
around your left shoulder which marks you as a man not to
be trifled with by colonels, brigadiers or MPs. That's the
way it is with aides. And, I don't know if you have any
outside interests, women or chess or drinking. The machinery didn't mention any. But you'll have to give them up if
you do."

"Yes, sir," said Kramer. And it seemed wildly possible
that he might never touch pencil to puzzle again. With
something to *do*—

"We're Operation Ripsaw," said the general. "So far,
that's me, Margaret out there in the office and you. In
addition to other duties, you'll keep a diary of Ripsaw, by
the way, and I want you to have a summary with you at all
times in case I need it. Now call in Margaret, make a pot
of coffee, there's a little stove thing in the washroom there,
and I'll start putting together my general staff."

It started as small and as quietly as that.

II

It was a week before Kramer got back to the 561st long
enough to pick up his possessions, and then he left the
stacks of newspapers and magazines where they lay, puzzles
and all. No time. The first person to hate him was Margaret,
the motherly major. For all her rank over him, she was a
secretary and he was an aide with a *fourragére* who had the
general's willing ear. She began a policy of nonresistance
that was non-cooperation, too; she would not deliberately
obstruct him, but she would allow him to poke through the
files for ten minutes before volunteering the information
that the folder he wanted was already on the general's desk.
This interfered with the smooth performance of Kramer's
duties, and, of course, the general spotted it at once.

"It's nothing," said Kramer when the general called him on it. "I don't like to say anything."

"Go on," General Grote urged. "You're not a soldier any more; you're a rat."

"I think I can handle it, sir."

The general motioned silently to the coffeepot and waited while Kramer fixed him a cup, two sugars, no cream. He said: "Tell me everything, always. All the dirty rumors about inefficiency and favoritism. Your suspicions and hunches. Anybody that gets in your way—or more important, in mine. In the underworld they shoot stool pigeons, but here we give them blue cords for their shoulders. Do you understand?"

Kramer did. He did not ask the general to intercede with the motherly major, or transfer her; but he did handle it himself. He discovered it was very easy. He simply threatened to have her sent to Narvik.

With the others it was easier. Margaret had resented him because she was senior in Operation Ripsaw to him, but as the others were sucked in they found him there already. Instead of resentment, their attitude toward him was purely fear.

The next people to hate him were the aides of Grote's general staff because he was a wild card in the deck. The five members of the staff—Chief, Personnel, Intelligence, Plans & Training and Operations—proceeded with their orderly, systematic jobs day by day, building Ripsaw . . . until the inevitable moment when Kramer would breeze in with, "Fine job, but the general suggests—" and the unhorsing of many assumptions, and the undoing of many days' work. That was his job also. He was a bird of ill omen, a coiled snake in fair grass, a hired killer and a professional betrayer of confidences—though it was not long before there were no confidences to betray, except from an occasional young, new officer who hadn't learned his way around, and those not worth betraying. That, as the general had said, was the way with aides. Kramer wondered sometimes if he liked what he was doing, or liked himself for doing it. But he never carried the thought through. No time.

Troops completed basic training or were redeployed from rest areas and entrained, emplaned, embussed or embarked for the scattered staging areas of Ripsaw. Great forty-wheeled trucks bore nuclear cannon up the Alcan Highway at a snail's pace. Air groups and missile sections launched on training exercises over Canadian wasteland that closely resembled tundra, with grid maps that bore names like Maina Pylgin and Kamenskoe. Yet these were not Ripsaw, not yet, only the separate tools that Ripsaw would some day pick up and use.

Ripsaw itself moved to Wichita and a base of its own when its headquarters staff swelled to fifteen hundred men and women. Most of them hated Kramer.

It was never perfectly clear to Kramer what his boss had to do with the show. Kramer made his coffee, carried his briefcase, locked and unlocked his files, delivered to him those destructive tales and delivered for him those devastating suggestions, but never understood just why there had to be a Commanding General of Ripsaw.

The time they went to Washington to argue an allocation of seventy rather than sixty armored divisions for Ripsaw, for instance, General Grote just sat, smiled and smoked his pipe. It was his chief of staff, the young and brilliant Major General Cartmill, who passionately argued the case before D. Beauregard Medway, though when Grote addressed his superior it still was as "Dan." (They did get the ten extra divisions, of course.)

Back in Wichita, it was Cartmill who toiled around the clock co-ordinating. A security lid was clamped down early in the game. The fifteen hundred men and women in the Wichita camp stayed in the Wichita camp. Commerce with the outside world, except via coded messages to other elements of Ripsaw, was a capital offense—as three privates learned the hard way. But through those coded channels Cartmill reached out to every area of the North American—and Allied—world.

Personnel scoured the globe for human components that might be fitted into Ripsaw. Intelligence gathered information about that track of Siberia which they were to invade, and the waters they were to cross. Plans & Training slaved at methods of effecting the crossing and invasion efficiently, with the least—or at any rate the optimum least, consistent with requirements of speed, security and so on—losses in men and matériel. Operations studied and restudied the various ways the crossing and invasion might go right or wrong, and how a good turn of fortune could be exploited, a bad turn minimized. General Cartmill was in constant touch with all of them, his fingers on every cord in the web. So was John Kramer.

Grote ambled about all this with an air of pleased surprise.

Kramer discovered one day that there had been books written about his boss—not best-sellers with titles like *"Bloody Larry" Grote, Sword of Freedom*, but thick, gray mimeographed staff documents, in Chinese and Russian, for top-level circulation among yute commanders. He surprised Grote reading one of them—in Chinese.

The general was not embarrassed. "Just refreshing my memory of what the yutes think I'm like so I can cross them up by doing something different. Listen: 'Characteristic of this officer's philosophy of attack is varied tactics. Reference his lecture, *Lee's 1862 Campaigns*, delivered at Fort Leavenworth Command & General Staff School, attached. Opposing commanders should not expect a force under him to—hm-m-m. *Tseung*, water radical—press the advance the same way twice.' Now all I have to do is make sure we attack by the book, like Grant instead of Lee, slug it out without any brilliant variations. See how easy it is, John? How's the message center?"

Kramer had been snooping around the message center at Grote's request. It was a matter of feeding out cigarettes and smiles in return for an occasional incautious word or a hint; gumshoe work. The message center was an underground complex of encoders, decoders, transmitters, receivers and switchboards. It was staffed by a Signal Corps WAC battalion in three shifts around the clock. The girls were worked hard—though a battalion should have been enough for the job. Messages went from and to the message center linking the Wichita brain with those seventy divisions training now from Capetown to Manitoba, a carrier task force conducting exercises in the Antarctic, a fleet of landing craft growing every day on the Gulf of California. The average time-lag between receipt of messages and delivery to the Wichita personnel at destination was 12.25 minutes. The average number of erroneous transmissions detected per day was three. Both figures General Grote considered intolerable.

"It's Colonel Bucknell who's lousing it up, General. She's trying too hard. No give. Physical training twice a day, for instance, and a very hard policy on excuses. A stern attitude's filtered down from her to the detachments. Everybody's chewing out subordinates to keep themselves covered. The working girls call Bucknell 'the monster.' Their feeling is the Army's impossible to please, so what the hell."

"Relieve her," Grote said amiably. "Make her mess officer; Ripsaw chow's rotten anyway." He went back to his Chinese text.

And suddenly it all began to seem as if it really might some day rise and strike out across the Strait. From Lieutenant Kramer's Ripsaw Diary:

> At AM staff meeting CG RIPSAW xmitted order CG NAAARMY designating RIPSAW D day 15 May 1986. Gen CARTMILL observed this date allowed 45 days to form troops in final staging areas assuming RIPSAW could be staged in 10 days. CG RIPSAW stated that a 10-day staging seemed feasible. Staff concurred. CG RIPSAW so ordered. At 1357 hours CG NAAARMY concurrence received.

They were on the way.

As the days grew shorter Grote seemed to have less and less to do, and curiously so did Kramer. He had not expected this. He had been aide-de-camp to the general for nearly a year now, and he fretted when he could find no fresh treason to bring to the general's ears. He redoubled his prowling tours of the kitchens, the BOQ, the motor pools, the message center, but not even the guard mounts or the shine on the shoes of the soldiers at Retreat parade was in any way at fault. Kramer could only imagine that he was missing things. It did not occur to him that, as at last they should be, the affairs of Ripsaw had gathered enough speed to keep them straight and clean, until the general called him in one night and ordered him to pack. Grote put on his spectacles and looked over them at Kramer. "D plus five," he said, "assuming all goes well, we're moving this headquarters to Kiska. I want you to take a look-see. Arrange a plane. You can leave tomorrow."

It was, Kramer realized that night as he undressed. Just Something to Do. Evidently the hard part of his job was at an end. It was now only a question of fighting the battle, and for that the field commanders were much more important than he. For the first time in many months he thought it would be nice to do a crossword puzzle, but instead fell asleep.

It was an hour before leaving the next day that Kramer met Ripsaw's "cover."

The "cover" was another lieutenant general, a bristling and wiry man named Clough, with a brilliant combat record staked out on his chest and sleeves for the world to read. Kramer came in when his buzzer sounded, made coffee for the two generals and was aware that Grote and Clough were old pals and that the Ripsaw general was kidding the pants off his guest.

"You always were a great admirer of Georgie Patton," Grote teased. "You should be glad to follow in his footsteps. Your operation will go down in history as big and important as his historic cross-Channel smash into Le Havre."

Kramer's thoughts were full of himself—he did not much like getting even so close to the yutes as Kiska, where he would be before the sun set that night—but his ears pricked up. He could not remember any cross-Channel smash into Le Havre—by Patton or anybody else.

"Just because I came to visit your show doesn't mean you have to rib me, Larry," Clough grumbled.

"But it's such a pleasure, Mick."

Clough opened his eyes wide and looked at Grote. "I've generaled against Novotny before. If you want to know what I think of him, I'll tell you."

Pause. Then Grote, gently: "Take it easy, Mick. Look at my boy there. See him quivering with curiosity?"

Kramer's back was turned. He hoped his blush would subside before he had to turn around with the coffee. It did not.

"Caught red-faced," Grote said happily, and winked at the other general. Clough looked stonily back. "Shall we put him out of his misery, Mick? Shall we fill him in on the big picture?"

"Might as well get it over with."

"I accept your gracious assent." Grote waved for Kramer to help himself to coffee and to sit down. Clearly he was unusually cheerful today, Kramer thought. Grote said: "Lieutenant Kramer, General Clough is the gun-captain of a Quaker cannon which covers Ripsaw. He looks like a cannon. He acts like a cannon. But he isn't loaded. Like his late idol George Patton at one point in his career, General Clough is the commander of a vast force which exists on paper and in radio transmissions alone."

Clough stirred uneasily, so Grote became more serious. "We're brainwashing Continental Defense Commissar Novotny by serving up to him his old enemy as the man he'll have to fight. The yute radio intercepts are getting a perfect picture of an assault on Polar Nine being prepared under old Mick here. That's what they'll prepare to counter, of course. Ripsaw will catch them flatfooted."

Clough stirred again but did not speak.

Grote grinned. "All right. We *hope*," he conceded. "But there's a lot of planning in this thing. Of course, it's a waste of the talent of a rather remarkably able general"—Clough gave him a lifted-eyebrow look—"but you've got to have a real man at the head of the fake army group or they won't believe it. Anyway, it worked with Patton and the Nazis. Some unkind people have suggested that Patton never did a better bit of work than sitting on his knapsack in England and letting his name be used."

"Wait'll the shooting starts," Clough said sourly.

"Ike never commanded a battalion before the day he invaded North Africa, Mick. He did all right."

"Ike wasn't up against Novotny," Clough said heavily. "I can talk better while I'm eating, Larry. Want to buy me a lunch?"

General Grote nodded. "Lieutenant, see what you can charm out of Colonel Bucknell for us to eat, will you? We'll have it sent in here, of course, and the best girls she's got to serve it." Then, unusually, he stood up and looked appraisingly at Kramer.

"Have a nice flight," he said.

III

Kramer's blue *fourragére* won him cold handshakes but a seat at the first table in the Headquarters Officers Mess in Kiska. He didn't have quite enough appetite to appreciate it.

Approaching the island from the air had taken appetite away from him as the GOA autocontroller rocked the plane in a carefully calculated zigzag in its approach. They were, Kramer discovered, under direct visual observation from any chance-met bird from yute eyries across the Strait until they got below five hundred feet. Sometimes the yutes sent over a flight of birds to knock down a transport. Hence the zigzags.

Captain Mabry, a dark, tall Georgian who had been designated to make the general's aide feel at home, noticed Kramer wasn't eating, pushed his own tray into the center strip and, as it sailed away, stood up. "Get it off the pad, shall we? Cain't keep the Old Man waiting."

The captain took Kramer through clanging corridors to an elevator and then up to the eyrie. It was only a room. From it the spy-bird missiles—rockets, they were really, but the services like to think of them as having a punch, even though the punch was only a television camera—were controlled. To it the birds returned the pictures their eyes saw.

Brigadier Spiegelhauer shook Kramer's hand. "Make yourself at home, Lieutenant," he boomed. He was short and almost skeletally thin, but his voice was enormous. "Everything satisfactory for the general, I hope?"

"Why, yes, sir. I'm just looking around."

"Of course," Spiegelhauer shouted. "Care to monitor a ride?"

"Yes, sir." Mabry was looking at him with amusement, Kramer saw. Confound him, what right did *he* have to think Kramer was scared—even if he was? Not a physical fear; he was not insane. But . . . scared.

The service life of a spy-bird over yute territory was something under twenty minutes, by then the homing heads on the ground-to-air birds would have sniffed out its special fragrance and knocked it out. In that twenty-minute period it would see what it could see. Through its eyes the observers in the eyrie would learn just that much more about yute dispositions—so long as it remained in direct line-of-sight to the eyrie, so long as everything in its instrumentation worked, so long as yute jamming did not penetrate its microwave control.

Captain Mabry took Kramer's arm. "Take 'er off the pad," Mabry said negligently to the launch officer. He conducted Kramer to a pair of monitors and sat before them.

On both eight-inch screens the officers saw a diamond-sharp scan of the inside of a silo plug. There was no sound. The plug lifted off its lip without a whisper, dividing into two semicircles of steel. A two-inch circle sky showed. Then, abruptly, the circle widened; the lip irised out and disappeared; the gray surrounded the screen and blanked it out, and then it was bright blue, and a curl of cirro-cumulus in one quadrant of the screen.

Metro had promised no cloud over the tactical area, but there was cloud there. Captain Mabry frowned and tapped a tune on the buttons before him; the cirro-cumulus disappeared and a line of gray-white appeared at an angle on the screen. "Horizon," said Mabry. "Labble to make you sea-sick, Lootenant." He tapped some more and the image righted itself. A faint yellowish stain not bright against the bright cloud, curved up before them and burst into spidery black smoke. "Oh, they are anxious," said Mabry, sounding nettled. "General, weather has busted it again. Cain't see a thing."

Spiegelhauer bawled angrily. "I'm going to the weather station," and stamped out. Kramer knew what he was angry about. It was not the waste of a bird; it was that he had been made to lose face before the general's aide-de-camp. There would be a bad time for the Weather Officer because Kramer had been there that day.

The telemetering crew turned off their instruments. The whining eighteen-inch reel that was flinging tape across a row of fifteen magnetic heads, recording the picture the spy-bird took, slowed and droned and stopped. Out of instinct and habit Kramer pulled out his rough diary and jotted down *Brig. Spiegelhauer—Permits bad wea. sta. situation?* But it was little enough to have learned on a flight to Kiska, and everything else seemed going well.

Captain Mabry fetched over two mugs of hot cocoa. "Sorry," he said. "Cain't be helped, I guess."

Kramer put his notebook away and accepted the cocoa.

"Beats U-2in'," Mabry went on. "Course, you don't get to see as much of the country."

Kramer could not help a small, involuntary tremor. For just a moment there, looking out of the sky-bird's eyes, he had imagined himself actually in the air above yute territory and conceived the possibility of being shot down, parachuting, interment, the Blank Tanks. "Yankee! Why not be good fellow? You *proud* you murderer?"

"No," Kramer said, "you don't get to see as much of the country." But he had already seen all the yute country he ever wanted.

Kramer got back in the elevator and descended rapidly, his mind full. Perhaps a psychopath, a hungry cat or a child would have noticed that the ride downward lasted a second or two less than the ride up. Kramer did not. If the sound echoing from the tunnel he walked out into was a bit more clangorous than the one he had entered from, he didn't notice that either.

Kramer's mind was occupied with the thought that, all in all, he was pleased to find that he had approached this close to yute territory, and to yute Blank Tanks, without feeling *particularly* afraid. Even though he recognized that there was nothing to be afraid of, since, of course, the yutes could not get hold of him here.

Then he observed that the door Mabry opened for him led to a chamber he knew he had never seen before.

They were standing on an approach stage and below them forty-foot rockets extended downward into their pit. A gantry-bridge hung across space from the stage to the nearest rocket, which lay open, showing a clumsily padded compartment where there should have been a warhead or an instrument capsule.

Kramer turned around and was not surprised to find that Mabry was pointing a gun at him. He had almost expected it. He started to speak. But there was someone else in the shadowed chamber, and the first he knew of *that* was when the sap struck him just behind the ear.

It was all coming true: "Yankee! Why not be honest man? You *like* to murder babies?" Kramer only shook his head. He knew it did no good to answer. Three years before he had answered. He knew it also did no good to keep quiet; because he had done that, too. What he knew most of all was that nothing was going to do him any good because the yutes had him now, and who would have thought Mabry would have been the one to do him in?

They did not beat him at this point, but then they did not need to. The nose capsule Mabry had thrust him into had never been designed for carrying passengers. With ingenuity Kramer could only guess that Mabry had contrived to fit it with parachutes and water-tight seals and flares so the yute gunboat could find it in the water and pull out their captive alive. But he had taken 15- and 20-G accelerations, however briefly. He seemed to have no serious broken bones, but he was bruised all over. Secretly he found that almost amusing. In the preliminary softening up the yutes did not expect their captives to be in physical pain. By being in pain he was in some measure upsetting their schedule. It was not much of a victory but it was all he had.

Phase Two was direct questioning: What was Ripsaw exactly? How many divisions? Where located? Why had Lieutenant General Grote spent so much time with Lieutenant General Clough? When Mary Elizabeth Grote, before her death, entertained the Vietnamese UNESCO delegate's aunt in Sag Harbor, had she known her husband had just been passed over for promotion to brigadier? And was resentment over that the reason she had subsequently donated twenty-five dollars to a mission hospital in Laos? What were the Bering Straits rendezvous points for missile submarines supporting Ripsaw? Was the transfer of Lieutenant Colonel Carolyn S. Bucknell from Message Center Battalion C.O. to Mess Officer a cover for some CIC complexity? What air support was planned for D plus one? D plus two? Did Major Somebody-or-other's secret drinking account for the curious radio intercept in clear logged at 0834 on 6 October 1985? Or was "Omobray for my eadhay" the code designation for some nefarious scheme to be launched against the gallant, the ever-victorious forces of Neo-Utilitarianism?

Kramer was alternately cast into despondency by the amount of knowledge his captors displayed and puzzled by the psychotic irrelevance of some of the questions they asked him. But most of all he was afraid. As the hours of Phase Two became days, he became more and more afraid—afraid of Phase Three—and so he was ready for Phase Three when the yutes were ready for him.

Phase Three was physical. They beat the living be-hell out of First Lieutenant John Kramer, and then they shouted at him and starved him and kicked him and threw him into bathtubs filled half with salt water and half with shaved ice. He was in constant pain. But he didn't think much about the pain. What he thought about was what came next. For the bad thing about Phase Three was Phase Four.

He remembered. First they would let him sleep. Then they would wake him up and feed him quickly, and bandage his worst bruises, and bandage his ears with cotton tampons, and bandage his eyes, and bandage his mouth, so he couldn't bite his tongue, and bandage his arms and legs, so he couldn't move them or touch them together . . .

And then the short superior-private who was kicking him while he thought all this stopped and talked briefly to a noncom. The two of them helped him to a mattress and left.

Ten hours later he was back in the Blank Tanks.

Sit back and listen. What do you hear?

Perhaps you think you hear nothing. You are wrong. You discount the sound of a distant car's tires, or the crackle of metal as steam expands the pipes. Listen more carefully to these sounds; others lie under them. From the kitchen there is a grunt and hum as the electric refrigerator switches itself on. You change position; your chair creaks, the leather of your shoes slip-slides with a faint sound. Listen more carefully still and hear the tiny roughness in the main bearing of the electric clock in the next room, or the almost inaudible hum of wind in a television antenna.

In the Blank Tanks a man hears nothing at all.

The pressure of the tampons in the ear does not allow stirrup to strike anvil; teeth cannot touch teeth, hands cannot clap, he cannot make a noise if he tries to, or hear it if he did.

That is deafness. The Blank Tanks are more than deafness. In them a man is blind, even to the red fog that reaches through closed eyelids. There is nothing to smell. There is nothing to taste. There is nothing to feel except the swaddling cloths, and through time the nerve ends tire and stop registering this constant touch.

Kramer was ready for the Blank Tank and did not at once panic. He remembered the tricks he had employed before. He swallowed his own sputum and it made a gratifying popping sound in his inner ear; he hummed until his throat was raw and gasped through flaring nostrils until he became dizzy. But each sound he was able to produce lasted only a moment. He might have dropped them like snowflakes onto wool. They were absorbed and they died.

It was actually worse, he remembered tardily, to produce a sound because you could not help but listen for the echo and no echo came. So he stopped.

In three years he *must* have acquired some additional resources, he thought. Of course. He had! He settled down to construct a crossword puzzle in his head. Let 1 Across be a tropical South American bird, *hoatzin*. Let 1 Down be a medieval diatonic series of tones, *hexachord*. Let 2 Down be the Asiatic wild ass, or *onagin*, which might make the first horizontal word under 1 Across be, let's see, E–N– . . . well, why not the ligature of couplets in verse writing, or *enjambment*. That would make 3 Down— He began to cry, because he could not remember 1 Across.

Something was nagging at his mind, so he stopped crying and waited for it to take form, but it would not. He thought of General Grote, by now surely aware that his aide had been taken; he thought of the consternation that must be shuddering through all the tentacles of Ripsaw. It was not actually going to be so hard, he thought pathetically, because he didn't actually have to *hold out* against the Blank Tanks, he only had to *wait*. After D day, or better, say D plus 7, it wouldn't much matter what he told them. Then the divisions would be across. Or not across. Breakthrough or failure, it would be decided by then and he could talk.

He began to count off Ripsaw's division officers to himself, as he had so often seen the names on the morning reports. Catton of the XLIst Armored, with Colonels Bogart, Ripner and Bletterman. M'Cleargh of the Highland & Lowland, with Brigadiers Douglass and McCloud. Leventhal of the Vth Israeli, with Koehne, Meier and—he stopped, because it had occurred to him that he might be speaking aloud. He could not tell. All right. Think of something else.

But what?

There was nothing dangerous about sensory deprivation, he lied. It was only a test. Nobody was hurting him. Looked at in the right way, it was a chance to do some *solid* thinking like you never got time for in real life—strike that. In *outside* life. For instance, what about freshing up on French irregular verbs? Start with *avoir*. Tu as, vous avez, nous avons. Voi avete, noi abbiamo, du hast . . . Du hast? How did that get in there? Well, how about poetry?

It is an ancient Mariner, and he stops the next of kin.
The guests are met, the feast is set, and sisters under the
     skin
Are rag and bone and hank of hair, and beard and
     glittering eye.
Invite the sight of patient Night, etherized under the sky.
I should have been a ragged claw; I should have said 'I
     love you';
But—here the brown eyes lower fell—I hate to go above
     you.
If Ripsaw fail and yutes prevail, what price Clough's
     Quaker cannon?
So Grote—

Kramer stopped himself, barely in time. Were there throat mikes? Were the yutes listening in?

He churned miserably in his cotton bonds, because, as near as he could guess, he had probably been in the Blank Tank for less than an hour. D day, he thought to himself, praying that it was only to himself, was still some six weeks away and a week beyond that was seven. Seven weeks, forty-nine days, eleven hundred and seventy-six hours, sixty-six thousand minutes plus. He had only to wait those minutes out. What about the diary? And then he could talk all he wanted. Talk, confess, broadcast, anything, what difference would it make then?

He paused, trying to remember. That furtive thought had struggled briefly to the surface but he had lost it again. It would not come back.

He tried to fall asleep. It should have been easy enough. His air was metered and the CO_2 content held to a level that would make him torpid; his wastes catheterized away; water and glucose valved into his veins; he was all but *in utero,* and unborn babies slept, didn't they? Did they? He would have to look in the diary, but it would have to wait until he could remember what thought it was that was struggling for recognition. And that was becoming harder with every second.

Sensory deprivation in small doses is one thing; it even has its therapeutic uses, like shock. In large doses it produces a disorientation of psychotic proportions, a melancholia that is all but lethal; Kramer never knew when he went loopy.

IV

He never quite knew when he went sane again, either, except that one day the fog lifted for a moment and he asked a WAC corporal, "When did I get back to Utah." The corporal had dealt with returning yute prisoners before. She said only: "It's Fort Hamilton, sir. Brooklyn."

He was in a private room, which was bad, but he wore a maroon bathrobe, which was good—at least it meant he was in a hospital instead of an Army stockade. (Unless the private room meant he was in the detention ward of the hospital.)

Kramer wondered what he had done. There was no way to tell, at least not by searching his memory. Everything went into a blurry alternation of shouting relays of yutes and the silence of the Blank Tanks. He was nearly sure he had finally told the yutes everything they wanted to know. The question was, when? He would find out at the court-martial, he thought. Or he might have jotted it down, he thought crazily, in the diary.

Jotted it down in the . . . ?

Diary!

That was the thought that had struggled to come through to the surface!

Kramer's screams brought the corporal back in a hurry, and then two doctors who quickly prepared knockout needles. He fought against them all the way.

"Poor old man," said the WAC, watching him twitch and shudder in unconsciousness. (Kramer had just turned forty.) "Second dose of the Blank Tanks for him, wasn't it? I'm not surprised he's having nightmares." She didn't know that his nightmares were not caused by the Blank Tanks themselves, but by his sudden realization that his last stay in the Tanks was totally unnecessary. It didn't matter what he told the yutes, or when! They had had the diary all along, for it had been on him when Mabry thrust him in the rocket; and all Ripsaw's secrets were in it!

The next time the fog lifted for Kramer it was quick, like the turning on of a light, and he had distorted memories of dreams before it. He thought he had just dreamed that General Grote had been with him. He was alone in the same room, sun streaming in a window, voices outside. He felt pretty good, he thought tentatively, and had no time to think more than that because the door opened and a ward boy looked in, very astonished to find Kramer looking back at him.

"Holy heaven," he said. "Wait there!"

He disappeared. Foolish, Kramer thought. Of course he would wait. Where else would he go?

And then, surprisingly, General Grote did indeed walk in.

"Hello, John," he said mildly, and sat down beside the bed, looking at Kramer. "I was just getting in my car when they caught me."

He pulled out his pipe and stuffed it with tobacco, watching Kramer. Kramer could think of nothing to say. "They said you were all right, John. Are you?"

"I . . . think so." He watched the general light his pipe. "Funny," he said. "I dreamed you were here a minute ago."

"No, it's not so funny; I was. I brought you a present."

Kramer could not imagine anything more wildly improbable in the world than that the man whose combat operation he had betrayed should bring him a box of chocolates, bunch of flowers, light novel or whatever else was appropriate. But the general glanced at the table by Kramer's bed.

There was a flat, green-leather-covered box on it. "Open it up," Grote invited.

Kramer took out a glittering bit of metal depending from a three-barred ribbon. The gold medallion bore a rampant eagle and lettering he could not at first read.

"It's your D.S.M.," Grote said helpfully. "You can pin it on if you like. I tried," he said, "to make it a Medal of Honor. But they wouldn't allow it, logically enough."

"I was expecting something different," Kramer mumbled foolishly.

Grote laughed. "We smashed them, boy," he said gently. "That is, Mick did. He went straight across Polar Nine, down the Ob with one force and the Yenisei with another. General Clough's got his forward command in Chebarkul now, loving every minute of it. Why, I was in Karpinsk myself last week—they let me get that far—of course, it's a rest area. It was a brilliant, bloody, back-breaking show. Completely successful."

Kramer interrupted in sheer horror: "Polar *Nine*? But that was the cover—the Quaker cannon!"

General Grote looked meditatively at his former aide. "John," he said after a moment, "didn't you ever wonder why the cardsorters pulled you out for my staff? A man who was sure to crack in the Blank Tanks, because he already had?"

The room was very silent for a moment.

"I'm sorry, John. Well, it worked—had to, you know; a lot of thought went into it. Novotny's been relieved. Mick's got his biggest victory, no matter what happens now; he was the man that led *the* invasion."

The room was silent again.

Carefully Grote tapped out his pipe into a metal waste-basket. "You're a valuable man, John. We traded a major general to get you back."

Silence.

Grote sighed and stood up. "If it's any consolation to you, you held out four full weeks in the Tanks. Good thing we'd made sure you had the diary with you. Otherwise our Quaker cannon would have been a bust."

He nodded good-by and was gone. He was a good officer, was General Grote. He would use a weapon in any way he had to, to win a fight; but if the weapon was destroyed, and had feelings, he would come around to bring it a medal afterward.

Kramer contemplated his Distinguished Service Medal for a while. Then he lay back and considered ringing for a Sunday *Times,* but fell asleep instead.

Novotny was now a sour, angry corps commander away off on the Baltic periphery because of him; a million and a half NAAARMY troops were dug in the heart of the enemy's homeland; the greatest operation of the war was an unqualified success. But when the nurse came in that night, the Quaker cannon—the man who had discovered that the greatest service he could perform for his country was to betray it—was moaning in his sleep.

THE MOON MOTH

BY JACK VANCE (1916-)

GALAXY SCIENCE FICTION
AUGUST

Jack Vance is perhaps the finest practitioner of what is called "science-fantasy," a hybrid form that combines science fictional elements with fantasy—what is sometimes referred to as "swords and spaceships." But with Vance, it means richly detailed worlds populated by well characterized protaganists, both human and alien. Mr. Vance is one of the few individuals to have won the Hugo, the Nebula, the World Fantasy Award, and the Edgar Allan Poe Award of the Mystery Writers of America (he is a fine mystery writer, although he hasn't written a pure mystery in many years).

"The Moon Moth" shows us a little of his ability to plot a mystery, along with his other great qualities—the ability to entertain and excite his readers. (MHG)

I think that the hardest and most rewarding job a science fiction writer can have is to devise an alien society.

Such a society must be dense; that is, it must be different from ours in myriad different ways, large and small (compare the society of fifteenth century England with that of fifteenth century China, for instance.) It is not enough to color the aliens green, or to give them antennae, or pointed ears and then leave everything else the same.

Such a society must also be unlectured. The writer can't sit down and give the reader a travelogue and a sociological treatise. The story must move steadily forward and the social strangenesses must be explained by the events. (The use of *footnotes as in Vance's story is unusual, but it is only there to explain the innards of the different musical instruments.)*

And such a society must be self-consistent. If the society has the equivalent of guns, they don't fight with swords except as a matter of ritual. If it has power machinery, it doesn't have gangs with shovels except as punishment, and so on. This is very difficult to do.

I can work up an alien society that will pass muster, but there are others that are better than I am in this respect. Vance's story here and Aldiss' earlier in the book are each better than I can do. (IA)

The houseboat had been built to the most exacting standards of Sirenese craftmanship, which is to say, as close to the absolute as human eye could detect. The planking of waxy dark wood showed no joints, the fastenings were platinum rivets countersunk and polished flat. In style, the boat was massive, broad-beamed, steady as the shore itself, without ponderosity or slackness of line. The bow bulged like a swan's breast, the stem rising high, then crooking forward to support an iron lantern. The doors were carved from slabs of a mottled black-green wood; the windows were many-sectioned, paned with squares of mica, stained rose, blue, pale green, and violet. The bow was given to service facilities and quarters for the slaves; amidships were a pair of sleeping cabins, a dining saloon, and a parlor saloon, opening upon an observation deck at the stern.

Such was Edwer Thissell's houseboat, but ownership brought him neither pleasure nor pride. The houseboat had become shabby. The carpeting had lost its pile; the carved screens were chipped; the iron lantern at the bow sagged with rust. Seventy years ago the first owner, on accepting the boat, had honored the builder and had been likewise honored; the transaction (for the process represented a great deal more than simple giving and taking) had augmented the prestige of both. That time was far gone; the houseboat now commanded no prestige whatever. Edwer Thissell, resident on Sirene only three months, recognized the lack but could do nothing about it: this particular houseboat was the best he could get. He sat on the rear deck practicing the *ganga*, a zitherlike instrument not much larger than his hand. A hundred yards inshore, surf defined a strip of white beach; beyond rose jungle, with the silhouette of craggy black hills against the sky. Mireille shone hazy and white overhead, as if through a tangle of spider web; the face of the ocean pooled and puddled with mother-of-pearl luster. The scene had become as familiar, though not as boring, as the *ganga,* at which he had worked two hours, twanging out the Sirenese scales, forming chords, traversing simple progressions. Now he put down the *ganga* for the *zachinko,* this a small sound box studded with keys, played with the right hand. Pressure on the keys forced air through reeds in the keys themselves, producing a concertinalike tone. Thissell ran off a dozen quick scales, making very few mistakes. Of the six instruments he had set himself to learn, the *zachinko* had proved the least refractory (with the exception, of course, of the *hymerkin,* that clacking, slapping, clattering device of wood and stone used exclusively with the slaves).

Thissell practiced another ten minutes, then put aside the *zachinko.* He flexed his arms, wrung his aching fingers. Every waking moment since his arrival had been given to the instruments: the *hymerkin,* the *ganga,* the *zachinko,* the *kiv,* the *strapan,* the *gomapard.* He had practiced scales in nineteen keys and four modes, chords without number, intervals never imagined on the Home Planets. Trills, arpeggios, slurs; click-stops, and nasalization; damping and augmentation of overtones; vibratos and wolf-tones; concavities and convexities. He practiced with a dogged, deadly diligence, in which his original concept of music as a source of pleasure had long become lost. Looking over the instruments, Thissell resisted an urge to fling all six into the Titanic.

He rose to his feet, went forward through the parlor saloon, the dining saloon, along a corridor past the galley and came out on the foredeck. He bent over the rail, peered down into the underwater pens where Toby and Rex, the slaves, were harnessing the dray-fish for the weekly trip to Fan, eight miles north. The youngest fish, either playful or captious, ducked and plunged. Its streaming black muzzle broke water, and Thissell, looking into its face felt a peculiar qualm: the fish wore no mask!

Thissell laughed uneasily, fingering his own mask, the Moon Moth. No question about it, he was becoming acclimated to Sirene! A significant stage had been reached when the naked face of a fish caused him shock!

The fish were finally harnessed; Toby and Rex climbed aboard, red bodies glistening, black cloth masks clinging to their faces. Ignoring Thissell, they stowed the pen, hoisted anchor. The dray-fish strained, the harness tautened, the houseboat moved north.

Returning to the afterdeck, Thissell took up the *strapan*— this a circular sound box eight inches in diameter. Forty-six wires radiated from a central hub to the circumference where they connected to either a bell or a tinkle-bar. When plucked, the bells rang, the bars chimed; when strummed, the instrument gave off a twanging, jingling sound. When played with competence, the pleasantly acid dissonances produced an expressive effect; in an unskilled hand, the results were less felicitous, and might even approach random noise. The *strapan* was Thissell's weakest instrument and he practiced with concentration during the entire trip north.

In due course the houseboat approached the floating city. The dray-fish were curbed, the houseboat warped to a mooring. Along the dock a line of idlers weighed and gauged every aspect of the houseboat, the slaves, and Thissell himself, according to Sirenese habit. Thissell, not yet accustomed to such penetrating inspection, found the scrutiny unsettling, all the more so for the immobility of the masks. Self-consciously adjusting his own Moon Moth, he climbed the ladder to the dock.

A slave rose from where he had been squatting, touched knuckles to the black cloth at his forehead, and sang on a three-tone phrase of interrogation: "The Moon Moth before me possibly expresses the identity of Ser Edwer Thissell."

Thissell tapped the *hymerkin* which hung at his belt and sang: "I am Ser Thissell."

"I have been honored by a trust," sang the slave. "Three days from dawn to dusk I have waited on the dock; three nights from dusk to dawn I have crouched on a raft below this same dock listening to the feet of the Night-men. At last I behold the mask of Ser Thissell."

Thissell evoked an impatient clatter from the *hymerkin*. "What is the nature of this trust?"

"I carry a message, Ser Thissell. It is intended for you."

Thissell held out his left hand, playing the *hymerkin* with his right. "Give me the message."

"Instantly, Ser Thissell."

The message bore a heavy superscription:

EMERGENCY COMMUNICATION! RUSH!

Thissell ripped open the envelope. The message was signed by Castel Cromartin, Chief Executive of the Interworld Policies Board, and after the formal salutation read:

ABSOLUTELY URGENT the following orders be executed! Aboard *Carina Cruzeiro*, destination Fan, date of arrival January 10 U.T., is notorious assassin, Haxo Angmark. Meet landing with adequate authority, effect detention, and incarceration of this man. These instructions must be successfully implemented. Failure is unacceptable.

ATTENTION! Haxo Angmark is superlatively dangerous. Kill him without hesitation at any show of resistance.

Thissell considered the message with dismay. In coming to Fan as Consular Representative he had expected nothing like this; he felt neither inclination nor competence in the matter of dealing with dangerous assassins. Thoughtfully he rubbed the fuzzy gray cheek of his mask. The situation was not completely dark; Esteban Rolver, director of the spaceport, would doubtless cooperate, and perhaps furnish a platoon of slaves.

More hopefully, Thissell reread the message. January 10, Universal Time. He consulted a conversion calendar. Today, fortieth in the Season of Bitter Nectar—Thissell ran his finger down the column, stopped. January 10. Today.

A distant rumble caught his attention. Dropping from the mist came a dull shape: the lighter returning from contact with the *Carina Cruzeiro*.

Thissell once more reread the note, raised his head, studied the descending lighter. Aboard would be Haxo Angmark. In five minutes he would emerge upon the soil of Sirene. Landing formalities would detain him possibly twenty minutes. The landing field lay a mile and a half distant, joined to Fan by a winding path through the hills.

Thissell turned to the slave. "When did this message arrive?"

The slave leaned forward uncomprehendingly. Thissell reiterated his question, singing to the clack of the *hymerkin*: "This message: you have enjoyed the honor of its custody how long?"

The slave sang: "Long days have I waited on the wharf, retreating only to the raft at the onset of dusk. Now my vigil is rewarded; I behold Ser Thissell."

Thissell turned away, walked furiously up the dock. Ineffective, inefficient Sirenese! Why had they not delivered the message to his houseboat? Twenty-five minutes—twenty-two now . . .

At the esplanade Thissell stopped, looked right then left, hoping for a miracle: some sort of air-transport to whisk him to the spaceport, where with Rolver's aid, Haxo Angmark might still be detained. Or better yet, a second message canceling the first. Something, anything . . . But aircars were not to be found on Sirene, and no second message appeared.

Across the esplanade rose a meager row of permanent structures, built of stone and iron and so proof against the efforts of the Night-men. A hostler occupied one of these structures, and as Thissell watched a man in a splendid pearl and silver mask emerged riding one of the lizard-like mounts of Sirene.

Thissell sprang forward. There was still time; with luck he might yet intercept Haxo Angmark. He hurried across the esplanade.

Before the line of stalls stood the hostler, inspecting his stock with solicitude, occasionally burnishing a scale or whisking away an insect. There were five of the beasts in prime condition, each as tall as a man's shoulder, with massive legs, thick bodies, heavy wedge-shaped heads. From their forefangs, which had been artificially lengthened and curved into near-circles, gold rings depended; the scales of each had been stained in diaper-pattern: purple and green, orange and black, red and blue, brown and pink, yellow and silver.

Thissell came to a breathless halt in front of the hostler.

He reached for his *kiv*,* then hesitated. Could this be considered a casual personal encounter? The *zachinko* perhaps? But the statement of his needs hardly seemed to demand the formal approach. Better the *kiv* after all. He struck a chord, but by error found himself stroking the *ganga*. Beneath his mask Thissell grinned apologetically; his relationship with this hostler was by no means on an intimate basis. He hoped that the hostler was of sanguine disposition, and in any event the urgency of the occasion allowed no time to select an exactly appropriate instrument. He struck a second chord, and, playing as well as agitation, breathlessness, and lack of skill allowed, sang out a request: "Ser Hostler, I have immediate need of a swift mount. Allow me to select from your herd."

The hostler wore a mask of considerable complexity which Thissell could not identify: a construction of varnished brown cloth, pleated gray leather and high on the forehead two large green and scarlet globes, minutely segmented like insect eyes. He inspected Thissell a long moment, then, rather ostentatiously selecting his *stimic*,** executed a brilliant progression of trills and rounds, of an import Thissell failed to grasp. The hostler sang, "Ser Moon Moth, I fear that my steeds are unsuitable to a person of your distinction."

Thissell earnestly twanged at the *ganga*. "By no means; they all seem adequate. I am in great haste and will gladly accept any of the group."

The hostler played a brittle cascading crescendo. "Ser Moon Moth," he sang, "the steeds are ill and dirty. I am flattered that you consider them adequate to your use. I cannot accept the merit you offer me. And"—here, switching instruments, he struck a cool tinkle from his

---

Kiv: five banks of resilient metal strips, fourteen to the bank, played by touching, twisting, twanging.

**Stimic*: three flutelike tubes equipped with plungers. Thumb and forefinger squeeze a bag to force air across the mouth-pieces; the second, third, and fourth little fingers manipulate the slide. The *stimic* is an instrument well adapted to the sentiments of cool withdrawal, or even disapproval.

krodatch*—"somehow I fail to recognize the boon-companion and cocraftsman who accosts me so familiarly with his *ganga.*"

The implication was clear. Thissell would receive no mount. He turned, set off at a run for the landing field. Behind him sounded a clatter of the hostler's *hymerkin*—whether directed toward the hostler's slaves, or toward himself Thissell did not pause to learn.

The previous Consular Representative of the Home Planets on Sirene had been killed at Zundar. Masked as a Tavern Bravo he had accosted a girl beribboned for the Equinoctial Attitudes, a solecism for which he had been instantly beheaded by a Red Demiurge, a Sun Sprite, and a Magic Hornet. Edwer Thissell, recently graduated from the Institute, had been named his successor, and allowed three days to prepare himself. Normally of a contemplative, even cautious, disposition, Thisscll had regarded the appointment as a challenge. He learned the Sirenese language by subcerebral techniques, and found it uncomplicated. Then, in the *Journal of Universal Anthropology,* he read:

> The population of the Titanic littoral is highly individualistic, possibly in response to a bountiful environment which puts no premium upon group activity. The language, reflecting this trait, expresses the individual's mood, his emotional attitude toward a given situation. Factual information is regarded as a secondary concomitant. Moreover, the language is sung, characteristically to the accompaniment of a small instrument. As a result, there is great difficulty in ascertaining fact from a native of Fan, or the forbidden city Zundar. One will be regaled with elegant arias and demonstrations of astonishing virtuosity upon one or another of the numerous musical instruments. The visitor to this fasci-

---

*Krodatch: a small square sound-box strung with resined gut. The musician scratches the strings with his fingernail, or strokes them with his fingertips, to produce a variety of quietly formal sounds. The *krodatch* is also used as an instrument of insult.

nating world, unless he cares to be treated with the most consummate contempt, must therefore learn to express himself after the approved local fashion.

Thissell made a note in his memorandum book: *Procure small musical instrument, together with directions as to use.* He read on.

There is everywhere and at all times a plentitude, not to say, superfluity of food, and the climate is benign. With a fund of racial energy and a great deal of leisure time, the population occupies itself with intricacy. Intricacy in all things: intricate craftmanship, such as the carved panels which adorn the houseboat; intricate symbolism, as exemplified in the masks worn by everyone; the intricate half-musical language which admirably expresses subtle moods and emotions; and above all the fantastic intricacy of interpersonal relationships. Prestige, face, *mana,* repute, glory: the Sirenese word is *strakh.* Every man has his characteristic *strakh,* which determines whether, when he needs a houseboat, he will be urged to avail himself of a floating palace, rich with gems, alabaster lanterns, peacock faïence, and carved wood, or grudgingly permitted an abandoned shack on a raft. There is no medium of exchange on Sirene; the single and sole currency is *strakh* . . .

Thissell rubbed his chin and read further.

Masks are worn at all times, in accordance with the philosophy that a man should not be compelled to use a similitude foisted upon him by factors beyond his control; that he should be at liberty to choose that semblance most consonant with his *strakh.* In the civilized areas of Sirene—which is to say the Titanic littoral—a man literally never shows his face; it is his basic secret.

Gambling, by this token, is unknown on Sirene; it would be catastrophic to Sirenese self-respect to gain advantage by means other than the exercise of *strakh.* The word "luck" has no counterpart in the Sirenese language.

Thissell made another note: *Get mask. Museum? Drama guild?*

He finished the article, hastened forth to complete his preparations, and the next day embarked aboard the *Robert Astroguard* for the first leg of the passage to Sirene.

The lighter settled upon the Sirenese spaceport, a topaz disk isolated among the black, green and purple hills. The lighter grounded, and Edwer Thissell stepped forth. He was met by Esteban Rolver, the local agent for Spaceways. Rolver threw up his hands, stepped back. "Your mask," he cried huskily. "Where is your mask?"

Thissell held it up rather self-consciously. "I wasn't sure—"

"Put it on," said Rolver, turning away. He himself wore a fabrication of dull green scales, blue-lacquered wood. Black quills protruded at the cheeks, and under his chin hung a black and white checked pom-pom, the total effect creating a sense of sardonic supple personality.

Thissell adjusted the mask to his face, undecided whether to make a joke about the situation or to maintain a reserve suitable to the dignity of his post.

"Are you masked?" Rolver inquired over his shoulder.

Thissell replied in the affirmative and Rolver turned. The mask hid the expression of his face, but his hand unconsciously flicked a set of keys strapped to his thigh. The instrument sounded a trill of shock and polite consternation. "You can't wear that mask!" sang Rolver. "In fact—how, where, did you get it?"

"It's copied from a mask owned by the Polypolis museum," declared Thissell stiffly. "I'm sure it's authentic."

Rolver nodded, his own mask more sardonic-seeming than ever. "It's authentic enough. It's a variant of the type known as the Sea Dragon Conqueror, and is worn on ceremonial occasions by persons of enormous prestige: princes, heroes, master craftsmen, great musicians."

"I wasn't aware—"

Rolver made a gesture of languid understanding. "It's something you'll learn in due course. Notice my mask. Today I'm wearing a Tarn-Bird. Persons of minimal prestige—such as you, I, any other out-worlder—wear this sort of thing."

"Odd," said Thissell as they started across the field toward a low concrete blockhouse. "I assumed that a person wore whatever mask he liked."

"Certainly," said Rolver. "Wear any mask you like—if you can make it stick. This Tarn-Bird for instance. I wear it to indicate that I presume nothing. I make no claims to wisdom, ferocity, versatility, musicianship, truculence, or any of a dozen other Sirenese virtues."

"For the sake of argument," said Thissell, "what would happen if I walked through the streets of Zundar in this mask?"

Rolver laughed, a muffled sound behind his mask. "If you walked along the docks of Zundar—there are no streets—in any mask, you'd be killed within the hour. That's what happened to Benko, your predecessor. He didn't know how to act. None of us out-worlders know how to act. In Fan we're tolerated—so long as we keep our place. But you couldn't even walk around Fan in that regalia you're sporting now. Somebody wearing a Fire-snake or a Thunder Goblin—masks, you understand—would step up to you. He'd play his *krodatch*, and if you failed to challenge his audacity with a passage on the *skaranyi*,* a devilish instrument, he'd play his *hymerkin*—the instrument we use with the slaves. That's the ultimate expression of contempt. Or he might ring his duelling gong and attack you then and there."

"I had no idea that people here were quite so irascible," said Thissell in a subdued voice.

Rolver shrugged and swung open the massive steel door into his office. "Certain acts may not be committed on the Concourse at Polypolis without incurring criticism."

"Yes, that's quite true," said Thissell. He looked around the office. "Why the security? The concrete, the steel?"

"Protection against the savages," said Rolver. "They come down from the mountains at night, steal what's available, kill anyone they find ashore." He went to a closet,

---

Skaranyi: a miniature bagpipe, the sac squeezed between thumb and palm, the four fingers controlling the stops along four tubes.

brought forth a mask. "Here. Use this Moon Moth; it won't get you in trouble."

Thissell unenthusiastically inspected the mask. It was constructed of mouse-colored fur; there was a tuft of hair at each side of the mouth-hole, a pair of featherlike antennae at the forehead. White lace flaps dangled beside the temples and under the eyes hung a series of red folds, creating an effect at once lugubrious and comic.

Thissell asked, "Does this mask signify any degree of prestige?"

"Not a great deal."

"After all, I'm Consular Representative," said Thissell. "I represent the Home Planets, a hundred billion people—"

"If the Home Planets want their representative to wear a Sea-Dragon Conqueror mask, they'd better send out a Sea-Dragon Conqueror type of man."

"I see," said Thissell in a subdued voice. "Well, if I must . . ."

Rolver politely averted his gaze while Thissell doffed the Sea-Dragon Conqueror and slipped the more modest Moon Moth over his head. "I suppose I can find something just a bit more suitable in one of the shops," Thissell said. "I'm told a person simply goes in and takes what he needs, correct?"

Rolver surveyed Thissell critically. "That mask—temporarily, at least—is perfectly suitable. And it's rather important not to take anything from the shops until you know the *strakh* value of the article you want. The owner loses prestige if a person of low *strakh* makes free with his best work."

Thissell shook his head in exasperation. "Nothing of this was explained to me! I knew of the masks, of course, and the painstaking integrity of the craftsmen, but this insistence on prestige—*strakh*, whatever the word is . . ."

"No matter," said Rolver. "After a year or two you'll begin to learn your way around. I suppose you speak the language?"

"Oh, indeed. Certainly."

"And what instruments do you play?"

"Well—I was given to understand that any small instrument was adequate, or that I could merely sing."

"Very inaccurate. Only slaves sing without accompaniment. I suggest that you learn the following instruments as quickly as possible: the *hymerkin* for your slaves. The *ganga* for conversation between intimates or one a trifle lower than yourself in *strakh*. The *kiv* for casual polite intercourse. The *zachinko* for more formal dealings. The *strapan* or the *krodatch* for your social inferiors—in your case, should you wish to insult someone. The *gomapard** or the *double-kamanthil*** for ceremonials." He considered a moment. "The *crebarin*, the water-lute, and the *slobo* are highly useful also—but perhaps you'd better learn the other instruments first. They should provide at least a rudimentary means of communication."

"Aren't you exaggerating?" suggested Thissell. "Or joking?"

Rolver laughed his saturnine laugh. "Not at all. First of all, you'll need a houseboat. And then you'll want slaves."

Rolver took Thissell from the landing field to the docks of Fan, a walk of an hour and a half along a pleasant path under enormous trees loaded with fruit, cereal pods, sacs of sugary sap.

"At the moment," said Rolver, "there are only four outworlders in Fan, counting yourself. I'll take you to Welibus, our Commercial Factor. I think he's got an old houseboat he might let you use."

Cornely Welibus had resided fifteen years in Fan, acquiring sufficient *strakh* to wear his South Wind mask with authority. This consisted of a blue disk inlaid with cabochons of lapis-lazuli, surrounded by an aureole of shimmering snakeskin. Heartier and more cordial than Rolver, he not only provided Thissell with a houseboat, but also a score of various musical instruments and a pair of slaves.

Embarrassed by the largesse, Thissell stammered something about payment, but Welibus cut him off with an

---

*Gomopard: one of the few electric instruments used on Sirene. An oscillator produces an oboelike tone which is modulated, choked, vibrated, raised and lowered in pitch by four keys.

**Double-kamanthil: an instrument similar to the *ganga*, except the tones are produced by twisting and inclining a disk of resined leather against one or more of the forty-six strings.

expansive gesture. "My dear fellow, this is Sirene. Such trifles cost nothing."

"But a houseboat—"

Welibus played a courtly little flourish on his *kiv*. "I'll be frank, Ser Thissell. The boat is old and a trifle shabby. I can't afford to use it; my status would suffer." A graceful melody accompanied his words. "Status as yet need not concern you. You require merely shelter, comfort, and safety from the Night-men."

"Night-men?"

"The cannibals who roam the shore after dark."

"Oh yes. Ser Rolver mentioned them."

"Horrible things. We won't discuss them." A shuddering little trill issued from his *kiv*. "Now, as to slaves." He tapped the blue disk of his mask with a thoughtful forefinger. "Rex and Toby should serve you well." He raised his voice, played a swift clatter on the *hymerkin*. "*Avan esx trobu!*"

A female slave appeared wearing a dozen tight bands of pink cloth, and a dainty black mask sparkling with mother-of-pearl sequins.

"*Fascu etz Rex ae Toby.*"

Rex and Toby appeared, wearing loose masks of black cloth, russet jerkins. Welibus addressed them with a resonant clatter of *hymerkin*, enjoining them to the service of their new master, on pain of return to their native islands. They prostrated themselves, sang pledges of servitude to Thissell in soft husky voices. Thissell laughed nervously and essayed a sentence in the Sirenese language. "Go to the houseboat, clean it well, bring aboard food."

Toby and Rex stared blankly through the holes in their masks. Welibus repeated the orders with *hymerkin* accompaniment. The slaves bowed and departed.

Thissell surveyed the musical instruments with dismay. "I haven't the slightest idea how to go about learning these things."

Welibus turned to Rolver. "What about Kershaul? Could he be persuaded to give Ser Thissell some basic instruction?"

Rolver nodded judicially. "Kershaul might undertake the job."

Thissell asked, "Who is Kershaul?"

"The third of our little group of expatriates," replied Welibus, "an anthropologist. You've read *Zundar the Splendid? Rituals of Sirene? The Faceless Folk?* No? A pity. All excellent works. Kershaul is high in prestige, and I believe visits Zundar from time to time. Wears a Cave Owl, sometimes a Star-wanderer or even a Wise Arbiter."

"He's taken to an Equatorial Serpent," said Rolver. "The variant with the gilt tusks."

"Indeed!" marveled Welibus. "Well, I must say he's earned it. A fine fellow, good chap indeed." And he strummed his *zachinko* thoughtfully.

Three months passed. Under the tutelage of Mathew Kershaul, Thissell practiced the *hymerkin*, the *ganga*, the *strapan*, the *kiv*, the *gompard*, and the *zachinko*. The *double-kamanthil*, the *krodatch*, the *slobo*, the water-lute, and a number of others could wait, said Kershaul, until Thissell had mastered the six basic instruments. He lent Thissell recordings of noteworthy Sirenese conversing in various moods and to various accompaniments, so that Thissell might learn the melodic conventions currently in vogue, and perfect himself in the niceties of intonation, the various rhythms, cross-rhythms, compound rhythms, implied rhythms, and suppressed rhythms. Kershaul professed to find Sirenese music a fascinating study, and Thissell admitted that it was a subject not readily exhausted. The quarter-tone tuning of the instruments admitted the use of twenty-four tonalities which multiplied by the five modes in general use, resulted in one hundred and twenty separate scales. Kershaul, however, advised that Thissell primarily concentrate on learning each instrument in its fundamental tonality, using only two of the modes.

With no immediate business at Fan except the weekly visits to Mathew Kershaul, Thissell took his houseboat eight miles south and moored it in the lee of a rocky promontory. Here, if it had not been for the incessant practicing, Thissell lived an idyllic life. The sea was calm and crystal-clear; the beach, ringed by the gray, green and purple foliage of the forest, lay close at hand if he wanted to stretch his legs.

Toby and Rex occupied a pair of cubicles forward, Thissell had the aftercabins to himself. From time to time he toyed with the idea of a third slave, possibly a young female, to contribute an element of charm and gaiety to the menage, but Kershaul advised against the step, fearing that the intensity of Thissell's concentration might somehow be diminished. Thissell acquiesced and devoted himself to the study of the six instruments.

The days passed quickly. Thissell never became bored with the pageantry of dawn and sunset; the white clouds and blue sea of noon; the night sky blazing with the twenty-nine stars of Cluster SI 1-715. The weekly trip to Fan broke the tedium. Toby and Rex foraged for food; Thissell visited the luxurious houseboat of Mathew Kershaul for instruction and advice. Then, three months after Thissell's arrival, came the message completely disorganizing the routine: Haxo Angmark, assassin, *agent provacateur,* ruthless and crafty criminal, had come to Sirene. *Effective detention and incarceration of this man!* read the orders. *Attention! Haxo Angmark superlatively dangerous. Kill without hesitation!*

Thissell was not in the best of condition. He trotted fifty yards until his breath came in gasps, then walked: through low hills crowned with white bamboo and black tree-ferns; across meadows yellow with grass-nuts, through orchards and wild vineyards. Twenty minutes passed, twenty-five minutes; with a heavy sensation in his stomach Thissell knew that he was too late. Haxo Angmark had landed, and might be traversing this very road toward Fan. But along the way Thissell met only four persons: a boy-child in a mock-fierce Alk-Islander mask; two young women wearing the Red-bird and the Green-bird; a man masked as a Forest Goblin. Coming upon the man, Thissell stopped short. Could this be Angmark?

Thissell essayed a strategem. He went boldly to the man, stared into the hideous mask. "Angmark," he called in the language of the Home Planets, "you are under arrest!"

The Forest Goblin stared uncomprehendingly, then started forward along the track.

Thissell put himself in the way. He reached for his *ganga,* then recalling the hostler's reaction, instead struck a chord on the *zachinko.* "You travel the road from the spaceport," he sang. "What have you seen there?"

The Forest Goblin gasped his hand-bugle, an instrument used to deride opponents on the field of battle, to summon animals, or occasionally to evince a rough and ready truculence. "Where I travel and what I see are the concern solely of myself. Stand back or I walk upon your face." He marched forward, and had not Thissell leapt aside the Forest Goblin might well have made good his threat.

Thissell stood gazing after the retreating back. Angmark? Not likely, with so sure a touch on the hand-bugle. Thissell hesitated, then turned and continued on his way.

Arriving at the spaceport, he went directly to the office. The heavy door stood ajar; as Thissell approached, a man appeared in the doorway. He wore a mask of dull green scales, mica plates, blue-lacquered wood and black quills—the Tarn-Bird.

"Ser Rolver," Thissell called out anxiously, "who came down from the *Carina Cruzeiro?*"

Rolver studied Thissell a long moment. "Why do you ask?"

"Why do I ask?" demanded Thissell. "You must have seen the spacegram I received from Castel Cromartin!"

"Oh yes," said Rolver. "Of course. Naturally."

"It was delivered only half an hour ago," said Thissell bitterly. "I rushed out as fast as I could. Where is Angmark?"

"In Fan, I assume," said Rolver.

Thissell cursed softly. "Why didn't you hold him up, delay him in some way?"

Rolver shrugged. "I had neither authority, inclination, nor the capability to stop him."

Thissell fought back his annoyance. In a voice of studied calm he said, "On the way I passed a man in rather a ghastly mask—saucer eyes, red wattles."

"A Forest Goblin," said Rolver. "Angmark brought the mask with him."

"But he played the hand-bugle," Thissell protested. "How could Angmark—"

"He's well acquainted with Sirene; he spent five years here in Fan."

Thissell grunted in annoyance. "Cromartin made no mention of this."

"It's common knowledge," said Rolver with a shrug. "He was Commercial Representative before Welibus took over."

"Were he and Welibus acquainted?"

Rolver laughed shortly. "Naturally. But don't suspect

poor Welibus of anything more venial than juggling his accounts; I assure you he's no consort of assassins."

"Speaking of assassins," said Thissell, "do you have a weapon I might borrow?"

Rolver inspected him in wonder. "You came out here to take Angmark barehanded?"

"I had no choice," said Thissell. "When Cromartin gives orders he expects results. In any event you were here with your slaves."

"Don't count on me for help," Rolver said testily. "I wear the Tarn-Bird and make no pretensions of valor. But I can lend you a power pistol. I haven't used it recently; I won't guarantee its charge."

"Anything is better than nothing," said Thissell.

Rolver went into the office and a moment later returned with the gun. "What will you do now?"

Thissell shook his head wearily. "I'll try to find Angmark in Fan. Or might he head for Zundar?"

Rolver considered. "Angmark might be able to survive in Zundar. But he'd want to brush up on his musicianship. I imagine he'll stay in Fan a few days."

"But how can I find him? Where should I look?"

"That I can't say," replied Rolver. "You might be safer not finding him. Angmark is a dangerous man."

Thissell returned to Fan the way he had come.

Where the path swung down from the hills into the esplanade a thick-walled *pisé-de-terre* building had been constructed. The door was carved from a solid black plank; the windows were guarded by enfoliated bands of iron. This was the office of Cornely Welibus, Commercial Factor, Importer and Exporter. Thissell found Welibus sitting at his ease on the tiled verandah, wearing a modest adaptation of the Waldemar mask. He seemed lost in thought, and might or might not have recognized Thissell's Moon Moth; in any event he gave no signal of greeting.

Thissell approached the porch. "Good morning, Ser Welibus."

Welibus nodded abstractedly and said in a flat voice, plucking at his *krodatch*. "Good morning."

Thissell was rather taken aback. This was hardly the instrument to use toward a friend and fellow out-worlder, even if he did wear the Moon Moth.

Thissell said coldly, "May I ask how long you have been sitting here?"

Welibus considered half a minute, and now when he spoke he accompanied himself on the more cordial *crebarin*. But the recollection of the *krodatch* chord still rankled in Thissell's mind.

"I've been here fifteen or twenty minutes. Why do you ask?"

"I wonder if you noticed a Forest Goblin pass?"

Welibus nodded. "He went on down the esplanade— turned into that first mask shop, I believe."

Thissell hissed between his teeth. This would naturally be Angmark's first move. "I'll never find him once he changes masks," he muttered.

"Who is this Forest Goblin?" asked Welibus, with no more than casual interest.

Thissell could see no reason to conceal the name. "A notorious criminal: Haxo Angmark."

"Haxo Angmark!" croaked Welibus, leaning back in his chair. "You're sure he's here?"

"Reasonably sure."

Welibus rubbed his shaking hands together. "This is bad news—bad news indeed! He's an unscrupulous scoundrel."

"You knew him well?"

"As well as anyone." Welibus was now accompanying himself with the *kiv*. "He held the post I now occupy. I came out as an inspector and found that he was embezzling four thousand UMI's a month. I'm sure he feels no great gratitude toward me." Welibus glanced nervously up the esplanade. "I hope you catch him."

"I'm doing my best. He went into the mask shop, you say?"

"I'm sure of it."

Thissell turned away. As he went down the path he heard the black plank door thud shut behind him.

He walked down the esplanade to the mask-maker's shop, paused outside as if admiring the display: a hundred miniature masks, carved from rare woods and minerals, dressed with emerald flakes, spider-web silk, wasp wings, petrified fish scales and the like. The shop was empty except for the mask-maker, a gnarled knotty man in a yellow robe, wearing a deceptively simple Universal Expert mask, fabricated from over two thousand bits of articulated wood.

Thissell considered what he would say, how he would accompany himself, then entered. The mask-maker, noting the Moon Moth and Thissell's diffident manner, continued with his work.

Thissell, selecting the easiest of his instruments, stroked his *strapan*—possibly not the most felicitous choice, for it conveyed a certain degree of condescension. Thissell tried to counteract this flavor by singing in warm, almost effusive, tones, shaking the *strapan* whimsically when he struck a wrong note: "A stranger is an interesting person to deal with; his habits are unfamiliar, he excites curiosity. Not twenty minutes ago a stranger entered this fascinating shop, to exchange his drab Forest Goblin for one of the remarkable and adventurous creations assembled on the premises."

The mask-maker turned Thissell a side-glance, and without words played a progression of chords on an instrument Thissell had never seen before: a flexible sac gripped in the palm with three short tubes leading between the fingers. When the tubes were squeezed almost shut and air forced through the slit, an oboelike tone ensued. To Thissell's developing ear, the instrument seemed difficult, the mask-maker expert, and the music conveyed a profound sense of disinterest.

Thissell tried again, laboriously manipulating the *strapan*. He sang, "To an out-worlder on a foreign planet, the voice of one from his home is like water to a wilting plant. A person who could unite two such persons might find satisfaction in such an act of mercy."

The mask-maker casually fingered his own *strapan*, and drew forth a set of rippling scales, his fingers moving faster than the eyes could follow. He sang in the formal style: "An artist values his moments of concentration; he does not care to spend time exchanging banalities with persons of at best average prestige." Thissell attempted to insert a counter melody, but the mask-maker struck a new set of complex chords whose portent evaded Thissell's understanding, and continued: "Into the shop comes a person who evidently has picked up for the first time an instrument of unparalleled complication, for the execution of his music is open to criticism. He sings of homesickness and longing for the sight of others like himself. He dissembles his enormous *strakh* behind a Moon Moth, for he plays the *strapan* to a Master Craftsman, and sings in a voice of contemptuous raillery. The refined and creative artist ignores the provocation. He plays a polite instrument, remains noncommittal, and trusts that the stranger will tire of his sport and depart."

Thissell took up his *kiv*. "The noble mask-maker completely misunderstands me—"

He was interrupted by staccato rasping of the mask-maker's *strapan*. "The stranger now sees fit to ridicule the artist's comprehension."

Thissell scratched furiously at his *strapan:* "To protect myself from the heat, I wander into a small and unpretentious mask-shop. The artisan, though still distracted by the novelty of his tools, gives promise of development. He works zealously to perfect his skill, so much so that he refuses to converse with strangers, no matter what their need."

The mask-maker carefully laid down his carving tool. He rose to his feet, went behind a screen, and shortly returned wearing a mask of gold and iron, with simulated flames licking up from the scalp. In one hand he carried a *skaranyi*, in the other a scimitar. He struck off a brilliant series of wild tones, and sang: "Even the most accomplished artist can augment his *strakh* by killing sea-monsters, Night-men, and importunate idlers. Such an occasion is at hand. The artist delays his attack. exactly ten seconds, because the offender wears a Moon Moth." He twirled his scimitar, spun it in the air.

Thissell desperately pounded the *strapan*. "Did a Forest Goblin enter the shop? Did he depart with a new mask?"

"Five seconds have lapsed," sang the mask-maker in steady ominous rhythm.

Thissell departed in frustrated rage. He crossed the square, stood looking up and down the esplanade. Hundreds of men and women sauntered along the docks, or stood on the decks of their houseboats, each wearing a mask chosen to express his mood, prestige and special attributes, and everywhere sounded the twitter of musical instruments.

Thissell stood at a loss. The Forest Goblin had disappeared. Haxo Angmark walked at liberty in Fan, and Thissell had failed the urgent instructions of Castel Cromartin.

Behind him sounded the casual notes of a *kiv*. "Ser Moon
Moth Thissell, you stand engrossed in thought."

Thissell turned, to find beside him a Cave Owl, in a somber cloak of black and gray. Thissell recognized the mask,
which symbolized erudition and patient exploration of
abstract ideas; Mathew Kershaul had worn it on the occasion of their meeting a week before.

"Good morning, Ser Kershaul," muttered Thissell.

"And how are the studies coming? Have you mastered
the C-Sharp Plus scale on the *gomapard?* As I recall, you
were finding those inverse intervals puzzling."

"I've worked on them," said Thissell in a gloomy voice.
"However, since I'll probably be recalled to Polypolis, it
may be all time wasted."

"Eh? What's this?"

Thissell explained the situation in regard to Haxo
Angmark. Kershaul nodded gravely. "I recall Angmark.
Not a gracious personality, but an excellent musician, with
quick fingers and a real talent for new instruments."
Thoughtfully, he twisted the goatee of his Cave-Owl mask.
"What are your plans?"

"They're nonexistent," said Thissell, playing a doleful
phrase on the *kiv*. "I haven't any idea what masks he'll be
wearing and if I don't know what he looks like, how can I
find him?"

Kershaul tugged at his goatee. "In the old days he
favored the Exo Cambian Cycle, and I believe he used an
entire set of Nether Denizens. Now of course his tastes may
have changed."

"Exactly," Thissell complained. "He might be twenty feet
away and I'd never know it." He glanced bitterly across the
esplanade toward the mask-maker's shop. "No one will tell
me anything; I doubt if they care that a murderer is walking
their docks."

"Quite correct," Kershaul agreed. "Sirenese standards
are different from ours."

"They have no sense of responsibility," declared Thissell.
"I doubt if they'd throw a rope to a drowning man."

"It's true that they dislike interference," Kershaul agreed.
"They emphasize individual responsibility and self-
sufficiency."

"Interesting," said Thissell, "but I'm still in the dark about Angmark."

Kershaul surveyed him gravely. "And should you locate Angmark, what will you do then?"

"I'll carry out the orders of my superior," said Thissell doggedly.

"Angmark is a dangerous man," mused Kershaul. "He's got a number of advantages over you."

"I can't take that into account. It's my duty to send him back to Polypolis. He's probably safe, since I haven't the remotest idea how to find him."

Kershaul reflected. "An out-worlder can't hide behind a mask, not from the Sirenese, at least. There are four of us here at Fan—Rolver, Welibus, you and me. If another out-worlder tries to set up housekeeping the news will get around in short order."

"What if he heads for Zundar?"

Kershaul shrugged. "I doubt if he'd dare. On the other hand—" Kershaul paused, then noting Thissell's sudden inattention, turned to follow Thissell's gaze.

A man in a Forest Goblin mask came swaggering toward them along the esplanade. Kershaul laid a restraining hand on Thissell's arm, but Thissell stepped out into the path of the Forest Goblin, his borrowed gun ready. "Haxo Angmark," he cried, "don't make a move, or I'll kill you. You're under arrest."

"Are you sure this is Angmark?" asked Kershaul in a worried voice.

"I'll find out," said Thissell. "Angmark, turn around, hold up your hands."

The Forest Goblin stood rigid with surprise and puzzlement. He reached to his *zachinko*, played an interrogatory arpeggio, and sang, "Why do you molest me, Moon Moth?"

Kershaul stepped forward and played a placatory phrase on his *slobo*. "I fear that a case of confused identity exists, Ser Forest Goblin. Ser Moon Moth seeks an out-worlder in a Forest Goblin mask."

The Forest Goblin's music became irritated, and he suddenly switched to his *stimic*. "He asserts that I am an out-worlder? Let him prove his case, or he has my retaliation to face."

Kershaul glanced in embarrassment around the crowd

which had gathered and once more struck up an ingratiating melody. "I am sure that Ser Moon Moth—"

The Forest Goblin interrupted with a fanfare of *skaranyi* tones. "Let him demonstrate his case or prepare for the flow of blood."

Thissell said, "Very well, I'll prove my case." He stepped forward, grasped the Forest Goblin's mask. "Let's see your face, that'll demonstrate your identity!"

The Forest Goblin sprang back in amazement. The crowd gasped, then set up an ominous strumming and toning of various instruments.

The Forest Goblin reached to the nape of his neck, jerked the cord to his duel-gong, and with his other hand snatched forth his scimitar.

Kershaul stepped forward, playing the *slobo* with great agitation. Thissell, now abashed, moved aside, conscious of the ugly sound of the crowd.

Kershaul sang explanations and apologies, the Forest Goblin answered; Kershaul spoke over his shoulder to Thissell: "Run for it, or you'll be killed! Hurry!"

Thissell hesitated; the Forest Goblin put up his hand to thrust Kershaul aside. "Run!" screamed Kershaul. "To Welibus' office, lock yourself in!"

Thissell took to his heels. The Forest Goblin pursued him a few yards, then stamped his feet, sent after him a set of raucous and derisive blasts of the hand-bugle, while the crowd produced a contemptuous counterpoint of clacking *hymerkins*.

There was no further pursuit. Instead of taking refuge in the Import-Export office, Thissell turned aside and after cautious reconnaissance proceeded to the dock where his houseboat was moored.

The hour was not far short of dusk when he finally returned aboard. Toby and Rex squatted on the forward deck, surrounded by the provisions they had brought back: reed baskets of fruit and cereal, blue-glass jugs containing wine, oil and pungent sap, three young pigs in a wicker pen. They were cracking nuts between their teeth, spitting the shells over the side. They looked up at Thissell, and it seemed that they rose to their feet with a new casualness. Toby muttered something under his breath; Rex smothered a chuckle.

Thissell clacked his *hymerkin* angrily. He sang, "Take the boat offshore; tonight we remain at Fan."

In the privacy of his cabin he removed the Moon Moth, stared into a mirror at his almost unfamiliar features. He picked up the Moon Moth, examined the detested lineaments: the furry gray skin, the blue spines, the ridiculous lace flaps. Hardly a dignified presence for the Consular Representative of the Home Planets. If, in fact, he still held the position when Cromartin learned of Angmark's winning free!

Thissell flung himself into a chair, stared moodily into space. Today he'd suffered a series of setbacks, but he wasn't defeated yet, not by any means. Tomorrow he'd visit Mathew Kershaul; they'd discuss how best to locate Angmark. As Kershaul had pointed out, another out-world establishment could not be camouflaged; Haxo Angmark's identity would soon become evident. Also, tomorrow he must procure another mask. Nothing extreme or vainglorious, but a mask which expressed a modicum of dignity and self-respect.

At this moment one of the slaves tapped on the doorpanel, and Thissell hastily pulled the hated Moon Moth back over his head.

Early next morning, before the dawn-light had left the sky, the slaves sculled the houseboat back to that section of the dock set aside for the use of out-worlders. Neither Rolver nor Welibus nor Kershaul had yet arrived and Thissell waited impatiently. An hour passed, and Welibus brought his boat to the dock. Not wishing to speak to Welibus, Thissell remained inside his cabin.

A few moments later Rolver's boat likewise pulled in alongside the dock. Through the window Thissell saw Rolver, wearing his usual Tarn-Bird, climb to the dock. Here he was met by a man in a yellow-tufted Sand Tiger mask, who played a formal accompaniment on his *gomapard* to whatever message he brought Rolver.

Rolver seemed surprised and disturbed. After a moment's thought he manipulated his own *gomapard*, and as he sang, he indicated Thissell's houseboat. Then, bowing, he went on his way.

The man in the Sand Tiger mask climbed with rather

heavy dignity to the float and rapped on the bulwark of Thissell's houseboat.

Thissell presented himself. Sirenese etiquette did not demand that he invite a casual visitor aboard, so he merely struck an interrogation on his *zachinko*.

The Sand Tiger played his *gomapard* and sang: "Dawn over the bay of Fan is customarily a splendid occasion; the sky is white with yellow and green colors; when Mireille rises, the mists burn and writhe like flames. He who sings derives a greater enjoyment from the hour when the floating corpse of an out-worlder does not appear to mar the serenity of the view."

Thissell's *zachinko* gave off a startled interrogation almost of its own accord; the Sand Tiger bowed with dignity. "The singer acknowledges no peer in steadfastness of disposition; however, he does not care to be plagued by the antics of a dissatisfied ghost. He therefore has ordered his slaves to attach a thong to the ankle of the corpse, and while we have conversed they have linked the corpse to the stern of your houseboat. You will wish to administer whatever rites are prescribed in the Out-world. He who sings wishes you a good morning and now departs."

Thissell rushed to the stern of his houseboat. There, near-naked and mask-less, floated the body of a mature man, supported by air trapped in his pantaloons.

Thissell studied the dead face, which seemed characterless and vapid—perhaps in direct consequence of the mask-wearing habit. The body appeared of medium stature and weight, and Thissell estimated the age as between forty-five and fifty. The hair was nondescript brown, the features bloated by the water. There was nothing to indicate how the man had died.

This must be Haxo Angmark, thought Thissell. Who else could it be? Mathew Kershaul? Why not? Thissell asked himself uneasily. Rolver and Welibus had already disembarked and gone about their business. He searched across the bay to locate Kershaul's houseboat, and discovered it already tying up to the dock. Even as he watched, Kershaul jumped ashore, wearing his Cave-Owl mask.

He seemed in an abstracted mood, for he passed Thissell's houseboat without lifting his eyes from the dock.

Thissell turned back to the corpse. Angmark, then, beyond a doubt. Had not three men disembarked from the houseboats of Rolver, Welibus, and Kershaul, wearing masks characteristic of these men? Obviously, the corpse of Angmark . . . The easy solution refused to sit quiet in Thissell's mind. Kershaul had pointed out that another out-worlder would be quickly identified. How else could Angmark maintain himself unless he . . . Thissell brushed the thought aside. The corpse was obviously Angmark. And yet . . .

Thissell summoned his slaves, gave orders that a suitable container be brought to the dock, that the corpse be transferred therein, and conveyed to a suitable place of repose. The slaves showed no enthusiasm for the task and Thissell was forced to thunder forcefully, if not skillfully, on the *hymerkin* to emphasize his orders.

He walked along the dock, turned up the esplanade, passed the office of Cornely Welibus and set out along the pleasant little lane to the landing field.

When he arrived, he found that Rolver had not yet made an appearance. An over-slave, given status by a yellow rosette on his black cloth mask, asked how he might be of service. Thissell stated that he wished to dispatch a message to Polypolis.

There was no difficulty here, declared the slave. If Thissell would set forth his message in clear block-print it would be dispatched immediately.

Thissell wrote:

OUT-WORLDER FOUND DEAD, POSSIBLY ANGMARK. AGE 48, MEDIUM PHYSIQUE, BROWN HAIR. OTHER MEANS OF IDENTIFICATION LACKING. AWAIT ACKNOWL-EDGMENT AND/OR INSTRUCTIONS.

He addressed the message to Castel Cromartin at Polypolis and handed it to the over-slave. A moment later he heard the characteristic sputter of trans-space discharge.

An hour passed. Rolver made no appearance. Thissell paced restlessly back and forth in front of the office. There was no telling how long he would have to wait: trans-space transmission time varied unpredictably. Sometimes the message snapped through in micro-seconds; sometimes it wandered through unknowable regions for hours; and there were several authenticated examples of messages being received before they had been transmitted.

Another half-hour passed, and Rolver finally arrived, wearing his customary Tarn-Bird. Coincidentally Thissell heard the hiss of the incoming message.

Rolver seemed surprised to see Thissell. "What brings you out so early?"

Thissell explained. "It concerns the body which you referred to me this morning. I'm communicating with my superiors about it."

Rolver raised his head and listened to the sound of the incoming message. "You seem to be getting an answer. I'd better attend to it."

"Why bother?" asked Thissell. "Your slave seems efficient."

"It's my job," declared Rolver. "I'm responsible for the accurate transmission and receipt of all space-grams."

"I'll come with you," said Thissell. "I've always wanted to watch the operation of the equipment."

"I'm afraid that's irregular," said Rolver. He went to the door which led into the inner compartment. "I'll have your message in a moment."

Thissell protested, but Rolver ignored him and went into the inner office.

Five minutes later he reappeared, carrying a small yellow envelope. "Not too good news," he announced with unconvincing commiseration.

Thissell glumly opened the envelope. The message read:

BODY NOT ANGMARK. ANGMARK HAS BLACK HAIR.
WHY DID YOU NOT MEET LANDING. SERIOUS INFRAC-
TION, HIGHLY DISSATISFIED. RETURN TO POLYPOLIS
NEXT OPPORTUNITY.

                                        CASTEL CROMARTIN

Thissell put the message in his pocket. "Incidentally, may I inquire the color of your hair?"

Rolver played a surprised little trill on his *kiv*. "I'm quite blond. Why do you ask?"

"Mere curiosity."

Rolver played another run on the *kiv*. "Now I understand. My dear fellow, what a suspicious nature you have!

Look!" He turned and parted the folds of his mask at the nape of his neck. Thissell saw that Rolver was blond indeed.

"Are you reassured?" asked Rolver jocularly.

"Oh, indeed," said Thissell. "Incidentally, have you another mask you could lend me? I'm sick of this Moon Moth."

"I'm afraid not," said Rolver. "But you need merely go into a mask-maker's shop and make a selection."

"Yes, of course," said Thissell. He took his leave of Rolver and returned along the trail to Fan. Passing Welibus' office he hesitated, then turned in. Today Welibus wore a dazzling confection of green glass prisms and silver beads, a mask Thissell had never seen before.

Welibus greeted him cautiously to the accompaniment of a *kiv*. "Good morning, Ser Moon Moth."

"I won't take too much of your time," said Thissell, "but I have a rather personal question to put to you. What color is your hair?"

Welibus hesitated a fraction of a second, then turned his back, lifted the flap of his mask. Thissell saw heavy black ringlets. "Does that answer your question?" inquired Welibus.

"Completely," said Thissell. He crossed the esplanade, went out on the dock to Kershaul's houseboat. Kershaul greeted him without enthusiasm, and invited him aboard with a resigned wave of the hand.

"A question I'd like to ask," said Thissell; "What color is your hair?"

Kershaul laughed woefully. "What little remains is black. Why do you ask?"

"Curiosity."

"Come, come," said Kershaul with an unaccustomed bluffness. "There's more to it than that."

Thissell, feeling the need of counsel, admitted as much. "Here's the situation. A dead out-worlder was found in the harbor this morning. His hair was brown. I'm not entirely certain, but the chances are—let me see, yes, two out of three that Angmark's hair is black."

Kershaul pulled at the Cave-Owl's goatee. "How do you arrive at that probability?"

"The information came to me through Rolver's hands. He has blond hair. If Angmark has assumed Rolver's identity, he would naturally alter the information which came to me this morning. Both you and Welibus admit to black hair."

"Hm," said Kershaul. "Let me see if I follow your line of reasoning. You feel that Haxo Angmark has killed either Rolver, Welibus, or myself and assumed the dead man's identity. Right?"

Thissell looked at him in surprise. "You yourself emphasized that Angmark could not set up another outworld establishment without revealing himself! Don't you remember?"

"Oh, certainly. To continue. Rolver delivered a message to you stating that Angmark was dark, and announced himself to be blond."

"Yes. Can you verify this? I mean for the old Rolver?"

"No," said Kershaul sadly. "I've seen neither Rolver nor Welibus without their masks."

"If Rolver is not Angmark," Thissell mused, "if Angmark indeed has black hair, then both you and Welibus come under suspicion."

"Very interesting," said Kershaul. He examined Thissell warily. "For that matter, you yourself might be Angmark. What color is your hair?"

"Brown," said Thissell curtly. He lifted the gray fur of the Moon Moth mask at the back of his head.

"But you might be deceiving me as to the text of the message," Kershaul put forward.

"I'm not," said Thissell wearily. "You can check with Rolver if you care to."

Kershaul shook his head. "Unnecessary. I believe you. But another matter: what of voices? You've heard all of us before and after Angmark arrived. Isn't there some indication there?"

"No. I'm so alert for any evidence of change that you all sound rather different. And the masks muffle your voices."

Kershaul tugged the goatee. "I don't see any immediate solution to the problem." He chuckled. "In any event, need there be? Before Angmark's advent, there were Rolver, Welibus, Kershaul, and Thissell. Now—for all practical purposes—there are still Rolver, Welibus, Kershaul, and Thissell. Who is to say that the new member may not be an improvement upon the old?"

"An interesting thought," agreed Thissell, "but it so happens that I have a personal interest in identifying Angmark. My career is at stake."

"I see," murmured Kershaul. "The situation then becomes an issue between yourself and Angmark."

"You won't help me?"

"Not actively. I've become pervaded with Sirenese individualism. I think you'll find that Rolver and Welibus will respond similarly." He sighed. "All of us have been here too long."

Thissell stood deep in thought. Kershaul waited patiently a moment, then said, "Do you have any further questions?"

"No," said Thissell. "I have merely a favor to ask you."

"I'll oblige if I possibly can," Kershaul replied courteously.

"Give me, or lend me, one of your slaves, for a week or two."

Kershaul played an exclamation of amusement on the *ganga*. "I hardly like to part with my slaves; they know me and my ways—"

"As soon as I catch Angmark you'll have him back."

"Very well," said Kershaul. He rattled a summons on his *hymerkin*, and a slave appeared. "Anthony," sang Kershaul, "you are to go with Ser Thissell and serve him for a short period."

The slave bowed, without pleasure.

Thissell took Anthony to his houseboat, and questioned him at length, noting certain of the responses upon a chart. He then enjoined Anthony to say nothing of what had passed, and consigned him to the care of Toby and Rex. He gave further instructions to move the houseboat away from the dock and allow no one aboard until his return.

He set forth once more along the way to the landing field, and found Rolver at a lunch of spiced fish, shredded bark of the salad tree, and a bowl of native currants. Rolver clapped an order on the *hymerkin*, and a slave set a place for Thissell. "And how are the investigations proceeding?"

"I'd hardly like to claim any progress," said Thissell. "I assume that I can count on your help?"

Rolver laughed briefly. "You have my good wishes."

"More concretely," said Thissell, "I'd like to borrow a slave from you. Temporarily."

Rolver paused in his eating. "Whatever for?"

"I'd rather not explain," said Thissell. "But you can be sure that I make no idle request."

Without graciousness Rolver summoned a slave and consigned him to Thissell's service.

On the way back to his houseboat, Thissell stopped at Welibus' office.

Welibus looked up from his work. "Good afternoon, Ser Thissell."

Thissell came directly to the point. "Ser Welibus, will you lend me a slave for a few days?"

Welibus hesitated, then shrugged. "Why not?" He clacked his *hymerkin*; a slave appeared. "Is he satisfactory? Or would you prefer a young female?" He chuckled rather offensively, to Thissell's way of thinking.

"He'll do very well. I'll return him in a few days."

"No hurry." Welibus made an easy gesture and returned to his work.

Thissell continued to his houseboat, where he separately interviewed each of his two new slaves and made notes upon his chart.

Dusk came soft over the Titanic Ocean. Toby and Rex sculled the houseboat away from the dock, out across the silken waters. Thissell sat on the deck listening to the sound of soft voices, the flutter and tinkle of musical instruments. Lights from the floating houseboats glowed yellow and wan watermelon-red. The shore was dark; the Night-men would presently come slinking to paw through refuse and stare jealously across the water.

In nine days the *Buenaventura* came past Sirene on its regular schedule; Thissell had his orders to return to Polypolis. In nine days, could he locate Haxo Angmark?

Nine days weren't too many, Thissell decided, but they might possibly be enough.

Two days passed, and three and four and five. Every day Thissell went ashore and at least once a day visited Rolver, Welibus, and Kershaul.

Each reacted differently to his presence. Rolver was sardonic and irritable; Welibus formal and at least superficially affable; Kershaul mild and suave, but ostentatiously impersonal and detached in his conversation.

Thissell remained equally bland to Rolver's dour jibes,

Welibus' jocundity, Kershaul's withdrawal. And every day, returning to his houseboat he made marks on his chart.

The sixth, the seventh, the eighth day came and passed. Rolver, with rather brutal directness, inquired if Thissell wished to arrange for passage on the *Buenaventura*. Thissell considered, and said, "Yes, you had better reserve passage for one."

"Back to the world of faces," shuddered Rolver. "Faces! Everywhere pallid, fish-eyed faces. Mouths like pulp, noses knotted and punctured; flat, flabby faces. I don't think I could stand it after living here. Luckily you haven't become a real Sirenese."

"But I won't be going back," said Thissell.

"I thought you wanted me to reserve passage."

"I do. For Haxo Angmark. He'll be returning to Polypolis, in the brig."

"Well, well," said Rolver. "So you've picked him out."

"Of course," said Thissell. "Haven't you?"

Rolver shrugged. "He's either Welibus or Kershaul, that's as close as I can make it. So long as he wears his mask and calls himself either Welibus or Kershaul, it means nothing to me."

"It means a great deal to me," said Thissell. "What time tomorrow does the lighter go up?"

"Eleven twenty-two sharp. If Haxo Angmark's leaving, tell him to be on time."

"He'll be here," said Thissell.

He made his usual call upon Welibus and Kershaul, then returning to his houseboat, put three final marks on his chart.

The evidence was here, plain and convincing. Not absolutely incontrovertible evidence, but enough to warrant a definite move. He checked over his gun. Tomorrow, the day of decision. He could afford no errors.

The day dawned bright white, the sky like the inside of an oyster shell; Mireille rose through iridescent mists. Toby and Rex sculled the houseboat to the dock. The remaining three out-world houseboats floated somnolently on the slow swells.

One boat Thissell watched in particular, that whose owner Haxo Angmark had killed and dropped into the harbor. This boat presently moved toward the shore, and Haxo

Angmark himself stood on the front deck, wearing a mask Thissell had never seen before: a construction of scarlet feathers, black glass, and spiked green hair.

Thissell was forced to admire his poise. A clever scheme, cleverly planned and executed—but marred by an insurmountable difficulty.

Angmark returned within. The houseboat reached the dock. Slaves flung out mooring lines, lowered the gangplank. Thissell, his gun ready in the pocket flap of his robes, walked down the dock, went aboard. He pushed open the door to the saloon. The man at the table raised his red, black and green mask in surprise.

Thissell said, "Angmark, please don't argue or make any—"

Something hard and heavy tackled him from behind; he was flung to the floor, his gun wrested expertly away.

Behind him the *hymerkin* clattered; a voice sang, "Bind the fool's arms."

The man sitting at the table rose to his feet, removed the red, black and green mask to reveal the black cloth of a slave. Thissell twisted his head. Over him stood Haxo Angmark, wearing a mask Thissell recognized as a Dragon-Tamer, fabricated from black metal, with a knife-blade nose, socketed-eyelids, and three crests running back over the scalp.

The mask's expression was unreadable, but Angmark's voice was triumphant. "I trapped you very easily."

"So you did," said Thissell. The slave finished knotting his wrists together. A clatter of Angmark's *hymerkin* sent him away. "Get to your feet," said Angmark. "Sit in that chair."

"What are we waiting for?" inquired Thissell.

"Two of our fellows still remain out on the water. We won't need them for what I have in mind."

"Which is?"

"You'll learn in due course," said Angmark. "We have an hour or so on our hands."

Thissell tested his bonds. They were undoubtedly secure.

Angmark seated himself. "How did you fix on me? I admit to being curious . . . Come, come," he chided as Thissell sat silently. "Can't you recognize that I have defeated you? Don't make affairs unpleasant for yourself."

Thissell shrugged. "I operated on a basic principle. A man can mask his face, but he can't mask his personality."

"Aha," said Angmark. "Interesting. Proceed."

"I borrowed a slave from you and the other two out-worlders, and I questioned them carefully. What masks had their masters worn during the month before your arrival? I prepared a chart and plotted their responses. Rolver wore the Tarn-Bird about eighty percent of the time, the remaining twenty percent divided between the Sophist Abstraction and the Black Intricate. Welibus had a taste for the heroes of Kan-Dachan Cycle. He wore the Chalekun, the Prince Intrepid, the Seavain most of the time: six days out of eight. The other two days he wore his South-Wind or his Gay Companion. Kersaul, more conservative, pre-ferred the Cave Owl, the Star Wanderer, and two or three other masks he wore at odd intervals.

"As I say, I acquired this information from possibly its most accurate source, the slaves. My next step was to keep watch upon the three of you. Every day I noted what masks you wore and compared it with my chart. Rolver wore his Tarn-Bird six times, his Black Intricate twice. Kershaul wore his Cave Owl five times, his Star Wanderer once, his Quincunx once and his Ideal of Perfection once. Welibus wore the Emerald Mountain twice, the Triple Phoenix three times, the Prince Intrepid once, and the Shark-God twice."

Angmark nodded thoughtfully. "I see my error. I selected from Welibus' masks, but to my own taste—and as you point out, I revealed myself. But only to you." He rose and went to the window. "Kershaul and Rolver are now coming ashore; they'll soon be past and about their business—though I doubt if they'd interfere in any case; they've both become good Sirenese."

Thissell waited in silence. Ten minutes passed. Then Angmark reached to a shelf and picked up a knife. He looked at Thissell. "Stand up."

Thissell slowly rose to his feet. Angmark approached from the side, reached out, lifted the Moon Moth from Thissell's head. Thissell gasped and made a vain attempt to seize it. Too late; his face was bare and naked.

Angmark turned away, removed his own mask, donned the Moon Moth. He struck a call on his *hymerkin*. Two slaves entered, stopped in shock at the sight of Thissell.

Angmark played a brisk tattoo, sang, "Carry this man up to the dock."

"Angmark," cried Thissell. "I'm maskless!"

The slaves seized him and in spite of Thissell's desperate struggles, conveyed him out on the deck, along the float and up on the dock.

Angmark fixed a rope around Thissell's neck. He said, "You are now Haxo Angmark, and I am Edwer Thissell. Welibus is dead, you shall soon be dead. I can handle your job without difficulty. I'll play musical instruments like a Night-man and sing like a crow. I'll wear the Moon Moth till it rots and then I'll get another. The report will go to Polypolis, Haxo Angmark is dead. Everything will be serene."

Thissell barely heard. "You can't do this," he whispered. "My mask, my face . . ." A large woman in a blue and pink flower mask walked down the dock. She saw Thissell and emitted a piercing shriek, flung herself prone on the dock.

"Come along," said Angmark brightly. He tugged at the rope, and so pulled Thissell down the dock. A man in a Pirate Captain mask coming up from his houseboat stood rigid in amazement.

Angmark played the *zachinko* and sang, "Behold the notorious criminal Haxo Angmark. Through all the outer-worlds his name is reviled; now he is captured and led in shame to his death. Behold Haxo Angmark!"

They turned into the esplanade. A child screamed in fright; a man called hoarsely. Thissell stumbled; tears tumbled from his eyes; he could see only disorganized shapes and colors. Angmark's voice belled out richly: "Everyone behold, the criminal of the out-worlds, Haxo Angmark! Approach and observe his execution!"

Thissell feebly cried out, "I'm not Angmark; I'm Edwer Thissell; he's Angmark." But no one listened to him; there were only cries of dismay, shock, disgust at the sight of his face. He called to Angmark, "Give me my mask, a slave-cloth . . ."

Angmark sang jubilantly, "In shame he lived, in maskless shame he dies."

A Forest Goblin stood before Angmark. "Moon Moth, we meet once more."

Angmark sang, "Stand aside, friend Goblin; I must execute this criminal. In shame he lived, in shame he dies!"

A crowd had formed around the group; masks stared in morbid titillation at Thissell.

The Forest Goblin jerked the rope from Angmark's hand, threw it to the ground. The crowd roared. Voices cried, "No duel, no duel! Execute the monster!"

A cloth was thrown over Thissell's head. Thissell awaited the thrust of a blade. But instead his bonds were cut. Hastily he adjusted the cloth, hiding his face, peering between the folds.

Four men clutched Haxo Angmark. The Forest Goblin confronted him, playing the *skaranyi*. "A week ago you reached to divest me of my mask; you have now achieved your perverse aim!"

"But he is a criminal," cried Angmark. "He is notorious, infamous!"

"What are his misdeeds?" sang the Forest Goblin.

"He has murdered, betrayed; he has wrecked ships; he has tortured, blackmailed, robbed, sold children into slavery; he has—"

The Forest Goblin stopped him. "Your religious differences are of no importance. We can vouch however for your present crimes!"

The hostler stepped forward. He sang fiercely, "This insolent Moon Moth nine days ago sought to pre-empt my choicest mount!"

Another man pushed close. He wore a Universal Expert, and sang, "I am a Master Mask-maker; I recognize this Moon Moth out-worlder! Only recently he entered my shop and derided my skill. He deserves death!"

"Death to the out-world monster!" cried the crowd. A wave of men surged forward. Steel blades rose and fell, the deed was done.

Thissell watched, unable to move. The Forest Goblin approached, and playing the *stimic* sang sternly, "For you we have pity, but also contempt. A true man would never suffer such indignities!"

Thissell took a deep breath. He reached to his belt and found his *zachinko*. He sang, "My friend, you malign me! Can you not appreciate true courage? Would you prefer to die in combat or walk maskless along the esplanade?"

The Forest Goblin sang, "There is only one answer. First I would die in combat; I could not bear such shame."

Thissell sang, "I had such a choice. I could fight with my hands tied, and so die—or I could suffer shame, and through this shame conquer my enemy. You admit that you lack sufficient *strakh* to achieve this deed. I have proved myself a hero of bravery! I ask, who here has courage to do what I have done?"

"Courage?" demanded the Forest Goblin. "I fear nothing, up to and beyond death at the hands of the Nightmen!"

"Then answer."

The Forest Goblin stood back. He played his *double-kamanthil*. "Bravery indeed, if such were your motives."

The hostler struck a series of subdued *gomapard* chords and sang, "Not a man among us would dare what this maskless man has done."

The crowd muttered approval.

The mask-maker approached Thissell, obsequiously stroking his *double-kamanthil*. "Pray Lord Hero, step into my nearby shop, exchange this vile rag for a mask befitting your quality."

Another mask-maker sang, "Before you choose, Lord Hero, examine my magnificent creations!"

A man in a Bright Sky Bird mask approached Thissell reverently. "I have only just completed a sumptuous houseboat; seventeen years of toil have gone into its fabrication. Grant me the good fortune of accepting and using this splendid craft; aboard waiting to serve you are alert slaves and pleasant maidens; there is ample wine in storage and soft silken carpets on the decks."

"Thank you," said Thissell, striking the *zachinko* with vigor and confidence. "I accept with pleasure. But first a mask."

The mask-maker struck an interrogative trill on the *gomapard*. "Would the Lord Hero consider a Sea-Dragon Conqueror beneath his dignity?"

"By no means," said Thissell. "I consider it suitable and satisfactory. We shall go now to examine it."

A PLANET NAMED SHAYOL

BY CORDWAINER SMITH
(PAUL M. A. LINEBARGER; 1913-1966)

GALAXY SCIENCE FICTION
OCTOBER

The remarkable Professor Linebarger returns with this stunning novelette set in his own special universe. One of the main differences between Campbellian science fiction of the Golden Age and what followed is that the nature of the protaganists shifted (in some, but not all, cases) from active "cando" scientists and astronauts to more passive, reactive people much closer to the real world and the tenor of the times.

This shift is quite obvious in the person of "Mercer" in "A Planet Named Shayol," one of Smith's longest and best works. (MHG)

As is true of everyone else, science fiction writers differ in temperament.

Some science fiction writers are loud and extroverted and make their presence felt wherever they go. Harlan Ellison is the supreme example of this, although I am no slouch myself.

Some science fiction writers attend science fiction conventions, give talks, win awards, but are very quiet and even retiring. Harry Stubbs ("Hal Clement") is the supreme example of this. Robert Silverberg is another prominent science fiction writer who is not noisy or exhibitionistic.

And there are some science fiction writers whose writing is all that is known about them. They make no mark whatever on the s.f. world as personalities. And Cordwainer Smith is one of these.

Human nature being what it is, the loud noisy ones are

invariably judged as perhaps better than they are. Quiet and retiring ones are judged as less good than they are.

Cordwainer Smith has written enormously unusual and high-quality stories and yet to the average fan he is almost unknown. It is purely a matter of personality and the result, in Cordwainer's case, is terribly unjust. (IA)

1

There was a tremendous difference between the liner and the ferry in Mercer's treatment. On the liner, the attendants made gibes when they brought him his food.

"Scream good and loud," said one rat-faced steward, "and then we'll know it's you when they broadcast the sounds of punishment on the Emperor's birthday."

The other, fat steward ran the tip of his wet, red tongue over his thick, purple-red lips one time and said, "Stands to reason, man. If you hurt all the time, the whole lot of you would die. Something pretty good must happen, along with the—whatchamacallit. Maybe you turn into a woman. Maybe you turn into two people. Listen, cousin, if it's real crazy fun, let me know . . ." Mercer said nothing. Mercer had enough troubles of his own not to wonder about the daydreams of nasty men.

At the ferry it was different. The biopharmaceutical staff was deft, impersonal, quick in removing his shackles. They took off all his prison clothes and left them on the liner. When he boarded the ferry, naked, they looked him over as if he were a rare plant or a body on the operating table. They were almost kind in the clinical deftness of their touch. They did not treat him as a criminal, but as a specimen.

Men and women, clad in their medical smocks, they looked at him as though he were already dead.

He tried to speak. A man, older and more authoritative than the others, said firmly and clearly, "Do not worry about talking. I will talk to you myself in a very little time. What we are having now are the preliminaries, to determine your physical condition. Turn around, please."

Mercer turned around. An orderly rubbed his back with a very strong antiseptic.

"This is going to sting," said one of the technicians, "but

it is nothing serious or painful. We are determining the toughness of the different layers of your skin."

Mercer, annoyed by this impersonal approach, spoke up just as a sharp little sting burned him above the sixth lumbar vertebra. "Don't you know who I am?"

"Of course we know who you are," said a woman's voice. "We have it all in a file in the corner. The chief doctor will talk about your crime later, if you want to talk about it. Keep quiet now. We are making a skin test, and you will feel much better if you do not make us prolong it."

Honesty forced her to add another sentence: "And we will get better results as well."

They had lost no time at all in getting to work.

He peered at them sidewise to look at them. There was nothing about them to indicate that they were human devils in the antechambers of hell itself. Nothing was there to indicate that this was the satellite of Shayol, the final and uttermost place of chastisement and shame. They looked like medical people from his life before he committed the crime without a name.

They changed from one routine to another. A woman, wearing a surgical mask, waved her hand at a white table.

"Climb up on that, please."

No one had said "please" to Mercer since the guards had seized him at the edge of the palace. He started to obey her and then he saw that there were padded handcuffs at the head of the table. He stopped.

"Get along, please," she demanded. Two or three of the others turned around to look at both of them.

The second "please" shook him. He had to speak. These were people, and he was a person again. He felt his voice rising, almost cracking into shrillness as he asked her, "Please, Ma'am, is the punishment going to begin?"

"There's no punishment here," said the woman. "This is the satellite. Get on the table. We're going to give you your first skin-toughening before you talk to the head doctor. Then you can tell him all about your crime—"

"You know my crime?" he said, greeting it almost like a neighbor.

"Of course not," said she, "but all the people who come through here are believed to have committed crimes. Somebody thinks so or they wouldn't be here. Most of them want

to talk about their personal crimes. But don't slow me
down. I'm a skin technician, and down on the surface of
Shayol you're going to need the very best work that any of
us can do for you. Now get on that table. And when you
are ready to talk to the chief you'll have something to talk
about besides your crime."

He complied.

Another masked person, probably a girl, took his hands
in cool, gentle fingers and fitted them to the padded cuffs
in a way he had never sensed before. By now he thought
he knew every interrogation machine in the whole empire,
but this was nothing like any of them.

The orderly stepped back. "All clear, Sir and Doctor."

"Which do you prefer?" said the skin technician. "A
great deal of pain or a couple of hours' unconsciousness?"

"Why should I want pain?" said Mercer.

"Some specimens do," said the technician, "by the time
they arrive here. I suppose it depends on what people have
done to them before they got here. I take it you did not
get any of the dream-punishments."

"No," said Mercer. "I missed those." He thought to himself, I didn't know that I missed anything at all.

He remembered his last trial, himself wired and plugged
in to the witness stand. The room had been high and dark.
Bright blue light shone on the panel of judges, their judicial
caps a fantastic parody of the episcopal mitres of long, long
ago. The judges were talking, but he could not hear them.
Momentarily the insulation slipped and he heard one of
them say, "Look at that white, devilish face. A man like
that is guilty of everything. I vote for Pain Terminal." "Not
Planet Shayol?" said a second voice. "The dromozoa
place," said a third voice. "That should suit him," said the
first voice. One of the judicial engineers must then have
noticed that the prisoner was listening illegally. He was cut
off. Mercer then thought that he had gone through everything which the cruelty and intelligence of mankind could
devise.

But this woman said he had missed the dream-punishments. Could there be people in the universe even worse
off than himself? There must be a lot of people down on
Shayol. They never came back.

He was going to be one of them; would they boast to him

of what they had done, before they were made to come to this place?

"You asked for it," said the woman technician. "It is just an ordinary anesthetic. Don't panic when you awaken. Your skin is going to be thickened and strengthened chemically and biologically."

"Does it hurt?"

"Of course," said she. "But get this out of your head. We're not punishing you. The pain here is just ordinary medical pain. Anybody might get it if they needed a lot of surgery. The punishment, if that's what you want to call it, is down on Shayol. Our only job is to make sure that you are fit to survive after you are landed. In a way, we are saving your life ahead of time. You can be grateful for that if you want to be. Meanwhile, you will save yourself a lot of trouble if you realize that your nerve endings will respond to the change in the skin. You had better expect to be very uncomfortable when you recover. But then, we can help that, too." She brought down an enormous lever and Mercer blacked out.

When he came to, he was in an ordinary hospital room, but he did not notice it. He seemed bedded in fire. He lifted his hand to see if there were flames on it. It looked the way it always had, except that it was a little red and a little swollen. He tried to turn in the bed. The fire became a scorching blast which stopped him in mid-turn. Uncontrollably, he moaned.

A voice spoke, "You are ready for some pain-killer."

It was a girl nurse. "Hold your head still," she said, "and I will give you half an amp of pleasure. Your skin won't bother you then."

She slipped a soft cap on his head. It looked like metal but it felt like silk.

He had to dig his fingernails into his palms to keep from threshing about on the bed.

"Scream if you want to," she said. "A lot of them do. It will just be a minute or two before the cap finds the right lobe in your brain."

She stepped to the corner and did something which he could not see.

There was the flick of a switch.

The fire did not vanish from his skin. He still felt it; but suddenly it did not matter. His mind was full of delicious pleasure which throbbed outward from his head and seemed to pulse down through his nerves. He had visited the pleasure palaces, but he had never felt anything like this before.

He wanted to thank the girl, and he twisted around in the bed to see her. He could feel his whole body flash with pain as he did so, but the pain was far away. And the pulsating pleasure which coursed out of his head, down his spinal cord and into his nerves was so intense that the pain got through only as a remote, unimportant signal.

She was standing very still in the corner.

"Thank you, nurse," said he.

She said nothing.

He looked more closely, though it was hard to look while enormous pleasure pulsed through his body like a symphony written in nerve-messages. He focused his eyes on her and saw that she too wore a soft metallic cap.

He pointed at it.

She blushed all the way down to her throat.

She spoke dreamily, "You looked like a nice man to me. I didn't think you'd tell on me . . ."

He gave her what he thought was a friendly smile, but with the pain in his skin and the pleasure bursting out of his head, he really had no idea of what his actual expression might be. "It's against the law," he said. "It's terribly against the law. But it is nice."

"How do you think *we* stand it here?" said the nurse. "You specimens come in here talking like ordinary people and then you go down to Shayol. Terrible things happen to you on Shayol. Then the surface station sends up parts of you, over and over again. I may see your head ten times, quick-frozen and ready for cutting up, before my two years are up. You prisoners ought to know how we suffer," she crooned, the pleasure-charge still keeping her relaxed and happy, "you ought to die as soon as you get down there and not pester us with your torments. We can hear you screaming, you know. You keep on sounding like people even after Shayol begins to work on you. Why do you do it, Mr. Specimen?" She giggled sillily. "You hurt our feelings so. No wonder a girl like me has to have a little jolt now and then. It's real, real dreamy and I don't mind getting you ready to go down on Shayol." She staggered over to his bed. "Pull this cap off me, will you? I haven't got enough will power left to raise my hands."

Mercer saw his hand tremble as he reached for the cap.

His fingers touched the girl's soft hair through the cap. As he tried to get his thumb under the edge of the cap, in order to pull it off, he realized that this was the loveliest girl he had ever touched. He felt that he had always loved her, that he always would. Her cap came off. She stood erect, staggering a little before she found a chair to hold to. She closed her eyes and breathed deeply.

"Just a minute," she said in her normal voice. "I'll be with you in just a minute. The only time I can get a jolt of this is when one of you visitors gets a dose to get over the skin trouble."

She turned to the room mirror to adjust her hair. Speaking with her back to him, she said, "I hope I didn't say anything about downstairs."

Mercer still had the cap on. He loved this beautiful girl who had put it on him. He was ready to weep at the thought that she had had the same kind of pleasure which he still enjoyed. Not for the world would he say anything which could hurt her feelings. He was sure she wanted to be told that she had not said anything about "downstairs"—probably shop talk for the surface of Shayol—so he assured her warmly, "You said nothing. Nothing at all."

She came over to the bed, leaned, kissed him on the lips. The kiss was as far away as the pain; he felt nothing; the Niagara of throbbing pleasure which poured through his head left no room for more sensation. But he liked the friendliness of it. A grim, sane corner of his mind whispered to him that this was probably the last time he would ever kiss a woman, but it did not seem to matter.

With skilled fingers she adjusted the cap on his head. "There, now. You're a sweet guy. I'm going to pretend-forget and leave the cap on you till the doctor comes."

With a bright smile she squeezed his shoulder.

She hastened out of the room.

The white of her skirt flashed prettily as she went out the door. He saw that she had very shapely legs indeed.

She was nice, but the cap . . . ah, it was the cap that mattered! He closed his eyes and let the cap go on stimulating the pleasure centers of his brain. The pain in his skin was still there, but it did not matter any more than did the chair standing in the corner. The pain was just something that happened to be in the room.

A firm touch on his arm made him open his eyes.

The older, authoritative-looking man was standing beside the bed, looking down at him with a quizzical smile.

"She did it again," said the old man.

Mercer shook his head, trying to indicate that the young nurse had done nothing wrong.

"I'm Doctor Vomact," said the older man, "and I am going to take this cap off you. You will then experience the pain again, but I think it will not be so bad. You can have the cap several more times before you leave here."

With a swift, firm gesture he snatched the cap off Mercer's head.

Mercer promptly doubled up with the inrush of fire from his skin. He started to scream and then saw that Doctor Vomact was watching him calmly.

Mercer gasped, "It is—easier now."

"I knew it would be," said the doctor. "I had to take the cap off to talk to you. You have a few choices to make."

"Yes, Doctor," gasped Mercer.

"You have committed a serious crime and you are going down to the surface of Shayol."

"Yes," said Mercer.

"Do you want to tell me your crime?"

Mercer thought of the white palace walls in perpetual sunlight, and the soft mewing of the little things when he reached them. He tightened his arms, legs, back and jaw. "No," he said, "I don't want to talk about it. It's the crime without a name. Against the Imperial family . . ."

"Fine," said the doctor, "that's a healthy attitude. The crime is past. Your future is ahead. Now, I can destroy your mind before you go down—if you want me to."

"That's against the law," said Mercer.

Doctor Vomact smiled warmly and confidently. "Of course it is. A lot of things are against human law. But there are laws of science, too. Your body, down on Shayol, is going to serve science. It doesn't matter to me whether that body has Mercer's mind or the mind of a low-grade shellfish. I have to leave enough mind in you to keep the body going, but I can wipe out the historic you and give

your body a better chance of being happy. It's your choice,
Mercer. Do you want to be you or not?"

Mercer shook his head back and forth, "I don't know."

"I'm taking a chance," said Doctor Vomact, "in giving
you this much leeway. I'd have it done if I were in your
position. It's pretty bad down there."

Mercer looked at the full, broad face. He did not trust
the comfortable smile. Perhaps this was a trick to increase
his punishment. The cruelty of the Emperor was proverbial.
Look at what he had done to the widow of his predecessor,
the Dowager Lady Da. She was younger than the Emperor
himself, and he had sent her to a place worse than death.
If he had been sentenced to Shayol, why was this doctor
trying to interfere with the rules? Maybe the doctor himself
had been conditioned, and did not know what he was
offering.

Doctor Vomact read Mercer's face. "All right. You
refuse. You want to take your mind down with you. It's all
right with me. I don't have you on my conscience. I suppose
you'll refuse the next offer too. Do you want me to take
your eyes out before you go down? You'll be much more
comfortable without vision. I *know* that, from the voices
that we record for the warning broadcasts. I can sear the
optic nerves so that there will be no chance of your getting
vision again."

Mercer rocked back and forth. The fiery pain had become
a universal itch, but the soreness of his spirit was greater
than the discomfort of his skin.

"You refuse that, too?" said the doctor.

"I suppose so," said Mercer.

"Then all I have to do is to get ready. You can have the
cap for a while, if you want."

Mercer said, "Before I put the cap on, can you tell me
what happens down there?"

"Some of it," said the doctor. "There is an attendant. He
is a man, but not a human being. He is a homunculus fash-
ioned out of cattle material. He is intelligent and very con-
scientious. You specimens are turned loose on the surface
of Shayol. The dromozoa are a special life-form there.
When they settle in your body, B'dikkat—that's the attendant—carves them out with an anesthetic and sends them
up here. We freeze the tissue cultures, and they are compat-

ible with almost any kind of oxygen-based life. Half the surgical repair you see in the whole universe comes out of buds that we ship from here. Shayol is a very healthy place, so far as survival is concerned. You won't die."

"You mean," said Mercer, "that I am getting perpetual punishment."

"I didn't say that," said Doctor Vomact. "Or if I did, I was wrong. You won't die soon. I don't know how long you will live down there. Remember, no matter how uncomfortable you get, the samples which B'dikkat sends up will help thousands of people in all the inhabited worlds. Now take the cap."

"I'd rather talk," said Mercer. "It may be my last chance."

The doctor looked at him strangely. "If you can stand that pain, go ahead and talk."

"Can I commit suicide down there?"

"I don't know," said the doctor. "It's never happened. And to judge by the voices, you'd think they wanted to."

"Has anybody ever come back from Shayol?"

"Not since it was put off limits about four hundred years ago."

"Can I talk to other people down there?"

"Yes," said the doctor.

"Who punishes me down there?"

"Nobody does, you fool," cried Doctor Vomact. "It's not punishment. People don't like it down on Shayol, and it's better, I guess, to get convicts instead of volunteers. But there isn't anybody *against* you at all."

"No jailers?" asked Mercer, with a whine in his voice.

"No jailers, no rules, no prohibitions. Just Shayol, and B'dikkat to take care of you. Do you still want your mind and your eyes?"

"I'll keep them," said Mercer. "I've gone this far and I might as well go the rest of the way."

"Then let me put the cap on you for your second dose," said Doctor Vomact.

The doctor adjusted the cap just as lightly and delicately as had the nurse; he was quicker about it. There was no sign of his picking out another cap for himself.

The inrush of pleasure was like a wild intoxication. His burning skin receded into distance. The doctor was near in space, but even the doctor did not matter. Mercer was not afraid of Shayol. The pulsation of happiness out of his brain was too great to leave room for fear or pain.

Doctor Vomact was holding out his hand.

Mercer wondered why, and then realized that the wonderful, kindly cap-giving man was offering to shake hands. He lifted his own. It was heavy, but his arm was happy, too.

They shook hands. It was curious, thought Mercer, to feel the handshake beyond the double level of cerebral pleasure and dermal pain.

"Goodbye, Mr. Mercer," said the doctor. "Goodbye and a good goodnight . . ."

2

The ferry satellite was a hospitable place. The hundreds of hours that followed were like a long, weird dream.

Twice again the young nurse sneaked into his bedroom with him when he was being given the cap and had a cap with him. There were baths which calloused his whole body. Under strong local anesthetics, his teeth were taken out and stainless steel took their place. There were irradiations under blazing lights which took away the pain of his skin. There were special treatments for his fingernails and toenails. Gradually they changed into formidable claws; he found himself stropping them on the aluminum bed one night and saw that they left deep marks.

His mind never became completely clear.

Sometimes he thought that he was home with his mother, that he was little again, and in pain. Other times, under the cap, he laughed in his bed to think that people were sent to this place for punishment when it was all so terribly much fun. There were no trials, no questions, no judges. Food was good, but he did not think about it much; the cap was better. Even when he was awake, he was drowsy.

At last, with the cap on him, they put him into an adiabatic pod—a one-body missile which could be dropped from the ferry to the planet below. He was all closed in, except for his face.

Doctor Vomact seemed to swim into the room. "You are

strong, Mercer," the doctor shouted, "you are very strong!
Can you hear me?"

Mercer nodded.

"We wish you well, Mercer. No matter what happens,
remember you are helping other people up here."

"Can I take the cap with me?" said Mercer.

For an answer, Doctor Vomact removed the cap himself.
Two men closed the lid of the pod, leaving Mercer in total
darkness. His mind started to clear, and he panicked against
his wrappings.

There was the roar of thunder and the taste of blood.

The next thing that Mercer knew, he was in a cool, cool
room, much chillier than the bedrooms and operating rooms
of the satellite. Someone was lifting him gently onto a table.

He opened his eyes.

An enormous face, four times the size of any human face
Mercer had ever seen, was looking down at him. Huge
brown eyes, cowlike in their gentle inoffensiveness, moved
back and forth as the big face examined Mercer's wrappings. The face was that of a handsome man of middle
years, clean-shaven, hair chestnut-brown, with sensual, full
lips and gigantic but healthy yellow teeth exposed in a half-
smile. The face saw Mercer's eyes open, and spoke with a
deep friendly roar.

"I'm your best friend. My name is B'dikkat, but you don't
have to use that here. Just call me Friend, and I will always
help you."

"I hurt," said Mercer.

"Of course you do. You hurt all over. That's a big drop,"
said B'dikkat.

"Can I have a cap, please," begged Mercer. It was not a
question; it was a demand; Mercer felt that his private
inward eternity depended on it.

B'dikkat laughed. "I haven't any caps down here. I might
use them myself. Or so they think. I have other things,
much better. No fear, fellow, I'll fix you up."

Mercer looked doubtful. If the cap had brought him happiness on the ferry, it would take at least electrical stimulation of the brain to undo whatever torments the surface of
Shayol had to offer.

B'dikkat's laughter filled the room like a bursting pillow.
"Have you ever heard of condamine?"

"No," said Mercer.

"It's a narcotic so powerful that the pharmacopoeias are not allowed to mention it."

"You have that?" said Mercer hopefully.

"Something better. I have super-condamine. It's named after the New French town where they developed it. The chemists hooked in one more hydrogen molecule. That gave it a real jolt. If you took it in your present shape, you'd be dead in three minutes, but those three minutes would seem like ten thousand years of happiness to the inside of your mind." B'dikkat rolled his brown cow eyes expressively and smacked his rich red lips with a tongue of enormous extent.

"What's the use of it, then?"

"*You* can take it," said B'dikkat. "You can take it after you have been exposed to the dromozoa outside this cabin. You get all the good effects and none of the bad. You want to see something?"

What answer is there except *yes*, thought Mercer grimly; does he think I have an urgent invitation to a tea party?

"Look out the window," said B'dikkat, "and tell me what you see."

The atmosphere was clear. The surface was like a desert, ginger-yellow with streaks of green where lichen and low shrubs grew, obviously stunted and tormented by high, dry winds. The landscape was monotonous. Two or three hundred yards away there was a herd of bright pink objects which seemed alive, but Mercer could not see them well enough to describe them clearly. Further away, on the extreme right of his frame of vision, there was the statue of an enormous human foot, the height of a six-story building. Mercer could not see what the foot was connected to. "I see a big foot," said he, "but—"

"But what?" said B'dikkat, like an enormous child hiding the denouement of a hugely private joke. Large as he was, he could have been dwarfed by any one of the toes on that tremendous foot.

"But it can't be a real foot," said Mercer.

"It is," said B'dikkat. "That's Go-Captain Alvarez, the man who found this planet. After six hundred years he's still in fine shape. Of course, he's mostly dromozootic by now, but I think there is some human consciousness inside him. You know what I do?"

"What?" said Mercer.

"I give him six cubic centimeters of super-condamine and he snorts for me. Real happy little snorts. A stranger might think it was a volcano. That's what super-condamine can do. And you're going to get plenty of it. You're a lucky, lucky man, Mercer. You have me for a friend, and you have my needle for a treat. I do all the work and you get all the fun. Isn't that a nice surprise?"

Mercer thought, You're lying! Lying! Where do the screams come from that we have all heard broadcast as a warning on Punishment Day? Why did the doctor offer to cancel my brain or to take out my eyes?

The cow-man watched him sadly, a hurt expression on his face. "You don't believe me," he said, very sadly.

"It's not quite that," said Mercer, with an attempt at heartiness, "but I think you're leaving something out."

"Nothing much," said B'dikkat. "You jump when the dromozoa hit you. You'll be upset when you start growing new parts—heads, kidneys, hands. I had one fellow in here who grew thirty-eight hands in a single session outside. I took them all off, froze them and sent them upstairs. I take good care of everybody. You'll probably yell for a while. But remember, just call me Friend, and I have the nicest treat in the universe waiting for you. Now, would you like some fried eggs? I don't eat eggs myself, but most true men like them."

"Eggs?" said Mercer. "What have eggs got to do with it?"

"Nothing much. It's just a treat for you people. Get something in your stomach before you go outside. You'll get through the first day better."

Mercer, unbelieving, watched as the big man took two precious eggs from a cold chest, expertly broke them into a little pan and put the pan in the heat-field at the center of the table Mercer had awakened on.

"Friend, eh?" B'dikkat grinned. "You'll see I'm a good friend. When you go outside, remember that."

An hour later, Mercer did go outside.

Strangely at peace with himself, he stood at the door. B'dikkat pushed him in a brotherly way, giving him a shove which was gentle enough to be an encouragement.

"Don't make me put on my lead suit, fellow." Mercer

had seen a suit, fully the size of an ordinary space-ship cabin, hanging on the wall of an adjacent room. "When I close this door, the outer one will open. Just walk on out."

"But what will happen?" said Mercer, the fear turning around in his stomach and making little grabs at his throat from the inside.

"Don't start that again," said B'dikkat. For an hour he had fended off Mercer's questions about the outside. A map? B'dikkat had laughed at the thought. Food? He said not to worry. Other people? They'd be there. Weapons? What for, B'dikkat had replied. Over and over again, B'dikkat had insisted that he was Mercer's friend. What would happen to Mercer? The same that happened to everybody else.

Mercer stepped out.

Nothing happened. The day was cool. The wind moved gently against his toughened skin.

Mercer looked around apprehensively.

The mountainous body of Captain Alvarez occupied a good part of the landscape to the right. Mercer had no wish to get mixed up with that. He glanced back at the cabin. B'dikkat was not looking out the window.

Mercer walked slowly, straight ahead.

There was a flash on the ground, no brighter than the glitter of sunlight on a fragment of glass. Mercer felt a sting in the thigh, as though a sharp instrument had touched him lightly. He brushed the place with his hand.

It was as though the sky fell in.

A pain—it was more than a pain; it was a living throb—ran from his hip to his foot on the right side. The throb reached up to his chest, robbing him of breath. He fell, and the ground hurt him. Nothing in the hospital-satellite had been like this. He lay in the open air, trying not to breathe, but he did breathe anyhow. Each time he breathed, the throb moved with his thorax. He lay on his back, looking at the sun. At last he noticed that the sun was violet-white.

It was no use even thinking of calling. He had no voice. Tendrils of discomfort twisted within him. Since he could not stop breathing, he concentrated on taking air in the way that hurt him least. Gasps were too much work. Little tiny sips of air hurt him least.

The desert around him was empty. He could not turn his

head to look at the cabin. Is this it? he thought. Is an eternity of this the punishment of Shayol?

There were voices near him.

Two faces, grotesquely pink, looked down at him. They might have been human. The man looked normal enough, except for having two noses side by side. The woman was a caricature beyond belief. She had grown a breast on each cheek and a cluster of naked baby-like fingers hung limp from her forehead.

"It's a beauty," said the woman, "a new one."

"Come along," said the man.

They lifted him to his feet. He did not have strength enough to resist. When he tried to speak to them a harsh cawing sound, like the cry of an ugly bird, came from his mouth.

They moved with him efficiently. He saw that he was being dragged to the herd of pink things.

As they approached, he saw that they were people. Better, he saw that they had once been people. A man with the beak of a flamingo was picking at his own body. A woman lay on the ground; she had a single head, but beside what seemed to be her original body, she had a boy's naked body growing sidewise from her neck. The boy-body, clean, new, paralytically helpless, made no movement other than shallow breathing. Mercer looked around. The only one of the group who was wearing clothing was a man with his overcoat on sidewise. Mercer stared at him, finally realizing that the man had two—or was it three?—stomachs growing on the outside of his abdomen. The coat held them in place. The transparent peritoneal wall looked fragile.

"New one," said his female captor. She and the two-nosed man put him down.

The group lay scattered on the ground.

Mercer lay in a state of stupor among them.

An old man's voice said, "I'm afraid they're going to feed us pretty soon."

"Oh, no!" "It's too early!" "Not again!" Protests echoed from the group.

The old man's voice went on, "Look, near the big toe of the mountain!"

The desolate murmur in the group attested their confirmation of what he had seen.

Mercer tried to ask what it was all about, but produced only a caw.

A woman—was it a woman?—crawled over to him on her hands and knees. Beside her ordinary hands, she was covered with hands all over her trunk and halfway down her thighs. Some of the hands looked old and withered. Others were as fresh and pink as the baby-fingers on his captress' face. The woman shouted at him, though it was not necessary to shout.

"The dromozoa are coming. This time it hurts. When you get used to the place, you can dig in—"

She waved at a group of mounds which surrounded the herd of people.

"They're dug in," she said.

Mercer cawed again.

"Don't you worry," said the hand-covered woman, and gasped as a flash of light touched her.

The lights reached Mercer too. The pain was like the first contact but more probing. Mercer felt his eyes widen as odd sensations within his body led to an inescapable conclusion: these lights, these things, these whatever they were, were feeding him and building him up.

Their intelligence, if they had it, was not human, but their motives were clear. In between the stabs of pain he felt them fill his stomach, put water in his blood, draw water from his kidneys and bladder, massage his heart, move his lungs for him.

Every single thing they did was well meant and beneficent in intent.

And every single action hurt.

Abruptly, like the lifting of a cloud of insects, they were gone. Mercer was aware of a noise somewhere outside—a brainless, bawling cascade of ugly noise. He started to look around. And the noise stopped.

It had been himself, screaming. Screaming the ugly screams of a psychotic, a terrified drunk, an animal driven out of understanding or reason.

When he stopped, he found he had his speaking voice again.

A man came to him, naked like the others. There was a spike sticking through his head. The skin had healed around it on both sides. "Hello, fellow," said the man with the spike.

"Hello," said Mercer. It was a foolishly commonplace thing to say in a place like this.

"You can't kill yourself," said the man with the spike through his head.

"Yes, you can," said the woman covered with hands.

Mercer found that his first pain had disappeared. "What's happening to me?"

"You got a part," said the man with the spike. "They're always putting parts on us. After a while B'dikkat comes and cuts most of them off, except for the ones that ought to grow a little more. Like her," he added, nodding at the woman who lay with the boy-body growing from her neck.

"And that's all?" said Mercer. "The stabs for the new parts and the stinging for the feeding?"

"No," said the man. "Sometimes they think we're too cold and they fill our insides with fire. Or they think we're too hot and they freeze us, nerve by nerve."

The woman with the boy-body called over, "And sometimes they think we're unhappy, so they try to force us to be happy. *I* think that's the worst of all."

Mercer stammered, "Are you people—I mean—are you the only herd?"

The man with the spike coughed instead of laughing. "Herd! That's funny. The land is full of people. Most of them dig in. We're the ones who can still talk. We stay together for company. We get more turns with B'dikkat that way."

Mercer started to ask another question, but he felt the strength run out of him. The day had been too much.

The ground rocked like a ship on water. The sky turned black. He felt someone catch him as he fell. He felt himself being stretched out on the ground. And then, mercifully and magically, he slept.

3

Within a week, he came to know the group well. They were an absentminded bunch of people. Not one of them ever knew when a dromozoon might flash by and add another part. Mercer was not stung again, but the incision he had

obtained just outside the cabin was hardening. Spike-head
looked at it when Mercer modestly undid his belt and lowered the edge of his trouser-top so they could see the
wound.

"You've got a head," he said. "A whole baby head.
They'll be glad to get that one upstairs when B'dikkat cuts
it off you."

The group even tried to arrange his social life. They introduced him to the girl of the herd. She had grown one body
after another, pelvis turning into shoulders and the pelvis
below that turning into shoulders again until she was five
people long. Her face was unmarred. She tried to be
friendly to Mercer.

He was so shocked by her that he dug himself into the
soft dry crumbly earth and stayed there for what seemed
like a hundred years. He found later that it was less than a
full day. When he came out, the long many-bodied girl was
waiting for him.

"You didn't have to come out just for me," said she.

Mercer shook the dirt off himself.

He looked around. The violet sun was going down, and
the sky was streaked with blues, deeper blues and trails of
orange sunset.

He looked back at her. "I didn't get up for you. It's no
use lying there, waiting for the next time."

"I want to show you something," she said. She pointed
to a low hummock. "Dig that up."

Mercer looked at her. She seemed friendly. He shrugged
and attacked the soil with his powerful claws. With tough
skin and heavy digging-nails on the ends of his fingers, he
found it was easy to dig like a dog. The earth cascaded
beneath his busy hands. Something pink appeared down in
the hole he had dug. He proceeded more carefully.

He knew what it would be.

It was. It was a man, sleeping. Extra arms grew down
one side of his body in an orderly series. The other side
looked normal.

Mercer turned back to the many-bodied girl, who had
writhed closer.

"That's what I think it is, isn't it?"

"Yes," she said. "Doctor Vomact burned his brain out
for him. And took his eyes out, too."

Mercer sat back on the ground and looked at the girl. "You told me to do it. Now tell me what for."

"To let you see. To let you know. To let you think."

"That's all?" said Mercer.

The girl twisted with startling suddenness. All the way down her series of bodies, her chests heaved. Mercer wondered how the air got into all of them. He did not feel sorry for her; he did not feel sorry for anyone except himself. When the spasm passed the girl smiled at him apologetically.

"They just gave me a new plant."

Mercer nodded grimly.

"What now, a hand? It seems you have enough."

"Oh, those," she said, looking back at her many torsos. "I promised B'dikkat that I'd let them grow. He's *good*. But that man, stranger. Look at that man you dug up. Who's better off, he or we?"

Mercer stared at her. "Is that what you had me dig him up for?"

"Yes," said the girl.

"Do you expect me to answer?"

"No," said the girl, "not now."

"Who are you?" said Mercer.

"We never ask that here. It doesn't matter. But since you're new, I'll tell you. I used to be the Lady Da—the Emperor's stepmother."

"You!" he exclaimed.

She smiled, ruefully. "You're still so fresh you think it matters! But I have something more important to tell you." She stopped and bit her lip.

"What?" he urged. "Better tell me before I get another bite. I won't be able to think or talk then, not for a long time. Tell me now."

She brought her face close to his. It was still a lovely face, even in the dying orange of this violet-sunned sunset. "People never live forever."

"Yes," said Mercer. "I knew that."

"*Believe* it," ordered the Lady Da.

Lights flashed across the dark plain, still in the distance. Said she, "Dig in, dig in for the night. They may miss you."

Mercer started digging. He glanced over at the man he had dug up. The brainless body, with motions as soft as those of a starfish under water, was pushing its way back into the earth.

Five or seven days later, there was a shouting through the herd.

Mercer had come to know a half-man, the lower part of whose body was gone and whose viscera were kept in place with what resembled a translucent plastic bandage. The half-man had shown him how to lie still when the dromozoa came with their inescapable errands of doing good.

Said the half-man, "You can't fight them. They made Alvarez as big as a mountain, so that he never stirs. Now they're trying to make us happy. They feed us and clean us and sweeten us up. Lie still. Don't worry about screaming. We all do."

"When do we get the drug?" said Mercer.

"When B'dikkat comes."

B'dikkat came that day, pushing a sort of wheeled sled ahead of him. The runners carried it over the hillocks; the wheels worked on the surface.

Even before he arrived, the herd sprang into furious action. Everywhere, people were digging up the sleepers. By the time B'dikkat reached their waiting place, the herd must have uncovered twice their own number of sleeping pink bodies—men and women, young and old. The sleepers looked no better and no worse than the waking ones.

"Hurry!" said the Lady Da. "He never gives any of us a shot until we're all ready."

B'dikkat wore his heavy lead suit.

He lifted an arm in friendly greeting, like a father returning home with treats for his children. The herd clustered around him but did not crowd him.

He reached into the sled. There was a harnessed bottle which he threw over his shoulders. He snapped the locks on the straps. From the bottle there hung a tube. Midway down the tube there was a small pressure-pump. At the end of the tube there was a glistening hypodermic needle.

When ready, B'dikkat gestured for them to come closer. They approached him with radiant happiness. He stepped through their ranks and past them, to the girl who had the boy growing from her neck. His mechanical voice boomed through the loudspeaker set in the top of his suit

"Good girl. Good, good girl. You get a big, big present."

He thrust the hypodermic into her so long that Mercer could see an air bubble travel from the pump up to the bottle.

Then he moved back to the others, booming a word now and then, moving with improbable grace and speed amid the people. His needle flashed as he gave them hypodermics under pressure. The people dropped to sitting positions or lay down on the ground as though half-asleep.

He knew Mercer. "Hello, fellow. Now you can have the fun. It would have killed you in the cabin. Do you have anything for me?"

Mercer stammered, not knowing what B'dikkat meant, and the two-nosed man answered for him, "I think he has a nice baby head, but it isn't big enough for you to take yet."

Mercer never noticed the needle touch his arm.

B'dikkat had turned to the next knot of people when the super-condamine hit Mercer.

He tried to run after B'dikkat, to hug the lead space suit, to tell B'dikkat that he loved him. He stumbled and fell, but it did not hurt.

The many-bodied girl lay near him. Mercer spoke to her. "Isn't it wonderful? You're beautiful, beautiful, beautiful. I'm so happy to be here."

The woman covered with growing hands came and sat beside them. She radiated warmth and good fellowship. Mercer thought that she looked very distinguished and charming. He struggled out of his clothes. It was foolish and snobbish to wear clothing when none of these nice people did.

The two women babbled and crooned at him.

With one corner of his mind he knew that they were saying nothing, just expressing the euphoria of a drug so powerful that the known universe had forbidden it. With most of his mind he was happy. He wondered how anyone could have the good luck to visit a planet as nice as this. He tried to tell the Lady Da, but the words weren't quite straight.

A painful stab hit him in the abdomen. The drug went after the pain and swallowed it. It was like the cap in the hospital, only a thousand times better. The pain was gone, though it had been crippling the first time.

He forced himself to be deliberate. He rammed his mind

into focus and said to the two ladies who lay pinkly nude beside him in the desert, "That was a good bite. Maybe I will grow another head. That would make B'dikkat happy!"

The Lady Da forced the foremost of her bodies in an upright position. Said she, "I'm strong, too. I can talk. Remember, man, remember. People never live forever. We can die, too, we can die like real people. I do so believe in death!"

Mercer smiled at her through his happiness.

"Of course you can. But isn't this nice . . ."

With this he felt his lips thicken and his mind go slack. He was wide awake, but he did not feel like doing anything. In that beautiful place, among all those companionable and attractive people, he sat and smiled.

B'dikkat was sterilizing his knives.

Mercer wondered how long the super-condamine had lasted him. He endured the ministrations of the dromozoa without screams or movement. The agonies of nerves and itching of skin were phenomena which happened somewhere near him, but meant nothing. He watched his own body with remote, casual interest. The Lady Da and the hand-covered woman stayed near him. After a long time the half-man dragged himself over to the group with his powerful arms. Having arrived he blinked sleepily and friendlily at them, and lapsed back into the restful stupor from which he had emerged. Mercer saw the sun rise on occasion, closed his eyes briefly, and opened them to see stars shining. Time had no meaning. The dromozoa fed him in their mysterious way: the drug canceled out his needs for cycles of the body.

At last he noticed a return of the inwardness of pain.

The pains themselves had not changed; he had.

He knew all the events which could take place on Shayol. He remembered them well from his happy period. Formerly he had noticed them—now he felt them.

He tried to ask the Lady Da how long they had had the drug, and how much longer they would have to wait before they had it again. She smiled at him with benign, remote happiness; apparently her many torsos, stretched out along the ground, had a greater capacity for retaining the drug than did his body. She meant him well, but was in no condition for articulate speech.

The half-man lay on the ground, arteries pulsating prettily behind the half-transparent film which protected his abdominal cavity.

Mercer squeezed the man's shoulder.

The half-man woke, recognized Mercer and gave him a healthily sleepy grin.

" 'A good morrow to you, my boy.' That's out of a play. Did you ever see a play?"

"You mean a game with cards?"

"No," said the half-man, "a sort of eye-machine with real people doing the figures."

"I never saw that," said Mercer, "but I—"

"But you want to ask me when B'dikkat is going to come back with the needle."

"Yes," said Mercer, a little ashamed of his obviousness.

"Soon," said the half-man. "That's why I think of plays. We all know what is going to happen. We all know when it is going to happen. We all know what the dummies will do—" he gestured at the hummocks in which the decorticated men were cradled—"and we all know what the new people will ask. But we never know how long a scene is going to take."

"What's a 'scene'?" asked Mercer. "Is that the name for the needle?"

The half-man laughed with something close to real humor. "No, no, no. You've got the lovelies on the brain. A scene is just part of a play. I mean we know the order in which things happen, but we have no clocks and nobody cares enough to count days or to make calendars and there's not much climate here, so none of us know how long anything takes. The pain seems short and the pleasure seems long. I'm inclined to think that they are about two Earth-weeks each."

Mercer did not know what an "Earth-week" was, since he had not been a well-read man before his conviction, but he got nothing more from the half-man at that time. The half-man received a dromozootic implant, turned red in the face, shouted senselessly at Mercer, "Take it out, you fool! Take it out of me!"

While Mercer looked on helplessly, the half-man twisted over on his side, his pink dusty back turned to Mercer, and wept hoarsely and quietly to himself.

Mercer himself could not tell how long it was before B'dikkat came back. It might have been several days. It might have been several months.

Once again B'dikkat moved among them like a father; once again they clustered like children. This time B'dikkat smiled pleasantly at the little head which had grown out of Mercer's thigh—a sleeping child's head, covered with light hair on top and with dainty eyebrows over the resting eyes. Mercer got the blissful needle.

When B'dikkat cut the head from Mercer's thigh, he felt the knife grinding against the cartilage which held the head to his own body. He saw the child-face grimace as the head was cut; he felt the far, cool flash of unimportant pain, as B'dikkat dabbed the wound with a corrosive antiseptic which stopped all bleeding immediately.

The next time it was two legs growing from his chest.

Then there had been another head beside his own.

Or was that after the torso and legs, waist to toe-tips, of the little girl which had grown from his side?

He forgot the order.

He did not count time.

Lady Da smiled at him often, but there was no love in this place. She had lost the extra torsos. In between teratologies, she was a pretty and shapely woman; but the nicest thing about their relationship was her whisper to him, repeated some thousands of times, repeated with smiles and hope, "People never live forever."

She found this immensely comforting, even though Mercer did not make much sense out of it.

Thus events occurred, and victims changed in appearance, and new ones arrived. Sometimes B'dikkat took the new ones, resting in the everlasting sleep of their burned-out brains, in a ground-truck to be added to other herds. The bodies in the truck threshed and bawled without human speech when the dromozoa struck them.

Finally, Mercer did manage to follow B'dikkat to the door of the cabin. He had to fight the bliss of super-condamine to do it. Only the memory of previous hurt, bewilderment and perplexity made him sure that if he did not ask B'dikkat when he, Mercer, was happy, the answer would no longer be available when he needed it. Fighting pleasure itself, he begged B'dikkat to check the records and to tell him how long he had been there.

B'dikkat grudgingly agreed, but he did not come out of the doorway. He spoke through the public address box built into the cabin, and his gigantic voice roared out over the empty plain, so that the pink herd of talking people stirred gently in their happiness and wondered what their friend B'dikkat might be wanting to tell them. When he said it, they thought it exceedingly profound, though none of them understood it, since it was simply the amount of time that Mercer had been on Shayol:

"Standard years—eighty-four years, seven months, three days, two hours, eleven and one half minutes. Good luck, fellow."

Mercer turned away.

The secret little corner of his mind, which stayed sane through happiness and pain, made him wonder about B'dikkat. What persuaded the cow-man to remain on Shayol? What kept him happy without super-condamine? Was B'dikkat a crazy slave to his own duty or was he a man who had hopes of going back to his own planet some day, surrounded by a family of little cow-people resembling himself? Mercer, despite his happiness, wept a little at the strange fate of B'dikkat. His own fate he accepted.

He remembered the last time he had eaten—actual eggs from an actual pan. The dromozoa kept him alive, but he did not know how they did it.

He staggered back to the group. The Lady Da, naked in the dusty plain, waved a hospitable hand and showed that there was a place for him to sit beside her. There were unclaimed square miles of seating space around them, but he appreciated the kindliness of her gesture none the less.

4

The years, if they were years, went by. The land of Shayol did not change.

Sometimes the bubbling sound of geysers came faintly across the plain to the herd of men; those who could talk declared it to be the breathing of Captain Alvarez. There was night and day, but no setting of crops, no change of season, no generations of men. Time stood still for these people, and their load of pleasure was so commingled with the shocks and pains of the dromozoa that the words of the Lady Da took on very remote meaning.

"People never live forever."

Her statement was a hope, not a truth in which they could believe. They did not have the wit to follow the stars in their courses, to exchange names with each other, to harvest the experience of each for the wisdom of all. There was no dream of escape for these people. Though they saw the old-style chemical rockets lift up from the field beyond B'dik-kat's cabin, they did not make plans to hide among the frozen crop of transmuted flesh.

Far long ago, some other prisoner than one of these had tried to write a letter. His handwriting was on a rock. Mercer read it, and so had a few of the others, but they could not tell which man had done it. Nor did they care.

The letter, scraped on stone, had been a message home. They could still read the opening: "Once, I was like you, stepping out of my window at the end of day, and letting the winds blow me gently toward the place I lived in. Once, like you, I had one head, two hands, ten fingers on my hands. The front part of my head was called a face, and I could talk with it. Now I can only write, and that only when I get out of pain. Once, like you, I ate foods, drank liquid, had a name. I cannot remember the name I had. You can stand up, you who get this letter. I cannot even stand up. I just wait for the lights to put my food in me molecule by molecule, and to take it out again. Don't think that I am punished any more. This place is not a punishment. It is something else."

Among the pink herd, none of them ever decided what was "something else."

Curiosity had died among them long ago.

Then came the day of the little people.

It was a time—not an hour, not a year: a duration somewhere between them—when the Lady Da and Mercer sat wordless with happiness and filled with the joy of super-condamine. They had nothing to say to one another; the drug said all things for them.

A disagreeable roar from B'dikkat's cabin made them stir mildly.

Those two, and one or two others, looked toward the speaker of the public address system.

The Lady Da brought herself to speak, though the matter was unimportant beyond words. "I do believe," said she, "that we used to call that the War Alarm."

They drowsed back into their happiness.

A man with two rudimentary heads growing beside his own crawled over to them. All three heads looked very happy, and Mercer thought it delightful of him to appear in such a whimsical shape. Under the pulsing glow of super-condamine, Mercer regretted that he had not used times when his mind was clear to ask him who he had once been. He answered it for them. Forcing his eyelids open by sheer will power, he gave the Lady Da and Mercer the lazy ghost of a military salute and said, "Suzdal, Ma'am and Sir, former cruiser commander. They are sounding the alert. Wish to report that I am . . . I am . . . I am not quite ready for battle."

He dropped off to sleep.

The gentle peremptorinesses of the Lady Da brought his eyes open again.

"Commander, why are they sounding it here? Why did you come to us?"

"You, Ma'am, and the gentleman with the ears seem to think best of our group. I thought you might have orders."

Mercer looked around for the gentleman with the ears. It was himself. In that time his face was almost wholly obscured with a crop of fresh little ears, but he paid no attention to them, other than expecting that B'dikkat would cut them all off in due course and that the dromozoa would give him something else.

The noise from the cabin rose to a higher, ear-splitting intensity.

Among the herd, many people stirred.

Some opened their eyes, looked around, murmured. "It's a noise," and went back to the happy drowsing with super-condamine.

The cabin door opened.

B'dikkat rushed out, *without his suit*. They had never seen him on the outside without his protective metal suit.

He rushed up to them, looked wildly around, recognized the Lady Da and Mercer, picked them up, one under each arm, and raced with them back to the cabin. He flung them into the double door. They landed with bone-splitting crashes, and found it amusing to hit the ground so hard. The floor tilted them into the room. Moments later, B'dikkat followed.

He roared at them, "You're people, or you were. You understand people; I only obey them. But this I will not obey. Look at that!"

Four beautiful human children lay on the floor. The two smallest seemed to be twins, about two years of age. There was a girl of five and a boy of seven or so. All of them had slack eyelids. All of them had thin red lines around their temples and their hair, shaved away, showed how their brains had been removed.

B'dikkat, heedless of danger from dromozoa, stood beside the Lady Da and Mercer, shouting.

"You're real people. I'm just a cow. I do my duty. My duty does not include this. These are *children*."

The wise, surviving recess of Mercer's mind registered shock and disbelief. It was hard to sustain the emotion, because the super-condamine washed at his consciousness like a great tide, making everything seem lovely. The forefront of his mind, rich with the drug, told him, "Won't it be nice to have some children with us!" But the undestroyed interior of his mind, keeping the honor he knew before he came to Shayol, whispered, "This is a crime worse than any crime we have committed! *And the Empire has done it*."

"What have you done?" said the Lady Da. "What can we do?"

"I tried to call the satellite. When they knew what I was talking about, they cut me off. After all, I'm not people. The head doctor told me to do my work."

"Was it Doctor Vomact?" Mercer asked.

"Vomact?" said B'dikkat. "He died a hundred years ago, of old age. No, a new doctor cut me off. I don't have people-feeling, but I am Earthborn, of Earth blood. I have emotions myself. Pure cattle emotions! *This* I cannot permit."

"What have you done?"

B'dikkat lifted his eyes to the window. His face was illuminated by a determination which, even beyond the edges of the drug which made them love him, made him seem like the father of this world—responsible, honorable, unselfish.

He smiled. "They will kill me for it, I think. But I have put in the Galactic Alert—*all ships here.*"

The Lady Da, sitting back on the floor, declared, "But that's only for new invaders! It is a false alarm." She pulled herself together and rose to her feet. "Can you cut these things off me, right now, in case people come? And get me a dress. And do you have anything which will counteract the effect of the super-condamine?"

"That's what I wanted!" cried B'dikkat. "I will not take these children. You give me leadership."

There and then, on the floor of the cabin, he trimmed her down to the normal proportions of mankind.

The corrosive antiseptic rose like smoke in the air of the cabin. Mercer thought it all very dramatic and pleasant, and dropped off in catnaps part of the time. Then he felt B'dikkat trimming him too. B'dikkat opened a long, long drawer and put the specimens in; from the cold in the room it must have been a refrigerated locker.

He sat them both up against the wall.

"I've been thinking," he said. "There is no antidote for super-condamine. Who would want one? But I can give you the hypos from my rescue boat. They are supposed to bring a person back, no matter what has happened to that person out in space."

There was a whining over the cabin roof. B'dikkat knocked a window out with his fist, stuck his head out of the window and looked up.

"Come on in," he shouted.

There was the thud of a landing craft touching ground quickly. Doors whirred. Mercer wondered, mildly, why people dared to land on Shayol. When they came in he saw that they were not people; they were Customs Robots, who could travel at velocities which people could never match. One wore the insigne of an inspector.

"Where are the invaders?"

"There are no—" began B'dikkat.

The Lady Da, imperial in her posture though she was completely nude, said in a voice of complete clarity, "I am a former Empress, the Lady Da. Do you know me?"

"No, Ma'am," said the robot inspector. He looked as

uncomfortable as a robot could look. The drug made Mercer think that it would be nice to have robots for company, out on the surface of Shayol.

"I declare this Top Emergency, in the ancient words. Do you understand? Connect me with the Instrumentality."

"We can't—" said the inspector.

"You can ask," said the Lady Da.

The inspector complied.

The Lady Da turned to B'dikkat. "Give Mercer and me those shots now. Then put us outside the door so the dromozoa can repair these scars. Bring us in as soon as a connection is made. Wrap us in cloth if you do not have clothes for us. Mercer can stand the pain."

"Yes," said B'dikkat, keeping his eyes away from the four soft children and their collapsed eyes.

The injection burned like no fire ever had. It must have been capable of fighting the super-condamine, because B'dikkat put them through the open window, so as to save time going through the door. The dromozoa, sensing that they needed repair, flashed upon them. This time the super-condamine had something else fighting it.

Mercer did not scream but he lay against the wall and wept for ten thousand years; in objective time, it must have been several hours.

The Customs robots were taking pictures. The dromozoa were flashing against them too, sometimes in whole swarms, but nothing happened.

Mercer heard the voice of the communicator inside the cabin calling loudly for B'dikkat. "Surgery Satellite calling Shayol. B'dikkat, get on the line!"

He obviously was not replying.

There were soft cries coming from the other communicator, the one which the customs officials had brought into the room. Mercer was sure that the eye-machine was on and that people in other worlds were looking at Shayol for the first time.

B'dikkat came through the door. He had torn navigation charts out of his lifeboat. With these he cloaked them.

Mercer noted that the Lady Da changed the arrangement of the cloak in a few minor ways and suddenly looked like a person of great importance.

They re-entered the cabin door.

B'dikkat whispered, as if filled with awe, "The Instrumentality has been reached, and a lord of the Instrumentality is about to talk to you."

There was nothing for Mercer to do, so he sat back in a corner of the room and watched. The Lady Da, her skin healed, stood pale and nervous in the middle of the floor.

The room filled with an odorless intangible smoke. The smoke clouded. The full communicator was on.

A human figure appeared.

A woman, dressed in a uniform of radically conservative cut, faced the Lady Da.

"This is Shayol. You are the Lady Da. You called me."

The Lady Da pointed to the children on the floor. "This must not happen," she said. "This is a place of punishments, agreed upon between the Instrumentality and the Empire. No one said anything about children."

The woman on the screen looked down at the children.

"This is the work of insane people!" she cried.

She looked accusingly at the Lady Da, "Are you imperial?"

"I was an Empress, madam," said the Lady Da.

"And you permit this!"

"Permit it?" cried the Lady Da. "I had nothing to do with it." Her eyes widened. "I am a prisoner here myself. Don't you understand?"

The image-woman snapped, "No, I don't."

"I," said the Lady Da, "am a specimen. Look at the herd out there. I came from them a few hours ago."

"Adjust me," said the image-woman to B'dikkat. "Let me see that herd."

Her body, standing upright, soared through the wall in a flashing arc and was placed in the very center of the herd.

The Lady Da and Mercer watched her. They saw even the image lose its stiffness and dignity. The image-woman waved an arm to show that she should be brought back into the cabin. B'dikkat tuned her back into the room.

"I owe you an apology," said the image. "I am the Lady Johanna Gnade, one of the lords of the Instrumentality."

Mercer bowed, lost his balance and had to scramble up from the floor. The Lady Da acknowledged the introduction with a royal nod.

The two women looked at each other.

"You will investigate," said the Lady Da, "and when you have investigated, please put us all to death. You know about the drug?"

"Don't mention it," said B'dikkat, "don't even say the name into a communicator. It is a secret of the Instrumentality!"

"I am the Instrumentality," said the Lady Johanna. "Are you in pain? I did not think that any of you were alive. I had heard of the surgery banks on your off-limits planet, but I thought that robots tended parts of people and sent up the new grafts by rocket. Are there any people with you? Who is in charge? Who did this to the children?"

B'dikkat stepped in front of the image. He did not bow. "I'm in charge."

"You're underpeople!" cried the Lady Johanna. "You're a cow!"

"A bull, Ma'am. My family is frozen back on Earth itself, and with a thousand years' service I am earning their freedom and my own. Your other questions, Ma'am. I do all the work. The dromozoa do not affect me much, though I have to cut a part off myself now and then. I throw those away. They don't go into the bank. Do you know the secret rules of this place?"

The Lady Johanna talked to someone behind her on another world. Then she looked at B'dikkat and commanded, "Just don't name the drug or talk too much about it. Tell me the rest."

"We have," said B'dikkat very formally, "thirteen hundred and twenty-one people here who can still be counted on to supply parts when the dromozoa implant them. There are about seven hundred more, including Go-Captain Alvarez, who have been so thoroughly absorbed by the planet that it is no use trimming them. The Empire set up this place as a point of uttermost punishment. But the Instrumentality gave secret orders for *medicine*—" he accented the word strangely, meaning super-condamine—"to be issued so that the punishment would be counteracted. The Empire supplies our convicts. The Instrumentality distributes the surgical material."

The Lady Johanna lifted her right hand in a gesture of silence and compassion. She looked around the room. Her eyes came back to the Lady Da. Perhaps she guessed what effort the Lady Da had made in order to remain standing erect while the two drugs, the super-condamine and the lifeboat drug, fought within her veins.

"You people can rest. I will tell you now that all things possible will be done for you. The Empire is finished. The Fundamental Agreement, by which the Instrumentality surrendered the Empire a thousand years ago, has been set aside. We did not know that you people existed. We would have found out in time, but I am sorry we did not find out sooner. Is there anything we can do for you right away?"

"Time is what we all have," said the Lady Da. "Perhaps we cannot ever leave Shayol, because of the dromozoa and the *medicine*. The one could be dangerous. The other must never be permitted to be known."

The Lady Johanna Gnade looked around the room. When her glance reached him, B'dikkat fell to his knees and lifted his enormous hands in complete supplication.

"What do you want?" said she.

"These," said B'dikkat, pointing to the mutilated children. "Order a stop on children. Stop it now!" He commanded her with the last cry, and she accepted his command. "And Lady—" he stopped as if shy.

"Yes? Go on."

"Lady, I am unable to kill. It is not in my nature. To work, to help, but not to kill. What do I do with these?" He gestured at the four motionless children on the floor.

"Keep them," she said. "Just keep them."

"I can't," he said. "There's no way to get off this planet alive. I do not have food for them in the cabin. They will die in a few hours. And governments," he added wisely, "take a long, long time to do things."

"Can you give them the *medicine*?"

"No, it would kill them if I give them that stuff first before the dromozoa have fortified their bodily processes."

The Lady Johanna Gnade filled the room with tinkling laughter that was very close to weeping. "Fools, poor fools, and the more fool I! If super-condamine works only *after* the dromozoa, what is the purpose of the secret?"

B'dikkat rose to his feet, offended. He frowned, but he could not get the words with which to defend himself.

The Lady Da, ex-empress of a fallen empire, addressed the other lady with ceremony and force: "Put them outside, so they will be touched. They will hurt. Have B'dikkat give them the drug as soon as he thinks it safe. I beg your leave, my Lady . . ."

Mercer had to catch her before she fell.

"You've all had enough," said the Lady Johanna. "A storm ship with heavily armed troops is on its way to your ferry satellite. They will seize the medical personnel and find out who committed this crime against children."

Mercer dared to speak. "Will you punish the guilty doctor?"

"*You* speak of punishment," she cried. "You!"

"It's fair. I was punished for doing wrong. Why shouldn't he be?"

"Punish—punish!" she said to him. "We will cure that doctor. And we will cure you too, if we can."

Mercer began to weep. He thought of the oceans of happiness which super-condamine had brought him, forgetting the hideous pain and the deformities on Shayol. Would there be no next needle? He could not guess what life would be like off Shayol. Was there to be no more tender, fatherly B'dikkat coming with his knives?

He lifted his tear-stained face to the Lady Johanna Gnade and choked out the words, "Lady, we are all insane in this place. I do not think we want to leave."

She turned her face away, moved by enormous compassion. Her next words were to B'dikkat. "You are wise and good, even if you are not a human being. Give them all of the drug they can take. The Instrumentality will decide what to do with all of you. I will survey your planet with robot soldiers. Will the robots be safe, cow-man?"

B'dikkat did not like the thoughtless name she called him, but he held no offense. "The robots will be all right, Ma'am, but the dromozoa will be excited if they cannot feed them and heal them. Send as few as you can. We do not know how the dromozoa live or die."

"As few as I can," she murmured. She lifted her hand in command to some technician unimaginable distances away. The odorless smoke rose about her and the image was gone.

A shrill cheerful voice spoke up. "I fixed your window," said the customs robot. B'dikkat thanked him absentmindedly. He helped Mercer and the Lady Da into the doorway.

When they had gotten outside, they were promptly stung by the dromozoa. It did not matter.

B'dikkat himself emerged, carrying the four children in his two gigantic, tender hands. He lay the slack bodies on the ground near the cabin. He watched as the bodies went into spasm with the onset of the dromozoa. Mercer and the Lady Da saw that his brown cow eyes were rimmed with red and that his huge cheeks were dampened by tears.

Hours or centuries.

Who could tell them apart?

The herd went back to its usual life, except that the intervals between needles were much shorter. The once-commander, Suzdal, refused the needle when he heard the news. Whenever he could walk, he followed the customs robots around as they photographed, took soil samples, and made a count of the bodies. They were particularly interested in the mountain of the Go-Captain Alvarez and professed themselves uncertain as to whether there was organic life there or not. The mountain did appear to react to super-condamine, but they could find no blood, no heart-beat. Moisture, moved by the dromozoa, seemed to have replaced the once-human bodily process.

5

And then, early one morning, the sky opened.

Ship after ship landed. People emerged, wearing clothes.

The dromozoa ignored the newcomers. Mercer, who was in a state of bliss, confusedly tried to think this through until he realized that the ships were loaded to their skins with communications machines; the "people" were either robots or images of persons in other places.

The robots swiftly gathered together the herd. Using wheelbarrows, they brought the hundreds of mindless people to the landing area.

Mercer heard a voice he knew. It was the Lady Johanna Gnade. "Set me high," she commanded.

Her form rose until she seemed one-fourth the size of Alvarez. Her voice took on more volume.

"Wake them all," she commanded.

Robots moved among them, spraying them with a gas which was both sickening and sweet. Mercer felt his mind go clear. The super-condamine still operated in his nerves and veins, but his cortical area was free of it. He thought clearly.

"I bring you," cried the compassionate feminine voice of the gigantic Lady Johanna, "the judgment of the Instrumentality on the planet Shayol.

"Item: the surgical supplies will be maintained and the dromozoa will not be molested. Portions of human bodies will be left here to grow, and the grafts will be collected by robots. Neither man nor homunculus will live here again.

"Item: the underman B'dikkat, of cattle extraction, will be rewarded by an immediate return to Earth. He will be paid twice his expected thousand years of earnings."

The voice of B'dikkat, without amplification, was almost as loud as hers through the amplifier. He shouted his protest, "Lady, Lady!"

She looked down at him, his enormous body reaching to ankle height on her swirling gown, and said in a very informal tone, "What do you want?"

"Let me finish my work first," he cried, so that all could hear. "Let me finish taking care of these people."

The specimens who had minds all listened attentively. The brainless ones were trying to dig themselves back into the soft earth of Shayol, using their powerful claws for the purpose. Whenever one began to disappear, a robot seized him by a limb and pulled him out again.

"Item: cephalectomies will be performed on all persons with irrecoverable minds. Their bodies will be left here. Their heads will be taken away and killed as pleasantly as we can manage, probably by an overdosage of super-condamine."

"The last big jolt," murmured Commander Suzdal, who stood near Mercer. "That's fair enough."

"Item: the children have been found to be the last heirs of the Empire. An over-zealous official sent them here to prevent their committing treason when they grew up. The doctor obeyed orders without questioning them. Both the official and the doctor have been cured and their memories of this have been erased, so that they need have no shame or grief for what they have done."

"It's unfair," cried the half-man. "They should be punished as we were!"

The Lady Johanna Gnade looked down at him. "Punishment is ended. We will give you anything you wish, but not the pain of another. I shall continue.

"Item: since none of you wish to resume the lives which you led previously, we are moving you to another planet nearby. It is similar to Shayol, but much more beautiful. There are no dromozoa."

At this an uproar seized the herd. They shouted, wept, cursed, appealed. They all wanted the needle, and if they had to stay on Shayol to get it, they would stay.

"Item," said the gigantic image of the lady, overriding their babble with her great but feminine voice, "you will not have super-condamine on the new planet, since without dromozoa it would kill you. But there will be caps. *Remember the caps*. We will try to cure you and to make people of you again. But if you give up, we will not force you. Caps are very powerful; with medical help you can live under them many years."

A hush fell on the group. In their various ways, they were trying to compare the electrical caps which had stimulated their pleasure-lobes with the drug which had drowned them a thousand times in pleasure. Their murmur sounded like assent.

"Do you have any questions?" said the Lady Johanna.

"When do we get the caps?" said several. They were human enough that they laughed at their own impatience.

"Soon," said she reassuringly, "very soon."

"Very soon," echoed B'dikkat, reassuring his charges even though he was no longer in control.

"Question," cried the Lady Da.

"My Lady . . . ?" said the Lady Johanna, giving the ex-empress her due courtesy.

"Will we be permitted marriage?"

The Lady Johanna looked astonished. "I don't know." She smiled. "I don't know any reason why not—"

"I claim this man Mercer," said the Lady Da. "When the drugs were deepest, and the pain was greatest, he was the one who always tried to think. May I have him?"

Mercer thought the procedure arbitrary but he was so happy that he said nothing. The Lady Johanna scrutinized him and then she nodded. She lifted her arms in a gesture of blessing and farewell.

The robots began to gather the pink herd into two groups. One group was to whisper in a ship over to a new world, new problems and new lives. The other group, no matter how much its members tried to scuttle into the dirt, was gathered for the last honor which humanity could pay their manhood.

B'dikkat, leaving everyone else, jogged with his bottle across the plain to give the mountain-man Alvarez an especially large gift of delight.

RAINBIRD

BY R. A. LAFFERTY (1914-   )

GALAXY SCIENCE FICTION
DECEMBER

Raphael Aloysius Lafferty is one of the quirkiest, funniest, off-center writers in the history of science fiction. Although he enjoys a considerable critical reputation and won a Hugo Award in 1973, he never achieved the commercial success of many writers who could not carry his typewriter. Perhaps strangeness just doesn't sell in this country. His more than a dozen novels, and especially marvelous collections like Nine Hundred Grandmothers *(1970),* Strange Doings *(1971), and* Does Anyone Else Have Something Further to Add? *(1974), contain some of the most rewarding (and fun) fiction to be found anywhere.*

"Rainbird" is early Lafferty, and like much of his work, defies easy summation. (MHG)

H.G. Wells popularized the time-travel story with his first great success, The Time Machine, *published in 1895.*

Since then, innumerable time-travel stories have been written, in which people moved up and down the time-axis much as they would travel from America to Asia.

The concept is quite impossible. To be sure, scientists sometimes talk of quirky methods of achieving the equivalent of time-travel but that would involve the simultaneous passage from one part of the Universe to a far distant part, and would not be practical for use in the H.G. Wells' sense. Besides, I think scientists who think up methods of time-travel are probably all wrong.

However, nothing will prevent its use in science fiction.

I've used it myself, notably in my novel, The End of Eternity, *and the reason for that is that it is the mother of an infinite number of plots, some serious, some funny, some merely odd.*

Lafferty's story is a very interesting example of what I mean. (IA)

Were scientific firsts truly tabulated the name of the Yankee inventor, Higgston Rainbird, would surely be without peer. Yet today he is known (and only to a few specialists, at that) for an improved blacksmith's bellows in the year 1785, for a certain modification (not fundamental) in the moldboard plow about 1805, for a better (but not good) method of reefing the lanteen sail, for a chestnut roaster, for the Devil's Claw Wedge for splitting logs, and for a nutmeg grater embodying a new safety feature; this last was either in the year 1816 or 1817. He is known for such, and for no more.

Were this all that he achieved his name would still be secure. And it *is* secure, in a limited way, to those who hobby in technological history.

But the glory of which history has cheated him, or of which he cheated himself, is otherwise. In a different sense it is without parallel, absolutely unique.

For he pioneered the dynamo, the steam automobile, the steel industry, ferro-concrete construction, the internal combustion engine, electric illumination and power, the wireless, the televox, the petroleum and petro-chemical industries, monorail transportation, air travel, worldwide monitoring, fissionable power, space travel, group telepathy, political and economic balance; he built a retrogressor; and he made great advances towards corporal immortality and the apotheosis of mankind. It would seem unfair that all this is unknown of him.

Even the once solid facts—that he wired Philadelphia for light and power in 1799, Boston the following year, and New York two years later—are no longer solid. In a sense they are no longer facts.

For all this there must be an explanation; and, if not that, then an account at least; and if not that, well—something anyhow.

Higgston Rainbird made a certain decision on a June

afternoon in 1779 when he was quite a young man, and by this decision he confirmed his inventive bent.

He was hawking from the top of Devil's Head Mountain. He flew his falcon (actually a tercel hawk) down through the white clouds, and to him it was the highest sport in the world. The bird came back, climbing the blue air, and brought a passenger pigeon from below the clouds. And Higgston was almost perfectly happy as he hooded the hawk.

He could stay there all day and hawk from above the clouds. Or he could go down the mountain and work on his sparker in his shed. He sighed as he made the decision, for no man can have everything. There was a fascination about hawking. But there was also a fascination about the copper-strip sparker. And he went down the mountain to work on it.

Thereafter he hawked less. After several years he was forced to give it up altogether. He had chosen his life, the dedicated career of an inventor, and he stayed with it for sixty-five years.

His sparker was not a success. It would be expensive, its spark was uncertain and it had almost no advantage over flint. People could always start a fire. If not, they could borrow a brand from a neighbor. There was no market for the sparker. But it was a nice machine, hammered copper strips wrapped around iron teased with lodestone, and the thing turned with a hand crank. He never gave it up entirely. He based other things upon it; and the retrogressor of his last years could not have been built without it.

But the main thing was steam, iron, and tools. He made the finest lathes. He revolutionized smelting and mining. He brought new things to power, and started the smoke to rolling. He made mistakes, he ran into dead ends, he wasted whole decades. But one man can only do so much.

He married a shrew, Audrey, knowing that a man cannot achieve without a goad as well as a goal. But he was without issue or disciple, and this worried him.

He built a steamboat and a steamtrain. His was the first steam thresher. He cleared the forests with wood-burning giants, and designed towns. He destroyed southern slavery with a steampowered cotton picker, and power and wealth followed him.

For better or worse he brought the country up a long road, so there was hardly a custom of his boyhood that still continued. Probably no one man had ever changed a country so much in his lifetime.

He fathered a true machine-tool industry, and brought rubber from the tropics and plastic from the laboratory. He pumped petroleum, and used natural gas for illumination and steam power. He was honored and enriched; and, looking back, he had no reason to regard his life as wasted.

"Yes, I've missed so much. I wasted a lot of time. If only I could have avoided the blind alleys, I could have done many times as much. I brought machine tooling to its apex. But I neglected the finest tool of all, the mind. I used it as it is, but I had not time to study it, much less modify it. Others after me will do it all. But I rather wanted to do it all myself. Now it is too late."

He went back and worked on his old sparker and its descendents, now that he was old. He built toys along the line of it that need not always have remained toys. He made a televox, but the only practical application was that now Audrey could rail at him over a greater distance. He fired up a little steam dynamo in his house, ran wires and made it burn lights in his barn.

And he built a retrogressor.

"I would do much more along this line had I the time. But I'm pepper-bellied pretty near the end of the road. It is like finally coming to a gate and seeing a whole greater world beyond it, and being too old and feeble to enter."

He kicked a chair and broke it.

"I never even made a better chair. Never got around to it. There are so clod-hopping many things I meant to do. I have maybe pushed the country ahead a couple of decades faster than it would otherwise have gone. But what couldn't I have done if it weren't for the blind alleys! Ten years lost in one of them, twelve in another. If only there had been a way to tell the true from the false, and to leave to others what they could do, and to do myself only what nobody else could do. To see a link (however unlikely) and to go out and get it and set it in its place. Oh, the waste, the wilderness that a talent can wander in! If I had only had a mentor! If I had had a map, a clue, a hatful of clues. I was born shrewd, and I shrewdly cut a path and went a grand ways. But always there was a clearer path and a faster way that I did not see till later. As my name is Rainbird, if I had it to do over, I'd do it infinitely better."

He began to write a list of the things that he'd have done better. Then he stopped and threw away his pen in disgust.

"Never did even invent a decent ink pen. Never got around to it. Dog-eared damnation, there's so much I didn't do!"

He poured himself a jolt, but he made a face as he drank it.

"Never got around to distilling a really better whiskey. Had some good ideas along that line, too. So many things I never did do. Well, I can't improve things by talking to myself here about it."

Then he sat and thought.

"But I burr-tailed *can* improve things by talking to myself *there* about it."

He turned on his retrogressor, and went back sixty-five years and up two thousand feet.

Higgston Rainbird was hawking from the top of Devil's Head Mountain one June afternoon in 1779. He flew his bird down through the white fleece clouds, and to him it was sport indeed. Then it came back, climbing the shimmering air, and brought a pigeon to him.

"It's fun," said the old man, "but the bird is tough, and you have a lot to do. Sit down and listen, Higgston."

"How do you know the bird is tough? Who are you, and how did an old man like you climb up here without my seeing you? And how in hellpepper did you know that my name was Higgston?"

"I ate the bird and I remember that it was tough. I am just an old man who would tell you a few things to avoid in your life, and I came up here by means of an invention of my own. And I know your name is Higgston, as it is also my name; you being named after me, or I after you, I forget which. Which one of us is the older, anyhow?"

"I had thought that you were, old man. I am a little interested in inventions myself. How does the one that carried you up here work?"

"It begins, well it begins with something like your sparker, Higgston. And as the years go by you adapt and add. But it is all tinkering with a force field till you are able to warp it a little. Now then, you are an ewer-eared galoot and not as handsome as I remembered you; but I happen to know that you have the makings of a fine man. Listen now as hard as ever you listened in your life. I doubt that I will be able to repeat. I will save you years and decades; I will tell you the best road to take over a journey which it was once said that a man could travel but once. Man, I'll pave a path for you over the hard places and strew palms before your feet."

"Talk, you addlepated old gaff. No man ever listened so hard before."

The old man talked to the young one for five hours. Not a word was wasted; they were neither of them given to wasting words. He told him that steam wasn't everything, this before he knew that it was anything. It was a giant power, but it was limited. Other powers, perhaps, were not. He instructed him to explore the possibilities of amplification and feedback, and to use always the lightest medium of transmission of power: wire rather than mule-drawn coal cart, air rather than wire, ether rather than air. He warned against time wasted in shoring up the obsolete, and of the bottomless quicksand of cliché, both of word and of thought.

He admonished him not to waste precious months in trying to devise the perfect apple corer; there will never be a perfect apple corer. He begged him not to build a battery bobsled. There would be things far swifter than a bobsled.

Let others make the new hide scrapers and tanning salts. Let others aid the carter and the candle molder and the cooper in their arts. There was need for a better hame, a better horse block, a better stile, a better whetstone. Well, let others fill those needs. If our buttonhooks, our firedogs, our whiffletrees, our bootjacks, our cheese presses are all badly designed and a disgrace, then let someone else remove that disgrace. Let others aid the cordwainer and the cobbler. Let Higgston do only the high work that nobody else would be able to do.

There would come a time when the farrier himself would disappear, as the fletcher had all but disappeared. But new trades would open for a man with an open mind.

Then the old man got specific. He showed young Higgs-

R. A. Lafferty

ton a design for a lathe dog that would save time. He told him how to draw, rather than hammer wire; and advised him of the virtues of mica as insulator before other material should come to hand.

"And here there are some things that you will have to take on faith," said the old man, "things of which we learn the 'what' before we fathom the 'why'."

He explained to him the shuttle armature and the self-exciting field, and commutation; and the possibilities that alternation carried to its ultimate might open up. He told him a bejammed lot of things about a confounded huge variety of subjects.

"And a little mathematics never hurt a practical man," said the old gaffer. "I was self-taught, and it slowed me down."

They hunkered down there, and the old man cyphered it all out in the dust on the top of Devil's Head Mountain. He showed him natural logarithms and rotating vectors and the calculi and such; but he didn't push it too far, as even a smart boy can learn only so much in a few minutes. He then gave him a little advice on the treatment of Audrey, knowing it would be useless, for the art of living with a shrew is a thing that cannot be explained to another.

"Now hood your hawk and go down the mountain and go to work," the old man said. And that is what young Higgston Rainbird did.

The career of the Yankee inventor, Higgston Rainbird, was meteoric. The wise men of Greece were little boys to him, the Renaissance giants had only knocked at the door but had not tried the knob. And it was unlocked all the time.

The milestones that Higgston left are breathtaking. He built a short high dam on the flank of Devil's Head Mountain, and had hydroelectric power for his own shop in that same year (1779). He had an arc light burning in Horse-Head Lighthouse in 1781. He read by true incandescent light in 1783, and lighted his native village, Knobknocker, three years later. He drove a charcoal fueled automobile in 1787, switched to a distillate of whale oil in 1789, and used true rock oil in 1790. His gasoline powered combination reaper-thresher was in commercial production in 1793, the same year that he wired Centerville for light and power. His first diesel locomotive made its trial run in 1796, in which year he also converted one of his earlier coal burning steamships to liquid fuel.

In 1799 he had wired Philadelphia for light and power, a major breakthrough, for the big cities had manfully resisted the innovations. On the night of the turn of the century he unhooded a whole clutch of new things, wireless telegraphy, the televox, radio transmission and reception, motile and audible theatrical reproductions, a machine to transmit the human voice into print, and a method of sterilizing and wrapping meat to permit its indefinite preservation at any temperature.

And in the spring of that new year he first flew a heavier-than-air vehicle.

"He has made all the basic inventions," said the many-tongued people. "Now there remains only their refinement and proper utilization."

"Horse hokey," said Higgston Rainbird. He made a rocket that could carry freight to England in thirteen minutes at seven cents a hundredweight. This was in 1805. He had fissionable power in 1813, and within four years had the price down where it could be used for desalting seawater to the eventual irrigation of five million square miles of remarkably dry land.

He built a Think Machine to work out the problems that he was too busy to solve, and a Prediction Machine to pose him with new problems and new areas of breakthrough.

In 1821, on his birthday, he hit the moon with a marker. He bet a crony that he would be able to go up personally one year later and retrieve it. And he won the bet.

In 1830 he first put on the market his Red Ball Pipe Tobacco, an aromatic and expensive crimp cut made of Martian lichen.

In 1836 he founded the Institute for the Atmospheric Rehabilitation of Venus, for he found that place to be worse than a smokehouse. It was there that he developed that hacking cough that stayed with him till the end of his days.

He synthesized a man of his own age and disrepute who would sit drinking with him in the after-midnight hours and say, "You're so right, Higgston, so incontestably right."

His plan for the Simplification and Eventual Elimination

of Government was adopted (in modified form) in 1840, a fruit of his Political and Economic Balance Institute.

Yet, for all his seemingly successful penetration of the field, he realized that man was the only truly cantankerous animal, and that Human Engineering would remain one of the never completely resolved fields.

He made a partial breakthrough in telepathy, starting with the personal knowledge that shrews are always able to read the minds of their spouses. He knew that the secret was not in sympathetic reception, but in arrogant break-in. With the polite it is forever impossible, but he disguised this discovery as politely as he could.

And he worked toward corporal immortality and the apotheosis of mankind, that cantankerous animal.

He designed a fabric that would embulk itself on a temperature drop, and thin to an airy sheen in summery weather. The weather itself he disdained to modify, but he did evolve infallible prediction of exact daily rainfall and temperature for decades in advance.

And he built a retrogressor.

One day he looked in the mirror and frowned.

"I never did get around to making a better mirror. This one is hideous. However (to consider every possibility) let us weigh the thesis that it is the image and not the mirror that is hideous."

He called up an acquaintance.

"Say, Ulois, what year is this anyhow?"

"1844."

"Are you sure?"

"Reasonably sure."

"How old am I?"

"Eighty-five, I think, Higgston."

"How long have I been an old man?"

"Quite a while, Higgston, quite a while."

Higgston Rainbird hung up rudely.

"I wonder how I ever let a thing like that slip up on me?" he said to himself. "I should have gone to work on corporal immortality a little earlier. I've bungled the whole business now."

He fiddled with his prediction machine and saw that he was to die that very year. He did not seek a finer reading.

"What a saddle-galled splay-footed situation to find myself in! I never got around to a tenth of the things I really wanted to do. Oh, I was smart enough; I just ran up too many blind alleys. Never found the answers to half the old riddles. Should have built the Prediction Machine at the beginning instead of the end. But I didn't know how to build it at the beginning. There ought to be a way to get more done. Never got any advice in my life worth taking except from that nutty old man on the mountain when I was a young man. There's a lot of things I've only started on. Well, every man doesn't hang, but every man does come to the end of his rope. I never did get around to making that rope extensible. And I can't improve things by talking to myself here about it."

He filled his pipe with Red Ball crimp cut and thought a while.

"But I hill-hopping *can* improve things by talking to myself *there* about it."

Then he turned on his retrogressor and went back and up.

Young Higgston Rainbird was hawking from the top of Devil's Head Mountain on a June afternoon in 1779. He flew his hawk down through the white clouds, and decided that he was the finest fellow in the world and master of the finest sport. If there was earth below the clouds it was far away and unimportant.

The hunting bird came back, climbing the tall air, with a pigeon from the lower regions.

"Forget the bird," said the old man, "and give a listen with those outsized ears of yours. I have a lot to tell you in a very little while, and then you must devote yourself to a concentrated life of work. Hood the bird and clip him to the stake. Is that bridle clip of your own invention? Ah yes, I remember now that it is."

"I'll just fly him down once more, old man, and then I'll have a look at what you're selling."

"No. No. Hood him at once. This is your moment of decision. That is a boyishness that you must give up. Listen to me, Higgston, and I will orient your life for you."

"I rather intended to orient it myself. How did you get

up here, old man, without my seeing you? How, in fact, did you get up here at all? It's a hard climb."

"Yes, I remember that it is. I came up here on the wings of an invention of my own. Now pay attention for a few hours. It will take all your considerable wit."

"A few hours and a perfect hawking afternoon will be gone. This may be the finest day ever made."

"I also once felt that it was, but I manfully gave it up. So must you."

"Let me fly the hawk down again and I will listen to you while it is gone."

"But you will only be listening with half a mind, and the rest will be with the hawk."

But young Higgston Rainbird flew the bird down through the shining white clouds, and the old man began his rigmarole sadly. Yet it was a rang-dang-do of a spiel, a mummy-whammy of admonition and exposition, and young Higgston listened entranced and almost forgot his hawk. The old man told him that he must stride half a dozen roads at once, and yet never take a wrong one; that he must do some things earlier that on the alternative had been done quite late; that he must point his technique at the Think Machine and the Prediction Machine, and at the unsolved problem of corporal immortality.

"In no other way can you really acquire elbow room, ample working time. Time runs out and life is too short if you let it take its natural course. Are you listening to me, Higgston?"

But the hawk came back, climbing the steep air, and it had a gray dove. The old man sighed at the interruption, and he knew that his project was in peril.

"Hood the hawk. It's a sport for boys. Now listen to me, you spraddling jack. I am telling you things that nobody else would ever be able to tell you! I will show you how to fly falcons to the stars, not just down to the meadows and birch groves at the foot of this mountain."

"There is no prey up there," said young Higgston.

"There *is*. Gamier prey than you ever dreamed of. Hood the bird and snaffle him."

"I'll just fly him down one more time and listen to you till he comes back."

The hawk went down through the clouds like a golden bolt of summer lightning.

Then the old man, taking the cosmos, peeled it open layer by layer like an onion, and told young Higgston how it worked. Afterwards he returned to the technological beginning and he lined out the workings of steam and petro- and electromagnetism, and explained that these simple powers must be used for a short interval in the invention of greater power. He told him of waves and resonance and airy transmission, and fission and flight and over-flight. And that none of the doors required keys, only a resolute man to turn the knob and push them open. Young Higgston was impressed.

Then the hawk came back, climbing the towering air, and it had a rainbird.

The old man had lively eyes, but now they took on a new light.

"Nobody ever gives up pleasure willingly," he said, "and there is always the sneaking feeling that the bargain may not have been perfect. This is one of the things I have missed. I haven't hawked for sixty-five years. Let me fly him this time, Higgston."

"You know how?"

"I am adept. And I once intended to make a better gauntlet for hawkers. This hasn't been improved since Nimrod's time."

"I have an idea for a better gauntlet myself, old man."

"Yes. I know what your idea is. Go ahead with it. It's practical."

"Fly him if you want to, old man."

And old Higgston flew the tercel hawk down through the gleaming clouds, and he and young Higgston watched from the top of the world. And then young Higgston Rainbird was standing alone on the top of Devil's Head Mountain, and the old man was gone.

"I wonder where he went? And where in appleknocker's heaven did he come from? Or was he ever here at all? That's a danged funny machine he came in, if he did come in it. All the wheels are on the inside. But I can use the gears from it, and the clock, and the copper wire. It must have taken weeks to hammer that much wire out that fine. I wish I'd paid more attention to what he was saying, but he poured it on a little thick. I'd have gone along with him on it if only he'd have found a good stopping place a little sooner, and hadn't been so insistent on giving up hawking. Well, I'll just hawk here till dark, and if it dawns clear I'll be up again in the morning. And Sunday, if I have a little time, I may work on my sparker or my chestnut roaster."

Higgston Rainbird lived a long and successful life. Locally he was known best as a hawker and horse racer. But as an inventor he was recognized as far as Boston.

He is still known, in a limited way, to specialists in the field and period; known as contributor to the development of the moldboard plow, as the designer of the Nonpareil Nutmeg Grater with the safety feature, for a bellows, for a sparker for starting fires (little used), and for the Devil's Claw Wedge for splitting logs.

He is known for such, and for no more.

WALL OF CRYSTAL, EYE OF NIGHT

BY ALGIS BUDRYS (1931-   )

GALAXY SCIENCE FICTION
DECEMBER

Lithuanian-born Algis Budrys is one of the leading critical minds working in the science fiction field. His monthly column of criticism and book reviews in The Magazine of Fantasy and Science Fiction *is often the first thing read by veteran fans and readers in that wonderful publication. His many interests and activities, including his work on behalf of the Writers of the Future contests, has severely reduced his fiction writing. This is a real tragedy, since his short stories and novels are uniformly excellent and ambitious.*

I still "see" scenes from "Wall of Crystal, Eye of Night" at odd moments in my life; it is one of the most unforgettable stories I've ever read, a combination of high technology, big business, and mysticism that will long linger in your mind. (MHG)

The United States is a land of immigrants and their descendants, if you don't count the Native Americans.

As we all know, immigrants have come to the United States chiefly to achieve a better life, if not for themselves, then for their children. In so doing, they have enormously strengthened American society and given it a variety and a new character that differentiates us from other nations. (Not necessarily better in all respects, but different.)

Science fiction has been enriched, too, by American writers who are not too far removed from the immigrant generation and who bring to bear their own ethnic background in their

*stories. Naturally, there are even some first-generation immi-
grants among the writers.*

*I am notoriously one of them, having been born in the
Soviet Union and having been brought to the United States
at the age of three. Algis Budrys is another. He was born in
East Prussia (although an ethnic Lithuanian) and was
brought to the United States at the age of five.*

*There are others, I'm sure, but we're the two most promi-
nent examples and I think the science fiction world must be
glad we're here. (IA)*

I

Soft as the voice of a mourning dove, the telephone
sounded at Rufus Sollenar's desk. Sollenar himself was
standing fifty paces away, his leonine head cocked, his
hands flat in his hip pockets, watching the nighted world
through the crystal wall that faced out over Manhattan
Island. The window was so high that some of what he saw
was dimmed by low cloud hovering over the rivers. Above
him were stars; below him the city was traced out in light
and brimming with light. A falling star—an interplanetary
rocket—streaked down toward Long Island Facility like a
scratch across the soot on the doors of Hell.

Sollenar's eyes took it in, but he was watching the total
scene, not any particular part of it. His eyes were shining.

When he heard the telephone, he raised his left hand to
his lips. "Yes?" The hand glittered with utilijem rings; the
effect was that of an attempt at the sort of copper-binding
that was once used to reinforce the ribbing of wooden
warships.

His personal receptionist's voice moved from the air near
his desk to the air near his ear. Seated at the monitor board
in her office, wherever in this building her office was, the
receptionist told him:

"Mr. Ermine says he has an appointment."

"No." Sollenar dropped his hand and returned to his panorama. When he had been twenty years younger—managing
the modest optical factory that had provided the support of
three generations of Sollenars—he had very much wanted
to be able to stand in a place like this, and feel as he imag-

ined men felt in such circumstances. But he felt unimaginable, now.

To be here was one thing. To have almost lost the right, and regained it at the last moment, was another. Now he knew that not only could he be here today but that tomorrow, and tomorrow, he could still be here. He had won. His gamble had given him EmpaVid—and EmpaVid would give him all.

The city was not merely a prize set down before his eyes. It was a dynamic system he had proved he could manipulate. He and the city were one. It buoyed and sustained him; it supported him, here in the air, with stars above and light-thickened mist below.

The telephone mourned: "Mr. Ermine states he has a firm appointment."

"I've never heard of him." And the left hand's utilijems fell from Sollenar's lips again. He enjoyed such toys. He raised his right hand, sheathed in insubstantial midnight-blue silk in which the silver threads of metallic wiring ran subtly toward the fingertips. He raised the hand, and touched two fingers together: music began to play behind and before him. He made contact between another combination of finger circuits, and a soft, feminine laugh came from the terrace at the other side of the room, where connecting doors had opened. He moved toward it. One layer of translucent drapery remained across the doorway, billowing lightly in the breeze from the terrace. Through it, he saw the taboret with its candle lit; the iced wine in the stand beside it; the two fragile chairs; Bess Allardyce, slender and regal, waiting in one of them—all these, through the misty curtain, like either the beginning or the end of a dream.

"Mr. Ermine reminds you the appointment was made for him at the Annual Business Dinner of the International Association of Broadcasters, in 1998."

Sollenar completed his latest step, then stopped. He frowned down at his left hand. "Is Mr. Ermine with the IAB's Special Public Relations Office?"

"Yes," the voice said after a pause.

The fingers of Sollenar's right hand shrank into a cone. The connecting door closed. The girl disappeared. The music stopped. "All right. You can tell Mr. Ermine to come up." Sollenar went to sit behind his desk.

The office door chimed. Sollenar crooked a finger of his left hand, and the door opened. With another gesture, he kindled the overhead lights near the door and sat in shadow as Mr. Ermine came in.

Ermine was dressed in rust-colored garments. His figure was spare, and his hands were empty. His face was round and soft, with long dark sideburns. His scalp was bald. He stood just inside Sollenar's office and said: "I would like some light to see you by, Mr. Sollenar."

Sollenar crooked his little finger.

The overhead lights came to soft light all over the office. The crystal wall became a mirror, with only the strongest city lights glimmering through it. "I only wanted to see you first," said Sollenar; "I thought perhaps we'd met before."

"No," Ermine said, walking across the office. "It's not likely you've ever seen me." He took a card case out of his pocket and showed Sollenar proper identification. "I'm not a very forward person."

"Please sit down," Sollenar said. "What may I do for you?"

"At the moment, Mr. Sollenar, I'm doing something for you."

Sollenar sat back in his chair. "Are you? Are you, now?" He frowned at Ermine. "When I became a party to the By-Laws passed at the '98 Dinner, I thought a Special Public Relations Office would make a valuable asset to the organization. Consequently, I voted for it, and for the powers it was given. But I never expected to have any personal dealings with it. I barely remembered you people had carte blanche with any IAB member."

"Well, of course, it's been a while since '98," Ermine said. "I imagine some legends have grown up around us. Industry gossip—that sort of thing."

"Yes."

"But we don't restrict ourselves to an enforcement function, Mr. Sollenar. You haven't broken any By-Laws, to our knowledge."

"Or mine. But nobody feels one hundred percent secure. Not under these circumstances." Nor did Sollenar yet relax his face into its magnificent smile. "I'm sure you've found that out."

"I have a somewhat less ambitious older brother who's with the Federal Bureau of Investigation. When I embarked on my own career, he told me I could expect everyone in the world to react like a criminal, yes," Ermine said, paying no attention to Sollenar's involuntary blink. "It's one of the complicating factors in a profession like my brother's, or mine. But I'm here to advise you, Mr. Sollenar. Only that."

"In what matter, Mr. Ermine?"

"Well, your corporation recently came into control of the patents for a new video system. I understand that this in effect makes your corporation the licensor for an extremely valuable sales and entertainment medium. Fantastically valuable."

"EmpaVid," Sollenar agreed. "Various subliminal stimuli are broadcast with and keyed to the overt subject matter. The home receiving unit contains feedback sensors which determine the viewer's reaction to these stimuli, and intensify some while playing down others in order to create complete emotional rapport between the viewer and the subject matter. EmpaVid, in other words, is a system for orchestrating the viewer's emotions. The home unit is self-contained, semiportable, and not significantly bulkier than the standard TV receiver. EmpaVid is compatible with standard TV receivers—except, of course, that the subject matter seems thin and vaguely unsatisfactory on a standard receiver. So the consumer shortly purchases an EV unit." It pleased Sollenar to spell out the nature of his prize.

"At a very reasonable price. Quite so, Mr. Sollenar. But you had several difficulties in finding potential licensees for this system, among the networks."

Sollenar's lips pinched out.

Mr. Ermine raised one finger. "First, there was the matter of acquiring the patents from the original inventor, who was also approached by Cortwright Burr."

"Yes, he was," Sollenar said in a completely new voice.

"Competition between Mr. Burr and yourself is long-standing and intense."

"Quite intense," Sollenar said, looking directly ahead of him at the one blank wall of the office. Burr's offices were several blocks downtown, in that direction.

"Well, I have no wish to enlarge on that point, Mr. Burr being an IAB member in standing as good as yours, Mr. Sollenar. There was, in any case, a further difficulty in licensing EV, due to the very heavy cost involved in equipping broadcasting stations and network relay equipment for this sort of transmission."

"Yes, there was."

"Ultimately, however, you succeeded. You pointed out, quite rightly, that if just one station made the change, and if just a few EV receivers were put into public places within the area served by that station, normal TV outlets could not possibly compete for advertising revenue."

"Yes."

"And so your last difficulties were resolved a few days ago, when your EmpaVid Unlimited—pardon me; when EmpaVid, a subsidiary of the Sollenar Corporation—became a major stockholder in the Transworld TV Network."

"I don't understand, Mr. Ermine," Sollenar said. "Why are you recounting this? Are you trying to demonstrate the power of your knowledge? All these transactions are already matters of record in the IAB confidential files, in accordance with the By-Laws."

Ermine held up another finger. "You're forgetting I'm only here to advise you. I have two things to say. They are:

"These transactions are on file with the IAB because they involve a great number of IAB members, and an increasingly large amount of capital. Also, Transworld's exclusivity, under the IAB By-Laws, will hold good only until thirty-three percent market saturation has been reached. If EV is as good as it looks, that will be quite soon. After that, under the By-Laws, Transworld will be restrained from making effective defenses against patent infringement by competitors. Then all of the IAB's membership and much of their capital will be involved with EV. Much of that capital is already in anticipatory motion. So a highly complex structure now ultimately depends on the integrity of the Sollenar Corporation. If Sollenar stock falls in value, not just you but many IAB members will be greatly embarrassed. Which is another way of saying EV must succeed."

"I know all that! What of it? There's no risk. I've had every related patent on Earth checked. There will be no catastrophic obsolescence of the EV system."

Ermine said: "There are engineers on Mars. Martian engineers. They're a dying race, but no one knows what they can still do."

Sollenar raised his massive head.

Ermine said: "Late this evening, my office learned that Cortwright Burr has been in close consultation with the Martians for several weeks. They have made some sort of machine for him. He was on the flight that landed at the Facility a few moments ago."

Sollenar's fists clenched. The lights crashed off and on, and the room wailed. From the terrace came a startled cry, and a sound of smashed glass.

Mr. Ermine nodded, excused himself, and left.

—A few moments later, Mr. Ermine stepped out at the pedestrian level of the Sollenar Building. He strolled through the landscaped garden, and across the frothing brook toward the central walkway down the Avenue. He paused at a hedge to pluck a blossom and inhale its odor. He walked away, holding it in his naked fingers.

II

Drifting slowly on the thread of his spinneret, Rufus Sollenar came gliding down the wind above Cortwright Burr's building.

The building, like a spider, touched the ground at only the points of its legs. It held its wide, low bulk spread like a parasol over several downtown blocks. Sollenar, manipulating the helium-filled plastic drifter far above him, steered himself with jets of compressed gas from plastic bottles in the drifter's structure.

Only Sollenar himself, in all this system, was not effectively transparent to the municipal antiplane radar. And he himself was wrapped in long, fluttering streamers of dull black, metallic sheeting. To the eye, he was amorphous and nonreflective. To electronic sensors, he was a drift of static much like a sheet of foil picked by the wind from some careless trash heap. To all of the senses of all interested parties he was hardly there at all—and, thus, in an excellent position for murder.

He fluttered against Burr's window. There was the man,

crouched over his desk. What was that in his hands—a pomander?

Sollenar clipped his harness to the edges of the cornice. Swayed out against it, his sponge-soled boots pressed to the glass, he touched his left hand to the window and described a circle. He pushed; there was a thud on the carpeting in Burr's office, and now there was no barrier to Sollenar. Doubling his knees against his chest, he catapulted forward, the riot pistol in his right hand. He stumbled and fell to his knees, but the gun was up.

Burr jolted up behind his desk. The little sphere of orange-gold metal, streaked with darker bronze, its surface vermicular with encrustations, was still in his hands. "Him!" Burr cried out as Sollenar fired.

Gasping, Sollenar watched the charge strike Burr. It threw his torso backward faster than his limbs and head could follow without dangling. The choked-down pistol was nearly silent. Burr crashed backward to end, transfixed, against the wall.

Pale and sick, Sollenar moved to take the golden ball. He wondered where Shakespeare could have seen an example such as this, to know an old man could have so much blood in him.

Burr held the prize out to him. Staring with eyes distended by hydrostatic pressure, his clothing raddled and his torso grinding its broken bones, Burr stalked away from the wall and moved as if to embrace Sollenar. It was queer, but he was not dead.

Shuddering, Sollenar fired again.

Again Burr was thrown back. The ball spun from his splayed fingers as he once more marked the wall with his body.

Pomander, orange, whatever—it looked valuable.

Sollenar ran after the rolling ball. And Burr moved to intercept him, nearly faceless, hunched under a great invisible weight that slowly yielded as his back groaned.

Sollenar took a single backward step.

Burr took a step toward him. The golden ball lay in a far corner. Sollenar raised the pistol despairingly and fired again. Burr tripped backward on tiptoe, his arms like windmills, and fell atop the prize.

Tears ran down Sollenar's cheeks. He pushed one foot

forward . . . and Burr, in his corner, lifted his head and began to gather his body for the effort of rising.

Sollenar retreated to the window, the pistol sledging backward against his wrist and elbow as he fired the remaining shots in the magazine.

Panting, he climbed up into the window frame and clipped the harness to his body, craning to look over his shoulder . . . as Burr—shredded; leaking blood and worse than blood—advanced across the office.

He cast off his holds on the window frame and clumsily worked the drifter controls. Far above him, volatile ballast spilled out and dispersed in the air long before it touched ground. Sollenar rose, sobbing—

And Burr stood in the window, his shattered hands on the edges of the cut circle, raising his distended eyes steadily to watch Sollenar in flight across the enigmatic sky.

Where he landed, on the roof of a building in his possession, Sollenar had a disposal unit for his gun and his other trappings. He deferred for a time the question of why Burr had failed at once to die. Empty-handed, he returned uptown.

He entered his office, called and told his attorneys the exact times of departure and return, and knew the question of dealing with municipal authorities was thereby resolved. That was simple enough, with no witnesses to complicate the matter. He began to wish he hadn't been so irresolute as to leave Burr without the thing he was after. Surely, if the pistol hadn't killed the man—an old man, with thin limbs and spotted skin—he could have wrestled that thin-limbed, bloody old man aside—that spotted old man—and dragged himself and his prize back to the window, for all that the old man would have clung to him, and clutched at his legs, and fumbled for a handhold on his somber disguise of wrappings—that broken, immortal old man.

Sollenar raised his hand. The great window to the city grew opaque.

Bess Allardyce knocked softly on the door from the terrace. He would have thought she'd returned to her own apartments many hours ago. Tortuously pleased, he opened the door and smiled at her, feeling the dried tears crack on the skin of his cheeks.

He took her proffered hands. "You waited for me," he sighed. "A long time for anyone as beautiful as you to wait."

She smiled back at him. "Let's go out and look at the stars."

"Isn't it chilly?"

"I made spiced hot cider for us. We can sip it and think."

He let her draw him out onto the terrace. He leaned on the parapet, his arm around her pulsing waist, his cape drawn around both their shoulders.

"Bess, I won't ask if you'd stay with me no matter what the circumstances. But it might be a time will come when I couldn't bear to live in this city. What about that?"

"I don't know," she answered honestly.

And Cortwright Burr put his hand up over the edge of the parapet, between them.

Sollenar stared down at the straining knuckles, holding the entire weight of the man dangling against the sheer face of the building. There was a sliding, rustling noise, and the other hand came up, searched blindly for a hold and found it, fingers hooked over the stone. The fingers tensed and rose, their tips flattening at the pressure as Burr tried to pull his head and shoulders up to the level of the parapet.

Bess breathed: "Oh, look at them! He must have torn them terribly climbing up!" Then she pulled away from Sollenar and stood staring at him, her hand to her mouth. "But he *couldn't* have climbed! We're so high!"

Sollenar beat at the hands with the heels of his palms, using the direct, trained blows he had learned at his athletic club.

Bone splintered against the stone. When the knuckles were broken the hands instantaneously disappeared, leaving only streaks behind them. Sollenar looked over the parapet. A bundle shrank from sight, silhouetted against the lights of the pedestrian level and the Avenue. It contracted to a pinpoint. Then, when it reached the brook and water flew in all directions, it disappeared in a final sunburst, endowed with glory by the many lights which found momentary reflection down there.

"Bess, leave me! Leave me, please!" Rufus Sollenar cried out.

III

Rufus Sollenar paced his office, his hands held safely still in front of him, their fingers spread and rigid.

The telephone sounded, and his secretary said to him: "Mr. Sollenar, you are ten minutes from being late at the TTV Executives' Ball. This is a First Class obligation."

Sollenar laughed. "I thought it was, when I originally classified it."

"Are you now planning to renege, Mr. Sollenar?" the secretary inquired politely.

Certainly, Sollenar thought. He could as easily renege on the Ball as a king could on his coronation.

"Burr, you scum, what have you done to me?" he asked the air, and the telephone said: "Beg pardon?"

"Tell my valet," Sollenar said. "I'm going." He dismissed the phone. His hands cupped in front of his chest. A firm grip on emptiness might be stronger than any prize in a broken hand.

Carrying in his chest something he refused to admit was terror, Sollenar made ready for the Ball.

But only a few moments after the first dance set had ended, Malcolm Levier of the local TTV station executive staff looked over Sollenar's shoulder and remarked:

"Oh, there's Cort Burr, dressed like a gallows bird."

Sollenar, glittering in the costume of the Medici, did not turn his head. "Is he? What would he want here?"

Levier's eyebrows arched. "He holds a little stock. He has entrée. But he's late." Levier's lips quirked. "It must have taken him some time to get that makeup on."

"Not in good taste, is it?"

"Look for yourself."

"Oh, I'll do better than that," Sollenar said. "I'll go and talk to him a while. Excuse me, Levier." And only then did he turn around, already started on his first pace toward the man.

But Cortwright Burr was only a pasteboard imitation of himself as Sollenar had come to know him. He stood to one side of the doorway, dressed in black and crimson robes, with black leather gauntlets on his hands, carrying a staff of weathered, natural wood. His face was shadowed by a sackcloth hood, the eyes well hidden. His face was powdered gray, and some blend of livid colors hollowed his cheeks. He stood motionless as Sollenar came up to him.

As he had crossed the floor, each step regular, the eyes of bystanders had followed Sollenar, until, anticipating his course, they found Burr waiting. The noise level of the Ball shrank perceptibly, for the lesser revelers who chanced to be present were sustaining it all alone. The people who really mattered here were silent and watchful.

The thought was that Burr, defeated in business, had come here in some insane reproach to his adversary, in this lugubrious, distasteful clothing. Why, he looked like a corpse. Or worse.

The question was, what would Sollenar say to him? The wish was that Burr would take himself away, back to his estates or to some other city. New York was no longer for Cortwright Burr. But what would Sollenar say to him now, to drive him back to where he hadn't the grace to go willingly?

"Cortwright," Sollenar said in a voice confined to the two of them. "So your Martian immortality works."

Burr said nothing.

"You got that in addition, didn't you? You knew how I'd react. You knew you'd need protection. Paid the Martians to make you physically invulnerable? It's a good system. Very impressive. Who would have thought the Martians knew so much? But who here is going to pay attention to you now? Get out of town, Cortwright. You're past your chance. You're dead as far as these people are concerned— all you have left is your skin."

Burr reached up and surreptitiously lifted a corner of his fleshed mask. And there he was, under it. The hood retreated an inch, and the light reached his eyes; and Sollenar had been wrong, Burr had less left than he thought.

"Oh, no, no, Cortwright," Sollenar said softly. "No, you're right—I can't stand up to that."

He turned and bowed to the assembled company. "Good night!" he cried, and walked out of the ballroom.

Someone followed him down the corridor to the elevators. Sollenar did not look behind him.

"I have another appointment with you now," Ermine said at his elbow.

*　　*　　*

They reached the pedestrian level. Sollenar said: "There's a cafe. We can talk there."

"Too public, Mr. Sollenar. Let's simply stroll and converse." Ermine lightly took his arm and guided him along the walkway. Sollenar noticed then that Ermine was costumed so cunningly that no one could have guessed the appearance of the man.

"Very well," Sollenar said.

"Of course."

They walked together, casually. Ermine said: "Burr's driving you to your death. Is it because you tried to kill him earlier? Did you get his Martian secret?"

Sollenar shook his head.

"You didn't get it." Ermine sighed. "That's unfortunate. I'll have to take steps."

"Under the By-Laws," Sollenar said, "I cry *laissez faire.*"

Ermine looked up, his eyes twinkling. "*Laissez faire?* Mr. Sollenar, do you have any idea how many of our members are involved in your fortunes? *They* will cry *laissez faire,* Mr. Sollenar, but clearly you persist in dragging them down with you. No, sir, Mr. Sollenar, my office now forwards an immediate recommendation to the Technical Advisory Committee of the IAB that Mr. Burr probably has a system superior to yours, and that stock in Sollenar, Incorporated, had best be disposed of."

"There's a bench," Sollenar said. "Let's sit down."

"As you wish." Ermine moved beside Sollenar to the bench, but remained standing.

"What is it, Mr. Sollenar?"

"I want your help. You advised me on what Burr had. It's still in his office building, somewhere. You have resources. We can get it."

"*Laissez faire,* Mr. Sollenar. I visited you in advisory capacity. I can do no more."

"For a partnership in my affairs could you do more?"

"Money?" Ermine tittered. "For me? Do you know the conditions of my employment?"

If he had thought, Sollenar would have remembered. He reached out tentatively. Ermine anticipated him.

Ermine bared his left arm and sank his teeth into it. He displayed the arm. There was no quiver of pain in voice or stance. "It's not a legend, Mr. Sollenar. It's quite true. We of our office must spend a year, after the nerve surgery, learning to walk without the feel of our feet, to handle objects without crushing them or letting them slip, or damaging ourselves. Our mundane pleasures are auditory, olfactory, and visual. Easily gratified at little expense. Our dreams are totally interior, Mr. Sollenar. The operation is irreversible. What would you buy for me with your money?"

"What would I buy for myself?" Sollenar's head sank down between his shoulders.

Ermine bent over him. "Your despair is your own, Mr. Sollenar. I have official business with you."

He lifted Sollenar's chin with a forefinger. "I judge physical interference to be unwarranted at this time. But matters must remain so that the IAB members involved with you can recover the value of their investments in EV. Is that perfectly clear, Mr. Sollenar? You are hereby enjoined under the By-Laws, as enforced by the Special Public Relations Office." He glanced at his watch. "Notice was served at 1:27 AM, City time."

"1:27," Sollenar said. "City time." He sprang to his feet and raced down a companionway to the taxi level.

Mr. Ermine watched him quizzically.

He opened his costume, took out his omnipresent medical kit, and sprayed coagulant over the wound in his forearm. Replacing the kit, he adjusted his clothing and strolled down the same companionway Sollenar had run. He raised an arm, and a taxi flittered down beside him. He showed the driver a card, and the cab lifted off with him, its lights glaring in a Priority pattern, far faster than Sollenar's ordinary legal limit allowed.

IV

Long Island Facility vaulted at the stars in great kangaroo leaps of arch and cantilever span, jeweled in glass and metal as if the entire port were a mechanism for navigating interplanetary space. Rufus Sollenar paced its esplanades, measuring his steps, holding his arms still, for the short time until he could board the Mars rocket.

Erect and majestic, he took a place in the lounge and

carefully sipped liqueur, once the liner had boosted away from Earth and coupled in its Faraday main drives.

Mr. Ermine settled into the place beside him.

Sollenar looked over at him calmly. "I thought so."

Ermine nodded. "Of course you did. But I didn't almost miss you. I was here ahead of you. I have no objection to your going to Mars, Mr. Sollenar. *Laissez faire.* Provided I can go along."

"Well," Rufus Sollenar said. "Liqueur?" He gestured with his glass.

Ermine shook his head. "No, thank you," he said delicately.

Sollenar said: "Even your tongue?"

"Of course my tongue, Mr. Sollenar. I taste nothing, I touch nothing." Ermine smiled. "But I feel no pressure."

"All right, then," Rufus Sollenar said crisply. "We have several hours to landing time. You sit and dream your interior dreams, and I'll dream mine." He faced around in his chair and folded his arms across his chest.

"Mr. Sollenar," Ermine said gently.

"Yes?"

"I am once again with you by appointment as provided under the By-Laws."

"State your business, Mr. Ermine."

"You are not permitted to lie in an unknown grave, Mr. Sollenar. Insurance policies on your life have been taken out at a high premium rate. The IAB members concerned cannot wait the statutory seven years to have you declared dead. Do what you will, Mr. Sollenar, but I must take care I witness your death. From now on, I am with you wherever you go."

Sollenar smiled. "I don't intend to die. Why should I die, Mr. Ermine?"

"I have no idea, Mr. Sollenar. But I know Cortwright Burr's character. And isn't that he, seated there in the corner? The light is poor, but I think he's recognizable."

Across the lounge, Burr raised his head and looked into Sollenar's eyes. He raised a hand near his face, perhaps merely to signify greeting. Rufus Sollenar faced front.

"A worthy opponent, Mr. Sollenar," Ermine said. "A persevering, unforgiving, ingenious man. And yet—" Ermine seemed a little touched by bafflement. "And yet it

seems to me, Mr. Sollenar, that he got you running rather
easily. What *did* happen between you, after my advisory
call?"

Sollenar turned a terrible smile on Ermine. "I shot him
to pieces. If you'd peel his face, you'd see."

Ermine sighed. "Up to this moment, I had thought perhaps you might still salvage your affairs."

"Pity, Mr. Ermine? Pity for the insane?"

"Interest. I can take no part in your world. Be grateful,
Mr. Sollenar. I am not the same gullible man I was when I
signed my contract with IAB, so many years ago."

Sollenar laughed. Then he stole a glance at Burr's corner.

The ship came down at Abernathy Field, in Aresia, the
Terrestrial city. Industrialized, prefabricated, jerry-built,
and clamorous, the storm-proofed buildings huddled, but
huddled proudly, at the desert's edge.

Low on the horizon was the Martian settlement—the
buildings so skillfully blended with the landscape, so
eroded, so much abandoned that the uninformed eye saw
nothing. Sollenar had been to Mars—on a tour. He had
seen the natives in their nameless dwelling place; arrogant,
venomous, and weak. He had been told, by the paid guide,
they trafficked with Earthmen as much as they cared to,
and kept to their place on the rim of Earth's encroachment,
observing.

"Tell me, Ermine," Sollenar said quietly as they walked
across the terminal lobby. "You're to kill me, aren't you,
if I try to go on without you?"

"A matter of procedure, Mr. Sollenar," Ermine said
evenly. "We cannot risk the investment capital of so many
IAB members."

Sollenar sighed. "If I were any other member, how I
would commend you, Mr. Ermine! Can we hire a car for
ourselves, then, somewhere nearby?"

"Going out to see the engineers?" Ermine asked. "Who
would have thought they'd have something valuable for
sale?"

"I want to show them something," Sollenar said.

"What thing, Mr. Sollenar?"

They turned the corner of a corridor, with branching hall-
ways here and there, not all of them busy. "Come here,"
Sollenar said, nodding toward one of them.

They stopped out of sight of the lobby and the main corridor. "Come on," Sollenar said. "A little farther."

"No," Ermine said. "This is farther than I really wish. It's dark here."

"Wise too late, Mr. Ermine," Sollenar said, his arms flashing out.

One palm impacted against Ermine's solar plexus, and the other against the muscle at the side of his neck, but not hard enough to kill. Ermine collapsed, starved for oxygen, while Sollenar silently cursed having been cured of murder. Then Sollenar turned and ran.

Behind him Ermine's body struggled to draw breath by reflex alone.

Moving as fast as he dared, Sollenar walked back and reached the taxi lock, pulling a respirator from a wall rack as he went. He flagged a car and gave his destination, looking behind him. He had seen nothing of Cortwright Burr since setting foot on Mars. But he knew that, soon or late, Burr would find him.

A few moments later Ermine got to his feet. Sollenar's car was well away. Ermine shrugged and went to the local broadcasting station.

He commandeered a private desk, a firearm, and immediate time on the IAB interoffice circuit to Earth. When his call acknowledgement had come back to him from his office there, he reported:

"Sollenar is enroute to the Martian city. He wants a duplicate of Burr's device, of course, since he smashed the original when he killed Burr. I'll follow and make final disposition. The disorientation I reported previously is progressing rapidly. Almost all his responses now are inappropriate. On the flight out, he seemed to be staring at something in an empty seat. Quite often when spoken to he obviously hears something else entirely. I expect to catch one of the next few flights back."

There was no point in waiting for comment to wend its way back from Earth. Ermine left. He went to a cab rank and paid the exorbitant fee for transportation outside Aresian city limits.

Close at hand, the Martian city was like a welter of broken pots. Shards of wall and roof joined at savage angles and pointed to nothing. Underfoot, drifts of vitreous material, shaped to fit no sane configuration, and broken to fit such a mosaic as no church would contain, rocked and slid under Sollenar's hurrying feet.

What from Aresia had been a solid front of dun color was here a facade of red, green, and blue splashed about centuries ago and since then weathered only enough to show how bitter the colors had once been. The plum-colored sky stretched over all this like a frigid membrane, and the wind blew and blew.

Here and there, as he progressed, Sollenar saw Martian arms and heads protruding from the rubble. Sculptures.

He was moving toward the heart of the city, where some few unbroken structures persisted. At the top of a heap of shards he turned to look behind him. There was the dust-plume of his cab, returning to the city. He expected to walk back—perhaps to meet someone on the road, all alone on the Martian plain if only Ermine would forebear from interfering. Searching the flat, thin-aired landscape, he tried to pick out the plodding dot of Cortwright Burr. But not yet.

He turned and ran down the untrustworthy slope.

He reached the edge of the maintained area. Here the rubble was gone, the ancient walks swept, the statues kept upright on their pediments. But only broken walls suggested the fronts of the houses that had stood here. Knifing their sides up through the wind-rippled sand that only constant care kept off the street, the shadow-houses fenced his way and the sculptures were motionless as hope. Ahead of him, he saw the buildings of the engineers. There was no heap to climb and look to see if Ermine followed close behind.

Sucking his respirator, he reached the building of the Martian engineers.

A sounding strip ran down the doorjamb. He scratched his fingernails sharply along it, and the magnified vibration, ducted throughout the hollow walls, rattled his plea for entrance.

V

The door opened, and Martians stood looking. They were spindly limbed and slight, their faces framed by folds of leathery tissue. Their mouths were lipped with horn as hard as dentures, and pursed, forever ready to masticate. They were pleasant neither to look at nor, Sollenar knew, to deal with. But Cortwright Burr had done it. And Sollenar needed to do it.

"Does anyone here speak English?" he asked.

"I," said the central Martian, his mouth opening to the sound, closing to end the reply.

"I would like to deal with you."

"Whenever," the Martian said, and the group at the doorway parted deliberately to let Sollenar in.

Before the door closed behind him, Sollenar looked back. But the rubble of the abandoned sectors blocked his line of sight into the desert.

"What can you offer? And what do you want?" the Martian asked. Sollenar stood half-ringed by them, in a room whose corners he could not see in the uncertain light.

"I offer you Terrestrial currency."

The English-speaking Martian—the Martian who had admitted to speaking English—turned his head slightly and spoke to his fellows. There were clacking sounds as his lips met. The others reacted variously, one of them suddenly gesturing with what seemed a disgusted flip of his arm before he turned without further word and stalked away, his shoulders looking like the shawled back of a very old and very hungry woman.

"What did Burr give you?" Sollenar asked.

"Burr." The Martian cocked his head. His eyes were not multifaceted, but gave that impression.

"He was here and he dealt with you. Not long ago. On what basis?"

"Burr. Yes. Burr gave us currency. We will take currency from you. For the same thing we gave him?"

"For immortality, yes."

"Im— This is a new word."

"Is it? For the secret of not dying?"

"Not dying? You think we have not-dying for sale here?" The Martian spoke to the others again. Their lips clattered. Others left, like the first one had, moving with great precision and very slow step, and no remaining tolerance for Sollenar.

Sollenar cried out: "What did you sell him, then?"

The principal engineer said: "We made an entertainment device for him."

"A little thing. This size." Sollenar cupped his hands.

"You have seen it, then."

"Yes. And nothing more? That was all he bought here?"

"It was all we had to sell—or give. We don't yet know whether Earthmen will give us things in exchange for currency. We'll see, when we next need something from Aresia."

Sollenar demanded: "How did it work? This thing you sold him."

"Oh, it lets people tell stories to themselves."

Sollenar looked closely at the Martian. "What kind of stories?"

"Any kind," the Martian said blandly. "Burr told us what he wanted. He had drawings with him of an Earthman device that used pictures on a screen, and broadcast sounds, to carry the details of the story told to the auditor."

"He stole those patents! He couldn't have used them on Earth."

"And why should he? Our device needs to convey no precise details. Any mind can make its own. It only needs to be put into a situation, and from there it can do all the work. If an auditor wishes a story of contact with other sexes, for example, the projector simply makes it seem to him, the next time he is with the object of his desire, that he is getting positive feedback—that he is arousing a similar response in that object. Once that has been established for him, the auditor may then leave the machine, move about normally, conduct his life as usual—but always in accordance with the basic situation. It is, you see, in the end a means of introducing system into his view of reality. Of course, his society must understand that he is not in accord with reality, for some of what he does cannot seem rational from an outside view of him. So some care must be taken, but not much. If many such devices were to enter his society, soon the circumstances would become commonplace, and the society would surely readjust to allow for it," said the English-speaking Martian.

"The machine creates any desired situation in the auditor's mind?"

"Certainly. There are simple predisposing tapes that can

be inserted as desired. Love, adventure, cerebration—it makes no difference."

Several of the bystanders clacked sounds out to each other. Sollenar looked at them narrowly. It was obvious there had to be more than one English-speaker among these people.

"And the device you gave Burr," he asked the engineer, neither calmly nor hopefully, "what sort of stories could its auditors tell themselves?"

The Martian cocked his head again. It gave him the look of an owl at a bedroom window. "Oh, there was one situation we were particularly instructed to include. Burr said he was thinking ahead to showing it to an acquaintance of his.

"It was a situation of adventure; of adventure with the fearful. And it was to end in loss and bitterness." The Martian looked even more closely at Sollenar. "Of course, the device does not specify details. No one but the auditor can know what fearful thing inhabits his story, or precisely how the end of it would come. You would, I believe, be Rufus Sollenar? Burr spoke of you and made the noise of laughing."

Sollenar opened his mouth. But there was nothing to say.

"You want such a device?" the Martian asked. "We've prepared several since Burr left. He spoke of machines that would manufacture them in astronomical numbers. We, of course, have done our best with our poor hands."

Sollenar said: "I would like to look out your door."

"Pleasure."

Sollenar opened the door slightly. Mr. Ermine stood in the cleared street, motionless as the shadow buildings behind him. He raised one hand in a gesture of unfelt greeting as he saw Sollenar, then put it back on the stock of his rifle. Sollenar closed the door and turned to the Martian.

"How much currency do you want?"

"Oh, all you have with you. You people always have a good deal with you when you travel."

Sollenar plunged his hands into his pockets and pulled out his billfold, his change, his keys, his jeweled radio; whatever was there, he rummaged out onto the floor, listening to the sound of rolling coins.

"I wish I had more here," he laughed. "I wish I had the

amount that man out there is going to recover when he shoots me."

The Martian engineer cocked his head. "But your dream is over, Mr. Sollenar," he clacked dryly. "Isn't it?"

"Quite so. But you to your purposes and I to mine. Now give me one of those projectors. And set it to predispose a situation I am about to specify to you. Take however long it needs. The audience is a patient one." He laughed, and tears gathered in his eyes.

Mr. Ermine waited, isolated from the cold, listening to hear whether the rifle stock was slipping out of his fingers. He had no desire to go into the Martian building after Sollenar and involve third parties. All he wanted was to put Sollenar's body under a dated marker, with as little trouble as possible.

Now and then he walked a few paces backward and forward, to keep from losing muscular control at his extremities because of low skin temperature. Sollenar must come out soon enough. He had no food supply with him, and though Ermine did not like the risk of engaging a man like Sollenar in a starvation contest, there was no doubt that a man with no taste for fuel could outlast one with the acquired reflexes of eating.

The door opened and Sollenar came out.

He was carrying something. Perhaps a weapon. Ermine let him come closer while he raised and carefully sighted his rifle. Sollenar might have some Martian weapon or he might not. Ermine did not particularly care. If Ermine died, he would hardly notice it—far less than he would notice a botched ending to a job of work already roiled by Sollenar's break away at the space field. If Ermine died, some other SPRO agent would be assigned almost immediately. No matter what happened, SPRO would stop Sollenar before he ever reached Abernathy Field.

So there was plenty of time to aim an unhurried, clean shot.

Sollenar was closer, now. He seemed to be in a very agitated frame of mind. He held out whatever he had in his hand.

It was another one of the Martian entertainment machines. Sollenar seemed to be offering it as a token to Ermine. Ermine smiled.

"What can you offer me, Mr. Sollenar?" he said, and shot.

The golden ball rolled away over the sand. "There, now," Ermine said. "*Now*, wouldn't you sooner be me than you? And where is the thing that made the difference between us?"

He shivered. He was chilly. Sand was blowing against his tender face, which had been somewhat abraded during his long wait.

He stopped, transfixed.

He lifted his head.

Then, with a great swing of his arms, he sent the rifle whirling away. "The wind!" he sighed into the thin air. "I feel the wind." He leapt into the air, and sand flew away from his feet as he landed. He whispered to himself: "I feel the ground!"

He stared in tremblant joy at Sollenar's empty body. "What have you given me?" Full of his own rebirth, he swung his head up at the sky again, and cried in the direction of the sun: "Oh, you squeezing, nibbling people who made me incorruptible and thought that was the end of me!"

With love he buried Sollenar, and with reverence he put up the marker, but he had plans for what he might accomplish with the facts of this transaction, and the myriad others he was privy to.

A sharp bit of pottery had penetrated the sole of his shoe and gashed his foot, but he, not having seen it, hadn't felt it. Nor would he see it or feel it even when he changed his stockings; for he had not noticed the wound when it was made. It didn't matter. In a few days it would heal, though not as rapidly as if it had been properly attended to.

Vaguely, he heard the sound of Martians clacking behind their closed door as he hurried out of the city, full of revenge, and reverence for his savior.

REMEMBER THE ALAMO!

BY R.R. FEHRENBACH

ANALOG
DECEMBER

This is an alternate history story, a form that has attracted some of the best talent in the science fiction field. It is a story that questions myths and legends and one that asks some profound questions.

I don't know anything about Mr. Fehrenbach—this is apparently the only story he published in the sf magazines—but this effort would merit inclusion in anyone's anthology of one-story wonders. (MHG)

Alternate histories annoy some people. I know because in my magazine Isaac Asimov's Science Fiction Magazine, *we occasionally publish an alternate history story and there are always a smattering of letters from upset readers. Marty Greenberg thinks it's all his fault because he edited an anthology of alternate histories and he feels that may have given writers a push in that direction.*

For myself, I love alternate histories because when well-done they have to contain considerable surprises, mentioned, hopefully, merely in passing.

After all, any change in history, however slight, is bound to send out expanding ripples of change. That is what the new mathematical science of chaos is all about. The great classic of this sort of story is Ward Moore's "Bring the Jubilee," but Fehrenbach's story is one of the few that I think can be mentioned in the same breath.

I am amazed that Fehrenbach hasn't written more science fiction. (IA)

Toward sundown, in the murky drizzle, the man who called himself Ord brought Lieutenant colonel William Barrett Travis word that the Mexican light cavalry had completely invested Bexar, and that some light guns were being set up across the San Antonio River. Even as he spoke, there was a flash and bang from the west, and a shell screamed over the old mission walls. Travis looked worried.

"What kind of guns?" he asked.

"Nothing to worry about, sir," Ord said. "Only a few one-pounders, nothing of respectable siege caliber. General Santa Anna has had to move too fast for any big stuff to keep up." Ord spoke in his odd accent. After all, he was a Britainer, or some other kind of foreigner. But he spoke good Spanish, and he seemed to know everything. In the four or five days since he had appeared he had become very useful to Travis.

Frowning, Travis asked, "How many Mexicans, do you think, Ord?"

"Not more than a thousand, now," the dark-haired, blue-eyed young man said confidently. "But when the main body arrives, there'll be four, five thousand."

Travis shook his head. "How do you get all this information, Ord? You recite it like you had read it all some place—like it were history."

Ord merely smiled. "Oh, I don't know *everything*, colonel. That is why I had to come here. There is so much we don't know about what happened . . . I mean, sir, what will happen—in the Alamo." His sharp eyes grew puzzled for an instant. "And some things don't seem to match up, somehow—"

Travis looked at him sympathetically. Ord talked queerly at times, and Travis suspected he was a bit deranged. This was understandable, for the man was undoubtedly a Britainer aristocrat, a refugee from Napoleon's thousand-year Empire. Travis had heard about the detention camps and the charcoal ovens . . . but once, when he had mentioned the *Empereur's* sack of London in '06, Ord had gotten a very queer look in his eyes, as if he had forgotten completely.

But John Ord, or whatever his name was, seemed to be the only man in the Texas forces who understood what William Barrett Travis was trying to do. Now Travis looked around at the thick abode wall surrounding the old mission in which they stood. In the cold, yellowish twilight even the flaring cook fires of his hundred and eighty-two men could not dispel the ghostly air that clung to the old place. Travis shivered involuntarily. But the walls were thick, and they could turn one-pounders. He asked, "What was it you called this place, Ord . . . the Mexican name?"

"The Alamo, sir." A slow, steady excitement seemed to burn in the Britainer's bright eyes. "Santa Anna won't forget that name, you can be sure. You'll want to talk to the other officers now, sir? About the message we drew up for Sam Houston?"

"Yes, of course," Travis said absently. He watched Ord head for the walls. No doubt about it, Ord understood what William Barrett Travis was trying to do here. So few of the others seemed to care.

Travis was suddenly very glad that John Ord had shown up when he did.

On the walls, Ord found the man he sought, broad-shouldered and tall in a fancy Mexican jacket. "The commandant's compliments, sir, and he desires your presence in the chapel."

The big man put away the knife with which he had been whittling. The switchblade snicked back and disappeared into a side pocket of the jacket, while Ord watched it with fascinated eyes. "What's old Bill got his britches hot about this time?" the big man asked.

"I wouldn't know, sir," Ord said stiffly and moved on.

Bang-bang-bang roared the small Mexican cannon from across the river. *Pow-pow-pow!* The little balls only chipped dust from the thick adobe walls. Ord smiled.

He found the second man he sought, a lean man with a weathered face, leaning against a wall and chewing tobacco. This man wore a long, fringed, leather lounge jacket, and he carried a guitar slung beside his Rock Island ribe. He squinted up at Ord. "I know . . . I know," he muttered. "Willy Travis is in an uproar again. You reckon that colonel's commission the Congress up at Washington-on-the-Brazos give him swelled his head?"

Rather stiffly, Ord said, "Colonel, the commandant desires an officers' conference in the chapel, now." Ord was somewhat annoyed. He had not realized he would find these Americans so—distasteful. Hardly preferable to Mexicans, really. Not at all as he had imagined.

For an instant he wished he had chosen Drake and the Armada instead of this pack of ruffians—but no, he had never been able to stand sea sickness. He couldn't have taken the Channel, not even for five minutes.

And there was no changing now. He had chosen this place and time carefully, at great expense—actually, at great risk, for the X-4-A had aborted twice, and he had had a hard time bringing her in. But it had got him here at last. And, because for a historian he had always been an impetuous and daring man, he grinned now, thinking of the glory that was to come. And he was a participant—much better than a ringside seat! Only he would have to be careful, at the last, to slip away.

John Ord knew very well how this coming battle had ended, back here in 1836.

He marched back to William Barrett Travis, clicked heels smartly. Travis' eyes glowed; he was the only senior officer here who loved military punctilio. "Sir, they are on the way."

"Thank you, Ord." Travis hesitated a moment. "Look, Ord. There will be a battle, as we know. I know so little about you. If something should happen to you, is there anyone to write? Across the water?"

Ord grinned. "No, sir. I'm afraid my ancestor wouldn't understand."

Travis shrugged. Who was he to say that Ord was crazy? In this day and age, any man with vision was looked on as mad. Sometimes, he felt closer to Ord than to the others.

The two officers Ord had summoned entered the chapel. The big man in the Mexican jacket tried to dominate the wood table at which they sat. He towered over the slender, nervous Travis, but the commandant, straightbacked and arrogant, did not given an inch. "Boys, you know Santa Anna has invested us. We've been fired on all day—" He seemed to be listening for something. *Wham!* Outside, a cannon split the dusk with flame and sound as it fired from the walls. "There is my answer!"

The man in the lounge coat shrugged. "What I want to

know is what our orders are. What does old Sam say? Sam and me were in Congress once. Sam's got good sense; he can smell the way the wind's blowin'." He stopped speaking and hit his guitar a few licks. He winked across the table at the officer in the Mexican jacket who took out his knife. "Eh, Jim?"

"Right," Jim said. "Sam's a good man, although I don't think he ever met a payroll."

"General Houston's leaving it up to me," Travis told them.

"Well, that's that," Jim said unhappily. "So what you figurin' to do, Bill?"

Travis stood up in the weak, flickering candlelight, one hand on the polished hilt of his saber. The other two men winced, watching him. "Gentlemen, Houston's trying to pull his militia together while he falls back. You know Texas was woefully unprepared for a contest at arms. The general's idea is to draw Santa Anna as far into Texas as he can, then hit him when he's extended, at the right place and right time. But Houston needs more time—Santa Anna's moved faster than any of us anticipated. Unless we can stop the Mexican Army and take a little steam out of them, General Houston's in trouble."

Jim flicked the knife blade in and out. "Go on."

"This is where we come in, gentlemen. Santa Anna can't leave a force of one hundred eighty men in his rear. If we hold fast, he must attack us. But he has no siege equipment, not even large field cannon." Travis' eye gleamed. "Think of it, boys! He'll have to mount a frontal attack, against protected American riflemen. Ord, couldn't your Englishers tell him a few things about that!"

"Whoa, now," Jim barked. "Billy, anybody tell you there's maybe four or five thousand Mexicaners comin'?"

"Let them come. Less will leave!"

But Jim, sour-faced turned to the other man. "Davey? You got something to say?"

"Hell, yes. How do we get out, after we done pinned Santa Anna down? You thought of that, Billy boy?"

Travis shrugged. "There is an element of grave risk, of course. Ord, where's the document, the message you wrote up for me? Ah, thank you." Travis cleared his throat. "Here's what I'm sending on to General Houston." He

read, "Commandancy of the Alamo, February 24, 1836 . . .
are you sure of the date, Ord?"

"Oh, I'm sure of that," Ord said.

"Never mind—if you're wrong we can change it later. To
the People of Texas and all Americans in the World. Fellow
Freemen and Compatriots! I am besieged with a thousand
or more Mexicans under Santa Anna. I have sustained a
continual bombardment for many hours but have not lost
a man. The enemy has demanded surrender at discretion,
otherwise, the garrison is to be put to the sword, if taken.
I have answered the demand with a cannon shot, and our
flag still waves proudly over the walls. I shall never surrender or retreat. Then, I call on you in the name of liberty,
of patriotism and everything dear to the American character—" He paused, frowning. "This language seems pretty
old-fashioned, Ord—"

"Oh, no, sir. That's exactly right," Ord murmured.

" '. . . To come to our aid with all dispatch. The enemy
is receiving reinforcements daily and will no doubt increase
to three or four thousand in four or five days. If this call is
neglected, I am determined to sustain myself as long as
possible and die like a soldier who never forgets what is due
his honor or that of his homeland. VICTORY OR DEATH!' "

Travis stopped reading, looked up. "Wonderful! Wonderful!" Ord breathed. "The greatest words of defiance ever
written in the English tongue—and so much more literate
than that chap at Bastogne."

"You mean to send that?" Jim gasped.

The man called Davey was holding his head his hands.

"You object, Colonel Bowie?" Travis asked icily.

"Oh, cut that 'colonel' stuff, Bill," Bowie said. "It's only
a National Guard title, and I like 'Jim' better, even though
I am a pretty important man. Damn right I have an objection! Why, that message is almost aggressive. You'd think
we wanted to fight Santa Anna! You want us to be marked
down as warmongers? It'll give us trouble when we get to
the negotiation table—"

Travis' head turned. "Colonel Crockett?"

"What Jim says goes for me, too. And this: I'd change
that part about all Americans, et cetera. You don't want
anybody to think we think we're better than the Mexicans.

After all, Americans are a minority in the world. Why not make it 'all men who love security?' That'd have worldwide appeal—"

"Oh, Crockett," Travis hissed.

Crockett stood up. "Don't use that tone of voice to me, Billy Travis! That piece of paper you got don't make you no better'n us. I ran for Congress twice, and won. I know what the people want—"

"What the people want doesn't mean a damn right now," Travis said harshly. "Don't you realize the tyrant is at the gates?"

Crockett rolled his eyes heavenward. "Never thought I'd hear a good American say that! Billy, you'll never run for office—"

Bowie held up a hand, cutting into Crockett's talk. "All right, Davey. Hold up. You ain't runnin' for Congress now. Bill, the main thing I don't like in your whole message is that part about victory or death. That's got to go. Don't ask us to sell that to the troops!"

Travis closed his eyes briefly. "Boys, listen. We don't have to tell the men about this. They don't need to know the real story until it's too late for them to get out. And then we shall cover ourselves with such glory that none of us shall ever be forgotten. Americans are the best fighters in the world when they are trapped. They teach this in the Foot School back on the Chatahoochee. And if we die, to die for one's country is sweet—"

"Hell with that," Crockett drawled. "I don't mind dyin', but not for these big landowners like Jim Bowie here. I just been thinkin'—I don't own nothing in Texas."

"I resent that," Bowie shouted. "You know very well I volunteered, after I sent my wife off to Acapulco to be with her family." With an effort, he calmed himself. "Look, Travis. I have some reputation as a fighting man—you know I lived through the gang wars back home. It's obvious this Alamo place is indefensible, even if we had a thousand men."

"But we must delay Santa Anna at all costs—"

Bowie took out a fine, dark Mexican cigar and whittled at it with his blade. Then he lit it, saying around it, "All right, let's all calm down. Nothing a group of good men can't settle around a table. Now listen. I got in with this revolution at first because I thought old Emperor Iturbide would listen to reason and lower taxes. But nothin's worked out, because hotheads like you, Travis, queered the deal. All this yammerin' about liberty! Mexico is a Republic, under an Emperor, not some kind of democracy, and we can't change that. Let's talk some sense before it's too late. We're all too old and too smart to be wavin' the flag like it's the Fourth of July. Sooner or later, we're goin' to have to sit down and talk with the Mexicans. And like Davey said, I own a million hectares, and I've always paid minimum wage, and my wife's folks are way up there in the Imperial Government of the Republic of Mexico. That means I got influence in all the votin' groups, includin' the American Immigrant, since I'm a minority group member myself. I think I can talk to Santa Anna, and even to old Iturbide. If we sign a treaty now with Santa Anna, acknowledge the law of the land, I think our lives and property rights will be respected—" He cocked an eye toward Crockett.

"Makes sense, Jim. That's the way we do it in Congress. Compromise, everybody happy. We never allowed ourselves to be led nowhere we didn't want to go, I can tell you! And Bill, you got to admit that we're in better bargaining position if we're out in the open, than if old Santa Anna's got us penned up in this old Alamo."

"Ord," Travis said despairingly. "Ord, you understand. Help me! Make them listen!"

Ord moved into the candlelight, his lean face sweating. "Gentlemen, this is all wrong! It doesn't happen this way—"

Crockett sneered, "Who asked you, Ord? I'll bet you ain't even got a poll tax!"

Decisively, Bowie said, "We're free men, Travis, and we won't be led around like cattle. How about it, Davey? Think you could handle the rear guard, if we try to move out of here?"

"Hell, yes! Just so we're movin'!"

"O.K. Put it to a vote of the men outside. Do we stay, and maybe get croaked, or do we fall back and conserve our strength until we need it? Take care of it, eh, Davey?"

Crockett picked up his guitar and went outside.

Travis roared. "This is insubordination! Treason!" He drew his saber, but Bowie took it from him and broke it in two. Then the big man pulled his knife.

"Stay back, Ord. The Alamo isn't worth the bones of a Britainer, either."

"Colonel Bowie, please," Ord cried. "You don't understand! You *must* defend the Alamo! This is the turning point in the winning of the west! If Houston is beaten, Texas will never join the Union! There will be no Mexican War. No California, no nation stretching from sea to shining sea! This is the Americans' manifest destiny. You are the hope of the future . . . you will save the world from Hitler, from Bolshevism—"

"Crazy as a hoot owl," Bowie said sadly. "Ord, you and Travis got to look at it both ways. We ain't all in the right in this war—we Americans got our faults, too."

"But you are free men," Ord whispered. "Vulgar, opinionated, brutal—but free! You are still better than any breed who kneels to tyranny—"

Crockett came in. "O.K., Jim."

"How'd it go?"

"Fifty-one percent for hightailin' it right now."

Bowie smiled. "That's a flat majority. Let's make tracks."

"Comin', Bill?" Crockett asked. "You're O.K., but you just don't know how to be one of the boys. You got to learn that no dog is better'n any other."

"No," Travis croaked hoarsely. "I stay. Stay or go, we shall all die like dogs, anyway. Boys, for the last time! Don't reveal our weakness to the enemy—"

"What weakness? We're stronger than them. Americans could whip the Mexicans any day, if we wanted to. But the thing to do is make 'em talk, not fight. So long, Bill."

The two big men stepped outside. In the night there was a sudden clatter of hoofs as the Texans mounted and rode. From across the river came a brief spatter of musket fire, then silence. In the dark, there had been no difficulty in breaking through the Mexican lines.

Inside the chapel, John Ord's mouth hung slackly. He muttered, "Am I insane? It didn't happen this way—it couldn't! The books can't be *that* wrong—"

In the candlelight, Travis hung his head. "We tried, John. Perhaps it was a forlorn hope at best. Even if we had defeated Santa Anna, or delayed him, I do not think the Indian Nations would have let Houston get help from the United States."

Ord continued his dazed muttering, hardly hearing.

"We need a contiguous frontier with Texas," Travis continued slowly, just above a whisper. "But we Americans have never broken a treaty with the Indians, and pray God we never shall. *We* aren't like the Mexicans, always pushing, always grabbing off New Mexico, Arizona, California. *We* aren't colonial oppressors, thank God! No, it wouldn't have worked out, even if we American immigrants had secured our rights in Texas—" He lifted a short, heavy, percussion pistol in his hand and cocked it. "I hate to say it, but perhaps if we hadn't taken Payne and Jefferson so seriously— if we could only have paid lip service, and done what we really wanted to do, in our hearts . . . no matter. I won't live to see our final disgrace."

He put the pistol to his head and blew out his brains.

Ord was still gibbering when the Mexican cavalry stormed into the old mission, pulling down the flag and seizing him, dragging him before the resplendent little general in green and gold.

Since he was the only prisoner, Santa Anna questioned Ord carefully. When the sharp point of a bayonet had been thrust half an inch into his stomach, the Britainer seemed to come around. When he started speaking, and the Mexicans realized he was English, it went better with him. Ord was obviously mad, it seemed to Santa Anna, but since he spoke English and seemed educated, he could be useful. Santa Anna didn't mind the raving; he understood all about Napoleon's detention camps and what they had done to Britainers over there. In fact, Santa Anna was thinking of setting up a couple of those camps himself. When they had milked Ord dry, they threw him on a horse and took him along.

Thus John Ord had an execellent view of the battlefield when Santa Anna's cannon broke the American lines south of the Trinity. Unable to get his men across to safety, Sam Houston died leading the last, desperate charge against the Mexican regulars. After that, the American survivors were too tired to run from the cavalry that pinned them against the flooding river. Most of them died there. Santa Anna expressed complete indifference to what happened to the Texans' women and children.

Mexican soldiers found Jim Bowie hiding in a hut, wearing a plain linen tunic and pretending to be a civilian. They would not have discovered his identity had not some of the Texan women whom the cavalry had captured cried out, "Colonel Bowie—Colonel Bowie!" as he was led into the Mexican camp.

He was hauled before Santa Anna, and Ord was summoned to watch. "Well, don Jaime," Santa Anna remarked, "You have been a foolish man. I promised your wife's uncle to send you to Acapulco safely, though of course your lands are forfeit. You understand we must have lands for the veterans' program when this campaign is over—" Santa Anna smiled then. "Besides, since Ord here has told me how instrumental you were in the abandonment of the Alamo, I think the Emperor will agree to mercy in your case. You know, don Jaime, your compatriots had me worried back there. The Alamo might have been a tough nut to crack . . . *pues*, no matter."

And since Santa Anna had always been broadminded, not objecting to light skin or immigrant background, he invited Bowie to dinner that night.

Santa Anna turned to Ord. "But if we could catch this rascally war criminal, Crockett . . . however, I fear he has escaped us. He slipped over the river with a fake passport, and the Indians have interned him."

"Si, *Señor Presidente*," Ord said dully.

"Please, don't call me that," Santa Anna cried, looking around. "True, many of us officers have political ambitions, but Emperor Iturbide is old and vain. It could mean my head—"

Suddenly, Ord's head was erect, and the old, clear light was in his blue eyes. "Now I understand!" he shouted. "I thought Travis was raving back there, before he shot himself—and your talk of the Emperor! American respect for Indian rights! Jeffersonian form of government! Oh, those ponces who peddled me that X-4-A—the *track jumper!* I'm not back in my own past. I've jumped the time track—*I'm back in a screaming alternate!*"

"Please, not so loud, *Señor* Ord." Santa Anna sighed.

DAW

Don't Miss These Exciting DAW Anthologies

ANNUAL WORLD'S BEST SF
Donald A. Wollheim, editor
- [ ] 1990 Annual   UE2424—$4.50

ISAAC ASIMOV PRESENTS THE GREAT SF STORIES
Isaac Asimov & Martin H. Greenberg, editors
- [ ] Series 18 (1956)   UE2289—$4.50
- [ ] Series 19 (1957)   UE2326—$4.50
- [ ] Series 20 (1958)   UE2405—$4.95
- [ ] Series 21 (1959)   UE2428—$4.95
- [ ] Series 22 (1960)   UE2465—$4.50

SWORD AND SORCERESS
Marion Zimmer Bradley, editor
- [ ] Book I   UE2359—$3.95
- [ ] Book II   UE2360—$3.95
- [ ] Book III   UE2302—$3.95
- [ ] Book IV   UE2412—$4.50
- [ ] Book V   UE2288—$3.95
- [ ] Book VI   UE2423—$4.50
- [ ] Book VII   UE2457—$4.50

THE YEAR'S BEST HORROR STORIES
Karl Edward Wagner, editor
- [ ] Series XVII   UE2381—$3.95
- [ ] Series XVIII   UE2446—$4.95

PENGUIN USA
P.O. Box 999, Bergenfield, New Jersey 07621

Please send me the DAW BOOKS I have checked above. I am enclosing $_____
(check or money order—no currency or C.O.D.'s). Please include the list price plus
$1.00 per order to cover handling costs. Prices and numbers are subject to change
without notice. (Prices slightly higher in Canada.)

Name _____

Address _____

City _____ State _____ Zip _____
Please allow 4-6 weeks for delivery.

''Now, we must shoot a few more American officers, of course. I regret this, you understand, and I shall no doubt be much criticized in French Canada and Russia, where there are still civilized values. But we must establish the Republic of the Empire once and for all upon this continent, that aristocratic tyranny shall not perish from the earth. Of course, as an Englishman, you understand perfectly, Señor Ord.''

''Of course, excellency,'' Ord said.

''There are soft hearts—soft heads, I say—in Mexico who cry for civil rights for the Americans. But I must make sure that Mexican dominance is never again threatened north of the Rio Grande.''

''Seguro, excellency,'' Ord said, suddenly. If the bloody X-4-A had jumped the track, there was no getting back, none at all. He was stuck here. Ord's blue eyes narrowed. ''After all, it . . . it is manifest destiny that the Latin peoples of North America meet at the center of the continent. Canada and Mexico shall share the Mississippi.''

Santa Anna's dark eyes glowed. ''You say what I have often thought. You are a man of vision, and much sense. You realize the indios must go, whether they were here first or not. I think I will make you my secretary, with the rank of captain.''

''Gracias, Excellency.''

''Now, let us write my communique to the capital, Capitán Ord. We must describe how the American abandonment of the Alamo allowed me to press the traitor Houston so closely he had no chance to maneuver his men into the trap he sought. Ay, Capitán, it is a cardinal principle of the Anglo-Saxons, to get themselves into a trap from which they must fight their way out. This I never let them do, which is why I succeed where others fail . . . you said something, Capitán?''

''Sí, Excellency,'' I said, I shall title our communique: 'Remember the Alamo,' '' Ord said, standing at attention.

''Bueno! You have a gift for words. Indeed, if ever we feel the gringos are too much for us, your words shall once again remind us of the truth!'' Santa Anna smiled. ''I think I shall make you a major. You have indeed coined a phrase which shall live in history forever!